THE 20th OF JULY

On the 20th of July, 1944 a German officer, Colonel Count von Stauffenberg, walked into Hitler's field Headquarters, placed a briefcase under the table and waited for the bomb it contained to explode. When it went off, it failed to kill Hitler. This attempt on the Fuehrer's life was not the suicidal act of one man, but the culmination of a carefully planned operation involving many men and high-ranking army officers in Berlin, Paris and elsewhere.

H. H. Kirst has turned this dramatic and heroic attempt to overthrow Hitler into the stuff of a magnificent novel. Names, dates, places are all authentic; much of the dialogue is taken from official documents. From the initial stages of the plot to the hunt for the conspirators, from the savage interrogations to the People's Court and the execution of the heroes, the author has drawn an unforgettable picture of one of the most singular episodes in German history.

HANS HELLMUT KIRST

The 20th of July

TRANSLATED FROM THE GERMAN
BY J. MAXWELL BROWNJOHN

Collins
FONTANA BOOKS

Originally published in Germany under the title 'Aufstand der Soldaten'
First published in Great Britain, 1966
First issued in Fontana Books, 1968

© 1965 by Verlag Kurt Desch GmbH, Munchen
© 1966 in the English translation by
Wm. Collins, Sons & Co., Ltd.
Printed in Great Britain
Collins Clear-Type Press
London and Glasgow

CONTENTS

This book is based on fact.

Names, dates and events accord with reality, and numerous passages of dialogue have been quoted verbatim from official records.

If, despite this, the book is called a novel, it is principally because of the character known as Captain Count Fritz-Wilhelm von Brackwede, who corresponds in part, but not wholly, to the unique and historical figure of Lieutenant Count Fritz-Dietlof von der Schulenburg. The latter only served as a guide, however, not a blue-print.

PART ONE

THE DAYS BEFORE

"I won't do anything myself, but
I shan't object if someone else does."
Walter von Brauchitsch, Field Marshal

ONE

"I'm going to do the job myself," said the colonel.

The "job" was to assassinate his Supreme Commander, and the colonel was Claus, Count von Stauffenberg, Chief of Staff to the Commander-in-Chief, Replacement Army. He stood in his office in the Bendlerstrasse, Berlin, a tense, erect figure, facing a man who wore captain's insignia.

The captain said: "I saw this coming a mile off." He sat down with an expectant air as though further comment were unnecessary.

The colonel eyed his visitor with a touch of surprise. "I'm waiting to hear your objections, Fritz."

"Would they change your mind?"

"No, of course not." There was an affectionate undertone in Stauffenberg's cool and incisive voice. "All the same, I'd like your comments on the idea. Our mutual friends are bound to raise a number of objections, and you must know their arguments backwards by now."

Captain Count Fritz-Wilhelm von Brackwede cocked his head and regarded Stauffenberg quizzically. "You're already aware of my views on the subject, Claus. It's more than time the man was dealt with, but if you really want an objection, here's one: he'll die soon enough of his own accord—we won't have to wait much longer."

Stauffenberg frowned and shook his head vigorously. "More and more people are dying every day. The casualty lists are growing longer and our circle of friends is getting smaller all the time."

"But we've already managed to survive five years of war. Another nine or ten months, and that butcher will have shot his bolt. He's bound to die sooner or later."

"And what happens in the interval?" Stauffenberg leant forward. "Losses in human life may have doubled by then.

7

Germany may be battered past recognition—and meanwhile the gas ovens go on belching smoke day and night."

"You mean we've got to demonstrate the existence of another Germany—one that isn't run by a gang of thugs?"

"The world must know that we were prepared to stake our lives on one last throw." Stauffenberg spoke quietly but with immense conviction. Suddenly he smiled. "Forgive me, Fritz. Stating the obvious is a waste of time, I realise that. Go on, try to find some more drawbacks to my plan—and don't spare my feelings."

"All right." Brackwede's hawk-like nose jutted aggressively. "Hold out your right arm."

"My right arm's useless," Stauffenberg said coolly. "Added to that, I've only got one eye and three fingers on my left hand. I know I'm a cripple, technically speaking, but you don't imagine it makes me any less capable of killing, do you?"

"If anyone can do it, you can," Brackwede replied without hesitation. "All right, Claus, I'll try and give you some covering fire, but it won't be easy. We're not only dealing with that human hyena, don't forget. There are our friends to be considered as well."

Lieutenant Konstantin von Brackwede was lying under the table, fully dressed. His face looked as smooth and untroubled as a child's despite its deathly pallor, and there was a faint smile on his lips.

The man bending over him was wearing a jet-black uniform. He stood there for some time without moving, but his eyes were alert.

The black-clad figure belonged to SS-Sturmbannfuehrer Maier, head of the unofficial "Armed Forces Section" of the State Security Bureau. His rotund and rosy features looked as if they were padded with foam rubber and resembled those of a genial country landlord. Nothing ever disturbed his air of bloated equanimity, nor did his expression change now, as he abruptly moved towards the desk with the silent precision of a well-oiled machine.

The black-encased arms might have been performing some rhythmical exercise. One hand complemented the movements of the other, the right hand rummaging, the left hand tidying, eliminating traces, restoring a semblance of order. Papers were thumbed through with the dexterity of a cashier counting banknotes. Then, as suddenly as it had begun, all movement ceased.

Maier froze for several moments. He had found something which appeared to interest him—a requisition chit for three kilograms of caulking material addressed to Stores Depot SM3 in Berlin-Lankwitz.

Nothing could have been more apparently innocuous, except that, as Maier was aware, "SM3" meant "Special Materials, Intelligence." These included machine pistols, portable radio equipment—and explosives.

Slowly, Maier turned his head and subjected the inert lieutenant to a searching stare. Then he prodded his hind quarters with the toe of his boot. He had to repeat the process several times before his efforts were rewarded, but he was a man with inexhaustible reserves of patience.

Konstantin von Brackwede squirmed like a caterpillar and tried to sit up, staring vacantly at the brown Bokhara carpet he had been lying on. The ornamental design in the centre was wet with dribble. He shook himself, and his blond hair fell across his face in a thick silken fringe.

"I'm an old friend of your brother's," Maier announced. "I was hoping to have a chat with him. Any idea where he is?"

The lieutenant regarded his visitor unsteadily for some moments. His blue eyes were bloodshot. "Not a clue," he mumbled. "I only got back from the front last night."

"That explains a great deal and excuses everything," Maier said warmly. "Allow me to welcome you back to the seat of empire. I hope you enjoy your leave. You certainly won't find it boring—not with a brother like yours. Perhaps I can help to entertain you, too."

"Hitler's days are numbered." Captain von Brackwede stated this in the unemotional tones of a weather-forecaster. "Stauffenberg has decided to kill him—he proposes to do the job himself."

Julius Leber thoughtfully inclined his bony, angular head, and it was some time before he spoke. At last he said slowly: "When Colonel Stauffenberg appeared in Berlin last year I knew, after our very first meeting, that what we'd been planning and attempting to do all these years would finally become reality."

"You're worried, though," Brackwede insisted, "I can feel you are. Why?"

"Perhaps it's because I'm fond of the man. I want to be certain that if anyone survives, he does—I'm sure you can

9

understand that. It worries me to think of him making the attempt in person."

" Someone has to do it, and he's one of the few people who can still get close enough to Hitler. It'll take a lot of guts, too, and he's got more than his share."

Leber gave a nod of agreement. He was working as a coal merchant in Berlin-Schoeneberg, where he and his wife Annedore now ran a small business together. His " log cabin," as he called his office, served as a rendezvous for a wide circle of friends, not all of whom dated from the days when he was still a Socialist member of the Reichstag. The resistance movement looked upon him as the prospective Minister of the Interior of a liberated Germany, and Count von Brackwede was tipped to become his Secretary of State.

" I think I know what Beck and Goerdeler's objections to Stauffenberg's plan will be," Leber went on warily. " They'll probably say that no one can act as chief planner of an operation and lead it at the same time—and they'll have a valid point."

" Suggest one other way of eliminating Hitler at this stage and I'll buy it."

Leber pulled himself to his feet and walked to the window, where he peered round the curtain at the sparkling summer day outside. " When I think how often we've tried!" he murmured. " Time and time again for years now—even before they dreamed up this war."

" But this is the moment," Brackwede said firmly. " Who knows? Maybe this kind of venture never succeeded until the right man comes along. I suggest we back the attempt—all the way."

The gnome-like personage wearing corporal's chevrons eyed Captain von Brackwede with casual unconcern. " I've been looking for you for the past twenty-four hours. What the devil have you been doing?"

" Killing time," Brackwede smiled, seemingly unperturbed by this breach of military etiquette. " I'm a born idler—you ought to know that by now, Lehmann."

They grinned cheerfully at each other. The corporal continued to lounge in the chair behind the captain's desk and made no move to vacate it. The two men—both sworn members of the resistance movement—were alone in the office.

" Well now," Lehmann said briskly, " the explosives problem is all taken care of. Let's hope that's the last batch I have to squeeze out of our friends in Intelligence. They're getting cold feet at last—and no wonder, the way we've been pestering them all these years."

—"British-made again?" inquired Brackwede.

"Yes, top-grade plastic. The detonator's acid-operated as usual, but it's a pretty reliable one this time. There shouldn't be any more slip-ups provided the right man's in charge."

Captain von Brackwede knew all about these "slip-ups," which had preyed on the conspirators' nerves and caused a great deal of uncertainty. Although completely silent, acid-operated detonators were dependent upon the weather, and the rate at which the retaining-wire dissolved was affected by the prevailing temperature.

"It's no good using ham-fisted amateurs," Lehmann continued firmly. "This time it'll be an expert job. I didn't train under General von Tresckow all those weeks for nothing."

"By the way," Brackwede said, "where's the requisition chit?"

The corporal's impish face registered a mixture of surprise and reproach. "You mean to say you haven't got it yet? I handed it in at your flat yesterday evening—your brother took charge of it. Don't you ever sleep at home these days?"

"Man alive!" Brackwede exclaimed in alarm. "You must be mad, giving a thing like that to my brother."

"He's your brother, isn't he?" Lehmann looked surprised. "Isn't he supposed to know what you're up to?"

Brackwede merely shook his head, put his cap on at a defiant angle and walked to the door, where he paused. "Konstantin is one of those misguided people who still think Hitler and Germany mean the same thing—you ought to have allowed for that possibility."

Lehmann swore uneasily. "How the devil was I to know? The world must be a pretty lousy place if a man can't even trust his own brother any more."

Captain von Brackwede made it a point never to be dropped immediately outside his flat. His driver was regularly instructed to pull up in a side-street, each time at a different spot, whereupon the captain got out and completed the journey on foot.

On this particular occasion, while he was still a considerable distance away, he noticed a car parked outside. It was a dark grey car whose faded paintwork was covered with a mesh of fine cracks but gleamed dully, as though someone had whiled away many an idle hour by polishing it with an oily rag—in short, an official car.

Brackwede strode past without hesitation and turned into the entrance of the house next door, from which vantage-point he scrutinised the car more closely. Then he emerged from the doorway and advanced on the unprepossessing vehicle with a smile on his hawk-like features.

He put his head through the open front window and addressed the pale, thin, bespectacled face that stared back at him. "Won't you ever learn!" he said reprovingly. "You might as well put up a placard saying "the cops are here." Any self-respecting police chief would put you back on the beat."

The pallid man in spectacles looked genuinely distressed. His studious six-former's face did its best to assume an air of friendly surprise. "Oh, come now, Councillor—why should we try to hoodwink you of all people?"

Brackwede ignored the appellation "Councillor." The days when he had been a member of the Prussian Ministry of the Interior might lie in the far distant past but they were not entirely forgotten, neither by him nor by a number of police officers of which this pallid and bespectacled individual—Voglbronner by name—was one.

"How long has Maier been ferreting around in my flat?" he demanded.

"Two hours," Voglbronner replied promptly.

"What for?"

"Pure routine," the Gestapo man replied in his smooth falsetto. "We've got nothing better to do, so we're taking an interest in anything that comes along. In this case it's the activities of a corporal known as "Pixie" Lehmann—we've had our eye on him for some time. I can't think why he should have visited your flat yesterday evening, but he did. You ought to be worried."

"So you're taking an interest in anything that comes along, are you? I suppose that means you've reached a dead end again."

A smile flitted across the smooth expanse of Voglbronner's face. He nodded. "I didn't say so, mind."

Brackwede dismissed the very idea. "How could you have? We never exchanged a word—I didn't even see you. One more question, though. How come you know Lehmann?"

"From a photograph taken in the Goethestrasse a few

months back. We've got a whole series of them, all showing visitors to General Beck's house. They include one of you, Councillor."

"Quite possibly." Brackwede did not betray the slightest surprise. "If you're really collecting snaps of me I could look out dozens for you, some of them showing me with Count Helldorf, Police President of Greater Berlin."

"We know," Voglbronner hastened to assure him. "We appreciate that—at least, I do."

"You mean Maier doesn't?" Brackwede inquired with an amiable grin.

"Oh yes, he does too." The schoolboyish face looked positively deferential. "But he's head of the Armed Forces Section, so he's got to produce results. Between you and me, he's finding it hard going."

"Perhaps I ought to give him a little help," Brackwede said goodhumouredly. "I'm all in favour of mutual co-operation."

"I had the honour of knowing your friend Hammerstein's father intimately," General Olbricht said with a formal little bow. "He was a fine soldier and a very remarkable man."

"My friend's father was reputed to be a Red," the lieutenant seated opposite him replied with almost defiant candour. "He came to terms with the unions and was regarded as a sworn opponent of national restoration."

The subject of the conversation was General Kurt von Hammerstein, Commander-in-Chief of the Army from 1930 to 1934. His son, also an army officer, had been posted to the Bendlerstrasse after a number of combat assignments, and the lieutenant who had been politely ushered into General Olbricht's office was a friend of his.

Also in the room were two colonels, Stauffenberg, keenly observant despite his lone eye, and Mertz von Quirnheim, a rather more pensive and self-effacing figure. Olbricht himself gave an impression of elegance and urbanity. He had great charm when he chose to employ it.

"Baron von Hammerstein enjoyed a reputation for unlimited sang-froid," the general went on, watching the young officer's reactions closely. "Chancellor Bruening considered him to be the only man who could have succeeded in eliminating Hitler."

"You may be right," the lieutenant said. He began to have

an inkling of what was expected of him. "I was privileged to know him personally, sir—he was like a father to me. He advised President Hindenburg to have Hitler and his friends deposed by the Army as early as 1933."

"I'm aware of that." Olbricht gave the young officer an encouraging smile. "I'm also aware that the President vetoed any such project. The old gentleman was a staunch upholder of the Constitution. I imagine he assumed that Hitler was one too."

Mertz von Quirnheim inclined his balding, scholarly head. "After the outbreak of war, when General Baron von Hammerstein-Equord was commanding an army in the West, he planned to arrest Hitler during a tour of inspection."

"But the man never turned up," Stauffenberg broke in. "He's got the instincts of a rat. It's damned difficult to lure him out into the open, but one day we'll succeed—and that day isn't far hence. Well," he pursued relentlessly, "are you with us?"

The lieutenant nodded. "Yes."

"All the way?"

"All the way."

"What if I were to tell you to lock up your Commander-in-Chief, General Fromm?"

"I'd lock him up."

The scene that met Captain von Brackwede when he entered his flat was as peaceful as he had anticipated. He knew Maier well enough to realise that the man was adept at creating a harmonious atmosphere. Even his victims took some time to penetrate his mask of bland bonhomie.

"There you are at last!" Konstantin von Brackwede called. "We've been waiting for you."

Maier extended his hand and Brackwede shook it. "I've been having a most interesting conversation with your brother."

"Been trying to pump him, eh?" The captain seemed to find the notion entertaining. "Sorry you wasted your time. The boy's a dyed-in-the-wool idealist, but what he needs most of all at the moment is a cold shower." He turned to his brother. "Make yourself scarce, Konstantin. I'll see you later."

Konstantin nodded obediently and went out. Maier gazed after him benignly. "A nice youngster," he commented, "—so sincere, too. I've quite taken to him."

"Lay off the boy," Brackwede said warningly. "He's not

fair game. If you insist on poaching on the army's preserves, concentrate on me."

"Very well, my dear fellow," Maier rejoined, all sweetness and light. "Let's talk about SM3."

Brackwede did not blink. "So you've been rooting through my papers, have you? You ought to be ashamed of yourself, Maier. What about honour among thieves, and all that sort of thing?"

"The main item stocked by the Intelligence Depot is explosives," Maier continued in his most dulcet tones, "—in particular, high-grade British plastic explosives. There's virtually nothing you couldn't blow up with them."

"You've hit on quite an idea there, old friend. Perhaps I'll be able to congratulate you on the suggestion publicly one day."

Maier's right eyelid twitched, an almost imperceptible token of dismay which Brackwede noted with malicious pleasure. When beads of sweat broke out on the Sturmbannfuehrer's upper lip it signified profound agitation. Unfortunately, he was far from having reached that stage.

Maier summoned up a smile. "You never could resist a joke, could you?" he said heavily. "I know all about your little rackets. If I turned up at SM3 and presented that requisition chit the storeman would probably hand over a case of brandy—am I right?"

"Champagne," Brackwede amended amiably.

Maier sat back in his chair with a faint air of fatigue. "I thought as much. I'm afraid you misunderstand my motives," he said, injecting a note of intimacy into his voice. "I've no intention of making life difficult for you. On the contrary, my one ambition is that we should co-operate as we did in the old days."

Captain von Brackwede fanned himself with the grey-green requisition slip. The air in the room had grown oppressively close. "You wouldn't be thinking of ensuring my co-operation by blackmail, I suppose?"

"God forbid! I'd never dream of doing such a thing!" Maier's voice rang with comradely sincerity. "I know you too well for that, Brackwede. What I'm really hinting at is that I'd appreciate your help—or at least your expert advice."

Brackwede folded the requisition chit carefully and placed it in his wallet. "That sounds more like it. It's roughly what I expected. You want to stick your nose deeper than usual into army business—preferably into the Bendlerstrasse—and you're hoping I'll play copper's nark."

"No, no!" Maier protested. He sounded positively shocked. "There's no question of that. I was thinking more in terms of a deal—a two-way transaction."

They exchanged a lingering smile, which in Maier's case meant that he bared a row of chipped and discoloured teeth. Both men shared the same sense of mutual distrust, but neither hesitated to shake hands with apparent warmth.

"I make one stipulation in advance," Brackwede said, "and I insist on your honouring it. Leave my brother out of this. He's a babe-in-arms by our standards. Our sort of business doesn't concern him."

"Gestapo." Maier's lids drooped to conceal the gleam of interest that had come into his eyes. "You're fond of the boy, eh?" he said with bluff good-nature.

"Don't bother to try and unearth any emotional frailties in me, Maier!" Brackwede made a curt gesture of dismissal. "My own skin means more to me than anything or anyone else in the world, believe you me—so don't waste your time trying to prove otherwise!"

In Berlin's Goethestrasse stood a small and insignificant-looking house which might have belonged to an old-age pensioner with a passion for gardening. In fact, it was occupied by a man who was privately regarded as Germany's next Head of State. His name: Ludwig Beck.

"A Herr Leber wants to speak to you."

Beck glanced up sharply as his housekeeper made the announcement. For a man who seldom displayed emotion he seemed startled. Closing the file he had been perusing, he hurried out of his study into the passage with hands extended in welcome.

"If you're here it must be important," he said, trying to conceal his anxiety at this untoward visit. Beck was well aware of Julius Leber's standing and importance. He not only admired and respected the man's strong personality but acknowledged him to be one of the main pillars of the German resistance movement.

"I took every possible precaution, of course," Leber replied, running an interested eye over the crowded book-shelves that walled them in.

Beck liked to observe the conventions. He ordered tea, and

they exchanged a few remarks on general topics of conversation. For all the outward contrast between the two men, they had a surprising amount in common.

Beck smiled approvingly at his visitor. "Obviously, people are right when they call you a Prussian with Socialist leanings."

"About as right as they are when they call Stauffenberg and Brackwede Red aristos—lines of demarcation become blurred sometimes."

"Why did you come?" Beck demanded. "What has happened?"

Leber bowed his rugged head. "Are you aware that Colonel von Stauffenberg plans to execute the attempt on Hitler's life in person?"

The general hesitated for a few moments before replying, his lips compressed into a grim line. Then he said tersely: "The group of officers headed by Olbricht and Stauffenberg have assumed responsibility for that task. One of them must— and will—carry it out."

"But not Stauffenberg, surely?"

"Why not Stauffenberg?"

"Because he's one of the few men who are capable of changing the world around them!" Leber's bushy eyebrows contracted, deepening the furrows in his brow. "He mustn't expose himself to immediate danger. We need him here, both at the crucial moment and afterwards. I've studied every aspect of the man's character, and I can't bring myself to envisage the future of Germany without him."

Beck rose uneasily to his feet and leant against a bookcase as though in quest of support. "I second every one of your comments on Stauffenberg, Herr Leber, but the man has a will of iron as well as a strong sense of duty. If he's really determined to do this thing, no one will be able to dissuade him."

"I certainly couldn't, nor could anyone else in the movement—with one exception: you, General."

General Ludwig Beck was no ordinary man. When Hitler was appointed Chancellor by Hindenburg, even he could see "no other solution." For another five years he soldiered on, becoming one of the most senior officers in the German Army. Then, in 1938, as the danger of war became imminent, he wrote three monographs predicting the holocaust to come. Having openly and unmistakably advocated a putsch against Hitler in lectures to members of the General Staff, he took the characteristically consistent step of submitting his resignation—the only one of many dissatisfied generals to do so.

"You're the only person Stauffenberg would listen to!" Leber insisted. "You were the first to speak out openly against a policy of force and betrayal. You've attacked the crude fanaticism of this régime time and time again—we all know that. Stauffenberg looks upon you as Germany's rightful Head of State. He'd bow to your decision."

"Someone has to do it," Beck said sombrely.

"I'm not at home to anyone but my friends from the Gestapo," Captain von Brackwede announced boldly as he entered his office in the Bendlerstrasse. "If the C.-in-C. or anyone equally unimportant asks for me, you can give them the standard answer: unfit for duty owing to complete inebriation."

His personal assistant, Countess Oldenburg-Quentin, regarded him with a hint of indulgence. "You do make life difficult for me, Captain."

"It's the least complicated way of getting along with you." Brackwede thumbed through the papers on his desk with yawning indifference. "After all, you're in love with me, aren't you?"

The Countess stiffened. "What put that idea into your head?" Her lips barely moved as she added: "I've never implied anything of the kind."

"All right, so you're not in love with me. I'll make a note of that."

"Kindly do!" Elisabeth, Countess Oldenburg-Quentin, frowned. "I can't imagine why you should say such a thing."

Brackwede did not reply. Further inspection of his desk had disclosed a slip of paper which appeared to interest him. It was a note requesting him to telephone Koenigshof, "Koenigshof" being the current code-name for a general who was Chief of Staff to an Army Group fighting on the Russian front—a man with the energy of a human dynamo. "Please put a call through to General von Tresckow."

"I already did, just before you arrived."

"You're incomparable—where would men be without women like you!" The captain shot his personal assistant a look of smiling admiration. "Would it amuse you to have dinner at Horcher's this evening?"

"With you?" Elisabeth did her best to look entertained. "You may have some obscure motive for playing the man-about-town, but there's no reason why I should help you make a deliberate caricature of yourself. You manage well enough on your own."

"Glad to hear it," Brackwede said cheerfully. "However, I'm not only ambitious in the extreme—I occasionally suffer from fits of philanthropy. I'm feeling profoundly sorry for someone at the moment. He's a genuine idealist, and it's wretched to be an idealist in this day and age. I'm referring to my young brother."

"You want me to play the nursemaid?"

"Precisely, Countess. You've plumbed my innermost thoughts as usual. Do your good deed for the evening and allow one of our national heroes to buy you a slap-up dinner. You can try to extract his milk-teeth between courses. They're urgently in need of attention."

Having presided over his daily conference, the Fuehrer, Chancellor and Supreme Commander was receiving Heinrich Himmler in audience. Although still numbered among Hitler's most loyal supporters, the Reichsfuehrer-SS was already engaged in putting out clandestine peace-feelers.

"Be brief, Himmler!" Adolf Hitler was yearning for his regular afternoon nap. He clasped his hands tightly together to hide the persistent tremor that afflicted them these days.

"Things don't look good, my Fuehrer," Himmler said cautiously, endeavouring to strike the requisite note of comradely intimacy. "Trouble at every turn—some of it quite unnecessary."

Hitler nodded with the mechanical regularity of a marionette. He heard the same story every day. The Anglo-Saxon invasion was making unaccountable headway, the Balkan front was on the verge of collapse, and Russian armies were thrusting steadily towards Germany's eastern borders. A sudden wave of suppressed fury welled up inside him.

"We'll soon see whether the German people really deserve me or whether they're only fit for extinction."

This theme was familiar to all who were privileged to frequent the inner sanctum of the Fuehrer's Headquarters. They numbered only a few dozen these days.

"We must concentrate every last ounce of our available strength—every last ounce." Himmler submitted his suggestion with extreme deference. "The army's striking power has declined to a dangerous degree."

Hitler leant back in his capacious armchair. Wherever

he was residing, whether in Berchtesgaden, Munich or his headquarters of the moment, he was surrounded by gigantic, well-padded chairs of this sort. He closed his eyes wearily, but his voice retained its strong metallic timbre.

"I know, Himmler—you want to take over the Replacement Army."

"I wouldn't press the point if I didn't consider it urgently necessary in the interests of this concentration of strength I mentioned—quite apart from the fact that a lot of officers are still displaying reactionary tendencies. Now that we're committed to total war, absolute trustworthiness is the prime requirement."

Hitler's expression did not change, but the brush-like moustache twitched briefly on his ashen-grey face. "I've never thought very highly of General Fromm and his Bendlerstrasse set-up," he mused. "On the other hand, he does his job."

"It's been months since you invited him to a daily conference, my Fuehrer."

"I'm going to change that now he's got a new Chief of Staff. That man Stauffenberg has ideas."

Hitler's interest had immediately been aroused by Stauffenberg's first memorandum, to which some of his associates had drawn attention. It had obviously been drafted by someone with a talent for revolutionary thinking.

"I'm all in favour of a logical concentration of effort, Himmler," he continued with an undisguised yawn. His Alsatian bitch licked the hand that hung limply over the arm of his chair. "I don't think much of General Fromm, either, and I realise that there's no love lost between you. However, until you can bring me tangible proof of the Bendlerstrasse's inefficiency or disloyalty, things stay as they are."

"Very well, my Fuehrer," Himmler replied reluctantly.

Hitler rose with an effort, stumbling a little as the Alsatian bitch leapt at him in play. Ruffling the animal's fur, he said: "The last thing I want to do is dishearten you, Himmler. I view a certain type of officer with the utmost misgiving, and always have done, as you well know. I want facts, though, not vague conjectures. The principal thing is to win this war, and win it at any price."

"It's action stations, Eugen," Captain von Brackwede announced eagerly. "Tell your friends to hold themselves in readiness."

"Some of them have been doing that for the past eleven years, so you can't blame a few of them for feeling a bit sceptical. Remember when Halder, Witzleben and Oster announced the first big putsch? Nineteen-thirty-eight wasn't it?"

"I know, they've tried everything—revolvers, sniper's rifles, half a dozen concealed bombs. Some first-rate men volunteered, but they all failed in turn. Perhaps they didn't have the right mixture of intelligence and coldbloodedness.' '

"So it's Stauffenberg," Eugen G. said quietly.

Eugen G., universally known as "the Doctor," was a professor of philosophy, though he did not currently hold a university post. A pugnacious and comparatively youthful Swabian, he shuttled to and fro between the various resistance groups, highly esteemed in Christian-Democratic circles and trusted by Socialist groups. The soldiers who knew him paid him the compliment of calling him a Prussian, and Brackwede was a personal friend of his.

"When is it to be?"

"As soon as possible—in a matter of days or weeks, depending on circumstances. Inform our friends and tell them to be prepared."

"Are there any lists of contacts in existence, Fritz? Will I be given any names to work on?"

"In so far as there are lists, only one copy of them exists, and that's in General Olbricht's safe. Mertz von Quirnheim guards it like Cerberus. Very few initiates know all the details. That's part of Stauffenberg's technique, as you know."

Eugen G. eyed his friend keenly. "Does that mean some people are on the list and don't realise it?"

"Very perceptive of you, Eugen," Brackwede said. "When the time comes we shall merely issue orders and the army will carry them out. None of our friends will back down— Stauffenberg is positive of that. Only those who are at the centre of things and have to take direct action against leading Nazis will be informed of all details in advance."

"What if counter-orders are issued?"

"They'll be issued too late—we'll take care of that."

To the delight of Brackwede, who always relished facing a skilful cross-examination, Eugen G. went on probing. "What about the oath of allegiance to Hitler? A lot of people may find that an insuperable difficulty, wouldn't you say?"

This oath, first administered on 2 August 1934, shortly after Hindenburg's death, ran as follows: "I swear by God this sacred oath, that I will render unconditional obedience to the Fuehrer of the German Reich and people, Adolf Hitler, Supreme Commander of the Armed Forces, and that I will, as a courageous soldier, be prepared to risk my life at any time for this oath." Beck had described 2 August 1934 as "the darkest day of my life," and resistance circles had debated the subject for years.

"Hitler broke the oath himself," Brackwede said firmly. "He has invalidated it by his own criminal acts—isn't that your view, Eugen?"

"The Doctor" gave an emphatic nod. "And not only mine. I've found a number of passages in early Christian literature which explicitly state that no oath rendered to a tyrant has any validity."

"In fact the whole thing's far less complicated than it seems. Get rid of Hitler and you automatically render the oath null and void."

"True," Eugen G. said pensively. "It certainly doesn't present any problem to us, I realise that, but too many Germans favour blind obedience. Try explaining it to them!"

Fritz-Wilhelm, Count von Brackwede, did not reach his office until just before midday. This surprised no one, since he habitually came and went as he pleased, relying on his secretary to devise a series of excuses for his non-appearance. The Bendlerstrasse's personnel lists described him variously as a "liaison officer" or "Captain, Special Duties," but very few people knew what his work really entailed.

The Bendlerstrasse headquarters lay to the south of the Tiergarten. The surrounding ruins lent it an air of majestic isolation which belied the fact that it was a clumsy box-shaped administrative block of no great architectural merit. Although it had already received numerous direct hits and was littered with débris, the main fabric had so far survived intact.

Bendlerstrasse housed the present Commander-in-Chief, Replacement Army, General Fritz Fromm, whose entourage consisted of several dozen assorted generals and staff officers. The building also accommodated over a hundred soldiers, female employees and assistants, guard duties and security being taken care of by troops from the Berlin garrison.

"Well, Countess, how did you find my young brother?" Brackwede demanded with a touch of curiosity. "Did he arouse your maternal instincts?"

Elisabeth Oldenburg-Quentin frowned. "Your brother takes life very seriously. He seems to have all the ideals proper to a young German of today."

"In other words, you find him unutterably boring."

"No," she said thoughtfully. "I feel sorry for him, mainly because he's your brother. I've no doubt you'll try to involve him in your sort of existence, and no one could be less fitted for it."

"Let me worry about that, Countess—he's my brother, not yours. I'm pleased you've taken such an interest in the boy, though—genuinely pleased. I doubt if you'll guess why, but I'll explain when the time comes." Brackwede gave a mischievous grin. "As a matter of fact, you're going to have many more opportunities to sample the dubious delights of Brackwede family life. My brother will be staying in the neighbourhood for the time being. He's been attached to the School of Air Warfare at Bernau."

"It's lucky for him he's not in the army or you'd have had him posted to the Bendlerstrasse."

"Don't worry, I'll have an ample chance to rouse our Sleeping Beauty from his slumbers. He'll be here in half an hour or so. When he arrives, kindly give him the Gestapo files to read. You know which ones I mean—the treason cases."

Elisabeth's grey eyes clouded. "What good do you think that will do?"

"I want to start him thinking, damn it!"

Konstantin greeted Elisabeth Oldenburg-Quentin with a mixture of warmth and shyness. He did not seem unduly disappointed by his brother's absence.

"It was a lovely evening—at least, it was for me. Could I take you out again sometime? Anywhere you like."

"Why not?" she parried. "If another opportunity comes along . . ."

"Did I do something wrong?" Konstantin demanded in an anxious voice.

"Of course not," she said hastily. "What on earth gave you that idea?" Konstantin's clumsy advances were beginning to shake her equilibrium. She hurriedly handed him the files his brother had mentioned.

Reluctantly but obediently, the lieutenant began to leaf through the documents in front of him. He could scarcely believe his eyes. One case concerned a soldier who had used

" defeatist language " in an air-raid shelter. The remark in question—which had earned him the death penalty—was " That shit Goering and his lousy promises!" Another unfortunate had urinated—unintentionally, so he alleged—over the national emblem. The penalty: death. A third soldier had been caught in the act of looting a bombed house. His booty: three bottles of schnapps, five tins of corned beef and a bedspread. The penalty: once again, death.

" But this is frightful!"

" Utterly frightful," said Elisabeth. She stood by the window, looking down at the Bendlerstrasse. The lieutenant's reaction to what he had read seemed to disquiet her. " Is that all you have to say on the subject?"

Konstantin glanced up, and his eyes were shining with honest indignation. " As a soldier, this sort of thing disgusts me. I haven't the slightest sympathy for such creatures. I can only call them traitors to the Fuehrer and their fallen comrades. That's not why we're risking our necks at the front!"

Elisabeth marvelled at the naturalness and conviction with which Konstantin uttered the words. It seemed almost inconceivable that the two Brackwedes were of the same flesh and blood—but then anything was possible in Germany these days.

" You ought to realise that not everyone shares your convictions or natural characteristics, Lieutenant. You might see things differently if you did."

Elisabeth Oldenburg-Quentin gazed out of the open window, surveying the dusty pavements, heaps of débris and pale blue horizon with its jagged crenellation of gutted buildings. Suddenly, a man on a motor-cycle roared up the street, hotly pursued by a dark-grey saloon, its engine screaming in protest.

The man on the motor-cycle wrenched his handle-bars over and swooped boldly into the forecourt. The car behind him slammed on its brakes. Elisabeth picked up the 'phone with perceptible agitation and asked for Colonel Mertz von Quirnheim.

The colonel answered at once with his habitual calm, and Elisabeth reported: " Corporal Lehmann has just turned up, apparently with the Gestapo at his heels. They must be headed off at once."

Mertz von Quirnheim did not hesitate for a fraction of a second. " Get hold of the first officer in sight. Captain von

24

Brackwede isn't available—he's with Stauffenberg. I'll be down myself in a minute."

Corporal "Pixie" Lehmann stood in the guard-room doorway, breathing hard and endeavouring to grin cheerfully at SS-Sturmbannfuehrer Maier.

"How about that for speed!" he said. "I shouldn't be surprised if your radiator's boiling."

Maier's bar-parlour visage glowed like a sunset. His voice assumed an almost wheedling note as he advanced on Lehmann. "I'd like a word with you, if you don't mind."

"You'd like to get your claws on me, you mean," Lehmann retorted. He made a sweeping gesture of refusal. "I hope you're not thinking of trespassing on Army territory. Things haven't reached that stage yet, you know."

"I must request you to come with me," Maier said, vigorously now. Voglbronner, who had accompanied him, whispered a few words of warning in his ear, but Maier curtly shooed him back to the car. However, the Sturmbannfuehrer's steps became slower and more hesitant as he approached the entrance to the guard-room, until he finally came to a halt. The sergeant-major who functioned as the Bendlerblock's head porter emerged and stationed himself beside the grinning corporal.

At this moment an officer hurried up, almost at the double. This was Lieutenant Herbert, the "first officer in sight" referred to by Mertz von Quirnheim. Herbert, a round-faced, earnest-looking young man, produced a studiously deferential smile and an impeccable military salute.

The Sturmbannfuehrer returned the compliment in Greater German fashion by flourishing his outstretched right arm at eye-level. He followed this up by requesting an immediate interview with the fugitive corporal, who had been handed a note by an unknown man in the booking-hall of Friedrich-strasse Station. It could well be in the national interest to ascertain the contents of that note.

Corporal Lehmann laughed truculently. "Nothing on these premises has anything to do with the Gestapo. Anyway, this is a purely private matter—the note was a sort of love-letter. I may not look like it, but I'm quite a lady's man."

Lieutenant Herbert did his best to be conciliatory. Replacement Army Headquarters naturally had nothing to hide. He personally had the highest regard for the work of the State

Security Bureau, so it went without saying that he was ready to further its efforts. On the other hand, due regard had to be paid to certain basic principles, e.g., the delimitation of responsibility. Nevertheless, since the corporal himself conceded that the note in question was a personal one, it might be advisable for him to eliminate any possible suspicion by producing it for inspection.

The corporal rounded on Lieutenant Herbert with an air of outrage. "What's that! Are you trying to sell me out?"

Herbert's honest face turned puce. "How dare you speak to me like that! You must be out of your mind."

"I told you he was up to no good," Maier interjected, heaping fuel on the flames. "He's a crafty one, take it from me."

"Corporal Lehmann," Lieutenant Herbert said resolutely, "hand over that note at once."

"You'll be lucky," Lehmann replied, undeterred. He could afford this piece of insubordination because he had just caught sight of Colonel Mertz von Quirnheim approaching the group at a leisurely pace. Gleaming spectacles veiled the scorn in his eyes as he looked at Maier.

The colonel listened to each of the parties concerned, virtually without comment. Then he announced: "This matter will be investigated with every possible care. May I ask you to accompany me to my office, Sturmbannfuehrer? Then you can have a thorough discussion with the officer responsible for such questions."

"Would that be Captain von Brackwede?"

"Right first time, Sturmbannfuehrer." Mertz von Quirnheim sketched an amicable smile. "I can't think of anyone better qualified to deal with the matter, can you?"

"You're looking very thoughtful, Stauffenberg," General Olbricht said with a touch of concern. "Something's obviously worrying you. What is it?"

The colonel laid the three fingers of his left hand on a list in front of him. After a moment's hesitation he said: "I think we ought to go through the whole schedule for X-Day again—carefully. A lot of it strikes me as out of date."

"Including that list?" Olbricht inquired in dismay. The sheaf of papers contained the names of future members of the government. "You're not thinking of making alterations to that, are you?"

Friedrich Olbricht was a well-built man of medium height.

26

When he waxed sarcastic a faintly Saxonian intonation crept into his voice, but this had happened rarely of late. The swift repartee for which he had once been renowned had also become rarer in recent times. From May 1940 onwards he had been in charge of the General Army Office, one of the three main departments in the Bendlerstrasse, and ever since that time he had been the hub of the military resistance movement—until Colonel Stauffenberg appeared.

" I quite realise that our lists aren't ideal—the government list included. However, they were agreed upon after confidential discussions between the separate groups . . ."

" That was ages ago!" Stauffenberg interjected.

"Perhaps, but it's too late to introduce any major changes now."

" It'll only be too late when the bomb's gone off."

General of Infantry Friedrich Olbricht was fully prepared to respect the opinions of Stauffenberg, even though he was by far his senior. He was even prepared to subordinate himself to him during the crucial stages of the revolt, but he had been worried to see Stauffenberg's mutilated hand single out one name on the list of prospective government members: that of Carl Friedrich Goerdeler, who was to become Chancellor in the event of a successful attempt on Hitler's life.

" I know," Stauffenberg said, a trifle impatiently, " you've been well acquainted with Herr Goerdeler for a long time—since nineteen thirty-three, if my memory serves me."

Olbricht gave a wry smile. " Brackwede has briefed you well, I see. In those days I was Chief of Staff at Fourth Army Corps in the Dresden and Leipzig area. Herr Goerdeler was mayor at the time."

"None of us forgets past acquaintanceships readily, General, and that's as it should be. The bulk of the resistance movement depends on personal contacts. You have to possess the realism of a man like Brackwede before you can feel entirely free from sentimental attachments to the past."

" Does our ultra-sceptical friend think he's discovered your Achilles' heel as well?" Olbricht inquired with a chuckle.

" He does indeed, and I'm half inclined to think he may be right." Stauffenberg thoughtfully surveyed the lists in front of him. " Brackwede regards my nomination of General Hoepner as C.-in-C. Replacement Army as sentimental weakness. He's found out that Hoepner used to be my divisional commander and that I owe him a debt of gratitude."

" Brackwede objects to both of them, then?"

" He has done his best to convince me that Goerdeler is played out—an honest man, but worn down by five years of intensive conspiracy. Hoepner he simply regards as unreliable. He virtually called him a blabbermouth."

Olbricht wagged his head. " He wants to substitute Julius Leber for Goerdeler, doesn't he? They don't call him the Red Count for nothing. He'd like to shift the balance of the next government in favour of Socialism, but that would stir up a lot of misgivings among our mutual friends."

" We can't afford to wrangle—there isn't time. Let's seize every available opportunity and concentrate on producing tangible results. The most important job must go to the man best equipped for it. If Julius Leber looks like the best candidate for the Chancellorship, let him become Chancellor."

" Sturmbannfuehrer Maier can wait," Captain von Brackwede said, stretching his legs comfortably. " Let him stew in his own juice for a while."

" I don't understand." Lieutenant Konstantin von Brackwede looked bewildered. He sat in his brother's office, listening to his remarks with mounting astonishment. " I thought the Sturmbannfuehrer was a friend of yours."

" Friendship is a pale description of our relationship."

For all her youth—she was only just twenty-two—Elisabeth Oldenburg-Quentin had learnt how to control her reactions in Captain von Brackwede's presence. She seldom found it difficult, but she was finding it an effort at the moment. Konstantin eyed her with fond concern.

Brackwede leant back in his chair and studied his fingernails with some distaste. They were not as well-tended as they might have been.

" My dear, ingenuous friends," he said meditatively. " Naïvety is a lovesome thing—Schiller would have confirmed that, but then he never knew our unique Fuehrer. There's no clear-cut distinction between friend and foe. Self-styled friends can be the deadliest of enemies."

" Possibly," Konstantin said. " Just as self-styled patriots can turn out to be traitors."

The captain nodded. " And just as alleged traitors can turn out to be better Germans than self-styled patriots."

Elisabeth's silky hair gleamed softly as she bowed her head, and the delicate curve of her neck was enough to stir any young man's fancy. Konstantin gazed at her enraptured. He did not appear to have heard his brother's last remark.

"I'd be only too happy to let you sit there mooning at my personal assistant all day, but we actually do some work here from time to time." Brackwede smiled without undue warmth. "Here's another basic principle for you, Konstantin: very few people are what they seem to be."

There was a knock and the door opened to reveal Corporal Lehmann, explosives expert, despatch-rider and post-box for conspiratorial mail. He grinned amiably, nodded at all three and strode into the room as though it belonged to him. Sitting down unasked, he crossed his legs casually and waited.

"Well, where's this love-letter the Gestapo were so keen to see?" demanded Brackwede.

The corporal produced a folded sheet of paper and handed it to him. Brackwede put it down on the desk-top and smoothed it out carefully. His hawk-like face lit up as he read the contents.

"Why do these people have to put so much in writing?" Lehmann inquired with interest. "All they have to do is say "I'm with you" or "I don't like the idea"—but no, they scribble away like maniacs. The General makes a careful note of every last little thing, and as for our friend the Mayor— anyone would think he was organising a paper-chase. I call that an unnecessary luxury, don't you?"

"Possibly," conceded Brackwede. "All the same, one can't forbid that sort of thing—or I can't anyway. I'm merely doing a specific job. The General and the Mayor are working for posterity—for the future, if you like."

"That's all very well, but what if their future lies with the Gestapo?"

Brackwede gave a short laugh, but there was no mirth in his expression. Konstantin's face was pale and vacant. He found it impossible to grasp the drift of the conversation. Turning to Elisabeth for enlightenment, he saw that her lips were slightly parted in dismay.

"After the dance you've just led the Gestapo, my friend, you'd better go to ground at once." Brackwede spoke without rancour.

"I suppose that means I'm sacked," the corporal said judicially.

"On the contrary, your services are still urgently needed. I'm simply going to give you a temporary reassignment. Don't worry, I've got just the job for you."

Lehmann looked apprehensive. "I hope you're not thinking of posting me to General Tresckow's mob. I don't fancy the Russian front. I'd prefer something cushier—you know that."

"I do indeed. That's why I'm sending you to Paris."

"Done!" the corporal said, rubbing his hands contentedly. "Paris is just up my street. They can write notes to their heart's content—I'll deliver them, and I'll watch out for kid brothers, too."

"I've just come from the Russian front," said the officer. "I had instructions from General von Tresckow to report to General Beck, and he sent me to you."

The officer, a lieutenant, could not have been more than twenty-five, but there were deeply etched lines at the corners of the mouth and his eyes looked like an old man's. Only his forehead retained the smoothness of youth.

"I've seen it for myself," he said.

Someone offered him a cigarette and he lit it, pressing his hands together to hide the tremor that ran through them, but his voice had a firm, forcible ring, as though he had already told what he had to tell many times before.

Leber asked: "Did General Beck give you any specific reason why he wanted you to come and see us?"

"He wanted me to tell you what I've seen."

The lieutenant, whose name was Bahr, gazed round at Leber's "log cabin." Grouped about him on packing-cases, sacks and chairs were a dozen of Leber's most trusted friends, among them Wilhelm Leuschner, formerly Hessen's Minister of the Interior and now the proprietor of a small factory producing beer-taps. Ex-trade-union leaders, one-time Socialist members of parliament and two priests made up the remainder of the circle. Leber's wife Annedore bustled about refilling cups and glasses.

"They're being annihilated in gas-chambers and ovens," the lieutenant went on. "Everything is run on a mass-production basis. The number of dead is currently estimated at about four millions."

The rough wooden walls of Leber's office were shrouded in shadow, and the pale faces of his audience swam in the gloom, dimly illuminated by the light of a single lamp. A breathless and oppressive hush hung over the gathering.

"Several thousand people are dying every day at a place called Auschwitz," Bahr pursued. "Losses at the front are increasing too. In General von Tresckow's opinion, the

Russians may reach the German border in a matter of weeks. Another few months, and they could be at the gates of Berlin. That's what I've been told to tell you."

He sat down. There was no more to say. He had tried to convey the enormity of what had happened in the simplest possible terms. The silence had become almost tangible now.

"Thousands of people—every day," Annedore Leber murmured in a shocked undertone.

"And every day that goes by costs another few thousand human lives," Julius Leber said, staring down at his hands, which he had folded in an attitude of prayer. "That's what General Beck meant this young man to convey to us."

"What does he want?"

"My approval of Stauffenberg's plan of action—and he can have it. We must bring this appalling slaughter to an end at the earliest possible moment."

"Well," Captain von Brackwede asked his brother, when Corporal Lehmann had left the room, beaming with pleasure, "are you waiting for an explanation?"

"No," Konstantin said.

"Why not?"

"Because I don't see the slightest necessity for one, Fritz."

The two brothers looked at each other, and the elder man noted with a touch of compassion that Konstantin's pale face radiated boundless trust. Elisabeth Oldenburg-Quentin gave a relieved smile.

"We often have to deal with the oddest things in this office," she said, "that's why they sometimes call us the Bendlerstrasse rubbish-dump. Don't worry your head about it."

"You can tell Sturmbannfuehrer Maier to come in now," Brackwede said with a hint of reluctance. "No, stay here and keep your ears open," he told Konstantin, who had started to get up. "You never know, you may learn something."

Maier burst into the room like a bull. He took the requisite formalities at a gallop—a handshake for Captain von Brackwede, a curt bow for Elisabeth and a benevolent nod for Konstantin. Then he sat down in the chair recently vacated by Corporal Lehmann.

"Well, what's the score?" he demanded abruptly. "Are you going to hand him over or aren't you?"

Brackwede's manner was obliging in the extreme. "I don't quite follow you, Maier. Even if the man you're referring to has done something wrong, it's a matter for the military authorities, not the Gestapo."

"My dear fellow," Maier said, "let's not beat about the bush. There are ways of arranging these things, as you well know . . ."

"Not in a case like this, old friend. I'm here to protect the Army's interests, even if I'm occasionally compelled to act against my better judgment."

"All right—out with it!" Maier's voice sounded resentful and accusing, but his face preserved its usual equability. "What's behind all this?"

Brackwede gave an apologetic shrug. He centred his whole attention on the Sturmbannfuehrer, seemingly unaware of his secretary's apprehensive glances and his brother's air of frozen astonishment.

Corporal Lehmann's note was still lying on the desk. Brackwede made no attempt to conceal it. That would have been a piece of stupidity which Maier would have been quick to spot. His eyes travelled swiftly over it and back to Maier's face. "The corporal you were chasing has been interrogated and searched, but the only thing found on him was an item of personal correspondence which might roughly be described as a love-letter."

Maier gave a snort of indignation. "Then he must have worked a switch. It's just what I'd have expected of a sly bastard like that. Never mind, I'll get him all the same."

"I'm afraid I can't hand him over." Brackwede's voice rang with sincerity. "The corporal doesn't belong to this department any more. He's been posted—I can't say where to at the moment."

"But this is outrageous! Are you really telling me you can't produce him?"

"You've caught my meaning perfectly, as usual."

Maier jumped to his feet, and the chair he had been sitting on clattered, unheeded, to the floor. To Konstantin's delight, the flush of agitation on Elisabeth's golden-brown cheeks deepened. His brother sat there, unmoved and unmoving.

"I refuse to believe that you want to put paid to our working relationship," Maier growled.

"Ah," Brackwede said suavely, "it's only just beginning, Maier. It'll be mutually profitable, too, as long as we're not petty-minded—and that's the last thing we'd expect of each other, isn't it?"

TWO

"The Commanders-in-Chief will co-operate," General Henning von Tresckow said confidently, "—provided, of course, that the attempt succeeds."

"In other words," Stauffenberg retorted with mild sarcasm, "they're not only leaving the dirty work to us but shelving all the responsibility as well. They're prepared to swear a new oath to a new Constitution, but that's as far as they'll go."

"We shouldn't expect too much from some of these gentlemen," General Olbricht interposed with his customary gift for compromise. "It's a promising sign that there are at least some Army Commanders who view our efforts with favour."

"Not only that," Tresckow said firmly. "Field Marshal von Kluge will lend us his active support—he told me so himself."

General Henning von Tresckow, Chief of Staff to the C.-in-C., Army Group Centre, had just flown in from the Russian front. Alerted by news of Stauffenberg's decision, he had come to give his friends all the moral support he could offer in the few hours available to him.

Gathered in the Bendlerstrasse on that flawless summer day were the three mainstays of the military resistance movement: Olbricht, the planner, Tresckow, the man of action, and Stauffenberg, the human dynamo. It was these three, aided by Mertz von Quirnheim, who had jointly devised Operation "Valkyrie" in the course of days and nights of unremitting work—"Valkyrie," which was to facilitate and implement the coup d'état with traditional General Staff precision when X-Day dawned.

"I've had long and frequent discussions with Field Marshal von Kluge," Tresckow continued, directing his remarks at Stauffenberg. "We were absolutely frank with one another. I told him that Hitler had to be eliminated and that I and my friends would personally try to achieve this. His reaction was quite spontaneous and wholly convincing. "I'm with you!" were his actual words."

"That's easy enough to say," Stauffenberg commented sceptically.

"I realise Kluge isn't the sort of man to commit himself to

the hilt," Tresckow conceded. "All the same, he despises Hitler and abhors his methods. He won't hold back when the time comes."

"I'm sure you're right," Olbricht said. "Kluge realises perfectly well that the war is lost, and that is bound to strengthen his determination. Many people think as he does, and they'll act accordingly. Besides, we mustn't forget that generals like von Brauchitsch were prepared to bring the war to an end at any price in nineteen thirty-nine—even if it entailed opposing Hitler."

Von Stauffenberg sat back in his chair with a smile. Almost mechanically, his hand went to the black patch covering his sightless eye. "I know, Brauchitsch says he went to see the Fuehrer brimming with determination, but that didn't prevent him from being abused, threatened and—to use his own words—deeply impressed."

"But his attitude didn't change," declared Tresckow. "He simply resigned himself to the situation like a lot of other people. A few months ago I had another chat with him— Manstein, too. Both of them listened to what I had to say, and they both seemed extremely interested."

"But they're not prepared to do anything." Stauffenberg was a striver after clarity. He refused to be borne away on rosy wings of optimism. He wanted to know what was, not what might conceivably be.

"None of them will object if we do it ourselves," said Olbricht.

"The main thing is to do it properly." Tresckow nodded at the colonel. "It'll start a landslide, you mark my words. The vital thing is to get through to Hitler. You'll manage that all right, Stauffenberg. Manufacturing the bomb is another important job, but Corporal Lehmann knows his stuff. I've made sure of that."

"I'm afraid we'll have to make do without Lehmann," Olbricht said, eager to avoid any unnecessary delays. "However, there are plenty of other explosives experts available. Lehmann had to be posted to Paris in a hurry because the Gestapo started taking an interest in him."

"Who transferred him?" demanded Tresckow. "I don't like it."

"Captain von Brackwede," replied Stauffenberg. "I must confess I've been wondering whether his decision was influenced by our personal friendship. To be quite frank, I wouldn't put it past him to try and stop me carrying out this project."

" He's a stubborn customer," Olbricht said diffidently.

Tresckow looked thoughtful. " I'm sure he's with us all the way, but friendship takes strange forms. It's difficult for outsiders to recognise them sometimes."

" I've never tried to interfere in your personal affairs," said Elisabeth Oldenburg-Quentin. " I've always done my best to respect your privacy—I'm sure you'll admit that."

" Of course. You've been very discreet." Captain von Brackwede eyed his personal assistant—normally so reserved—with guarded interest. " What's worrying you exactly?"

" Your brother, and the way you're trying to drag him into your world by the scruff of his neck."

They eyed each other warily across one of the small tables in the Bendlerstrasse canteen, watched over by the inevitable photograph of Adolf Hitler. The large and ornate mess which had once accommodated the whole staff no longer existed, but few of the Bendlerstrasse officers regretted its passing. Allied air-raids had endowed their communal life with a rough-and-ready intimacy which was not without its compensations.

Brackwede smiled. " I was under the impression that we'd reached a basic understanding, Countess. You file my papers, but you don't know what's in them. You type documents for me, but you don't know what they mean. You take my 'phone calls, but you don't remember any names or particulars."

" I realise you want to protect me and I appreciate it, but I can't switch my mind off entirely. I've already forgotten most of the confidential material you've entrusted me with, but I can't remain indifferent to what you're doing to your brother."

" How delightful for him." Captain von Brackwede glanced round, but no one appeared to be listening. Few of the tables were occupied and the officers seated at them were working their way through the fixed menu in stolid silence, their jaws champing doggedly on the tough and stringy meat.

" I'm not much given to good works, Countess, as you know, but I respect people who are. If you're really determined to take my young brother in hand, far be it from me to stop you."

Elisabeth was spared the necessity of replying by the appearance of Colonel Mertz von Quirnheim, who walked over to their table and politely asked if he might join them. The light shone gently on his balding head as he sat down,

35

smiling almost diffidently and adjusting his professional-looking spectacles.

Having bowed gallantly to Elisabeth he abruptly turned his attention to Brackwede. He was feeling a little worried, he confessed. "Gestapo" Maier was not a man to be trifled with.

"I know he isn't," Brackwede conceded, "but that makes him all the easier to handle. Once you realise that he's a double-dyed villain, it's amazing what you can get out of him."

The colonel registered no reaction. He methodically spooned up the soup which a mess waiter had brought him—slimy water with a few grains of rice in it—until he had emptied his plate.

"The Gestapo is Himmler," he said at length, "and everyone knows that Himmler is angling for the job of Commander-in-Chief, Replacement Army. That means he'll exploit every opportunity to make things difficult for General Fromm—i.e., for us. Maier strikes me as just the man who might supply the Reichsfuehrer-SS with a pretext for moving into the Bendlerstrasse."

"He might, but he won't find it easy." Brackwede's eyes narrowed. "Membership of the Gestapo doesn't come naturally—except to blockheads, sadists, born intriguers and a few radical politicians. Maier may be a lot of things, but he certainly isn't a blockhead. What's more, I've established a certain measure of contact with him. We're in the process of forming a sort of mutual investment company——" he grinned "—with limited liability, of course."

"A risky game." Mertz von Quirnheim pushed his empty plate away and stared morosely into space for a moment. "It's becoming harder and harder to pick the right men these days," he said. "Here in the Bendlerstrasse we've spent years trying to keep our stable clean—and then suddenly a man like Lieutenant Herbert comes along. He was on the point of handing Lehmann over to the Gestapo, if you can imagine it."

"A confirmed idealist," Brackwede said equably. "As I see it, you not only have to allow for people like Herbert—you have to exploit them. Used properly, they provide a perfect smoke-screen—and what could suit our particular purposes better than a few lusty flag-wavers in the foreground?"

Mertz von Quirnheim looked amused, and a network of fine wrinkles appeared at the corners of his eyes. He rose with an air of decision.

"I have a short 'phone-call to make. I'll be back in a few minutes, if you care to wait."

Elisabeth Oldenburg-Quentin stared after the colonel's retreating figure with a worried frown. Captain von Brackwede continued to study the gravy-stained tablecloth as if it were a General Staff map. He wore an expression of brooding excitement.

"You seem to have given him a bright idea," Elisabeth said. "Isn't everything complicated enough already?"

"As long as a few individuals can thread their way through the jungle, that's good enough for me. Most people are satisfied with a crudely painted façade, and the fashionable décor at the moment is brown with a frieze of swastikas. We ought to have adopted that sort of camouflage years ago."

Mertz von Quirnheim reappeared. "I've just spoken to General Olbricht," he said, resuming his seat. "He approves of your suggestion. With effect from now, we're setting up a new department whose sole function will be to ensure the closest liaison with Party authorities of every description. This department is to be administered by Lieutenant Herbert, who will be directly responsible to General Olbricht. The General has selected you, Captain von Brackwede, as his permanent representative where Party liaison questions are concerned."

"Good," Brackwede said with evident relish. "If we're going to throw dust into people's eyes I'll be happy to supply it by the cart-load. One of the first deliveries will be made by my young brother. Even he has his uses."

"We mustn't overlook anything or take anything for granted," said the foreign office official. "You can't deny that Colonel von Stauffenberg used to be an ardent National Socialist."

"No, he wasn't!" Eugen G. retorted belligerently. "That's a slanderous allegation. What the devil do you mean by it?"

The foreign office official shot the temperamental young man a reproachful look, and his voice took on a note of gentle reproof. "I merely wanted to clear up any possible misunderstandings. Since objections of a more or less open nature have recently been lodged against Herr Goerdeler by certain parties, it would not be immaterial to identify their underlying cause."

"Very well!" Eugen G. snapped angrily. "I'd sooner say it now and have done with it: I used to be a Hitler Youth leader myself."

Count von Moltke, their tall and elegant host, gave a conciliatory laugh. Eager to avoid any resumption of internecine strife, he drew his guests' attention to the wine he had managed to procure for the occasion—a Kitzinger Mainleite 1933—and the half-dozen men in civilian clothes temporarily yielded to the distraction, Eugen G. included.

Von Moltke was only thirty-five, but he was one of the main co-ordinators of the resistance movement. Leber and Beck held him in equal esteem, Goerdeler trusted him, and even Communist groups spoke of him with respect. His circle of friends included Stauffenberg, Brackwede and Eugen G.

"Are you familiar with an incident which occurred in Bamberg on January thirty-first, nineteen-thirty-three?" demanded the foreign office official, clearly determined to lend indirect support to Goerdeler's position.

"Perfectly familiar!" parried Eugen G. "A young army officer joined the jubilant crowds and marched through the streets—namely, Stauffenberg. For that matter, Brackwede used to be Deputy Police President of Berlin and Dr. Goerdeler wrote reports on his travels abroad for the benefit of Hitler and Goering. So what?"

"So nothing," interposed Count von Moltke, trying to look amused. "Beck wasn't opposed either, to begin with. Professor Popitz semi-approved of the new régime and Professor Haushofer even supplied it with some theoretical advice, but they're all with us now—shoulder to shoulder. I'd go so far as to say that their rejection of Nazism is even better founded than ours. We and a lot of others opposed the Nazis from the outset on grounds of birth, upbringing or political conviction —quite apart from religion—but they had to wrestle with themselves to reach a decision, and for many of them it was a hard struggle. Their beliefs represent a triumph of conscience."

"Claus von Stauffenberg has gone on record on three occasions," Eugen G. said solemnly, "and he couldn't have been more explicit. In nineteen-thirty-nine he said: The fool's gone to war. In nineteen-forty-one: He's still winning too many victories. In nineteen-forty-two, his verdict was: Kill him!"

Lieutenant Herbert, Christian name Herbert, was convinced that he had joined the national élite. The sun of official favour seemed to be shining brightly on him. He had been appointed head of a department, allocated an office of his own and accorded the patronage of Captain von Brackwede.

"We're placing a great deal of faith in you," the captain told him. "We're confident you won't let us down."

"This is a job after my own heart, sir," Herbert replied with fervour. "I'll really put my back into it, don't you worry."

"You mustn't overestimate its importance, of course," Brackwede said goodnaturedly. "On the other hand, I'm quite certain you'll make a go of it. Your political convictions give you a head start—I know, I've got a brother who shares them. As a matter of fact, it was partly on his account that I recommended you. I'd be grateful if you'd give him a few hints on the real meaning of loyalty to the Fuehrer."

"I should be honoured," Herbert declared solemnly.

Well-chosen clichés floated round the new departmental chief's office for several minutes more, wreathing the air like incense.

With nonchalant ease, Brackwede laid what he hoped would be a monumental cuckoo's egg in the zealous young lieutenant's nest. Apart from telling Herbert to put out routine preliminary feelers where the Party and its various agencies were concerned, he advised him to devote particular attention to SS-Sturmbannfuehrer Maier.

Herbert bowed. "Your wish is my command."

"Sturmbannfuehrer Maier and I are friends, in a manner of speaking. I'm extremely anxious to ensure the closest cooperation between us—if you're agreeable."

"I shall do my utmost to achieve it, sir," Herbert assured him in the tones of one taking a solemn vow.

"You'll keep me regularly informed of all developments, of course. We'll cross our bridges when we come to them. All right, carry on, and let me see you come up with some bright ideas!"

"I'm afraid we can't count on General Oster," Olbricht reported. "He's been under surveillance for quite a time. The Gestapo are doing their best to isolate Intelligence altogether."

"And all because of that confounded list of names on his assistant's desk," Stauffenberg commented bitterly. "The Gestapo would never have spotted Oster if he hadn't tried to pocket it while they were actually searching the room."

Henning von Tresckow looked unperturbed. "We've got to allow for any eventuality—even the chance that those British acid detonators fail to function. I had a primed bomb put into Hitler's plane, if you remember, and it didn't go off."

The meeting had been going on for several hours now, but Tresckow was as indefatigable as his two friends. They marshalled arguments, explored counter-arguments, exchanged ideas and devised new proposals. Tresckow's arrival signalled the appearance on the scene of a man of action—a man who had already made nearly half a dozen attempts to rid Germany of Hitler.

The notorious *Kommissarbefehl*, a decree which sanctioned the shooting of Russians "on suspicion" and in direct contravention of international law, had ushered in a reign of terror which Tresckow refused to countenance. "Remember this moment," he had told his officers as they listened to him, frozen-faced with disgust. "If we don't succeed in getting these orders countermanded, Germany will have forfeited her honour once and for all, and the effects will be felt for centuries to come."

Today, in the Bendlerstrasse, Tresckow's manner was calm, composed and resolutely objective. "We've got to get the bomb into Hitler's presence without arousing suspicion—that's the first requirement."

"No difficulty there," said Stauffenberg. "I'm summoned to attend conferences at the Fuehrer's Headquarters fairly regularly these days, usually with General Fromm."

"A bomb is the only possibility, I suppose?"

"It is as far as I'm concerned." Stauffenberg held up the three remaining fingers on his left hand.

"I didn't mean that," Tresckow replied coolly. "Shooting is an unreliable method of assassination. Even the so-called successes—Sarajevo, for instance—left an awful lot to chance. We want to eliminate every element of uncertainty."

Olbricht gave a nod of agreement. "Besides, they never leave Hitler alone. Security measures are strict, and he seems to have a sixth sense for danger—always did have. Remember how he left the Munich beer-cellar before the bomb went off in nineteen-thirty-eight?"

Tresckow drummed his fingers on the desk. "There was a time when I and my fellow-officers thought the job would have to be done with pistols—it seemed to be more in the army tradition. Five men volunteered in order to eliminate slip-ups, but there was no way of getting them into Hitler's presence."

"Then we're agreed on this point," Stauffenberg said. "I

also share the view that a high-explosive bomb is the only possibility. The only thing I'm still vague about is how to set it off unobtrusively and effectively."

"You'll find a way," Tresckow told him confidently. "I'll bet you're thinking what I'm thinking, Stauffenberg. There's nothing more inconspicuous than our favourite national accoutrement—the briefcase!" He gave a sardonic smile and then looked grave again. "However, there's another point which strikes me as far more important. What's your personal reaction to Hitler?"

"How do you mean?"

Olbricht cleared his throat. "Hitler is universally credited with remarkable powers of persuasion, Stauffenberg. Even a man like Brauchitsch found them too much for him, and he's only one of many. Members of our group at Supreme Headquarters—General Stieff, for instance—have said that his presence would render them physically incapable of . . ."

Stauffenberg burst out laughing. Tresckow raised his bullet head sharply and Olbricht looked faintly surprised despite himself.

"Don't worry," Stauffenberg said. "The first time I saw him face to face my sole reaction was 'Can that really be our great Leader?' He left me completely cold. I felt then what I still feel: the man's redundant!"

Determined to justify his superiors' faith in him and earn Captain von Brackwede's approbation, Lieutenant Herbert prepared to step up his personal contribution to the war-effort.

On the evening of his very first day as "National Socialist Liaison Officer" he mobilised his girl-friend of the moment, Molly Ziesemann, who was currently doing switchboard duty in the Bendlerstrasse communications centre. "I'm counting on you," he told her. "If you really love me, you'll pull your weight."

The result was an "informal little gathering" in Ulmenstrasse, only three blocks from the Bendlerstrasse headquarters. Molly Ziesemann not only lent her flat for the occasion but showed a willingness to make any further sacrifices that might be required of her.

The two invited guests were SS-Sturmbannfuehrer Maier and Lieutenant von Brackwede. The former came direct from a Gestapo interrogation in the cellars of the Prinz Albrechtstrasse, the latter from his new quarters at the School of Air

41

Warfare in Bernau, just outside Berlin. Both ate with appetite, drank with enthusiasm and flirted with Molly, egged on in comradely fashion by Herbert.

After the third bottle of wine, Konstantin von Brackwede blossomed like a hot-house flower and began to sing his brother's praises. Herbert joined in the refrain while Maier lent an attentive ear. It seemed that Captain Count Fritz-Wilhelm von Brackwede was a loving brother, an exemplary superior and a remarkable man.

"I've always had the highest opinion of my friend Fritz," Maier said gravely. "Tell me more about him—I'm intrigued."

The Sturmbannfuehrer casually surveyed his surroundings. The ceiling was stained greyish-brown with smoke, the wallpaper blotched and wrinkled like a week-old tablecloth in a cheap café, the floor-boards warped and uneven. War swept away the trappings of bourgeois domesticity, he reflected. It paved the way for a new world, provided one survived long enough to see it.

Molly bustled about emptying ash-trays and refilling glasses, displaying her plump buttocks to Maier and Konstantin as she did so. Herbert noted her endeavours with satisfaction. His guests appeared to be appreciating the fare set before them. Contentedly, he uncorked the sixth bottle.

"What about women—pardon me—the ladies?" Maier hazarded with a jovial smile. "Everyone has his failings—even friend Fritz."

"Not him!" Konstantin insisted, trying to keep Molly at arm's length. "My brother's a gentleman in every respect."

Herbert's round red face glistened. "Yes, I can vouch for that! The captain's fire-proof. He could have it off with that Mona Lisa of a secretary of his any time he liked, but he won't play ball."

"That's a dirty lie!" Konstantin leapt to his feet, knocking a glass to the floor. "How dare you say such a thing!"

"Steady on!" Herbert looked taken aback. "I didn't mean any harm—it was just a way of expressing my admiration. Don't get me wrong."

Maier removed his hand from Molly's thigh and leant forward to refill their glasses. "Your brother's only human, after all . . ."

"But he's married!" Konstantin protested in a high, shaking voice. His pale-blue eyes shone with tipsy belligerence. "He loves his wife and children more than anything else in the world."

42

"Anything?" Maier inquired softly.

"He'd rather die than betray someone close to him."

"How admirable," said the Sturmbannfuehrer, smiling with relish. "I'm happy to hear that such sentiments still exist."

"We've worked out a few supplementary plans for Operation Valkyrie, sir," Olbricht said.

"Very good—if you've nothing better to do." Fromm's tone conveyed resentment at being interrupted. A monthly magazine devoted to hunting and shooting lay open on his desk.

"These supplementary plans are designed to achieve a tighter grip on Berlin itself, particularly in regard to cordoning off the administrative quarter."

General Fromm's fleshy features darkened. He disliked Operation Valkyrie, especially as it was not his own brainchild but had been devised by his chief of staff.

"Spare me the details," he grumbled. "I don't think much of your plan—in fact I've even recorded my objections to it in writing, so put that in your pipe!"

Olbricht remained silent for a few moments, digesting the fact that his wily commander-in-chief had characteristically taken out yet another insurance policy. "But the Fuehrer gave his personal approval . . ."

"He did indeed!" interjected Fromm. The thought seemed to amuse him, judging by the malicious glint in his shrewd little eyes. "The man's an amateur, and this proves it. He hasn't a clue what you smart lads are cooking up for him."

Olbricht registered no surprise at his chief's remarks. Fromm indulged in sacrilege often enough, as long as no third party was present. Officially, he was one of the Fuehrer's paladins; privately, he regarded Hitler as a cretin and Himmler as a "wild boar." The huntsman in him was never far below the surface.

In fact, Fromm himself had failed to see through Operation Valkyrie straight away, even though he was fully acquainted with its details. The basic idea was absolutely brilliant, he had to admit that. Once one granted the possibility that the Reich's millions of foreign labourers might rise in a concerted revolt against their overlords, Valkyrie became the logical response. At a given signal, all units under the control of Replacement Army Headquarters would converge on Berlin, ostensibly to protect members of the government, civil service and Party organisations, SS and Gestapo included.

43

"Do your own dirty work," Fromm said sturdily. "And don't bank on my support."

"The knowledge that you understand the situation will be quite enough, sir." Olbricht gave a slight bow. He had just won a not inconsiderable victory. The wily C.-in-C. knew what was afoot and had simply declined to take an active part. This meant that he was at least prepared to keep quiet.

Fromm bent over his magazine once more, seemingly uninterested in Olbricht's supplementary plans, but before his right-hand man withdrew he looked up. "If and when you start your putsch, don't forget Wilhelm Keitel."

Field Marshal Keitel was Hitler's lieutenant and Fromm's long-time opponent. To say that there was no love lost between the two men was an understatement. They circled each other like fighting-cocks, bent on each other's destruction but lacking the forcefulness to achieve it.

"Did I say something naughty, Olbricht?" Fromm inquired with an air of innocence. "All right, forget it—perhaps I was just thinking aloud. Carry on."

"Where's my brother?" demanded Konstantin von Brackwede. "I must speak to him—it's urgent."

"Good morning," Elisabeth said in a faintly reproving tone.

Konstantin blushed. "Please excuse me, but I really am in a hurry. It's very important."

Examining her visitor more closely, Elisabeth saw that he looked pale and tense.

"What's happened?"

Konstantin shook his head. "I'd prefer to tell my brother."

"I'm sorry," Elisabeth said, nervously rearranging some papers on the desk, "your brother's not here." Despite the rebuff, her voice was gentle as she added: "Don't you trust me, then?"

"What a question—of course I trust you! I don't want to bother you, that's all."

Elisabeth was touched by his apparent concern. "I'll be happy to help if I can."

"Thank you." Konstantin paused. "It's about General von Brackwede—my father—he's been badly wounded. Mother ought to be told at once, and my brother's the person to do it."

"I quite understand."

Elisabeth rose and walked to the window. The frown wrinkling her brow did not detract from the serene, grave beauty of her face.

At last she said: "I don't think your brother will put in an appearance here today. He's away on important business, but I realise you've got to speak to him."

She walked resolutely back to her desk, avoiding Konstantin's eye. Reaching for a slip of paper, she wrote a few words on it and thrust it into Konstantin's hand.

"I'm pretty certain you'll find your brother at that address. I'm not meant to give it to anyone—even you—but this is an exceptional case, so I suppose it's all right."

"I won't get you into trouble, will I?" Konstantin asked anxiously. "That's the last thing I want to do."

"Please don't worry. There is just one thing, though. Pieces of paper have a habit of falling into the wrong hands. Memorise the address and I'll destroy it."

Konstantin looked faintly bewildered. "If Fritz weren't my brother I might suspect he was up to no good."

"Take the Underground to Innsbrucker Platz. It's a ten-minute walk from there, but don't ask anyone the way or mention the address you're looking for. It would be best if you checked it on the street-map first."

Konstantin took Elisabeth's hand and bent over it in a courtly gesture which had rarity value, even in the Bendler-strasse. A lock of soft fair hair brushed her skin, but she did not feel his lips.

"You'd better go now," she said hurriedly. "Be careful for everyone's sake—and that includes your brother as well as the man whose address I've given you." She omitted to mention herself.

"What are the objections, Berthold? Come on, let's hear them."

Claus von Stauffenberg asked the question with quiet confidence, knowing that his brother would never lie, even to spare his feelings. Berthold was uncompromisingly honest.

"I can think of all sorts of objections," Berthold said thoughtfully. "The dictates of common sense, for a start, quite apart from the present mood of a large section of the population and certain officers' conception of their code of honour. What you're planning to do can't be judged by normal standards."

The two brothers, one an army colonel and the other an admiralty adviser on international law, were enjoying a rare

45

evening alone together in a relative's flat beside the Wannsee, where two rooms had been put at their disposal.

"Is that eye of yours still suppurating, Claus?" Berthold asked after a lengthy pause. "Are you in pain?"

"No," Stauffenberg replied, dabbing the socket with a pad of cotton-wool.

Berthold leant forward and examined it. "If it's still suppurating it means you haven't got rid of the infection yet."

"You mean the other eye might become affected?" Stauffenberg grimaced. "Let's hope not—not for the moment, anyway."

The incident which had transformed a man once nick-named "the darling of the gods" into a physical wreck had occurred in Africa on 7 April 1943. A low-level attack by Allied aircraft had shattered his face, both hands and one knee. Shrouded in total darkness for days and racked with high fever for weeks, he had barely regained consciousness when he dictated a letter to General Olbricht informing him that he would be available for duty within three months. By late September of the same year he was back in Berlin, a man with one eye, one good arm and only three usable fingers on his left hand.

"Our friend Brackwede doesn't approve of your carrying out this assignment in person. He thinks it should be anyone but you—Germany needs you without blood on your hands, he says."

"I didn't know he could be so dramatic," Stauffenberg said lightly. "However, even Brackwede will have to resign himself to the fact that—under the circumstances—I'm the only person who can still do the job. As soon as he does he'll calm down and take the appropriate measures."

Berthold glanced at his watch and switched on the radio. The two brothers had retired in order to listen to Haydn's C major 'Cello Concerto, and it was time for the scheduled broadcast.

The rich texture of sound enveloped them, conjuring up fragmentary recollections of a childhood made radiant by music and poetry, of the days when Claus used to play the 'cello and was planning to become an architect, of the days when they read Stefan George, played with their dogs and lay watching deer in the depths of the forest.

"Forget all that," Stauffenberg said brusquely, when the last notes of the Allegro had died away. "Haydn and Hitler can't coexist in the same world." He sat up and hooked his glass towards him with the three fingers of his left hand. "Next Tuesday, July the eleventh, I shall be at Berchtesgaden with a bomb in my briefcase."

Almost all the people Konstantin von Brackwede passed looked grey and haggard. Their faces betrayed exhaustion and malnutrition, anxiety and weary indifference. They stared at the ground, and their voices were gruff, hoarse, irritable, despairing, sometimes spiteful and ill-tempered—seldom loud. Seen amid these shabby, uniform-looking creatures, the few plump and well-nourished individuals he encountered stood out like mushrooms in a field. Very few people had been left unmarked by the five lost years of war.

The travellers on the Underground made room for the slim young air force lieutenant with the Knight's Cross dangling at his breast, some of them resentfully, but most of them with respect and many with looks of admiration. A little girl stared at him entranced, and an old man hissed approving comments through the gaps in his teeth.

Konstantin helped a woman to carry her battered suitcase on to the train. The woman, presumably an evacuee from one of the bombed-out quarters of the city, accepted his help with reluctance. "Good for something, at least," he heard her mumble, and politely raised his hand to his cap in an uncomprehending salute.

Half an hour later he found himself face to face with someone who made a profound and immediate impression on him. He was a sturdy-looking man of medium height with a rugged, angular face which might have been hewn out of granite. Konstantin was involuntarily reminded, in turn, of a Roman philosopher, a Brandenburg peasant and a Prussian civil servant. All three impressions were misleading. The man was Julius Leber.

"Is my brother with you?" Konstantin inquired, glancing round the simply-furnished room. It looked worn and shabby, as though it had been trodden by innumerable restless feet, but it somehow conveyed a feeling of reassuring informality.

"You're Brackwede junior, aren't you?" Leber said, after a brief but searching glance. "Yes, I can see you are."

"Really? I never thought there was much resemblance between Fritz and me—outwardly, anyway."

"You're wrong," Leber said. He sat down on the hard sofa between the two windows and gestured to the lieutenant to join him. "You've got the same eyes. Did he send you to me?"

"No, I was hoping to find him here. I've got to speak to him urgently."

"He said he was coming," Leber remarked after an almost imperceptible pause. "I expect he'll turn up in due course. You're welcome to keep me company until then, if you care to." Almost in the same breath, he asked: "Do you work with your brother?"

Konstantin replied in the negative. He told Leber that he had only got back from the front a few days before, and had since been posted to the School of Air Warfare at Bernau. Much as he regretted it, he knew next to nothing about his brother's actual duties.

The shrewd-eyed man asked a number of carefully chosen questions, but the replies he received seemed uninformative enough. "So you're at the School of Air Warfare," he said at length. "Tell me, do they teach you about Stein, Gneisenau and Scharnhorst these days?"

"Of course, but they're more of a subsidiary subject."

"I'm sorry to hear that," Leber said. "I doubt if Prussia ever received a more vigorous prod in the direction of national revival, transformation and true revolution in the whole of her existence, before or since. It was a turning-point in the history of the Prussian officer corps."

Konstantin listened with great attention, completely won over by the man's sage and kindly manner. He wondered vaguely if he were a general in civilian clothes.

"Have you met Colonel von Stauffenberg yet?" Leber inquired abruptly.

"No, who is he?"

"You'll meet him—your brother will see to that, I'm sure. Stauffenberg was born in nineteen-seven. He comes from an old family of South German aristocrats—loyal and trusted servants of Church and State. He's a descendant of Gneisenau on his mother's side."

The man on the sofa neither moved nor raised his voice and his eyes remained watchful—almost cool—but Konstantin felt increasingly drawn to him. He entirely forgot why he had come.

"Men like those—Gneisenau, Stein and Scharnhorst— were described by their contemporaries as a rebellious clique. They were condemned for being demagogues. Even their honour was impugned."

48

"It was shameful." Konstantin looked up at Leber trustingly. "But history proved them right, didn't it?"

"It's not easy to forgo the approval of the age you live in," Leber said, "but people who espouse a just cause sometimes have to. They even have to risk their lives and endure hatred and derision for its sake. They called Gneisenau a miserable yokel, don't forget."

"It was the same with Hitler, wasn't it?"

"With whom?" Leber asked in surprise.

Konstantin repeated the name. There were people who had dared to dismiss the Fuehrer as a "house-painter," he went on. It was typical of the world's indifference, obstinacy and imperviousness to change. "But there comes a time when someone manages to win through against all the odds—like the Fuehrer."

Leber drew on his abundant reserves of self-control and swallowed this line of thought without turning a hair. He merely said: "Every age has to discover by experience who its real villains and heroes are. It's not always easy, I'll admit—not for everyone—but it's unavoidable."

For all his determination, General of Infantry Friedrich Olbricht was a cautious man who did not, for example, possess the conspiratorial disposition of General Oster of Intelligence. He strove for tolerance, understanding and—wherever possible —harmony.

"We're all after the same fundamental thing," he said. "There really oughtn't to be any misunderstandings between us."

At the urgent request of several fellow-conspirators, Olbricht had arranged a meeting with a man named Erich Hoepner in a country inn north of Berlin. On the stained wooden table between them stood two untouched glasses of the war-time "light ale" which connoisseurs compared unfavourably with liquid manure.

"My friends and I are worried," Hoepner said. "Nothing ever moves. How much longer will we have to wait?"

"A matter of days." Olbricht offered his companion a cigar from the stocks of the Bendlerstrasse mess. He did not smoke himself. "Stauffenberg has made up his mind to force a decision."

"A good man," Hoepner commented. "So he should be. He used to be in my division."

Olbricht thought it wiser not to comment on this statement.

General Hoepner was a welcome addition to the resistance movement. Having led his tank forces to sweeping victories during the French campaign, he was unwise enough, in winter 1941, to yield ground to the Russians without permission. Hitler accused him of " cowardice in the face of the enemy " and he was officially dismissed the service. Unofficially, he continued to draw general's pay, but Hitler had earned his undying hostility and everyone in the army knew it.

" Much as I respect Stauffenberg," Hoepner went on, taking a pull at his light ale, " the fact remains that he's on record as having said one or two things which my friends view with a certain amount of misgiving."

Olbricht knew which remarks Hoepner was alluding to. They were always being quoted. Stauffenberg openly referred to Hitler's generals as " those people " and described them, with inexorable candour, as " spineless individuals." In October 1942 he had characterised the conditions tolerated by the generals as " scandalous " and appealed for " more courage and determination, even at the expense of one's own life."

" Don't forget," Olbricht said diplomatically, " that Colonel Stauffenberg's remarks are directed against a certain type of general officer. They're not aimed at you or your friends—or me, for that matter. There is a difference, you must admit."

There was. Those who appeared to obstruct the advance of the Third Reich were eliminated; those who toed the line received orders and decorations. Bonuses described as " honoraria " were bestowed on particularly meritorious generals, and reliable field marshals not only earned an extra fifty thousand marks per annum but were sometimes awarded the odd quarter of a million or a country estate as well.

" I've nothing against Stauffenberg personally," Hoepner conceded, " but I can well understand why some of my friends have reservations about him. Since he's our last hope of blowing Hitler up, he may make conditions. That's what worries them."

" General," Olbricht said solemnly, " we've assigned hundreds of government posts in the past few months, from chief executive downwards, and Stauffenberg has made no provision for himself whatsoever."

" What about me?" Hoepner inquired, unabashed.

" You will succeed General Fromm as Commander-in-Chief Replacement Army, as arranged. The opportunities for further advancement will be very great. May we count on your support?"

"On that basis, yes," Hoepner assured him. There was a mixture of caution and challenge in his voice as he added: "But only on that basis."

"I don't believe it!" exclaimed Captain von Brackwede. "What in God's name are you doing here?"

The normally elegant captain was clad in contemporary civilian dress: scuffed shoes, threadbare trousers and a baggy wood-fibre jacket worn over a dingy checked shirt. His appearance was hardly gentlemanly, and his reaction to the right of Konstantin was even less so. He stood waiting for the young officer's explanation with an air of casual indifference. When he heard that his father had been severely wounded he bowed his head in silence for a moment.

"You must tell Mother yourself. I haven't time now."
Konstantin looked bewildered. "You haven't time?"

"No," Brackwede said curtly, "and while we're on the subject, I think it's high time you got to grips with the realities of the present situation. One of them is death—in all its various forms. All right, you can go now—don't let me detain you. I'll worry about you later. Personally, I've got enough to do here for the time being."

Konstantin omitted to shake hands with his brother, who looked as if he would have regarded the gesture as superfluous anyway. Having been escorted to the back door by Leber, he bade him a respectful farewell and hurried off down the street, looking preoccupied.

Leber returned to the living-room, where Brackwede had already spread some papers on the table. He might have been a book-keeper waiting to submit his daily accounts.

"What is it this time?"

"The usual," Brackwede replied laconically. There was no point in discussing his brother or worrying about a *fait accompli*. "Let's get down to business."

Julius Leber resumed his place on the sofa with an air of deliberation. "Another treatise from our friend Goerdeler, I suppose?" he said, smiling resignedly. "Well, why not? I can think of worse things. Let's get started."

Doctor Carl Friedrich Goerdeler was the former mayor of Leipzig. Picked by the conspirators as Hitler's successor to the Chancellorship, he was reputed to be toying with the idea of giving Germany a hereditary or elective monarchy.

He had been "tramping round" Germany, as the Gestapo

later phrased it, for years now. Possessing no fixed abode, he lodged at friends' houses, in hotels and at the "Temperance Hostel" in Berlin—a frequent haunt of his. He also undertook arduous journeys to the Russian front, sought out like-minded people in the West and was even said to have been sighted in Scandinavia and the Balkans.

On this particular day he had been summoned to Count von Moltke's flat. He stood on the landing for a while with his head cocked like a hunted animal and his thin, pale, worried civil servant's face tense with the effort of listening. Scenting no danger, he knocked at the door.

Helmuth von Moltke appeared. The two men shook hands in silence and exchanged smiles, the Count a trifle apprehensively and Goerdeler with resolute optimism. He was always at pains to radiate confidence, though his manner had lost some of its conviction in recent months.

"Well, what is it?" he asked hurriedly, after a brief but cordial word with Eugen G., who was also present. "Why did you send for me? Has something happened?"

"I don't know," Moltke said apologetically. "I've no idea why, but Count von Brackwede insists on speaking to you. He should be here at any minute."

Goerdeler sat down wearily on the nearest chair. "Brackwede—that means Stauffenberg, doesn't it?"

"Not necessarily," Moltke replied. "Brackwede may have some information from the Gestapo. He has his contacts, you know. A man of many parts, Brackwede."

Goerdeler nervously adjusted his frayed tie. "They tell me Stauffenberg has evolved some entirely new ideas and made some surprise recommendations as well."

"Misleading rumours," Eugen G. said firmly. "You'd do well to ignore them. The last thing we want to do is broadcast them round the movement."

"All the same," Goerdeler persisted, "I've heard that Stauffenberg has conferred with Julius Leber recently— several times. I haven't seen him myself for weeks."

"But that's quite understandable," Moltke said confidently. "Your own position is absolutely clear. Unnecessary meetings would be pointless—dangerous, too, for that matter."

"If you think there's been a major change of tack at the last moment, you're quite wrong." Eugen G. spoke with assurance. "I know Brackwede as well as I know Stauffenberg, and they're both methodical men. They abhor precipitate action. Their attitude towards you hasn't changed, Herr Goerdeler, take my word for it."

"You're a young man, Doctor," Goerdeler said without rancour. "I was young myself not so many years ago. I had a great deal of ambition, but I never acted on impulse."

Moltke smiled. "You gave up your job as mayor of Leipzig because you refused to sanction the removal of the Mendelssohn Memorial from the front of the Gewandhaus."

"Perhaps I committed myself too hastily," Goerdeler replied with a touch of weariness. "Perhaps I resigned to save my face."

"You resigned because you stood by your beliefs," Eugen G. broke in. "Nothing could be more self-evident."

In 1932, when Chancellor Bruening had reached the end of the road, he recommended two potential successors to Hindenburg, then Reich President. Both men were mayors, one of Cologne and the other of Leipzig. Their names were Adenauer and Goerdeler respectively. Hindenburg chose Papen and, thus, indirectly, Hitler.

Adenauer retired in his rose-garden at Rhoendorf. Goerdeler stayed on as mayor for a while and continued to perform his duties as a State Price Controller before eventually joining the firm of Bosch, which welcomed him with open arms. He travelled widely and wrote accounts of his travels. He also wrote monographs. While praising the achievements of the German Army during the conquest of France in 1940, he simultaneously accused Hitler of a " Napoleonic lack of moderation."

Goerdeler's exchange with Moltke and Eugen G. was brusquely interrupted by the appearance of Captain von Brackwede. Scarcely allowing himself time to shake hands, he announced: "Herr Goerdeler, the Gestapo yesterday issued a warrant for your arrest."

Silence fell. Eugen G. shook his head angrily and Moltke looked perturbed, but Goerdeler merely closed his eyes for a few moments. Then, in a flat voice, he said: "It had to happen sooner or later."

Brackwede nodded. "I know, but later would have been preferable. The fact is that the Gestapo are looking for you. Another couple of days and the C.I.D. will probably be on your trail as well."

"It won't alter my way of life," Goerdeler replied with simple resignation. "I'm always on the move."

"I've already been in touch with Intelligence," Brackwede said. "They're prepared to fly you out of Germany within the next twenty-four hours."

"What?" Goerdeler drew himself up. "Is this an attempt to get me out of the way? Have you discussed this plan with Stauffenberg?"

"We want to get you to safety," Brackwede said firmly, "—nothing more."

"It's the best thing," Moltke assured him.

Eugen G. gave a nod of assent. "The only alternative, under these circumstances."

"I'm staying," Goerdeler said staunchly. "I want to be here when it happens—and it won't be long now, will it?"

The early days of July 1944 also witnessed the return to Berlin of Corporal "Pixie" Lehmann. His reappearance in the Bendlerstrasse was greeted with surprise and consternation by the dozen or so initiates among the hundred officers on the staff.

"Good morning, Madame," he called to Elisabeth Oldenburg-Quentin, putting his nose round the office door and grinning delightedly at the sight of her. He had always cherished a weakness for this "rose among the weeds," as he called her. "What's the matter—lost your tongue since I saw you last?"

"Lehmann!" Elisabeth exclaimed with a start of dismay. "How on earth did you get here?"

"By train, my heart's delight—straight from Paris—and my first act on reaching Berlin was to make a bee-line for you. I hope you're flattered." The corporal took her hand and shook it warmly. "I won't say you're looking lovelier than ever—that would be a physical impossibility—but you've certainly kept your looks."

Elisabeth mustered a smile. "Another few weeks in this job and I'll go grey-headed."

"Don't worry, it'll suit you fine—you're just the type." Lehmann behaved as though he had only been out of the room for five minutes. He went over to the filing-cabinet, rummaged among the high treason records and fished out a bottle of cognac. "Will you have a drop?"

Elisabeth nodded and took the proffered glass. "I don't understand, though," she said, sipping it, "—you shouldn't be here. What went wrong?"

" That's easy. I was posted to Paris all right but they forgot to hobble me, so here I am again—playing postman."

" You've brought news from Paris?"

" News isn't the word for it." The diminutive corporal tapped his chest proudly. " I'm bursting at the seams with inside information—quite a job to carry it all, too, in this sodding heat—I beg your pardon—warm weather."

Elisabeth laughed. There was something infectious about Lehmann's humorous unconcern. Even Brackwede found the little man's self-possession a source of amazement.

" What do you think the Captain's going to say when he sees you?"

" He won't exactly throw his arms round my neck, I don't suppose."

" I doubt if he'll be able to send you back to Paris straight away, either. I'm almost sorry, for your sake."

" You'll give me a swelled head," Lehmann smirked. " Don't tell me you've got a weak spot for me after all!"

Elisabeth stared at her desk. " There aren't many people I worry about, Corporal, but you're one of them. I don't like to see you in danger."

" I'm flattered." Lehmann refilled his glass thoughtfully, and his eyes were grave. " Strikes me I got back in the nick of time."

Corporal Lehmann passed the time until Captain von Brack-wede's return by chatting with Elisabeth, mainly about the delights of Paris. He was in full spate when Lieutenant Herbert appeared.

After a perfunctory bow to the Countess, Herbert turned to Lehmann. " So I wasn't mistaken!" he exclaimed in bright, comradely tones. " It really was you. This is a surprise, I must say."

Lehmann promptly switched on an ingenuous grin. " Surprised to see you still here, too, sir. I thought you might have been promoted." He noted out of the corner of his eye that Elisabeth had tucked his messages away in a file-cover with an air of routine.

Lieutenant Herbert's sojourn at the Bendlerstrasse had given him a nose for personal relationships that went beyond the bounds of rank. Colonel Stauffenberg conferred boldly with generals one minute and readily accepted Captain von Brack-wede's advice the next. He, Lieutenant Herbert, had recently had to deal with senior Party officials. He treated them—with all due respect—as equals, but there was no reason why he shouldn't indulge in a little friendly intercourse with one of his subordinates, especially one who so clearly enjoyed the favour of his immediate superior's personal assistant.

"I've been made liaison officer between G.H.Q. and Party authorities."

Lehmann gaped obediently. "You don't say!"

"An extremely interesting and responsible job," Herbert elaborated, "and one which I owe to the good offices of Captain von Brackwede."

"I'd never have believed it!" Lehmann commented with mock wonder.

"General Olbricht is expecting you," Elisabeth told the corporal in businesslike tones. She picked up the file-cover with its cache of secret messages. "Please take that with you— he needs it urgently."

"Certainly, Countess." Lehmann put the briefcase under his arm, saluted smartly, and made his exit.

Lieutenant Herbert stared after the corporal's departing figure with surprise. "Where did he pop up from? I thought he'd been posted to the front."

Elisabeth deemed it wise to make a show of affability. The situation was too delicate to risk any complications. "Orders are always being countermanded, Lieutenant—you know how it is."

"What does Olbricht want him for?"

"I really couldn't say," Elisabeth replied casually. "Perhaps you ought to ask General Olbricht," she added with a faint smile.

Herbert's reaction was spontaneous. "God forbid! It's none of my business, is it?"

The normal route to General Olbricht's office in the Bendlerstrasse led via that of his chief of staff, Colonel Mertz von Quirnheim. He too seemed surprised at the sight of Corporal Lehmann, but his surprise was not unmixed with satisfaction.

"Lehmann!" he said warmly. "You've arrived at the ideal moment."

Mertz reported Lehmann's arrival to Olbricht, who rose at once with an exclamation of pleasure and instructed his chief of staff to inform Stauffenberg. Then he went to meet the corporal at the door.

" Good to see you! " he said, gripping Lehmann's hand.
" How did you find Paris? "

" *Formidable,* sir," replied Lehmann, sitting down in the
arm-chair reserved for the C.-in-C. on the occasions when he
conferred with Olbricht. " A successful trip all round. The
place is really humming. General von Stuelpnagel and Lieutenant-Colonel von Hofacker are working at top pressure, and
so are a lot of other people."

He deposited the file on the desk. Olbricht and Mertz bent
over it and began to sort out its contents. When Stauffenberg walked in, Olbricht called out: " Paris seems to be doing
a good job."

Stauffenberg cast a brief glance at the papers on the desk
before turning to Lehmann with an expression of benevolent
interest. " Do you want to go back to Paris right away," he
asked, " or would it amuse you to stay on here for a day or
two?"

" Why bother to ask, sir?" Lehmann's face registered genuine
surprise. " All you've got to do is give an order."

" That's just what I don't want to do in this instance."
Stauffenberg leant forward confidentially. " The fact is, I
could use you here."

" Then there's no point in discussing it, sir. Of course I'll
stay—be glad to."

" Without knowing what's in store for you?"

Lehmann laughed. " I'll hope for the worst—where a
certain person is concerned. I'm pretty certain I won't be
disappointed."

Now it was Stauffenberg's turn to laugh, and Olbricht
and Mertz glanced up from their reading-matter in surprise.
At that moment Captain von Brackwede walked into the
room. He stationed himself in front of Corporal Lehmann
with his beaky nose tilted at an angle which, to those who knew
him well, signified extreme displeasure.

" I don't believe it!" he said angrily. " You really are here
—and I thought my P.A. was pulling my leg."

." How are you, sir?" Lehmann said. " You don't look too
happy. Is that brother of yours giving us trouble?"

" The corporal has brought us some really first-rate material."
Olbricht interposed, "—not only confirmation that all our
plans will be carried out to the letter but one or two excellent
new recommendations as well. Hofacker will be here himself
in a few days' time."

"He'll be welcome," Brackwede retorted sarcastically. "He isn't wanted by the Gestapo like our fun-loving friend here. You must make yourself scarce again, Lehmann," he added with a note of urgency, "—within the next few hours, before the hounds pick up your scent."

"Forgive me, Fritz," Stauffenberg said gently, "but I need him here."

Brackwede shrugged. "Very well. In that case he can stay, but only on one condition. As long as he's needed in Berlin he mustn't leave the Bendlerstrasse. This is the only place where he'll be safe from the Gestapo."

Allied bomber formations were droning over Berlin. They came day and night, with the regularity of a well-run bus service. Air-raids had been part of Berlin's daily life for some time now.

Captain von Brackwede strolled into his secretary's office and looked round. He seemed surprised to find Elisabeth alone. "Well, well? Where are your minions? I was just going to send you down to the cellar with my brother."

"Your brother and Corporal Lehmann went to see Lieutenant Herbert at my suggestion. I expect they've all gone down to the shelter together."

"You're really sticking your oar in these days, aren't you?" There was an undertone of warning in Brackwede's voice. "I thought we'd made a bargain."

"Was it part of the bargain that I have to act as a decoy when required?"

Brackwede chuckled. "I didn't plan it that way," he assured her gaily. "I must confess I'm pleased, all the same. You react on my brother like a magnet. Whenever he's got half an hour to spare he turns up here."

"And you exploit the fact—you make the most of any opportunity to work on him. I don't like it."

"You seem to have developed a soft spot for the boy already. —But forgive me, I didn't mean to embarrass you. Why did you send him to see Herbert?"

"To give him a rest. Your methods of enlightenment are bad enough, but when Lehmann starts on him as well it's too much of a good thing. Besides, Herbert welcomes any excuse to come snooping round here."

"Don't worry," Brackwede said confidently. "He thinks I'm a loyal Nazi—he even models himself on me."

"How much longer will that illusion last?" Elisabeth

pretended to study a file. "I should have thought your brother was the only person who'd swallow it indefinitely. He's got an infinite capacity for loyalty."

"Yes," snapped Brackwede, " —the sort of loyalty that has millions of deaths to its credit! It's a vice, not a virtue."

The bitterness in his voice shocked Elisabeth, who had never seen him so emotionally aroused before. Then, as suddenly as it had come, the outburst subsided. Brackwede shook his head and essayed a smile. "Forgive me," he said. "I get like this occasionally these days, but only when I'm alone or with close friends."

A faint blush rose to Elisabeth's cheeks. "Shall I call the communications centre?" she asked hurriedly. "I suppose you'd like to know where the main concentration of bombs is falling, as usual?"

"Please do that, Elisabeth."

A few moments elapsed before the exchange answered. "I'll go down to the shelter afterwards, if you like," she said cupping her hand over the receiver.

"I'd be glad if you did—for Lehmann's sake, apart from anything else. He adores playing idiotic games with Herbert, and heaven knows what'll happen if the worthy lieutenant wakes up to the fact that he's being baited. Also, as I told you, I like you to keep my brother company."

A metallic voice at the other end of the line gave Elisabeth the requisite information. "The bombing is concentrated south of the Tiergarten," she said, "in the region of Wittenberg-erplatz."

Brackwede glanced at a street map on the wall beside her desk. "Ask about Goethestrasse, please."

"Goethestrasse is in the centre of the affected area," she reported.

Brackwede hurried into the inner office and fetched his cap. "Ring down to the M.T. pool for a car," he said, buckling his belt, " —any car that's available, even if it belongs to the C.-in-C. I'll take the responsibility."

Goethestrasse, which Brackwede reached in a matter of minutes, was a wilderness of rubble. A dense pall of dust and blue-black smoke hung over the area. Shadowy figures scurried through the chaotic gloom carrying items of household equipment or dragging wounded with them. Civil defence squads were in action, heaving baulks of timber aside and demolishing shattered walls. Ambulances whined up the street in low gear, were loaded with human freight and crawled away again. Someone screamed close at hand, but his cries were suddenly smothered by a collapsing house-front.

As he threaded his way breathlessly through the steaming, smoking, stinking sea of rubble, Brackwede cannoned into the burly figure of a man. He was spitting and cursing, and he looked suspiciously like SS-Sturmbannfuehrer Maier.

The two men greeted one another with an almost jovial bonhomie which effectively concealed their mutual surprise.

" I wondered whether I'd find you here!" Brackwede shouted.

" It's a small world!" Maier yelled back. " Great minds think alike, eh? I don't suppose you're just out for an evening stroll."

" Hardly—I was thinking of going to the same party as you." Brackwede seemed to find this remark inordinately amusing, and Maier laughed too. Tears ran down his cheeks, though this was due more to dust than mirth.

Evidently making for the same objective, they trudged through the still-smoking rubble to a point half-way down Goethestrasse. Only one house remained standing.

" It's unbelievable," Maier said, wagging his head. " Why should he survive, of all people?"

" Perhaps it's a dispensation of Providence—to borrow our beloved Fuehrer's favourite phrase." The captain gave Maier a familiar wink and saw him return it in kind. " I suggest we take care of our own business first and then divide the spoils over a drink. All right?"

They went their separate ways, keeping a weather eye on each other. Brackwede walked up to the house that belonged to General Ludwig Beck.

The former Chief of the General Staff and prospective Head of State, the man who was acknowledged to be Germany's leading strategist and frequently mentioned in the same breath as Moltke and Schlieffen, emerged wearing a pair of soiled baggy trousers and a coarse linen shirt. He peered out into the smoke-filled gloom with sweat streaming down his face and a bucket of water dangling from one hand.

" You're still alive, then!" Brackwede said with relief.

" I'm alive all right," the general replied grimly. His lean face wore its usual expression of grave solemnity. " I'm just helping to put a fire out for my next-door neighbour—and the Gestapo men who have been billeted on him. I even helped them to rescue their files, including a mass of photographs they've had the impertinence to take of my visitors."

"I congratulate you, sir," Brackwede said. "That's what I call real community spirit."

"You congratulate me, do you?" Not for the first time, Beck found Brackwede's reactions puzzling. "Doesn't it alarm you that a squad of Gestapo agents have been sitting on my doorstep, watching me?"

"It's routine procedure, sir. There's nothing new about it, if that's any comfort to you." Brackwede scrutinised the house closely. "The main thing is, your place is intact. There's nothing missing, is there?"

"No documents, if that's what you mean."

Brackwede looked relieved. "In that case I won't keep you from your work. My Gestapo friends are waiting to have a chat with me. I wouldn't want to disappoint them."

"How big do you think the room will be?" inquired Corporal Lehmann. "It's important to know, so that I can work out the size of the charge required."

Stauffenberg stroked his chin thoughtfully. "I can't say for certain. There are two alternatives—either the conference room at Berchtesgaden or the command bunker at the Wolfsschanze headquarters at Rastenburg."

"Bunker—I like the sound of that. Thick walls and small windows are just what we need."

The two men were sitting side by side in Stauffenberg's office like art collectors examining a new acquisition, but all that lay on the desk in front of them were several blank sheets of paper, ready to receive Lehmann's calculations and formulae.

"We must allow for both possibilities," the colonel said. "The only clue I can give you is that these conferences never take place in large rooms. To give you a rough idea, the rooms don't hold more than twenty-five people or so."

"We'll manage," Lehmann replied. "General von Gersdorff's explosive is first-class stuff—top-grade British quality. A briefcase will easily hold the right amount. Do you have to pass any check-points?"

"Always," Stauffenberg said. "Officers attending the daily conference usually have to take off their belts, so they're unarmed when they go in."

"Does anyone check on that?"

"Regularly. It's the responsibility of Hitler's body-guard—that's SS-Oberfuehrer Rattenhuber and his men. They've been known to run their hands over general officers before now."

Lehmann looked unimpressed. Stauffenberg privately congratulated himself on having found the ideal person to handle this part of the plan. He appreciated the little man's prudent attention to detail.

"The people who attend these affairs must bring papers with them," Lehmann went on, " —briefcases and so on. Do Rattenhuber's men check the contents?"

"Not in my experience, but it's not beyond the bounds of possibility."

"There's a way round that. I can make up the charge in layers so that it looks like a bundle of documents." He jotted down a few notes.

"The trickiest point is the detonator," Stauffenberg said thoughtfully. "A lot of attempts have failed because of that."

"These acid detonators have to be crushed with pliers," the corporal said in professional tones. "The acid dissolves a locking device which releases the firing-pin. There's no noise at all until the whole thing goes up."

"I'm told it's extremely difficult to calculate the timing."

"At a time of year when temperatures vary from one hour to the next—yes, certainly—but not when it's mid-summer, like now. When it's a warm day—seventy to eighty-five degrees, say—you can guarantee the timing fairly accurately. How long will you need, more or less?"

"About fifteen minutes."

"Then you can bank on a very small variation, providing it's day-time—roughly a minute either way."

Stauffenberg looked relieved. "I feel much more confident, now I know you're on the job."

"This little chat is only a modest beginning, sir," Lehmann said cautiously. "There are all kinds of details to be settled yet."

"We must try not to overlook a thing—not the smallest point."

Having negotiated the rubble-strewn wilderness that used to be Goethestrasse, Brackwede and Maier met at their pre-arranged rendezvous, the last surviving tramway halt-sign. They grinned at each other, sweating, dusty and slightly exhausted.

"Well," Brackwede demanded, "were your little lambs successful?"

"It all depends what you mean," Maier replied evasively. "Perhaps we ought to have a chat about it—this seems to be as good a time as any. How would Handler's suit you? I'll foot the bill."

"Done!" Captain von Brackwede said with a smile. Maier's readiness to incur heavy expenditure at Handler's was an auspicious sign.

A good dinner at the Weinhaus Handler, situated in the centre of the city, cost the equivalent of an average mortal's monthly salary, but for this, even in the fifth year of the war he could choose from an astonishing range of delicacies, among them smoked goose-breast from Brandenburg, eel from Pomerania, venison from East Prussia. Admittance was by reservation only, except in the case of regular patrons who—like Maier—belonged to the ruling circles of the day.

"I'm told there's *caneton à l'orange* today," the Sturmbannfuehrer remarked. "What's more, a consignment of fresh lobster is due in from Hamburg."

"I hope you don't lose your appetite in the interval," quipped Brackwede.

The ruins around them were still smoking, and dead bodies lay in piles beside the road. Maier and Brackwede continued to converse while their drivers belaboured them with clothesbrushes.

"What do you fancy?" inquired Maier.

"I suggest a mushroom omelette instead of the ox-tail soup."

Flames spouted up behind them and the hoarse shouts of the heavy-rescue squads grew louder. Brackwede and Maier were enveloped in a cloud of fine dust. Sweat ran down the SS driver's face as he worked on Maier's black uniform, which required considerably more attention than the army officer's field-grey. Besides, Brackwede was not as particular. "Everyone gets dirty these days," he murmured, "—one way or another."

A respectful welcome awaited them at Handler's. Better still, Maier's favourite table in the far corner of the inner room, which afforded a view of the entire establishment, was vacant.

"Nothing but the best!" the Sturmbannfuehrer enjoined as the head waiter hurried up.

The restaurant was not over-crowded. It never was. The patrons included a few gentlemen from the Foreign Office disporting themselves with their ladies, a Minister complete with girl-friend, a Secretary of State entertaining a Japanese couple and a small group of officers gathered round a colonel wearing a brand-new Knight's Cross. "Gestapo" Maier knew most of those present. He even kept dossiers on some of them as an insurance against all eventualities.

By the time the main course arrived Maier felt ready to broach his chosen subject. "Tell me," he said, sipping his burgundy, "do you know General Beck well?" Wine did not appeal to him, but he liked to appear an *homme du monde*.

Captain von Brackwede was prepared for this question. "My opinion of Beck is roughly the same as yours," he said cautiously. "I know he's on your list, and I also know you well enough to realise that you'd like to get your hands on him."

"You're right," Maier said. "He'd be a real catch."

"But a risky one, don't you agree?"

The Sturmbannfuehrer nodded vigorously, chewing on a mouthful of duck. "That's the whole trouble. If I put the screws on him without producing any tangible results, it could be damned awkward."

"I quite understand. One crashing blunder on your part, and who knows where you might end up. What you need is some really convincing evidence, and you'd like me to help you find it."

"That shouldn't be too hard. The man spends his whole time writing—there must be piles of documents in that house of his. Some of them are bound to be incriminating."

"Your best bet would have been to organise a sort of salvage operation—today, after the bombing. You could have said you were protecting his papers from the risk of fire."

"There's still time," Maier said ruminatively. "My men are only waiting for the word—a 'phone call would be enough. That's why I'm sitting here with you, man. I need your advice. Shall I act or not—what do you think?"

Brackwede leant back in his chair. "I think we've reached an extremely interesting stage in our discussion. We ought to make the most of it. Bring on the champagne, my dear fellow. I propose we drink to a future radiant with promise!"

"Count von Brackwede sends his apologies," General Olbricht said, shaking hands. "He asked me to inform you that he's dining with 'Gestapo' Maier—an exercise in self-control, he called it."

The half-dozen men who had assembled at Count von Moltke's flat registered scant amusement. They were too well-acquainted with Brackwede's witticisms.

"The captain conveys his special apologies to you, Doctor," Olbricht continued. "He was most anxious to have a word with you in person."

"We're extremely worried," interposed another voice. The speaker was a man who worked for the existing Ministry of the Interior and had considerable misgivings about its prospective incumbent, Julius Leber. "The warrant for Goerdeler's arrest is an alarming development, particularly at this stage."

"In Captain von Brackwede's view, the move has been brewing for months," Olbricht said pacifically, "—more than a year, in fact. However, no general call has been issued yet, and I'm sure they won't catch up with our elusive Pimpernel as quickly as all that. It's only a matter of days now."

"A lot can happen in a few days," objected the man from the Ministry of the Interior. "Who will be next on the Gestapo's list? We've every reason to be worried—all of us, not just Goerdeler. It can't be mere coincidence."

"It may not be a coincidence, but it certainly isn't grounds for panic." As always in situations of mounting alarm and uncertainty, it was the youthful-looking Count von Moltke who leapt into the breach. His tone was courteous but incisive. "Goerdeler has been an avowed opponent of Hitler for years. The Gestapo have got a fat dossier on Leber and they're still adding to it. As for Beck, Hitler personally described him as a dangerous man, even before the outbreak of war. I can think of many similar examples."

"The number of executions for high treason, defeatism, defamation of the Fuehrer and similar crimes gets bigger and bigger every year," Olbricht said in a deliberately unemotional voice. "More than three thousand German civilians were officially sentenced to death and executed in 1943 alone. It's almost a miracle that our movement has lost such a comparatively small proportion of its membership so far."

"The miracle seems to have come to an end," persisted the civil servant.

"We can't exclude that possibility," Olbricht conceded. "Colonel von Stauffenberg shares your opinion. In view of the imminence of final action and the fact that all major points have already been settled, he feels that no more meetings should be held in the next few days or weeks. Extreme discretion . . ."

"Just a moment, please!" interrupted the official from the Ministry of the Interior. "Is that a request or an order? To be quite frank, some of my friends are uneasy about the arbitrary way in which Colonel von Stauffenberg has been trying to meddle in the decisions of the various resistance groups recently."

Stung by this, Olbricht looked across at Count von Moltke, who in turn shot an encouraging glance at Eugen G. However, the normally disputatious doctor of philosophy, who could always be relied on to take an independent line in the presence of officers from the Bendlerstrasse, was staring thoughtfully into space. It suddenly occurred to Moltke that he had so far taken no part in the discussion.

"Why, General Olbricht," Eugen G. asked at length, "did you tell me when you came in that Captain von Brackwede would have liked to speak to me personally? Is it what I suspect?"

"I'm afraid so." After a brief pause, Olbricht added: "I have to inform you, Doctor, that the Gestapo have issued a warrant for your arrest as well."

"What did I tell you!" exclaimed the ministry official.

Olbricht did not turn his head. Fixing his eyes on the silent figure of Eugen G., he continued: "It has nothing to do with our meetings here. The Gestapo conducted a search of Pastor Bonhoeffer's house. In the course of the search they found some manuscripts to which the Doctor contributed. That is the only reason they are looking for him."

"Very well," said Eugen G., "I'll go to ground—somewhere in the neighbourhood of Stuttgart, probably—but as soon as the balloon goes up I'll be back."

"All right, old man, out with it," Sturmbannfuehrer Maier said, when the champagne—a vintage bottle of Mumm Cordon Rouge—had been served. "Let's let our respective cats out of their bags, shall we? Can you put the finger on Beck or can't you?"

Captain von Brackwede seemed to hesitate. The colonel with the brand-new Knight's Cross called for another round of drinks in an imperious voice which rang through the small room like a trumpet: "Fill 'em up—to the top this time, if you don't mind!" Several patrons raised their eyebrows and the head waiter hurried over, looking apprehensive.

"Your instinct is correct," Brackwede said. "General Beck is far more than an eccentric old man."

"He's conspiring against the Fuehrer, isn't he?"

"That's not the half of it. He's regarded in some quarters as our future Head of State."

Maier breathed heavily as he devoured his sweet, a confection of honey, biscuit and whipped cream garnished with finely-chopped almonds. "Christ Almighty!" he muttered between mouthfuls. "If that's the case, the sooner we put him inside the better."

"You've got to have proof first, but I'm afraid the General's scribblings won't constitute sufficient evidence in themselves. He's a philosopher, after all, and philosophers can always prove they've been misinterpreted."

"Does that mean you advise against immediate action?"

"I'm merely questioning its expediency at this particular stage. Ask yourself this: which is more potentially valuable, another candidate for the firing-squad or the goodwill of a prospective Head of State?"

Maier's bland face betrayed no form of emotion, even now, but there was a hint of perplexity in his eyes. He drained his glass and stared into space, leaving Brackwede to study his finger-nails.

A moment later, their attention was violently distracted by the colonel with the gleaming Knight's Cross, who had just been presented with his bill.

"This is the bloody limit!" he bellowed indignantly. "What the hell do you take me for?"

The head waiter hurried over again, flanked by two waiters. They tried to form a human screen round the clamorous colonel, but in vain. His stentorian voice, which had often made itself heard above the din of battle, threatened to dislodge the plaster from the restaurant walls.

"How dare you stick this in front of me! I'm Colonel Bruchsal! My officers and I don't risk our necks in action every day just so that a lot of lily-livered bastards can eat and drink themselves silly at home! These prices are exorbitant, I tell you!"

"I beg of you, Colonel!" the head waiter entreated. "Please consider yourself a guest of the house."

"Guest be buggered!" yelled the war-hero, trembling with fury and nervous tension. "You can't get round me like that. This country has gone to the dogs!"

Maier raised his head as though snuffing the air. Brackwede sipped his coffee impassively, but his eyes were troubled.

Meanwhile, the enraged colonel's inhibitions had fled. "It's a shambles, this country!" he fumed. "And no wonder, with a bastard like Hitler in charge—skulking in corners with a gang of yes-men licking his arse!"

67

Colonel Bruchsal's fellow-officers hastily shepherded him towards the exit. The other diners behaved as though they had heard nothing.

"Well, well, never look a gift-horse in the mouth," murmured Maier, lighting a genuine Havana cigar taken from captured French stocks. "Even half a loaf is better than none, and I've got to fill my quota somehow." He blew out the match with a finality which symbolised that the vociferous Colonel Bruchsal had signed his own death warrant.

Captain von Brackwede leant forward. "Do I take it that you're suspending action against Beck?"

Maier nodded. "For the moment, yes—on condition that you and I continue to work in close harness."

Corporal Lehmann and Colonel von Stauffenberg were once more closeted in Stauffenberg's office. The glow of a shaded lamp half illuminated their faces, throwing the colonel's lean and angular features into sharp relief and turning the corporal's homely countenance into a wrinkled moonscape. Midnight was not far off, and the Bendler block seemed to be deserted. The room was shrouded in silence.

"Well, there's our gift package," said Lehmann. He was holding what appeared to be a bulky photograph album. "That ought to fit into any briefcase."

Stauffenberg took the article and examined it. On closer inspection, it resembled a concertina file weighing not more than fifteen or twenty pounds.

"Will that be enough?"

"More than enough." Lehmann drew a rough sketch of a room with a small circle in the centre. In this he inscribed a swastika. "If the performance takes place in the bunker it won't matter where the charge is placed. If it takes place in a normal room, the distance between the package and our birthday boy shouldn't be more than twenty-five or thirty feet."

Stauffenberg nodded. "That can be arranged."

"But watch out for one point which might easily come up at this time of year—open windows. They cut down the force of the explosion a lot. Under those conditions, you'll have to get pretty close to him—ten or fifteen feet at the outside."

"I'll put a few more documents in as camouflage."

"I wouldn't do that, sir. Take some blank paper, preferably, or newspapers—the *Voelkischer Beobachter*, let's say. They're bound to call in experts to examine every scrap of débris, so steer clear of anything which might identify you personally. You can never tell how things are going to work out. That's why I shouldn't leave any recognisable traces behind—and that includes the briefcase itself."

"You're very thorough, Lehmann."

"It still burns me up when I think of the bomb General von Tresckow's people stowed away in Hitler's 'plane, disguised as a bottle of cognac. The detonator didn't work, so they say, but I take that with a pinch of salt. Maybe they failed to set it off properly in all the excitement. We don't want anything like that to happen this time."

"May I ask you a personal question, Lehmann?"

The corporal nodded, looking faintly surprised.

"Why are you doing this?"

Lehmann gave an almost soundless chuckle. "I could ask you the same thing, sir. Someone's got to do it—but that's not the whole story. The thing is, I've got father-trouble. My old man's a local group-leader. He takes it very seriously—does his best to model himself on the Fuehrer. It spurs you on somehow, a thing like that."

Stauffenberg gave the corporal a friendly pat on the shoulder. Lehmann could not have guessed how rare it was for Stauffenberg, who had a horror of physical contact, to make such a gesture.

"Give me your hand, sir," the corporal said. "Now grip mine—press as hard as you can." After a moment's hesitation, Stauffenberg complied. "Good, you've got a lot of strength left in those three fingers of yours. You must have been a pretty tough youngster."

"Not particularly," Stauffenberg replied with a smile, " —at least, not when I was very young. I was a rather delicate child, but I got over it in time by systematic physical training. Why the trial of strength?"

"Because there's another important point." Lehmann unwrapped a cloth to reveal three pairs of pliers. After inspecting them carefully he selected one and handed it to Stauffenberg. Then he held out a thick pencil.

"Try and crush that."

Stauffenberg grasped the pliers and squeezed. The pencil broke in half.

"Now have another three goes, please, one after the other."

Stauffenberg complied, and three splintered sections of pencil pattered on to the desk-top in quick succession. Lehmann gave an approving nod.

" That's the last stage in the proceedings, sir—breaking the acid capsule. There's no turning back after that. You should be able to find room for the pliers in your left-hand trousers pocket—but don't put anything else in there. Everything must be spot-on. We'll practise it."

" And after that?"

" After that you can go into action as soon as you like—tomorrow, as far as I'm concerned."

" The day after tomorrow," Stauffenberg said.

THREE

On 11 July—a Tuesday—General Olbricht and Colonel Mertz von Quirnheim never stirred far from their telephones. They paced restlessly round Olbricht's office, avoiding each other's eye and wrestling with a mounting sense of anxiety.

Claus von Stauffenberg had flown off to Berchtesgaden with the bomb in his briefcase. The dream which had almost been abandoned seemed about to become reality.

" Hitler's so damned unpredictable," Olbricht said suddenly. " Whenever he leaves his headquarters, three itineraries have to be worked out—one by 'plane, one by train and one by car. He only makes up his mind at the last moment."

" But he's made of flesh and blood, sir," Mertz ventured. " Besides, he's never been up against a man like Stauffenberg before."

Olbricht's brow remained clouded. " This isn't the first time our friends have managed to get a bomb into his vicinity, Mertz. They've even been prepared to blow themselves to kingdom come and take him with them. Axel von der Busche, Ewald von Kleist, Helmuth Stieff—they all tried, but it was hopeless. Hitler either failed to turn up or left prematurely or postponed his engagements. The man eluded them each time."

Colonel Mertz von Quirnheim continued to circle the telephone on the desk between them. " Perhaps it was fate, sir —perhaps the right moment hadn't arrived. Now, defeat is inevitable. The Russians are bearing down on our frontiers, the Allied invasion is going according to plan and the Balkans are lost. Hitler must be eliminated at all costs, before the German nation bleeds to death or becomes completely brutalised."

Both men made a sudden dive for the desk as the telephone shrilled. Mertz picked up the receiver and handed it to the general, who listened in frozen silence. The colour drained from his cheeks.

" It didn't come off," he muttered after a long pause. " Himmler and Goering were both absent. Stauffenberg wanted to carry on anyway, but . . ."

" We'll have to make do with Hitler alone," the colonel said.

" Next time, perhaps." Olbricht sounded utterly exhausted.
" Whatever happens, it will have to be in the next few days."

" Where's my brother?" asked Captain von Brackwede.
" Doesn't he appreciate your company these days?"

" I've been busy, that's all," Elisabeth said. " General Olbricht ordered a complete re-check of the Valkyrie alert
plans, so I couldn't have devoted any time to Lieutenant von
Brackwede even if I'd wanted to."

" And would you have wanted to?" Brackwede was tactful
enough not to wait for a reply. " Anyway, it doesn't matter if
you do neglect your work a little in the interests of my
brother—nothing you do now will change anything."

" Is it coming off?"

" I didn't hear that question and you never asked it—you
know nothing about this business. Your contacts with Corporal
Lehmann have been of the slightest and you don't have any
detailed information about Stauffenberg or anyone else, nor
have you ever had access to the confidential files and documents
in this office. That was our arrangement and we're sticking to
it. And now, tell me where I can find that young brother of
mine."

" In the mess, attending an officers' instruction period."

" Oh, no!" Brackwede exclaimed in mock horror. " Don't
tell me Lieutenant Herbert's holding one of his indoctrination
classes!"

" His subject is Western civilisation and the preservation
of human values, I believe."

" What! A worm like that lecturing on Western civilisation?
Good God, it's almost inconceivable! Still, I suppose it's no
more inconceivable than the thought of a group of rational
human beings listening to him voluntarily—my brother among
them. Never mind, I'll soon bring him to heel."

Brackwede picked up the telephone and asked to be connected with Gestapo headquarters in Prinz Albrechtstrasse.

" Ah, Maier," he said, when the Sturmbannfuehrer answered,
" I was wondering if you'd do me a little favour. You know
my brother, don't you? I'm sure you have someone under
interrogation at the moment, and I'd appreciate it if he could
be present at one of your sessions. It's time our budding heroes
realised what a sterling job you people are doing on the home
front—the subject came up recently, if you remember. You
will? Splendid—I'll send him over."

"Pease don't do it," Elisabeth said softly, when he had replaced the receiver.

Brackwede rounded on her. "Don't look so reproachful! The boy's my brother, and I want him to behave like it."

"It's always a pleasure to see you, my boy," declared Sturmbannfuehrer Maier, "—and not only because you're the brother of an old comrade-in-arms, either. You're welcome in your own right as a representative of our lads at the front, so to speak."

"I'm much obliged, sir."

Konstantin had been given a punctilious reception on his arrival at the Prinz Albrechtstrasse, otherwise known as the Gestapo's "repair shop." The men on duty made an extremely favourable impression on him. They were polite in an unceremonious way, preserved a soldierly demeanour and limited speech to the minimum.

The building, too, looked solidly respectable—not in the least imposing, but clean as a new pin. There was an all-pervading smell of fresh paint and disinfectant which recalled a clinic rather than an administrative headquarters.

Maier's subtly modulated cordiality did not fail in its effect. Konstantin felt flattered at being on such friendly terms with one of the mighty of the Central State Security Bureau. The Sturmbannfuehrer introduced the much-decorated young officer to his closest associates: Voglbronner, looking as usual like a mild-eyed, bespectacled schoolboy, and another assistant who was resplendent in the raven-black uniform of an SS-Sturmfuehrer.

Over a cup of coffee Maier expatiated on his job, its responsibilities and difficulties and the proper method of coping with them.

"You have to master the art of isolated essentials. We're working on a typical case at the moment—a colonel who has finally confessed to being a treacherous swine."

"A colonel?" Konstantin said incredulously.

Maier explained the situation in his own way by dwelling at length on the subject of divided responsibility, the inconvenience of separate judicial machines and the burdens imposed on the security system by the army's misguided emphasis on tradition and independence.

"Recently, however, more progressive methods have been introduced. The Gestapo can arrest traitors and criminals of every description, anywhere except on army territory. After

73

all, what's at stake here is the Reich and our Fuehrer—and I'm sure you'd agree that no sacrifice can be too great where they're concerned."

Konstantin nodded. " Of course."

" Come with me, then."

They descended the stairs, crossed the hall and made for the entrance to the cellars. Maier's men sedulously opened every door as he approached with the lieutenant in tow.

Below ground-level, the whitewashed hospital atmosphere seemed to become even more accentuated. Maier's objective turned out to be a room brilliantly illuminated by a circular bank of lights in the ceiling, which gave it the look of an operating theatre. This illusion was heightened by the long narrow table in the centre, behind which stood a single chair. Having sent for a second chair, Maier invited Konstantin to sit beside him and commanded: " Bring in Bruchsal."

A moment later, one of the guards thrust a man through the door. He reeled across the room to the table and gripped it in an attempt to recover his balance. Finally, he heaved himself into a semi-erect position, swaying like a sapling in a gale.

" Well?" Maier said softy.

" Prisoner Bruchsal!" came the obedient response. The man was wearing a shabby, faded brown civilian suit. His shirt-collar protruded above the ill-fitting jacket, and he was supporting his baggy trousers with both hands. There were no shoes or socks on his feet. " Prisoner Bruchsal," he repeated hoarsely, " number-thirty-seven-thousand-eight-hundred-and-four, present!"

He bore little resemblance to the colonel who had been celebrating his newly-awarded Knight's Cross in Handler's a few nights before. His face was pallid and bore several days' growth of beard. His hands trembled like an alcoholic's, and he smelt of sweat, urine and blood.

" And that," Maier said with scorn, " —that thing—wanted to exterminate the Fuehrer!"

The Sturmbannfuehrer swung round to face Konstantin, who was staring at the human wreck in bewilderment. " This degenerate creature actually called the Fuehrer a madman who ought to be shot like a rabid dog." He turned back to Bruchsal. " Do you deny it, Bruchsal?" he inquired sarcastically.

" I plead guilty," said Bruchsal, staring at the whitewashed wall above Maier's head.

" That's typical of these swine." The Sturmbannfuehrer leant back complacently in his chair. " First of all they shoot off their mouths and then they shit themselves. Do you regret what you've done, Bruchsal?"

" I regret it."

" And? —Go on, man!"

" I regret it," the tottering figure said dully, " and I request the court to impose a just penalty."

Maier shot an oblique glance at Konstantin and snorted contemptuously. The lieutenant's stupefaction titillated him. He felt like a surgeon wielding his scalpel under the horrified eyes of a layman.

" This swine has disgracefully betrayed his men. While they were dying for their Reich and Fuehrer, he was sitting in the officers' mess calling Hitler a cretin. He even managed to find other treacherous swine with as little sense of honour as himself." Maier spoke with satisfaction. At last he had found someone who lent genuine meaning and purpose to his special task: the surveillance of the army. " Well, Bruschal, let's have some names!"

" Lieutenant Hasenclever," Bruchsal recited mechanically, " Major Samson, Major Edler von Hirth, Colonel Nassenreuth, Colonel Naetzel, General Fellmann, General Blumentritt, Field Marshal Rommel . . ."

" But that's quite absurd!" Konstantin burst out. " That can't be true! Field Marshal Rommel? Never!"

Even Maier appeared a shade uneasy at this. He stopped lolling in his chair, leant across the table, and shouted: " Shut your trap, Bruchsal!" Turning to Konstantin with a disingenuous laugh, he went on: " You're right—that's going a bit too far. The chap's evidently got a screw loose, but we can soon put that right."

" I need some fresh air," Konstantin said abruptly.

" Feeling off-colour, are you?"

Konstantin drew a deep breath. " Yes, I think I'm going to be sick."

Field Marshal Erwin Rommel rose and left the table without a word, as he always did when conversation turned to the progress of the Allied invasion. His staff officers knew him well enough to interpret this as a sign of bitterness and contempt.

He walked into the room where his chief of staff was working alone and sat down next to him. "It's just as I feared," he said morosely. "There's no way of staving off disaster. Only an imbecile could have failed to see this coming!"

The chief of staff, who was studying a map and making notes, did not look up from his work. "Lieutenant-Colonel von Hofacker is waiting in your quarters, sir," he said casually. "He's here from Paris on the orders of General von Stuelpnagel."

Rommel bent low over the map. The Allies were gaining ground hour by hour. Another few weeks and they would be at the gates of Paris; a few months, and they would be pouring across the German border. Such was the position and a soldier could draw only one inference from it, but Hitler seemed to have gone blind. It was a long time since he had listened to a military expert of Rommel's calibre.

"Abnormal situations necessitate abnormal measures," the chief of staff said slowly. "That's a quotation from General Beck, sir."

The field marshal raised his thoughtful face, the face of a hunter who has lost his bearings. He looked as if he were suffering from the effects of prolonged fatigue, but he squared his shoulders and strode out of the room as though in response to a military command.

He greeted Lieutenant-Colonel von Hofacker with a cordial handshake. "Let's make ourselves comfortable," he said. "What have you got for me—information or a request?"

Caesar von Hofacker was a tall, slim, vigorous-looking man who bore a distinct resemblance to his cousin, Colonel von Stauffenberg. "Have you come to a decision yet, sir? Can we count on your support?"

The hero of North Africa was aware of his personal worth. His name carried legendary weight, his courage was proverbial and his reputation had been lavishly boosted by every publication in the Third Reich. Even his enemies had referred to him in laudatory terms.

"I have always expressed my views frankly and openly," he began, "—in so far as it was possible to do so. I make no secret of the fact that I regard this war as lost, nor do I hesitate to demand that the guilty party be brought to book."

"That, sir," Hofacker declared, "is an indictment of Hitler."

Rommel got up, vainly trying to conceal his uneasiness. The oppressive awareness that he was being forced to take such a decision—a decision which in his view exceeded the competence of a normal soldier—made him nervous.

"I spoke to your general in the middle of May," he said. "We're in fundamental agreement. A few days later I met Field Marshal von Rundstedt—he was still in command of the Western Front at the time. I found him sympathetic to the cause but not unreservedly so."

"We can count on a much more favourable reaction from the new Commander-in-Chief, Field Marshal von Kluge."

"A logical assumption, I'm sure. Even hardbitten SS generals like Hauser seem to have lost their enthusiasm for the war in recent months. But as to killing Hitler . . . honestly, Hofacker, I find it hard to reconcile myself to the idea."

"What's the alternative, sir?"

"Well, I could envisage sending a reliable armoured force to take him into custody. After that we'd have to hand him over to a court for trial—something like that, anyway."

Lieutenant-Colonel von Hofacker closed his eye briefly, remembering what Claus von Stauffenberg had had to say about certain generals, but he quickly banished the bitter recollection from his mind. Remarks of that sort did not necessarily apply to a man like Rommel.

"Let's assume, sir, that you're presented with a fait accompli."

"In that case I'd join you—naturally."

"Might we use your name under such circumstances? It carries a great deal of weight in Germany, sir, as you must be aware."

"That's precisely why I feel we should keep our powder dry for the moment. I don't propose to go into action until the situation has become really crystallised. With all due modesty, I'm sure my contribution will have an effect."

"I've no doubt of it, sir," Hofacker said quietly and without irony. "One can only hope, for your sake, that it won't be too late by then."

"Please come in, you're not disturbing me." Julius Leber seemed quite unsurprised to see Konstantin, despite the lateness of the hour. "Your brother didn't send you, did he?"

"Far from it," Konstantin sat down beside Leber on the hard sofa, as he had on his previous visit. "As a matter of fact, he flatly forbade me to call here again, but I just had to come. I didn't know who else to talk things over with. Do you mind?"

Leber smiled, and his craggy features radiated secret amusement. "You're here now, so make the most of it."

"The thing is," Konstantin said hurriedly, "I've just come from the Prinz Albrechtsrasse."

"Alone?" asked Leber.

The lieutenant looked puzzled.

"I mean, were you followed?"

"Why should I have been?"

"Never mind—just tell me why you came. You look rather the worse for wear, not that I'm surprised, considering where you've been. Would you like to tell me about it? Do, if it'll make you feel any better."

"Thank you." Konstantin did not regret having chosen this paternal man as his confidant rather than his brother or Herbert, or even Elisabeth Oldenburg-Quentin. He related his experiences in detail.

Leber's initial surprise was replaced by a look of suppressed melancholy. "Was it your brother who sent you there?"

"Yes," Konstantin replied angrily, "and in my opinion he might have spared me a spectacle like that."

"If I understand you correctly," Leber said, "the main target of your wrath was this unfortunate colonel—Bruchsal, wasn't it?"

"The whole thing was simply ghastly!"

"I'm sure it was. However, there's just a chance that you were less outraged by what the colonel had done than by the spectacle he presented."

"That's just it!" Konstantin burst out. "The man's against the Fuehrer—all right, so it happens sometimes."

"Excellent," Leber said approvingly. "You're broadening your horizons, I see. I also begin to understand your brother's motives. Go on, Herr von Brackwede."

Konstantin stubbornly tried to collect his still chaotic thoughts. "Well, if someone is against the Fuehrer he ought to stand by his beliefs like a man."

"Agreed."

"But what does this fellow do? He turns yellow and tries to put the blame on others. He even had the nerve to implicate Field Marshal Rommel, of all people!"

Leber raised his massive head abruptly. "You must tell your brother all this as soon as possible—in the fullest detail. You'll find him quite as attentive an audience as I am."

Konstantin promised to do so and then plunged into a

further account of his experiences, stimulated by Leber's evident interest.

"I never thought I'd see a colonel in the German army reduced to a snivelling wreck."

"You underestimate the potentialities of brute force. All you saw was the end product. I don't suppose you devoted much thought to the techniques that produced it."

"But I did—that's why I find the whole thing so revolting!"

Leber got up and walked to the window furthest from the dim table-lamp. Cautiously, he pushed the heavy blackout curtain an inch or two aside and peered out into the night. The bright moonlight cast swathes of jet-black shadow, each of which might have concealed a lurking figure, but it was impossible to identify anything clearly.

"Almost everyone's resistance can be broken," Leber said. He turned and stood with his back to the curtain.

Konstantin could not know that the man facing him had spent years in concentration camps, including twelve months in total darkness. Leber had passed whole nights on a bare floor without benefit of blanket, coat or straw in thirty degrees of frost, yet his will had remained unbroken and his self-respect intact.

Konstantin said stubbornly: "I know it was shameful of the colonel to act as he did, but it was just as shameful to reduce a man to a condition like that."

"I'm glad you realise it." Leber gave him a warm smile. "What you've learnt today is no mean thing, believe me."

"But what's the answer?" insisted Konstantin. "What ought I to do?"

"Please don't expect me to answer that—I can't, much as I'm tempted to." Leber glanced round at the shrouded windows. "All I can do is offer you a piece of rather banal advice: consult your own conscience."

"But I'm completely at sea, Herr Leber."

"You won't always be—your brother will see to that. And now, if you're agreeable, let's continue the conversation we were having last time you came here. We were talking about wars of liberation, if I remember rightly."

Konstantin von Brackwede did not leave Leber's house until dawn. Birds were already singing in the leafless, bomb-blasted trees and the sun was climbing painfully over the horizon like a wounded man, staining the sky above Berlin blood-red.

"What a day!" breathed Konstantin.

It was the day on which Julius Leber was re-arrested by the Gestapo.

The assembled guests smiled doggedly and exchanged small-talk, inclining their bodies towards each other without sacrificing any of their dignified poise, like storks communing in a pool.

Dr. Josef Goebbels, Reich Minister for Popular Enlightenment and Propaganda, was giving a reception. He held a large number of social functions at his official headquarters and in its neighbouring annexes, but this particular one was devoted primarily to the military and to high-ranking government and Party officials from the Greater Berlin area whose jobs entailed co-operation with the army.

"I trust you're enjoying yourself," Goebbels said, beaming persuasively at a general.

"Immensely, Minister."

Goebbels, who was not anticipating any polished conversation this evening, had donned a mantle of guileless charm. He served hard liquor and methodically disseminated goodwill among the guests who buzzed around him like a swarm of bees.

The earlier part of the evening had been devoted to an hour-long show of war news-reels—most of them containing material which was not for release to public audiences. Goebbels was curious to observe how these professional soldiers reacted to them, though he felt fairly confident that their reaction would tell him little that he did not know already. A warm glow of superiority possessed him at the thought.

"Tell me," he said, turning to General von Hase, G.O.C. Berlin District, "do you think we ought to make our news-reels more harrowing or deliberately tone them down? I'd appreciate your views on the subject."

"It never does any harm to toughen people up," replied the general. "On the other hand, it might be equally beneficial to take their minds off things."

"Take their minds off things?" Goebbels inquired with an artless smile. "What things, General?"

General von Hase squared his shoulders. "I mean," he said in a firm but noncommittal tone, "it might be advisable to adopt a middle line, show both sides of the coin, present a carefully balanced picture—that sort of thing."

Goebbels nodded. He hadn't expected anything more un-ambiguous. His sharp eyes roved round the room, gauging the mood of the gathering. Harmony reigned wherever he looked—field-grey uniforms shoulder to shoulder with black and interspersed with brown. The lofty reception room was a sea of determinedly smiling faces. Goebbels was bored beyond measure, but he continued to radiate enthusiasm. He became aware that General von Kortzfleisch, a staunch Party supporter, was addressing him.

"Toughness is the watch-word, Minister," Kortzfleisch said, uninvited. "Bang the drum and keep 'em on their toes! For all that, people have got to be made to realise that there's a brighter side to the business of war—it takes their minds off the casualty lists. That's my humble opinion, anyway."

Goebbels smiled politely, but his gaze wandered to the neighbouring room where the bar and buffet were located. Conversation in there sounded much more animated, and he would have liked to listen in. He was boundlessly inquisitive.

In the room next door, Captain von Brackwede had just encountered SS-Sturmbannfuehrer Maier. They exchanged boisterous greetings.

"Well," Maier demanded, "how did your young brother enjoy his visit to the Gestapo?"

"I'm afraid I haven't had a chance to ask him yet."

"You've got a little treat in store, then. The youngster's stomach isn't as strong as it might be. By the way, have you tried old club-foot's champagne yet?" He nodded in the approximate direction of the limping Propaganda Minister. "It's top-notch—but then Jupp Goebbels has a nose for anything expensive."

Brackwede found Maier's high spirits suspect. He eyed the Gestapo man warily as he stood there preening himself, with his arms folded against the luminous black of his fulldress uniform tunic.

"You look as though you've hooked a big one."

"Two, my dear chap! That man Bruchsal has turned out to be a real winner. He's given me more names than I know what to do with at the moment. But apart from that," he continued, scrutinising the captain closely as he spoke, "a man named Leber has just taken up residence with us."

It was several seconds before Brackwede recovered his composure, but there was a note of steady menace in his voice when he spoke. "If you were responsible for this . . ."

"What an idea!" Maier protested. "I've no doubt it would have been the best way of crossing swords with you, and we want to avoid that, don't we? No, Leber was detained by another department, but I had him transferred into my keeping immediately. The surveillance reports list him as having been visited by a number of army officers, so he comes into my category."

"You're holding him as security against me—is that it?"

"Not directly, if you insist on being so frank. I'm not sure what my little fish is worth yet. Ought I to gut him, or give him away to someone else, or keep him on ice—or even throw him back into the pond? Or what about doing a swap—one Leber for two generals, let's say?"

Captain von Brackwede blinked momentarily, and an icy glint came into his eyes. "You can take it for granted that Hitler will be dead in a matter of days," he said grimly. "I should act on that assumption from now on."

The man standing before Goebbels had been introduced to him by one of his aides as Colonel Mertz von Quirnheim, "representing General Fromm, Commander-in-Chief, Replacement Army."

Goebbels found himself unexpectedly absorbed by the colonel's conversation. Far from uttering the usual platitudes, Mertz did his best to keep the ball in the Propaganda Minister's court.

"What is your experience of attempts to convey unpalatable truths to the German public, Minister? How do they react?"

"An extremely interesting question, Colonel," Goebbels said. "I'll answer it by asking you another: do senior officers make a habit of telling their men everything they know?"

"No."

"And why not, pray?"

Both men sensed that there was little point in pursuing the subject further. They were each aware, in their different ways, of the rules that governed the wielding of power and the waging of war. Private soldiers and/or citizens were not always capable of assimilating the truth. Genuine leaders of men took this into account.

"For all that," Mertz said, "the methods employed to enlighten people are not only crucially important but highly indicative—indicative of the nature of those who employ them."

"Most people are apathetic, stupid and credulous," Goebbels remarked with mild cynicism. "Anyone who aspires to govern must take that into account." He savoured his words for a moment. "The ancient Romans found that out long ago. No, we rely more on the idealism of the German people, their devotion to duty and sense of responsibility. To revert to your own professional sphere, Colonel, can you envisage any successful general deliberately spreading defeatism?"

"Tradition has it that the soldier must believe in victory."

Goebbels smiled. "Fundamentally speaking, we both operate on the same principle. Anyone who wants to achieve large-scale results must think in large-scale terms. We can safely leave emotionalism to poets and love-lorn virgins. By all means let the Church stake its claim to the world hereafter and allow retarded adolescents to dream heroic dreams and spout about love of country. They all obey our orders—that's the main thing. What was your name again?"

Mertz von Quirnheim . . . Goebbels tucked the item way in his capacious memory under the heading: noteworthy individuals of subordinate rank with scope for advancement. "We speak the same language, Colonel. I'm sure we shall hear from each other again before long."

Mertz's gleaming spectacles concealed the look in his eyes as he gave a small bow. Where the last remark was concerned, he and the Minister were at one. Mertz was equally certain that they would hear from each other again very soon.

A shadow fell on the sleeping face of Lieutenant von Brackwede as his brother bent over him. He watched Konstantin for some time, alert and motionless. Then he gently shook him by the shoulder.

Konstantin was fully awake within a matter of seconds. "Oh, it's you," he said ungraciously.

"Yes, it's me," Brackwede replied.

"What do you want this time?"

"I was going to suggest we went for a bathe. I've managed to get you the day off. Your commandant at the School of Air Warfare is a friend of Colonel Mertz von Quirnheim, and any friend of Mertz is a friend of mine. All right, get dressed."

An hour later they reached the Kleiner Wannsee, where Brackwede knew a place which offered comparatively undisturbed bathing in relatively pleasant surroundings. The Café Krause, "with private beach," enjoyed a certain reputation.

"I only came because I had to speak to you," Konstantin said.

He stared sullenly at the people who were devoting themselves to the meagre delights of bathing on the pocket-hand-kerchief-sized beach. The early July weather had been alternating between violent local downpours and glaring sunshine, sultry heat and cool, cloudy intervals, but the Berlin lakes still attracted their quota of femininity.

The female figures, too, failed to fit into the picture Konstantin had painted of the world. They were either on leave or night duty, war-widows or precocious adolescents, venturesome housewives or foreign workers in privileged jobs—not very many from any one category but more than enough to divert a young and unattached male.

"What was your connection with Colonel Bruchsal's arrest?" he asked.

Captain von Brackwede eyed his brother keenly. "That's quite simple. I happened to be present when Bruchsal delivered his last speech. Maier asked me to testify to the facts and I did so."

"You mean you were a party to this?"

"What a gratifying question! You actually seem to be absorbing something at last."

Konstantin looked incredulous. "You honestly mean to tell me you helped to betray a brother officer?"

"Some people might quarrel with your choice of phrase. However, allow me to put the situation in its proper perspective. In the first place there were dozens of witnesses, so Bruchsal was done for in any case. In the second place, the colonel's abuse of Hitler may demonstrate the excellence of his character, but the fact that he abused him in a favourite haunt of Party officials casts considerable doubt on his sanity."

Surrounding noises crowded in on them: a child's shrill squeals of delight, a woman's full-throated laughter, the inane giggling of two girls as they jumped up and ran down to the water's edge. A monotonous voice intoned: "Cigarettes, refreshments, cigarettes, refreshments!"

"I feel ashamed," Konstantin muttered, "ashamed for your sake."

"Congratulations," said Brackwede. "So in your opinion it wasn't right to hand over a man to the Gestapo for calling Hitler a lousy bastard."

"It's the methods they use!" Konstantin burst out impotently. "You make me sick—all of you!"

"What a fund of new discoveries you've made!" Brackwede seemed to be relishing this moment. "Keep it up and you may yet become the apple of my eye."

But Konstantin was not listening. He sprang to his feet, bundled his clothes together and hurried off. Heedless of wistful glances and blind to the flirtatious beckoning of a shapely blonde, he strode across a carpet of sun-warmed female bodies and made for the exit.

"Today's the day," Olbricht declared confidently. He glanced at his wrist-watch. "Another few minutes and we'll be open for business. I shall issue code-word Valkyrie at eleven hundred hours."

It was Saturday, 15 July 1944. Early that morning, Colonel von Stauffenberg had set off by 'plane for the Fuehrer's Headquarters at Rasternburg in East Prussia, accompanied by General Fromm. The requisite briefcase had been entrusted to Captain Friedrich-Karl Klauring.

Back in the Bendlerstrasse, Colonel Mertz von Quirnheim had already opened his safe and was beginning to stack the contents on his desk in neat piles. "Our first step," he told Captain von Brackwede, who was an interested spectator, "will be to alert all units stationed on the outskirts of Berlin. The rest will follow in due course."

"You've thought everything out very carefully, I see," Brackwede remarked in a faintly challenging voice. "But aren't other people capable of putting two and two together— the unit commanders advancing on Berlin, for instance?"

General Olbricht smiled. "We're all capable of constructive thought, my friend, you and the Gestapo included, but we need every man we can lay our hands on."

"Yes, when the time comes. To the best of my knowledge, the Fuehrer's daily conference doesn't start until one-thirty, but you're ringing up the curtain two-and-a-half hours early. I congratulate you on your nerve."

"We're relying on Stauffenberg . . ."

"But you can't rely on Hitler, sir."

Olbricht rounded on him, looking slightly indignant. "God Almighty, Brackwede, I know you only play the devil's advocate so as to keep us on our toes, but give it a rest occasionally."

"I will at one-thirty p.m., sir—if the attempt succeeds."

"Nothing will stop Stauffenberg now—all the signs point in that direction. Think of the disastrous state of our fronts! Rommel has sent Hitler a form of ultimatum. General von Falkenhausen, the military governor of Belgium, was removed from his post yesterday and replaced by a Gauleiter. —And

85

what about the arrest of Julius Leber! Stauffenberg was shattered by the news."

" It's time, sir," said Mertz von Quirnheim. " Eleven hundred hours."

Olbricht picked up the 'phone. " Valkyrie—the code-word for the suppression of internal disorder—will now be issued."

" In that case, sir," said Captain von Brackwede, " I shall initiate my own preparatory measures. If I'm needed before one-thirty I'll be in the mess, fortifying myself."

" Stand to!" Bellowed by powerful voices, the cry echoed and re-echoed along barrack passages. Whistles shrilled and sirens rent the air for a full minute.

This process was repeated in the tank training establishments at Krampnitz and Gross-Glienicke, the School of Infantry at Doeberitz, the Junior Leaders' School at Potsdam and a dozen other, smaller units stationed in the environs of Berlin.

There was nothing dramatic about the process. Alerts occurred quite frequently and formed part of the routine training schedule.

" All right, let's go," said the officers.

" Pull your fingers out and get moving!" yelled the N.C.O.s.

" Why now?" grumbled the other ranks. " Our dinners'll be cold by the time we get back."

They streamed obediently towards their assembly points from class-rooms, store depots and canteens. They converged from cellars, workshops and barrack squares. They dived into their battle-dress, clamped on their steel helmets and reached for their rifles.

Junior officers paced up and down with stop-watches in their hands, solely concerned with how long their men took to fall in after the issuing of the alert. It was essential to beat the average and desirable to beat the record. The atmosphere was that of a military sports day.

For the time being, company commanders stood waiting in the background, eyeing their charges critically. Battalion commanders betook themselves to battalion headquarters. School commandants assembled their officers and ordered their adjutants to hand them the Valkyrie file from their safes.

At Krampnitz, Colonel Gorn was saying: " In the first place, the existence of internal disorder must be assumed. This, in turn, presupposes that martial law has been imposed."

His audience listened casually, with the indifference of

men who had been compelled to take part in countless military charades in their time—fire-practices, imaginary paratroop attacks, mock searches for escaped prisoners of war, measures to combat hypothetical acts of sabotage. Now it was internal disorder.

"In the second place," the commandant continued, "three tank battalions will move to Berlin and take up their position in the Tiergarten-Bendlerstrasse area. Attached to them—see Appendix C—will be a unit made up of five companies of officer cadets from the School of Infantry at Potsdam— equivalent to one battalion. Also attached to them will be a battalion supplied by the Junior Leaders' School at Potsdam, this one consisting of only three companies."

Those present registered no perceptible emotion. Orders were orders. A question referring to the possible consumption of field rations, special distributions of canned food and cigarettes and the supply of beer was dismissed as "immaterial at this time."

"In the third place," said the commandant, leafing through his operational plans, "a special unit consisting of an armoured car company and a Panzergrenadier company will occupy the radio stations at Koenigswusterhausen and Zeesen." He bent lower over his papers as though to decipher them better. Then, with a hint of surprise, he went on: "Any resistance will be overcome by force."

Even this caused no stir. Phrases of this type were in current vogue and, anyway, nothing was impossible in war-time. His listeners waited with patient resignation for their marching orders.

"Issue live ammunition," ordered the commandant. "Any further details can be found in the schedules which the adjutant will give you. I myself will be reporting to the C.-in-C. Replacement Army, as instructed. I want everything to go like clockwork, gentlemen," he concluded. "Kindly see that it does!"

Shortly afterwards, at 12.15 a.m., dozens of engines roared into life. The motorised troops reached automatically for their grab-handles and the first tanks lurched forward, bound for Berlin.

General Erich Fellgiebel, chief of Signals and lord and master of all telephones, radio sets and teleprinters in the Fuehrer's Headquarters, leant nonchalantly against the concrete wall outside his bunker, blinking with apparent boredom at the greyish-yellow summer sky. He looked like the manager of a large Swiss hotel awaiting the arrival of distinguished guests. Glancing at his watch, he saw that it was just after one-thirty.

Fellgiebel concealed his sense of expectancy well, but his eyes wandered repeatedly in the direction of the Fuehrer's bunker, which was shielded from view by a dense screen of trees and barbed wire. He smoked his cigar as slowly as he could, and waited.

Suddenly, from the inner compound, there emerged an officer whom Fellgiebe recognised as Stauffenberg's companion, Captain Klauring. Controlling himsef with an effort, Klauring approached him at a rigidly conventional pace.

"What's gone wrong?" demanded the general.

Captain Klauring registered a mixture of agitation and nervous exhaustion. "Everything was going according to plan . . ." he said slowly.

"There have been dozens of plans, Klauring, if not hundreds—and all evolved by the finest brains in Germany. Theoretically, that man over there should have been dead by nineteen-thirty-eight at the latest." General Fellgiebel thrust himself away from the bunker wall by his shouders and stood there, slightly hunched. "But I'm as bad as the rest—standing here talking. What can I do to help?"

"I'm afraid there's nothing more to be done today." Klauring sounded almost ashamed. "Hitler left the conference almost as soon as it started—he was only in the room for a couple of minutes. No one knows why he went out."

"It's always the same," Fellgiebel grumbled, nervously smoothing the wrinkles from his leather gloves. "He hops around like a flea, that man. Sometimes I think his main occupation in life is upsetting schedules. He's been avoiding the limelight for months now."

"The Bendlerstrasse must be informed, General," Klauring said. "Colonel von Stauffenberg was most insistent on that point. He can't call them himself because he's been summoned to see Himmler."

"Why? Is it about those new Volksgrenadier divisions the Reichsfuehrer-SS is so keen to get his hands on?"

"Please, General, the Bendlerstrasse . . . Berlin was due to put parts of Operation Valkyrie into effect at eleven o'clock this morning."

"Christ Almighty!" exclaimed Fellgiebel. "That's all we

needed!" Then he turned and hurried into the communications bunker.

"Well, here I am," announced Eugen G., walking into Brackwede's office with a beaming smile. "How goes it?"

"Good God, man!" Brackwede ejaculated. "I thought you'd gone into hiding. What are you doing here?"

Eugen G. shrugged. "I wanted to be here, that's all."

Brackwede quickly concealed his consternation behind a mask of sarcasm. "If you came to gloat over the discomfiture of Olbricht and Mertz, you chose your moment carefully. The great day has been postponed."

"What, another flop?"

"It's been postponed," Brackwede repeated calmly. "But that's not all. It takes nerve to make two attempts and fail, but Stauffenberg's got plenty of that commodity. He'll have a third go—and a fourth and a fifth, too, if need be."

"You're not worried, then?"

"Not about that—I've had enough practice at waiting in my life. No, what worries me is that our military geniuses opened fire too soon. They're now trying to conjure their ammunition back into the barrel. Come and watch?"

Mertz von Quirnheim was telephoning when they entered his office. One after another, the calls went out: "Practice alert concluded, code-word Valkyrie cancelled. All units will return to base. Written reports to me by midday tomorrow."

"Not bad," commented Brackwede, "You seem to be pouring oil on the troubled waters very effectively. The only question is, did anyone drown?"

Olbricht looked a trifle pale but seemed calm and composed. Obviously, the worst was over, so he could leave his chief of staff to clear up the mess with his usual cold-blooded attention to detail. He greeted Eugen G. warmly.

"You're not only efficient, gentlemen," Brackwede remarked with gentle irony. "You're lucky into the bargain, I dread to think what would have happened if our revered Commander-in-Chief had been on the premises. Even he would have been bound to spot that something was up. On the other hand, it's quite possible that some officious sneak will try to open his bleary eyes to what's been going on—I can think of at least three generals in this building who are capable of it."

"I've allowed for that," Olbricht replied gravely. "I'll simply tell him we've been carrying out a spot-check in his absence."

"And you think he'll believe you?" Brackwede looked dubious. "Have you really gone through all the motions of a partial alert?"

Mertz von Quirnheim, who had been following the course of the conversation with half an ear, put down the 'phone and looked up.

"Brackwede may be a Job's comforter, but he has his uses," Olbricht said thoughtfully, "I believe he's given me a bright idea. I'll go and inspect some of the units we alerted and give them a little sermon on the subject of exercises, practice alerts, rehearsals and so on. That should be an additional safeguard."

Corporal Lehmann had spent the day roaming idly through the Bendlerstrasse block. No one took any notice of him, no one requested his assistance or advice, no one helped to speed the sluggish hands of the clock. Stauffenberg was still en route, Brackwede bustled busily up and down the corridors and Elisabeth Oldenburg-Quentin was occupied elsewhere on the captain's orders, so there was no likelihood of Konstantin's appearance either. Lehmann yawned.

Eventually he bumped into Lieutenant Herbert, who professed himself delighted at the encounter. "Come along to my office," he said. "I've just finished work for the day, if you'd like to keep me company for a while."

The corporal accepted Herbert's suggestion without demur. "As long as you've got a drop of the hard stuff tucked away somewhere—not that you ought to find that difficult, sir, with your connections."

Herbert was positively lavish in his hospitality. He emptied half the contents of his bottom desk drawer, which was where he kept his most treasured delicacies. Having opened a large tin of crayfish-tails, he produced a special bottle of Scotch whisky—guaranteed seven years old—and set it down beside Lehmann.

"Help yourself," he said cordially. "There's more where that came from. I'm just going to shake hands with the man I enlisted with—be back in a moment."

Having retired, not to the lavatory, but to make a 'phone call from the room next door, Herbert reappeared wearing a satisfied smile and began to discuss the Brackwede brothers, especially Konstantin.

Lehmann looked interested. "How's he doing?"

"Splendid," Lieutenant Herbert assured him. "We spend

a lot of time together. Lieutenant von Brackwede is a first-rate chap. My girl-friend thinks so too, worse luck."

Encouraged by Lehmann, Herbert developed the theme, heaping praises on all that bore the name Brackwede. Glancing covertly through the window, he saw a large black Mercedes saloon roll past and pull up at a discreet distance from the main entrance.

"I'm worried," Herbert lied convincingly. "I arranged to meet Lieutenant von Brackwede at my girl-friend's flat. It's only just round the corner, three blocks away, but the 'phone's out of order and I can't leave here yet. I'm expecting an important call from the Propaganda Ministry."

Lehmann felt amused. In his eyes, Herbert was a wind-bag, an opportunist, a boot-licker—in short, an officious bastard. He was fundamentally indifferent to Herbert—there were millions like him in Germany today—but Konstantin intrigued him, and so did the girl-friend who allegedly managed to distract the lieutenant's attention from a unique woman like Elisabeth, Countess von Oldenburg-Quentin. His curiosity was whetted.

"If it's only just down the road, and you'd really like me to, I could nip along there for you."

"Would you really, Corporal? I'd be most obliged." A brief glance through the window reassured Herbert that all was well: the hearse-like limousine was still waiting.

General Fritz Fromm, Commander-in-Chief of the Replacement Army, had his own band of henchmen, paladins and informers. When it was reported to him, immediately on his return from the Fuehrer's Headquarters, that code-word Valkyrie had been issued in his absence, his first reaction was to register the information and digest it in silence. After sitting motionless at his desk for some minutes, he began to make discreet inquiries. Slightly relieved to learn that General Olbricht was out on a tour of inspection, he summoned Colonel Mertz von Quirnheim to his office.

"Now, Mertz," he snapped, "what's the meaning of this tomfoolery?"

"A routine exercise, sir," the colonel replied coolly.

Fromm refrained from asking the cardinal question, namely, how such an order could have been issued at all without his approval. Instead, he behaved as though the whole operation was his idea but had been carried out inefficiently and without the requisite care.

"It sounds like a complete cock-up to me," he grumbled. "You ought to have laid it on more carefully."

Mertz von Quirnheim at once realised what Fromm was driving at. The general didn't want to commit himself. He wanted to eliminate the possibility of personal risk. "Any defects in the plan will be reported to us, sir," he said with relief, "—I've seen to that."

"I only hope you haven't stirred up any unnecessary dust," Fromm said resentfully. Injecting a note of fatherly concern into his voice, he continued: "Don't do anything foolish, for God's sake."

"The operation was carefully planned," Mertz insisted.

"I sincerely hope so," Fromm replied, swinging round to face the window. "However, I'm going to circulate a memorandum, initially—I repeat, initially—for internal consumption, stating that I vigorously disapprove of subordinates indulging in dubious experiments in command, that I strongly advise against them, and that I utterly refuse to tolerate them. Is that clear?"

Mertz von Quirnheim adjusted his glasses. "Quite clear, sir."

That day, the Bendlerstrasse witnessed an incident which caused a considerable stir.

The facts, as officially reported, were as follows: a corporal named Lehmann emerged from the Bendler block wheeling a bicycle. He mounted it and pedalled away at a leisurely pace, followed by a black government saloon. Suddenly, the corporal jumped off his bicycle, drew a pistol and punctured the front tyres of the saloon with two well-aimed shots. The occupants of the car ducked for cover, and by the time they ventured to raise their heads again the man with the bicycle had vanished.

Voglbronner, the chief occupant of the car in question, had arrived in response to a telephone call. Since he had been acting on his own initiative in the temporary absence of his superior, Sturmbannfuehrer Maier, he was satisfied that his failure to arrest Lehmann reflected no discredit on him. He hurried back to the Prinz Albrechtstrasse headquarters as fast as he could, but it was some time before he could submit his report.

"It's pitiful," was Maier's first comment. His voice rose abruptly to a leonine roar. "You're a miserable flop, Voglbronner! You've either got to capture people like that alive or shoot them down on the spot. What you did is tantamount to sabotage!"

Voglbronner ground his teeth. No one could have foreseen the course of events, he ventured to suggest. Such a thing had never happened before.

"The things one has to put up with when one's got a lot of useless dead-beats on one's staff!" Maier growled, with a withering glance at his assistant. "One more balls-up like that, my friend, and you're finished!"

Maier attempted to clarify the situation in person. He drove to the Bendlerstrasse in his official capacity and was referred, after much inter-departmental manoeuvring, to Captain von Brackwede. The result was predictable.

Brackwede registered consternation. "I can hardly believe it!" he exclaimed. A telephone call from Lehmann had meanwhile assured him that the corporal was safely installed in one of the movement's numerous bolt-holes in the Greater Berlin area. "It would be my duty to hand him over, of course, but I haven't got him."

Quickly realising the hopelessness of his position, Maier refrained from making any rash demands. "I was merely thinking of our mutual agreement to co-operate," he said mildly.

"I attach the greatest importance to it," Brackwede assured him. "However, where Lehmann's concerned I'm afraid there's nothing to be done. I can't lay hands on him."

"Why not? I require an official explanation—you must realise that."

"Of course. You'll get one, too. Unfortunately, Lehmann has absented himself from his post without permission. In plain language, he's a deserter."

"All right, all right," Maier said impatiently, "I get the picture—I wasn't born yesterday. I'll be glad to help you find him. We'll run him to earth sooner or later, don't you worry."

Brackwede sat back in his chair. "My dear fellow, you still seem to be unaware of how little time you have to evolve a correct approach to certain matters. From your point of view, tomorrow or the day after may be too late."

"That's the way it goes, Konstantin," Lieutenant Herbert declared. "It's part of the price we have to pay for living in an historic age. Renegades and people who slander the Fuehrer must be dealt with as they deserve."

93

Konstantin von Brackwede had been shocked by the news of Lehmann's brush with the Gestapo, just as he was still unable to banish the memory of Colonel Bruchsal. Julius Leber's arrest he regarded as a tragic mistake.

He had gone in search of his brother, who professed to be too busy to see him. Then he had inquired after Elisabeth, but she seemed to be away for the day. Finally, he had encountered Lieutenant Herbert, who welcomed him with open arms and bore him off to Molly's flat.

"Sacrifices have to be made—surely you must realise that, Konstantin." Herbert already made a point of addressing the younger Brackwede by his Christian name, not least because he was the influential captain's brother. "Besides, as I say, everything has its prices."

Molly, who was sitting beside them in her bath-robe, had just taken a shower. The water mains happened to be functioning in this quarter of the city, and it was advisable to make the most of the fact.

"Rub my back for me," she pouted coquettishly at Konstantin.

"Rub my back," mimicked Herbert. "That's how it always starts with her!" Konstantin's diffidence seemed to amuse him. "You needn't be bashful," he said with a confidential wink. "In the first place there's no one here but us, and in the second place I'm all for a policy of share alike."

He gave a proprietorial gesture which took in Molly's plump body and the battery of bottles on the drinks trolley beside him. After all, he ultimately owed the perquisities of his new job to Konstantin's brother.

"That brother of yours is a real card, Konstantin—you've got to hand it to him. It's marvellous, the way he talks to Colonel Mertz and General Olbricht. They say he even tore a strip off General Fromm at a conference recently, and the old boy just looked dazed and said nothing. But that's the way it ought to be. A good officer always speaks his mind, generals or no generals."

Molly purred like a contented cat as Konstantin gently rubbed her back, but the lieutenant's movements were mechanical. He found Molly distracting rather than exciting. However, Herbert devised a pleasant way of soothing his troubled mind by insisting that he sample every brand of French cognac on the trolley, from Hennessy, via Dubouchet and Monnet, to Courvoisier. The one he liked best would be reserved for him from then on.

"You've got to be a realist, Konstantin," he pursued. "We're fighting for total victory. If anyone doesn't toe the line a hundred per cent, there can only be one solution." He made a graphic chopping motion with his hand.

"You can rub harder if you like," Molly cooed, but Konstantin ignored the invitation. Stumbling a little over his words, he said: "What worries me is the methods they use . . ."

"We're struggling for survival, man! The enemy is trying to exterminate us—the Fuehrer says so."

Konstantin could not summon up the strength to reply. He watched Herbert get up, swaying slightly, with his arms crooked as if he were cradling a tommy-gun against his thick body.

"Mow 'em down!" he cried in a hoarse voice. "Mow down anyone who gets in the Fuehrer's way!"

"I'm going to take another shower," Molly announced, rising to her feet. "Who'll soap my back for me?"

Herbert opened a bottle of whisky and invited Konstantin to escort Molly to the bathroom. Konstantin, who was on the point of testing his twelfth brandy—three fingers of rare Jouvet Réserve slopped into a tumbler—tipped the liquor down his throat and made his way, stiff-legged and foggy-brained, to the bathroom.

Once there he addressed Molly as Elisabeth and tried to soap her back, but his strength failed him. He sat on the edge of the bath, slid slowly to the floor, and lay there.

Herbert tottered in, summoned by Molly. Surveying the lieutenant's inert form, he said ponderously: "What that boy needs is a woman!"

"Yes," Molly agreed, "a woman called Elisabeth."

"He shall have her," Herbert declared magnanimously. "I'll appeal to her conscience, the stuck-up bitch. What's she waiting for?"

General Beck said: "You did your best—I'd like to make that quite clear."

"I can do better," Stauffenberg replied grimly. "I won't give up."

It was Sunday, 16 July 1944, the day after the unsuccessful attempt on Hitler's life, and Stauffenberg had been summoned to Beck's house. The two men were sitting in the general's study, enclosed by a rampart of book-lined walls.

"I'm told that the Valkyrie alert was a doubtful success

in one or two respects," Beck said. "For instance, some units failed to maintain their schedules."

"I'm still not satisfied with our plans either, sir," Stauffenberg admitted. "One or two improvements are urgently required—Olbricht and Mertz are working on them at this moment. Brackwede has also expressed doubts. He doesn't like the phrasing of our public proclamations, but they'll be redrafted in the next few days."

"Perhaps we ought to abandon the idea of a radical solution altogether," mused Beck. "This is the safest method, I know, but there are others."

"Any other solution would take time and a fresh set of elaborate preparations, sir," Stauffenberg said firmly. "It would mean postponing the decision yet again. In the meantime, Goerdeler might be arrested and Leber tortured. A lot of important people would lose heart and cry off."

"I know," Beck said with evident reluctance, "—the war seems to have lasted an eternity, especially to those of us who opted for resistance."

"There's only one possibility left." Claus von Stauffenberg drew himself erect and laid the three fingers of his left hand on the breast of his uniform tunic, almost as though he had been transfixed by a sudden spasm of pain. "I'm being accused of making extravagant promises which I fail to keep. Himmler is threatening to put a stop to the activities of men like yourself and Goerdeler, and Brackwede has shown us a Reuter report stating that an officer of the German General Staff has already been selected to assassinate Hitler. We must act, and act quickly."

"What if I ordered you to abandon the project, Stauffenberg?"

"I beg you not to, sir."

There was a long pause. Then Beck said: "My orders to you are as follows: you will confer with your friends once more and acquaint them with my misgivings. If, after that, you still insist on carrying out your decision—do so, and God be with you!"

"I just happened to be passing," Sturmbannfuehrer Maier said jovially. "I had some official business to attend to in the neighbourhood, so I thought I'd drop in on you."

Maier's corpulent frame seemed to fill Konstantin's diminutive room in the School of Air Warfare at Bernau to bursting-point. He ran an interested eye over the lieutenant's primitive quarters—a sort of glorified prison cell—and lowered his bulk on to the camp-bed.

" Tell me," he inquired amiably, " when did you last see your brother?"

" Yesterday, but he was tied up—we scarcely exchanged a word." Almost bitterly, Konstantin added: " Perhaps it was just as well."

" I quite understand," Maier said with easy familiarity. " Old Fritz isn't exactly a run-of-the-mill type—he tends to rub people up the wrong way. I'd feel a bit uneasy about that, if I were you."

Konstantin shrugged. " What's the point—he does as he pleases."

" Gestapo " Maier assumed his most dulcet tone and cemented an affectionate smile to his face. " I'm genuinely fond of Fritz, believe me, but that's just why I worry about him. A lot of the things he does strike me as unwise."

" I get that impression too, sometimes," Konstantin replied with guileless sincerity. " I'm devoted to my brother, but I'm not his keeper."

The Sturmbannfuehrer nodded. He fumbled in his breast pocket and produced a slip of paper. It bore a diagram consisting of a large rectangle with a smaller rectangle in the centre. Beside the latter was inscribed a swastika, and near the swastika a cross. The sketch had been recovered from a waste-paper basket in the Bendlerstrasse by a cleaning-woman who drew supplementary pay from the Gestapo.

" Any idea what this is?"

Konstantin studied the piece of paper and shook his head.

" People can get caught up in dangerous situations without their knowledge or consent—believe me, I know about these things." Maier gripped Konstantin's arm in a gesture of friendly entreaty. " All I want you to promise me is this: if you see anything that strikes you as odd or suspicious, contact me straight away and I'll bail your brother out."

" I promised General Beck I'd present the facts of the matter with complete honesty," Stauffenberg said. " After that we must come to a decision, and our decision will be final and binding."

It was the evening of Sunday, 16 July 1944, and the following persons were assembled in Colonel von Stauffenberg's flat beside the Grosser Wannsee: Adam von Trott zu Solz, diplomatic adviser to the Foreign Office, Captain von Schwerin-

Schwanefeld, Councillor Yorck von Wartenburg, Colonel Mertz von Quirnheim, Colonel of the General Staff Georg Hansen, Lieutenant-Colonel Caesar von Hofacker from Paris, Stauffenberg's brother Berthold, and Captain von Brackwede—nine in all.

"General Beck believes—and he is not alone in his view—that there are three alternatives," Stauffenberg began. "Would you be kind enough to outline them for us, Fritz?"

"Under protest." Brackwede's smile did not quite disguise his latent concern. "We all know what alternative number one is," he said hurriedly, " —the so-called radical solution. Number two may be described as the Berlin solution—seizure of the entire chain of command and communication, withdrawal on all fronts and defiance of Supreme Headquarters. Thirdly, there's the so-called Western solution—disengagement in the West, withdrawal of troops to the Rhine and stepped-up defence in the East."

"What about the Commanders-in-Chief?"

Brackwede grinned sardonically. "Once Hitler is eliminated they'll need a new Head of State to swear allegiance to so that they can continue to serve with honour."

He looked across at Stauffenberg, but the colonel remained silent. His attitude toward certain military leaders needed no amplification in this company, and he was anxious not to intervene prematurely.

Adam von Trott cleared his throat. "We've made repeated attempts to establish contact with the other side."

"Himmler has been doing much the same thing," Brackwede said, " —without success, needless to say. No one wants to negotiate with a butcher. What have our own approaches yielded?"

"Polite expressions of interest and goodwill, nothing more. Our friends even managed to get into touch with Churchill direct, but without any definite result."

"Perhaps it's better that way," Berthold von Stauffenberg said reflectively. "We must handle this by ourselves."

Silence fell on the members of the group. Brackwede watched them intently. Claus von Stauffenberg sat there motionless, apparently lost in thought. He had forgotten to mop his infected eye, and a thin stream of pus was trickling down his lean cheek. He gave no sign of the pain that was raging in his head.

"I telephoned Henning von Tresckow today," Brackwede reported. "His attitude is this: Hitler must be assassinated at all costs. Even if the attempt fails, a coup d'état must be organised. It isn't merely a question of practicalities—not any longer. The world must be made to realise that members of the German resistance movement were ready to stake their lives on a final and decisive throw of the dice—all other considerations are secondary. So much for Henning von Tresckow."

"I agree," Stauffenberg said. "There's only one course of action open to us. It must and will be tried—again and again, until it succeeds."

Brick-dust covered the streets of Berlin like a shroud. It drifted over the buildings that still stood, coating window-panes and roof-tops with a dirty grey film. No one in the Kurfuerstendamm looked entirely clean any more—no one, that is, except Lieutenant Konstantin von Brackwede. His shoes gleamed, his gloves were freshly washed and his numerous medals and decorations shone with metallic splendour. He stood outside a cinema as he had done for the past half hour, waiting impatiently for Elisabeth Oldenburg-Quentin.

His gaze wandered past the Gedaechtniskirche and the Zoo Station in the direction of Tauentzienstrasse and its sombre skyscraper, but he did not see the patched and broken windows that stared out of it like sightless eyes, nor did he take in the people who jostled past him with desiccated faces, grey as dust themselves, sour-smelling and shabbily dressed. All he yearned to see was Elisabeth.

She appeared, wearing a dress made of some pale-blue silky material which moulded itself softly to the contours of her slender body. There was veiled affection in her smile of greeting.

"How wonderful," Konstantin said gratefully, "—wonderful that you exist and wonderful that you're here."

"I've been looking forward to it," she replied. She glanced over his shoulder at the dark shaft of the Underground, down which people were vanishing like mice into a hole. "There's bound to be an air-raid warning soon, but let's enjoy ourselves till then."

They set out for the Weinstock, a restaurant in a side-street just off the Kurfuerstendamm favoured by officers from the Bendlerstrasse. The proprietor, who acted as a post-box for the resistance movement, was always happy to reserve tables for his friends.

"I told your brother where we'd be," Elisabeth said. "It's

the usual rule in our department—we're on call twenty-four hours a day."

"I hope he didn't object to your coming here with me."

"He seemed pleased at the idea," Elisabeth replied with a smile. "Does that annoy you?"

Konstantin coloured slightly and shook his head. He had just started to study the modest menu when the proprietor appeared. He announced that he had taken the liberty of ordering the meal himself, and had also selected a wine from his private cellar. With a discreet smile at Elisabeth, he went on to inform Konstantin that the suggestion had emanated from Captain von Brackwede.

The food, when it arrived, was not unduly plentiful but as good as any Berlin restaurant could have produced in the fifth year of the war, and the wine was a Franconian from Kitzingen. Konstantin and Elisabeth chatted lightheartedly for almost an hour.

At the end of that time Brackwede appeared. He walked across to their table and sat down with a broad smile. "Sorry to interrupt you, but it's unavoidable—what's more, it may be worth-while."

Elisabeth reached for her handbag. "I'll come straight away."

"Thanks, but it's nothing to do with you this time. I want to borrow Konstantin from you, that's all. I have an appointment with Colonel von Stauffenberg, and he didn't object when I asked if I could bring my brother along. A splendid opportunity for him, don't you agree, Countess?"

"Is it really necessary?" Elisabeth asked quietly.

"I think so," Brackwede replied. "It may be a unique chance for Konstantin to improve his knowledge of human nature. I see you've no objection, Countess—many thanks." He turned to Konstantin. "All right, my boy, let's go."

"Come in, come in!" Stauffenberg called to Brackwede. "I'm just indulging in high treason—my favourite hobby."

Konstantin deduced from the cheerful smile which accompanied these words that the one-eyed colonel had cracked a joke. Extravagant language of this sort appeared to be commonplace among members of the General Staff, at least in the Bendlerstrasse.

Stauffenberg put down the receiver for a moment and walked swiftly over to the lieutenant. Extending his three fingers, he said: "It's a pleasure to meet you, Herr von Brackwede. Your brother has told me quite a bit about you."

The colonel's hearty laughter was seldom heard these days. Once upon a time his friends had been able to identify him from behind closed doors by his gusts of unaffected merriment, but now he radiated grim resolution, intense concentration and razor-sharp expectancy.

Striding quickly back to his desk, he picked up the receiver again and spoke to the chief of staff of an Army Group. "Your office confirmed receipt of the last consignment of supplies about a fortnight ago, at the beginning of July—kindly check on that." Turning to Brackwede, he went on, almost in the same breath: "The amended proclamation and the revised drafts of the preliminary teleprinter messages are ready, Fritz."

The captain went over to Stauffenberg's desk, extracted a file from the bottom of the right-hand pile and retired with it to an arm-chair. Konstantin remained standing by the door, electrified by the atmosphere of restless urgency that dominated the room.

Stauffenberg was talking into the 'phone again. No, he was quite unable to double allocations of supplies; yes, he knew it was desirable, but it was even unlikely that the present level would be able to be maintained in the near future. "This war is turning into a one-way trip to eternity, old man. Ever thought of jumping off before it's too late? No? In that case, happy landings!"

The receiver never left Stauffenberg's hand as one conversation followed hard on the heels of the next. Konstantin diffidently took a chair in the background near the door, where he could watch his brother and the youthful-looking Chief of Staff with equal facility. There seemed to be an unspoken understanding between the two men.

"No!" Stauffenberg said with a cold incisiveness which was in sharp contrast with his habitually quiet, almost gentle tone. "No, that's not on! Priority can't be limited to troops' wives and children only. If German nationals from the East are forced to flee to the Reich they must be helped, not turned away. There's no reason why civilians should suffer because our military leaders are making a hash of things."

Captain von Brackwede glanced up briefly from his perusal of the file on his lap. "You're becoming pretty outspoken these days."

"Not outspoken enough," replied Stauffenberg. He did not replace the receiver but asked for three more calls, one to an arms manufacturer, another to Rosenberg's Ministry and a third to Army Group B in the West. While waiting he lit a cigarette—unaided. Konstantin had been expressly warned by his brother not to leap to the colonel's assistance. Despite his disability, Stauffenberg dressed himself, fed himself and wrote his own memoranda.

Stauffenberg put the cigarette in his mouth, opened the matchbox on his desk and extracted a match with swift, unerring movements. He struck it dexterously against the box and it flared up at once. Almost at the same moment he picked up the telephone again. The signet-ring on his surviving forefinger bore the inscription: FINIS INITIUM.

Turning to Konstantin with the receiver clamped to his ear, Stauffenberg asked: "What's your opinion of the military situation, Herr von Brackwede?"

"I'm afraid I haven't a broad enough appreciation of it, sir."

"But he's optimistic," Captain von Brackwede interposed with amusement. "He's prepared to die for Germany like a good boy. The only trouble is, he identifies Germany with Hitler—it's a widespread fallacy."

Stauffenberg's attention was distracted by a voice at the other end of the line. He sat there with his broad shoulders slightly hunched, but his brow remained clear and serene. "I know conditions aren't normal," he told the armaments supplier. "We realise that, even in the Bendlerstrasse. I know all about your probems, too, but they're your problems, not mine. The men at the front need something to fight with, and you'll go on supplying it until your factory is completely bombed out."

A moment later he was addressing Konstantin again. "Army Group Centre is as good as done for," he said, as though stating an arithmetical problem. "The collapse of the Eastern front can be expected within a few weeks. Russian troops will shorty cross the Vistula, then the Oder. They'll be at the gates of Berlin in the foreseeable future. That, Lieutenant von Brackwede, is the position."

Konstantin crouched in his chair as though turned to stone. He shot an appealing look at his brother, but Brackwede appeared to be wholly absorbed in his papers. Meanwhile, Stauffenberg was telephoning again, first to a Party official about the distribution of clothing to destitute members of the civil population in military areas, then to the widow of a brother officer, to express his condolences on her husband's death.

"Well, Fritz," he said, putting down the 'phone at last, "how far have you got with your reading? Have you been able to form an opinion yet?"

"The proclamations are far too long-winded—completely lacking in impact. They won't make an immediate impression on the man in the street."

"Just what I've always said myself, Fritz. You can't found a new era with the help of a bunch of uniformed schoolmasters."

A dark glow seemed to emanate from Stauffenberg and his lone eye shone with steely brilliance. Konstantin watched him with fascination. He could not follow all the colonel said, but he was piercingly aware that the man possessed enormous and infectious strength—that he was a leader whose men would follow him through thick and thin.

"All these pieces of verbiage can be eliminated," Brackwede said briskly. "I'll make some radical cuts. The opening words of a proclamation of this sort are particularly important. For instance, I'd have no hesitation about changing the phrase 'Adolf Hitler is dead' to 'The Fuehrer is dead'—it sounds less provocative and conforms to current usage. The next sentence must provide an immediate reason for the Fuehrer's death and a plausible indication of who was responsible for it."

"What does the lieutenant think?" Stauffenberg inquired.

"Come on, Konstantin," Brackwede prompted, "tell us who would be most likely to bring about the Fuehrer's demise."

"I can't!" Konstantin burst out in bewilderment. "It's inconceivable."

"What do you mean, inconceivable?" Brackwede hardened his heart. "Nothing's inconceivable, especially when a lot of sheep-brained idiots believe it is. Come on, think . . . Who'd be a likely candidate?"

Konstantin had risen to his feet and was staring desperately round the room, scrutinised by three sharp eyes. He bowed his head, and his Knight's Cross dangled helplessly against his tunic. Eventually he said: "Well, unpatriotic elements, I suppose."

"Go on," urged his brother. "What do you mean by the phrase unpatriotic elements?"

Konstantin's boyish face shone with perspiration. "Unscrupulous people," he said laboriously. " A clique of some sort—one of the Party leaders, say."

Brackwede gave a triumphant nod. "There you are—precisely what I was thinking myself. The most plausible opening phrase, under the circumstances, is: An unscrupulous clique of unpatriotic Party leaders . . . Many thanks, Konstantin, you can go now—you've been a great help."

On the morning of 18 July 1944, news reached Colonel von Stauffenberg that Field Marshal Rommel had been severely wounded. Low-flying aircraft had shot up his car while he was returning from the Normandy front.

General Beck let it be known that he expected everyone to proceed with the utmost discretion. Goerdeler managed to shake off his pursuers yet again by spending several nights in the home of a former office employee. The interrogation of Julius Leber began. Maier privately deplored the fact to Brackwede and claimed that the matter was out of his hands. General von Tresckow despatched alarming reports from the Russian front. General Blumentritt announced the capture of Caen by the Allies, who had started to clear the route to Paris by bombing. There were disturbances in Hungary and partisan attacks in Italy. Hamburg was virtually destroyed, Munich fast becoming a sea of rubble, Berlin hammered unceasingly by day and night. Disaster seemed complete.

" And yet there are generals who still compare Hitler with Frederick the Great," Brackwede said. " They genuinely think he may be saved at the eleventh hour by a sort of miracle."

Stauffenberg smiled. " Just the sort of miracle I'm hoping for myself."

Shortly after 3 p.m., while he was in the process of noting down Brackwede's suggested amendments, the telephone rang and a member of Field Marshal Keitel's staff transmitted the following summons from the Fuehrer's Headquarters: Chief of Staff to the Commander-in-Chief Replacement Army: you are requested to attend the Fuehrer and Supreme Commander's daily conference on 20 July 1944.

" I'll be there," Stauffenberg promised.

On 19 July 1944, Captain Fritz-Wilhelm von Brackwede asked his brother to call at the Bendlerstrasse after working hours.

When Konstantin arrived, late in the afternoon, he found Elisabeth Oldenburg-Quentin already gone and his brother seated at his desk sorting through bundles of papers.

"I've been thinking a lot about you and Colonel Stauffenberg," he said.

"Excellent," Brackwede replied. "What conclusion have you come to?"

"Well, your sort of work and my humble military duties belong to two entirely different worlds. You have to allow for things which would never enter my mind in a thousand years. In your job, you have to be ready for any eventuality, however remote, even the Fuehrer's death. That's it, isn't it?"

"What if we're not only allowing for the possibility of the Fuehrer's death but systematically planning it? Didn't that occur to you?"

"It did for a while," Konstantin admitted without hesitation. "I suffered the tortures of the damned until I remembered two good reasons why it was totally out of the question."

"Two reasons?"

"You and the Colonel, of course." Konstantin spoke with utter conviction. "—Two people who merit unquestioning respect and affection, like the Fuehrer.'

"Thanks for the bouquet, my boy—let's hope it doesn't turn out to be a wreath." Brackwede gave an abrupt laugh and bent over his work again with an air of concentration.

"I was at home yesterday," he said casually, without looking up. "We celebrated Maria's birthday."

"I thought her birthday was the day after tomorrow."

"It is, but who knows what'll have happened by then? I was able to get away yesterday, so I drove out to Brandenburg for a few hours. It's wiser to celebrate birthdays when you get the chance. Maria and the children sent their love, anyway, and so did Mother. She's pretty well, all things considered."

"Did she have any news of Father?"

"No." Nothing in Brackwede's expression betrayed the fact that he had learnt of their father's death three hours before. He decided to keep the information to himself for another day. "All the same, I think you ought to visit Mother tomorrow or the day after. It can be arranged—we're on good terms with your commandant, as you know. There's a three-day pass available any time you want it."

"Thanks." Konstantin had almost ceased to wonder at his brother's autocratic ways. "Anything else?"

"Yes, you can do me a favour. You see this briefcase here?" Brackwede pointed to a bulging brown leather bag which stood ready on his desk. "Would you mind taking charge of it and delivering it to Countess Oldenburg with a covering note which I'll give you?"

"Of course," Konstantin said eagerly, "I'd be glad to. I don't know her address, though. Do you think she'll mind if I drop in unannounced at this hour?"

Brackwede pushed the briefcase across to his brother with a faint smile. "Countess Oldenburg is always available when she's needed. She's a reliable person—haven't you found that out yet?"

Konstantin weighed the briefcase in his hand. It felt quite light despite its bulk. "I can go straight away if you like."

Brackwede gave an approving nod. Spreading a blank sheet of white, unheaded, unwatermarked paper on his blotter, he began to write:

The time has come, my dear. I'm sending you this briefcase and my brother. Do your best to take care of them both for as long as you possibly can—twenty-four hours at least.

You won't be needed here for the next few days, and my brother's on leave. Make the best possible use of your time. I know I can rely on you—in every respect. I wish us luck. We need it, and so does Konstantin. All the very best.

Yours

B.

Konstantin watched his brother seal the letter. He did not know what was in it, nor did he care. All that interested him was Elisabeth's address, which proved to be: "c/o Wallner, 3rd floor, 13 Schifferdamm."

"Hardly the most elegant part of Berlin," Brackwede observed, handing Konstantin the letter, his pass and the briefcase. "Gone are the days when every self-respecting countess owned a villa. However, one room's enough, provided it's got a door with a lock on it."

Konstantin smiled. "I'm used to roughing it."

"All the better." The captain ran an appraising eye over his brother. "You're not armed," he said abruptly. "Here, take this." He produced an object from the top drawer of his desk and tossed it across to Konstantin. It proved to be an 8 mm. automatic in a leather holster.

Konstantin caught it, looking faintly amused. "What's this in aid of?"

"Who knows?" Brackwede replied with a smile. "Thirteen Schifferdamm overlooks one of the tributaries of the Spree. There may be rats."

Konstantin von Brackwede reached No. 13 Schifferdamm at about eight o'clock the same evening—20.00 hours, Central European Time, to quote the subsequent official record.

According to the unanimous testimony of several eye-witnesses, the sequence of events was as follows:

Lieutenant von Brackwede, wearing air force uniform, a Knight's Cross and a holstered automatic pistol, approached the house with a bulky briefcase in his hand. He was accosted at the door by Joachim Jodler, caretaker and local Nazi group-leader. The two men conducted a brief conversation in what two witnesses described as a "rather acrimonious" fashion.

Jodler, wearing leather slippers, brown riding-breeches and open shirt traversed by broad, garishly embroidered braces, was smoking a cigar and staring out at the warm summer evening. He had sent his foreign servant-girl to fetch some butter from a fellow-Party member's house, and was impatiently awaiting her return.

The lieutenant gave Jodler a polite but suitably restrained good evening.

"Were you wanting me?" Jodler demanded in a faintly suspicious tone.

"No, I've come to see a lady."

"On the third floor, eh?" Jodler gave a knowing wink. The Fuehrer's war-heroes being his heroes, he didn't begrudge them a chance to recharge their batteries occasionally. On the other hand, it irked him to see his premises used so regularly for the distribution of feminine favours in which he was never permitted to share himself.

"Well, I'm not a spoil-sport. All the same, give the lady my best and ask her to try and be a bit quieter than she has been recently. I know the nights are warm, but I'd advise her to keep her windows shut."

Konstantin left Jodler without bestowing another word on him. He decided to forget the man's remarks, which hardly accorded with his rosy-hued picture of Elisabeth and her private life. Expectantly, he climbed the stairs to the third floor.

No. 13 Schifferdamm was shabby, dilapidated and uncared

for. Generations of inhabitants seemed to have immortalised themselves on the walls of the stair-well, and the banisters looked as if a thousand sweaty fingers had groped their way along them. The house smelt of stagnant water and stale cabbage, and the stairs, which were worn and scuffed, creaked at every step.

Just as Konstantin reached the second landing a crack of light appeared at one of the doors and a woman peered out.

Nothing escaped Frau Breitstrasser. She saw, as she later testified, a fair-haired young man creeping cautiously upstairs. He disappeared from view, but her lubricious and over-developed imagination enabled her to picture the rest. According to her evidence, the young officer reached the third-floor landing at approximately eight-twenty p.m. and stood there in apparent indecision for some minutes.

Konstantin examined the name-plates on the three doors. The first read " Johann Wolfgang Scheumer, Assistant Master," the second " Erika Elster " and the third, simply, " Wallner."

Konstantin rang the bell marked " Wallner " and waited. After a substantial pause the door opened to reveal a dwarfish little woman with straggling white hair.

" What do you want?" The woman's voice had a tinny quality, like the sound of water running into an enamel jug.

" May I speak to Countess Oldenburg, please?"

" No, I'm afraid you can't."

" Why not?"

" She's not here." Frau Wallner made as if to close the door again, but Konstantin put his foot in it.

" May I wait for the Countess? It's important."

Frau Wallner shrugged angrily. " You can wait as long as you like, but not inside my flat. I don't know who you are."

" My name's Brackwede."

" Nonsense! I happen to know Herr Brackwede—he looks nothing like you. Besides, he's a captain."

" That's my brother," Konstantin said patiently.

Frau Wallner hesitated. She studied the young man's face but could detect no resemblance.

" Anyone could say that!" she snapped, and slammed the door.

Evidence as to the above conversation was supplied by Frau Breitstrasser, still at her listening-post on the second floor. She further testified that the officer stood motionless on the landing for several minutes with the briefcase in his hand. After leaning against the wall for a while he started to pace restlessly up and down. Eventually—at about eight forty-five p.m.—he sat down on the top step.

"He looked like a man who was capable of anything," Frau Breitstrasser said later, "—though I naturally couldn't tell what he had in mind."

At about nine p.m. the centre door on the third-floor landing of No. 13 Schifferdamm—the door marked "Erika Elster"—opened and a woman in a dressing-gown emerged. She examined her letter-box and found it empty. As she did so, her gaze fell on Konstantin. She brightened perceptibly.

"Well I never! What are you doing there?" Erika Elster's husky, come-hither voice sounded sleepily seductive. She was an auburn-haired woman with plump, marzipan features and a baroque figure. "Waiting for me, were you?"

Konstantin replied politely in the negative. He rose, introduced himself and explained his predicament. Erika Elster listened sympathetically.

"Why sit around out here? You're welcome to come inside."

"Are you a friend of the Countess's," she demanded with disconcerting directness, as she led the way into her flat, "—a boy-friend, I mean?"

The lieutenant demurred vigorously. He sat down on the sofa, deposited his briefcase on the floor beside him and surveyed the room with some astonishment. Cushions lay beneath him, behind him, beside him, in front of him; they luxuriated over all the chairs, lay heaped on the gargantuan divan in the corner and sprawled across the thick woollen rug. A patchwork of pink, baby-blue and pale-green met his eye at every turn.

He was given a glass of cognac and treated to the strains of a gramophone record entitled "Stars above My Homeland." Erika sank languorously on to the sofa, well within arm's reach.

"Have you known the Countess long?"

Konstantin produced an evasive reply. He sat stiffly at the far end of the sofa with his right foot touching the briefcase and his hand resting casually on the handle.

"I'm extremely grateful to you for being so hospitable," he said formally, "but I really mustn't presume upon your kindness."

He got no opportunity to do so, because at that moment the door-bell rang and Elisabeth Oldenburg-Quentin appeared. She had not found it unduly hard to trace Konstantin, thanks to Frau Wallner's description and Frau Breitstrasser's avid account of how " The Elster woman " had lured him into her flat—not that one could expect anything else of a creature like that.

Staring past Erika Elster into the sitting-room, Elisabeth called: " If you want to speak to me, Konstantin, you'd better come next door."

Erika gave a scornful laugh, but Konstantin thanked her and followed Elisabeth down the narrow passage to her room. It was an oasis of cleanliness and light in a desert of gloom.

Elisabeth opened the letter which Captain von Brackwede had given Konstantin and read it with an expression of grave concentration. Then she said: " If you haven't any plans for the evening, why don't you stay and keep me company?— For as long as you like," she added bravely.

Colonel von Stauffenberg left his office in the Bendler block earlier than usual on the evening of 19 July 1944. It was only eight o'clock when he told his driver to drive him to his pied-à-terre beside the Grosser Wannsee. His brother Berthold travelled with him.

Berthold was probably the only person in whom Stauffenberg confided unreservedly. He loved his wife Nina with all his heart, but he had kept a great deal from her in order to spare her anxiety. Among his friends, Berthold had a reputation for nobility, warmth, intelligence and discernment. To Claus von Stauffenberg he seemed the perfect complement to himself—calm, meditative and profound—and he chose to spend what proved to be the last leisure hours of his life in Berthold's company.

Nineteenth July seemed to take its course like any other day. Berthold, the admiralty lawyer, worked in his office a few hundred yards from the Bendlerstrasse. At midday, Claus conducted one of his routine conferences as chief of staff to General Fromm. Some thirty officers were present, and none of them noticed anything out of the ordinary.

Berthold arrived at the Bendlerstrasse just before eight p.m., having walked there from his own office.

Claus von Stauffenberg gave his brother a nod of welcome and initialled a few more lists, letters and reports. Then he put his good arm round Berthold's shoulders and led him out into the courtyard, where his car was waiting.

At Dahlem, on the way to the Wannsee, they passed a church. Evensong was in progress, and the sound of organ music drifted out into the street through the open doors.

Claus told his driver to stop and climbed out without a word. For a moment he seemed to hesitate before entering the church. Then, squaring his shoulders, he strode inside.

He stood at the back of the nave for some minutes, still and motionless, with his head bowed in silent prayer.

He did not speak again until they reached their destination.

PART TWO

THE 20TH OF JULY

"Abnormal situations necessitate abnormal measures."
Ludwig Beck, General

ONE

Twentieth July 1944—a Thursday—slunk wearily into Central Europe like a hunted beast. The night sky spread its dull purple mantle over the ravaged countryside, heralding the hottest day of the year.

Death did not sleep. It mowed down soldiers at the front, fell from the sky like dew, stalked through hospital wards, crouched in fox-holes, droned overhead in bombers and burst uninvited into private homes—yet even at this stage there were some who could still sleep the sleep of tired children after a long day's play.

Now five years old, the war raged on like a maddened, bleeding bull. Yet, behind the scenes, preparations had aready been made to give it the *coup de grâce,* and it was as if world history were shouting its encouragement.

At his headquarters in the dark forests of East Prussia, Adolf Hitler was sitting in his personal bunker, protected by a triple cordon of barbed wire and security guards. He was addressing a select circle of political disciples.

The windows stood open, lapping the Fuehrer's weary audience in a stream of warm, humid air. The great man never retired to bed before two a.m., and until then he continued to pile one idea on another in a weird cloud-castle of speculation. No subject was beyond his scope, but his favourite hobby was self-comment. He *was* Germany, and Germany must prove itself worthy of him. The hour of trial was at hand, as it had been for months now.

"I've said the same thing myself," General Jodl, Chief of Operations, declared with manifest pride. "As I told an audience of regional and district Party leaders months ago, we shall win because we must win!"

"If we did not," supplemented Field Marshal Keitel, "world history would have lost its meaning."

"Victory or annihilation," murmured Hitler, fondling his Alsatian bitch with a mechanical tenderness which stirred the hearts of all present. "But we shall only merit annihilation if we have not deserved victory."

Ergo, we shall win! No one in the room appeared to doubt this. Reichsleiter Bormann had no need to bombard Hitler's audience with approval-seeking glances, but he did so just the same. He was gratified to see Keitel give an emphatic nod—an implicit vow of allegiance.

Hitler had not anticipated any other reaction.

Back in Berlin, the ruins seemed to glow with phosphorescent light. The leaden sky remained clear of bombers for the first time in weeks.

In a villa beside the Grosser Wannsee the Stauffenberg brothers sat facing one another, drinking a final glass of wine and reminiscing about their childhood days. The briefcase in the corner of the room contained a bomb.

"Is it true you passed up the chance of an operation?" Berthold asked. "Fritz Brackwede tells me that the doctors wanted to restore some movement to your right arm."

Claus von Stauffenberg nodded. "Yes, but it would have taken months, and that would have meant I shouldn't be here now—all on account of one miserable arm."

Captain Count Fritz-Wilhelm von Brackwede had lit a fire in his office in the Bendlerstrasse and was seated in front of it with his uniform jacket open. He carefully tore up a bundle of papers and tossed the pieces into the flames. Reflected light played spasmodically over his face, turning it into a mask of petrified lava. His eyes narrowed as he watched the dun-coloured smoke drifting up the chimney. A cousin of his had once predicted that he would either end up at the head of a Ministry or on the gallows. From his expression, he might have been remembering this back-handed compliment now.

Only a few kilometres away to the north, past the Tiergarten and Moabit, No. 13 Schifferdamm stood beside the Spree like a dark brown box, its blacked-out windows reminiscent of blind embrasures. No light was allowed to penetrate the Berlin night.

Sleep had not yet taken possession of the house, nor had death, but both waited in the wings.

Joachim A. Jodler, caretaker and Local Group-Leader, bore a certain well-cultivated resemblance to his beloved Fuehrer.

This resemblance extended from his toothbrush moustache to his predilection for inspiring discourse, even in the small hours.

"It's a privilege to live here in Germany, isn't it, my girl?"

The object of his attentions was Maria, last name unpronounceable, a Polish girl who was registered as an "alien worker" and had been allocated to him and his wife Hermine. Joachim and Hermine served the Reich, and Maria was privileged to serve them.

"Are you happy here with us?" he demanded. "Well, are you?"

"Yes, sir," Maria assured him hastily.

Hermine was not at home. She worked as an instructor for the National Socialist Women's League, a job which had lately claimed so much of her time that she was forced to spend whole days and nights away from Schifferdamm. Joachim not only accepted that such sacrifices had to be made but accepted them willingly—especially since Maria was there to mitigate the rigours of his arduous existence.

She crouched warily on a stool near the door with her legs drawn up and her skinny arms clasping her childish body. Large, misty-looking eyes dominated the sickly pallor of her face, and her thin lips were slightly parted as though to aid her breathing. A silken cascade of blue-black hair flowed down her back. Maria was sixteen years old.

"Glad you like it here," Joachim A. Jodler remarked graciously, stretching his legs. "You've every reason to be grateful, considering what might have happened to you. Come over here, girl."

Maria approached him with small, hesitant steps, trying to raise a smile. Jodler had conveyed to her that he set store by a cheerful demeanour. She refilled his glass and did her best to stay out of arm's reach.

"You wouldn't like to do factory work and sleep in a bug-ridden hut, would you? Don't worry, though, I'll make sure it doesn't happen."

Jodler's tone was rough and good-natured. The girl might be an alien worker, but she was Aryan. She ought to relish the privilege of consorting with a member of the Party hierarchy, however humble.

Without more ado, he grabbed at her knee and slid his hand upwards.

There was a moment's paralysed silence. Then Maria gave

an outraged scream and broke away from him, her childish eyes dilated with terror. Flinging open the door, she rushed out into the darkened hall.

Corporal Lehmann had spent the early hours of the new day with some new-found friends, painting slogans in Prenzlauer Allee, e.g., HOW MUCH LONGER?, HITLER NEEDS CANNON-FODDER, and—simple but refined—GERMANS AWAKE!

They were now sitting, slightly out of breath, in a gloomy basement room in Landwehrstrasse, near Alexanderplatz—a train-conductor, two girl students, a civil servant, a retired couple, a playwright and Corporal " Pixie " Lehmann, described in his forged identity papers as a crane-driver from the Kohle district of Westhafen. The records officer for Westhafen happened to be the civil servant sitting opposite him.

" Do we have to do this every night?" inquired Lehmann.

One of the girl students laughed. " Was it as exhausting. as all that?"

" No, just frustrating," Lehmann replied tersely. His new friends obviously had no idea what they had let themselves in for. " Those slogans looked as if they'd been daubed on in a hurry—it offends my aesthetic sense."

" I'm afraid we're not in the fine art business," the playwright said with an indulgent smile.

Lehmann proceeded to expound a comprehensive reorganisation scheme which provided for the manufacture of stencils, the training of slogan-painters, rationalised operating methods and the use of thinner, brighter and more weather-proof paints. He sat back, enjoying the sensation he had caused.

The old-age pensioner, who managed the clandestine depot jointly with his wife, said: " How do you propose to do all that, Comrade? Every kilo of paint has to be brought here by hand."

" In that case I'll lay on a bulk consignment," Lehmann replied easily. " Where there's a will there's a way—that's my personal slogan. I'll see if I can wangle a few drums of paint for you tonight."

A few minutes later he was making a call from a neutral 'phone in premises which his companions opened with the aid of a skeleton key. He was not unduly surprised when Captain von Brackwede answered.

" Warehouse No. 7 here," announced Lehmann. " May I place an urgent order?"

Brackwede took only a few seconds to recognise the identity

of his caller. "Are the perishable goods safely stowed away?" he inquired cheerfully.

"Safe and sound," Lehmann assured him, "—perfectly protected against all atmospheric conditions."

Brackwede hesitated for a moment. "There's no more caulking material here—it's all packed and ready to go. It should reach its destination at about midday tomorrow."

"Fine," said the corporal. "May I call in at the office sometime to check the invoice?"

"Do that," Brackwede replied, "but watch your step."

"I will." Lehmann grinned. Cupping the receiver, he turned to his friends and said: "I'll have barrels of the stuff here by tomorrow evening, or I'm not a crane-driver from Westhafen."

Lieutenant Konstantin von Brackwede had been sitting stiffly on a chair in the middle of the narrow room for hours now, immediately beneath the dimly-glowing centre light. In front of him stood a low table, roughly the size of an open *Voelkischer Beobachter,* and on it was an assortment of cups and glasses. Their contents had scarcely been touched. Elisabeth Oldenburg-Quentin sat opposite him, striving to match his rigidly formal manner, almost as if they were in her office in the Bendlerstrasse and the door might open at any moment.

"It must be very late," Konstantin said politely.

Elisabeth smiled. "Are you bored?"

"No, no, of course not!" Konstantin protested. "How could you possibly think that? I can't remember when I enjoyed myself so much."

Their main topic of conversation had been literature, but they had not got far beyond Shakespeare. Konstantin had been persuaded to quote whole passages from *Romeo and Juliet,* and he now showed signs of applying himself to Schiller with similar enthusiasm.

"Curious what a bent for poetry the military seem to have," said Elisabeth. "Colonel Stauffenberg can recite pages of obscure poetry by heart, and your brother knows his *Faust* almost better than his paper-work—and that's saying something!"

"You must be wanting to go to bed now. I should have left hours ago."

"Don't let me keep you if you've got something definite in mind." Elisabeth's tone was deliberately suggestive. "I shouldn't like you to miss anything for my sake."

Konstantin firmly dismissed the idea. "I can't think of anywhere I'd rather be . . ." He trailed off into embarrassed silence, then asked hurriedly: "What are we supposed to do with the briefcase my brother gave me?"

"Do you know what's inside it?" Elisabeth demanded, watching him keenly. "Wouldn't it intrigue you to know what you've been carrying around with you?"

"Why should it?" the lieutenant replied without hesitation. "My brother asked me to keep it for him—that's good enough for me."

"But it's not locked. Don't you feel like taking a peep inside?"

"Not in the least."

"How right your brother was!" Elisabeth said. She smiled, but her smile was not meant for him. "He always knows who can be trusted implicitly and who can't. It's a wonderful instinct."

She paused as though listening for something. There was a minute's oppressive silence. Then, like a star-shell bursting in the night, the silence was broken by a woman's shrill scream. A door slammed and a moment later there was the sound of hurried footsteps on the stairs. Konstantin looked up sharply.

"What was that?"

"Don't worry," Elisabeth told him. "In times like these, sleeping isn't the only thing people do at night. Did you realise that some people in this country spend their whole lives in fear and trembling? No, I can see your imagination doesn't stretch that far—not yet, anyway. Never mind, the day will come. Would you like to spend the night here, Konstantin?"

Adolf Hitler did not show signs of retiring to bed until almost a quarter of an hour later than usual, a fact which occasioned Bormann a certain amount of uneasiness. The Fuehrer—referred to by him as "The Chief"—needed every ounce of sleep he could get. Lack of it made him bad-tempered, and this had a detrimental effect on the carefully regulated routine of life at Supreme Headquarters.

Unfortunately for Bormann, Field Marshal Wilhelm Keitel was enjoying one of his finest hours and had no intention of bringing it to a premature end. With Hitler as a willing audience, he was wallowing in rose-tinted reminiscences.

"When I think, my Fuehrer, of the way you have won through again and again in the face of every kind of opposition and loathsome intrigue, I can only regard it as a dispensation of Providence!"

Wilhelm Keitel meant what he said. He was genuinely devoted to Hitler and firmly convinced that he was discharging his duty in an exemplary manner. Stimulated by the Fuehrer's evident approval, his voice rose to rhetoric pitch as he intoned his favourite catch-words. "Remember the Roehm putsch, the Fritsch crisis, the Blomberg affair? You survived them all!"

"That which fails to destroy us makes us stronger," observed Hitler.

His entourage greeted this axiom as if it were a divine revelation. Two secretaries, SS-Gruppenfuehrer Fegelein, a stenographer, a field marshal, an aide-de-camp, a general, a butler and Martin Bormann—all wrenched their weary eyelids apart in an attempt to simulate intense interest. In the corridor outside, the SS N.C.O. whose nightly task it was to walk Hitler's Alsatian among the trees and then deposit her in her kennel glanced at his watch and waited.

Meanwhile, the Fuehrer had taken up Keitel's thread. Roehm, one-time Chief of Staff of the S.A., had had to be eliminated in the national interest. General von Fritsch had been suspected of homosexuality—though this assumption had proved to be unfounded. Field Marshal von Blomberg had married a woman of dubious reputation. Such were the incidents which had paved the way for his, the Fuehrer's, assumption of the supreme command of the Wehrmacht. His authority was absolute and undivided. He had created the Supreme Command merely as an aid to his own conduct of military operations, but he had placed it in the best possible hands—those of Field Marshal Keitel.

"No one who aspires to greatness can afford to be pettyminded," Hitler concluded. "Every honest man has enemies. If he wishes to prevail he must eliminate them."

Maria, the Polish servant-girl, plunged into the dark, stuffy hall-way and collided with a wall. She lay where she had fallen, panting hard, with her open mouth pressed against the dirty linoleum. Then, scrabbling at the battered plaster, she tried to sit up.

"Now, now, my child! What's all this?"

A dim figure helped her to her feet and folded her spontaneously in its arms. Maria saw that it was one of the third-floor tenants, the schoolmaster Johann Wolfgang Scheumer, a venerable gentleman with the face of an heroic actor and an aureole of silver hair. Nocturnal roaming through No. 13 Schifferdamm had recently become a habit with Johann Wolfgang. His wife was confined to bed with a severe illness and the school where he taught had been destroyed by bombs a few days before, so he had taken to spending the small hours in silent meditation on exalted subjects.

Maria clung to him, trembling violently. His hands glided over her shoulders and stroked her back, and his words were soft as a caress.

"Never lose heart, my dear child—never lose faith in human nature under any circumstances. You trust me, don't you?"

Maria, who was prepared to regard anyone except Jodler as a paragon of virtue and nobility, nodded eagerly.

"Come upstairs with me, then. —My dear wife won't have any objection," he added, remembering that he had given her a powerful sedative which ought to keep her hors de combat until noon.

They climbed the stairs, passing the door behind which lurked the ever-observant Frau Breitstrasser.

"Where should we be without an occasional helping hand?" the schoolmaster murmured as he led Maria across the third-floor landing. "Where indeed!"

"Curious to take a look at our brain-repair shop, or were you wanting a bed for the night?" Maier laughed hugely at his own joke.

"I can't bear to let you out of my sight, that's all," Brackwede retorted sarcastically, glancing round the bare basement walls of the Gestapo palace in Prinz Albrechtstrasse.

"Gestapo" Maier was noted for being a night-worker. The humorous placard on his office wall—"The early bird catches the worm"—was not there by accident. His victims tended to become more communicative when a new day was dawning.

"Got something specific in mind, Brackwede, or did you come to help me kill time?"

The two men lit cigarettes, watching each other intently.

"Rumour has it that you've just scored a big success," Brackwede said. "Colonel Bruchsal has been singing like a male-voice choir, so I'm told."

"It's sickening," Maier replied. "I'm a patient man, but this chap Bruchsal would try the patience of an angel. He still insists on implicating Field Marshal Rommel."

" You find the idea absurd?"

" No—that's the whole trouble." Maier looked morose. " But if I went to the Fuehrer with the story he'd have my guts for garters."

" That's simple, then—don't pass it on." Brackwede made the suggestion in a low, confidential voice. There was no need for the sentry guarding the door to overhear.

" It's easy for you," Maier said resentfully. " It doesn't cost you anything to give me advice, but I'm in a cold draught. Himmler'll give me the sack if I don't produce some tangible results soon. He wants something to get his teeth into—and I'd rather it wasn't me."

" Take it easy," advised Brackwede. " It would be a dangerous mistake to rush things at this juncture, I can assure you."

The Sturmbannfuehrer drew his visitor into the far corner of the room. " The whole operation's under way already. The warrant for Goerdeler's arrest isn't just routine any more—Kaltenbrunner is putting out a general call to the C.I.D., obviously at Himmler's instigation. Beck has been at the top of my list for months now, and I'm itching to get my hands on him—purely in self-defence, you understand. We'll drum up some kind of evidence somehow."

Heaps of it, reflected Brackwede. All Maier had to do was clear out the General's desk and he'd find enough material for a dozen dossiers. " What about Julius Leber?"

Maier looked a trifle embarrassed. " He's been under interrogation since yesterday—entirely against my wishes, I may say, but I couldn't do a thing to stop it. He's a damned tough customer, if that's any comfort to you. It'll take weeks to wear him down."

" If you're wise you'll try to put a brake on the proceedings," Brackwede urged, " —and quickly at that! You won't have to mark time for more than twenty-four hours—possibly twelve."

Maier screwed up his eyes and studied Brackwede with interest. " Is that a threat or a promise?"

" Let's call it an offer. Think it over and work out what you're willing to pay. I'm not offering you a pig in a poke— I hope you realise that. The only question is, how much is a hide like yours or mine really worth?"

" Strange how quickly these summer nights seem to pass," Elisabeth said. She raised her arms and stretched delicately.

Konstantin watched her entranced. In the past few hours they had talked together as if they had known each other since childhood. Having grown up on country estates in Brandenburg and Pomerania, they had something in common.

"We often slept out of doors on nights like this—Fritz and I," Konstantin told her. "We used to take a tent into the garden or the woods and sleep rough."

"It must have been nice to have a brother like him. I was on my own nearly all the time—I haven't got any brothers or sisters."

Konstantin couldn't quite screw up enough courage to say "You've got me now," but his eyes shone with tenderness and Elisabeth seemed to take pleasure in his undisguised admiration.

"I am feeling a bit tired now," she said, looking him straight in the eye, "—not tired enough to sleep, though. I'd just like to lie down."

For the umpteenth time that night, Konstantin assured her that he didn't want to be a nuisance. "I could go for a stroll until the first train leaves for Bernau. For that matter, I'm sure I could find somewhere to put my head down in the Bendlerstrasse."

"I wouldn't do that," Elisabeth said quickly. "Doesn't the idea of staying here appeal to you, then?" she asked in a low voice.

"I'm only thinking of you—the neighbours . . ."

"Nonsense!" Elisabeth said firmly. "Reputations are a luxury in war-time. People are sleeping ten to a room these days—we ought to be glad to have one between the two of us. Take off your shoes and your jacket and we'll share my bed."

Konstantin's offer to sleep on the floor was dismissed as a gratuitous form of martyrdom.

"What about the briefcase?"

"We can put it between us, if you like." Elisabeth laughed. "Hurry up—it'll be daylight soon."

"It may not be much, this nocturnal painting of ours," the playwright said, "but one has to do something these days."

"I'm most impressed," Lehmann assured him. "You could get picked up any night of the week. How long have you been at it?"

"Three years," replied the playwright. "—On and off," he added, looking almost shamefaced.

They were still sitting in the basement of the house in Landwehrstrasse. The local members of the group had gone home, leaving Lehmann alone with the playwright and the two girl students, whose lodgings were a fair distance away. When daybreak came they would be able to leave the premises unobserved and mingle with the crowds on their way to work.

The two girls, one of whom was studying philosophy and the other medicine, maintained a weary silence. They normally dossed down on a pile of sacks in the corner of the cellar after a night's work, but the men's voices were not conductive to sleep. Lehmann was wide awake.

"Do you do all this on spec, so to speak?"

The playwright nodded. "Yes, I suppose we do."

Lehmann was lying on his back, blinking in the dim candlelight and plunging the far wall into darkness every so often as he raised his arm. The girls lay huddled in a corner like silent shadows, while the playwright squatted against the cracked and peeling wall near the door.

"Don't you ever get the feeling you're completely on your own?" Lehmann raised himself on one elbow. "Don't you ever feel you've been left in the lurch? Don't you ever ask yourself what good it is painting slogans on walls when people are dying like flies all over the place?"

"Why don't you go to sleep?" complained one of the girls. "It's not worth thinking too much about what's going on these days. If you've got any intelligence or convictions at all, you automatically end up doing something like this."

Her companion, a blonde blue-eyed girl with an intense-looking face, said: "You've heard of the Scholls, haven't you?"

"Sophie Scholl," the playwright recounted in an unemotional tone, "together with her brother and a friend of theirs, threw some leaflets into the assembly hall at Munich University. The Scholls abhorred Hitler and his régime. The circle which grew up round them and their professor, a man named Huber, was known as 'The White Rose.' They were all executed. Then there was the so-called 'Red Orchestra'—mostly officers from the Air Ministry, I believe. They were executed too—in the strictest secrecy. Hitler's victims include priests and school-teachers, civil servants and writers, trade union leaders and former members of parliament from almost every party. Countless other people have died at the rate of several thousand a year, but many have survived—like us."

"I know a general called von Tresckow," Lehmann said, "—a man who comes from one of the oldest families in Prussia. He's made several attempts to blow Hitler up. I also know Lieutenant-Colonel Heinz, who volunteered to lead a raiding-party into the Chancellery as long ago as nineteen-thirty-eight. Lieutenant Colonel von Boeselager also volunteered to bump Hitler off. General Stieff, Colonel von Gersdorff and Captain von dem Busche were all prepared to blow themselves to kingdom come and take Hitler with them."

"Then why in God's name is the man still alive?" the playwright asked quietly.

"Perhaps he never met his match before. He has now."

"Open up!" shouted SS-Scharfuehrer Josef Jodler, banging on the door.

It opened immediately, to reveal the figure of Johann Wolfgang Scheumer, swathed in a blue-and-white striped dressing-gown. The schoolmaster's silvery and senatorial locks looked slightly disarranged. "Heil Hitler, Herr Scharfuehrer," he said hastily. "How are you keeping?"

"Never mind the state of my health—you've got that little tart Maria in there!" Josef Jodler was an impressive sight, even in his billowing night-shirt. He looked vaguely like the naked bronze figure on a war memorial, shortly before the unveiling ceremony. "Are you going to hand her over, or do I have to lean on you a little?"

Josef was the son of Joachim, caretaker of No. 13 Schifferdamm and local Party functionary. He belonged to one of the Special Action Groups—better known as Extermination Squads—which had performed such sterling service behind the German lines in Russia. At the moment he was enjoying some well-earned leave in the other flat on the ground floor. He spent it in solitude for the most part, since his wife also served the State in her own way. She specialised in gold—notably gold teeth—and her department was a direct supplier of the State banks.

Shouldering the schoolmaster aside, Josef marched down the passage and through the open door into the living-room. Maria was lying on the sofa with a blanket pulled up to her chin. Her eyes shone with apprehension.

"Well take a look at that!" exclaimed the Scharfuehrer. "What a dirty old man you are, Scheumer!"

The schoolmaster tried to register righteous indignation. "I really must ask you, Herr Jodler . . ."

He got no further. Jodler junior, who cherished a strong belief in his own sense of humour, laughed uproariously and told Scheumer to shut his trap. Then he turned to Maria and said: " Give your arse an airing and come with me—just the way you are."

Maria pushed back the blanket and got up. She was naked. Collecting her sack-like dress, which lay neatly folded on a chair, she walked obediently to the door with downcast eyes. SS-Scharfuehrer Jodler studied her with mounting interest.

" My intentions were of the very best, I assure you . . ." Scheumer stammered apprehensively, aware that Jodler was not a man to be trifled with. " I feel obliged to point out . . ." Jodler junior left him there standing there, feebly flapping his hands. He smote Maria on the buttocks and shouted: " Get going, you little bitch! Back to the kennel where you belong!"

Colonel von Stauffenberg rose shortly after five a.m. He had slept for only a few hours, as he had done almost invariably during the past few weeks, but he was awake on the instant. His complexion looked fresh, his single eye clear.

He walked to the window and drew the curtains. The pale-blue waters of the Grosser Wannsee sparkled in the early morning sunlight. Stauffenberg surrendered himself to the gentle radiance of the spectacle for several minutes. Then he made for the bathroom, where he found Berthold. They nodded silently at each other, as though words were superfluous.

Stauffenberg's strong fingers grasped the collar of his pyjama-jacket and pulled it over his head. Berthold made no move to help him—he knew that his brother hated being treated like a cripple.

" The thermometer's shooting up already," Berthold remarked at length. " It looks as if we may be in for the hottest day for years."

Stauffenberg soaped his face and chest thoughtfully, his expression revealing none of the pain which this caused him. He was thirty-six years old—two-and-a-half years older than his brother—but the inexorable march of time had almost completely erased the age-difference between them.

" Everything will go according to plan," he said, running a razor over his face. " This time I'm certain of it."

"Yes," Berthold replied, "I can feel you are."

Claus von Stauffenberg's schedule for the day had been worked out with a meticulousness which was only to be expected in a plan that had been devised by members of the General Staff. The first phase was as follows: the colonel would leave his Wannsee flat at approximately 6 a.m., accompanied by his brother and carrying a briefcase. His driver was already waiting outside the house with an official car. On the drive to the airfield they would pick up Stauffenberg's aide, Lieutenant Werner von Haeften, also carrying a briefcase. This would contain a second explosive charge for use in an emergency. At Rangsdorf a Heinkel aircraft would be waiting for them. Take-off was scheduled for 7 a.m.

Berthold said: "It's time to go."

Before Claus von Stauffenberg left his room he glanced briefly at a photograph which stood on the small table beside his bed. It showed his wife Nina with their children. Stauffenberg smiled confidently at them.

Outside, the army driver saluted smartly when he saw Stauffenberg emerge. The colonel, he later recalled, looked as amiable and relaxed as he always did.

Large areas of Berlin were still lapped in the leaden embrace of sleep. The pale light of early morning played tremulously over the shattered ruins of the tormented, devastated city.

Captain von Brackwede had stretched out on a camp-bed in the Bendlerstrasse and lay there, completely inert. SS-Sturmbannfuehrer Maier had postponed two arrests scheduled for that morning and was asleep in his private lair, "on call." Lieutenant Herbert slumbered beside Molly, dreaming of heroic deeds but unaware of their imminence.

In the basement in Landwehrstrasse, Lehmann had accepted the girl students' invitation to share their pile of sacks and lay sprawled out, snoring. The playwright, who could not sleep, was jotting down notes on small scraps of paper. One of them read:

> It always amazes me
> that our faces still look the same
> as they did three thousand years ago,
> when so much hatred and suffering
> has passed across them.

General Beck was sweating profusely, a frequent phenomenon in recent weeks. His housekeeper had more than once
found his bed " sopping wet." The general's drawn and haggard expression had aroused fears among his friends that he
was gravely ill.

Julius Leber, Minister of the Interior designate, had passed
the night as he had done on numerous other occasions in his
career—handcuffed and lying on the floor of a prison cell.
He wondered why he had not been dragged off for his usual
bout of early morning interrogation, and decided that there
must be some special reason for this unexpected reprieve.
Even torturers adhered to a routine.

Carl Friedrich Goerdeler, Chancellor designate, had taken
refuge with a former government official. The night before,
his host had been a diplomat, and tonight it would be a priest.
He did not know that Colonel von Stauffenberg had already
embarked on his attempt to force a final decision.

Doctor Eugen G. had arrived in Berlin from Stuttgart the
day before and was staying at the home of his friend Helmuth
von Moltke. He had received a postcard inscribed with the
words: " The marriage will soon take place" It was signed by
Peter Yorck, i.e., Peter, Count Yorck von Wartenburg, Councillor and Doctor of Law, another of Stauffenberg's intimates.
Since it had to be assumed that Moltke's house was under
surveillance, Eugen G. had crept in via the garden. Now he
was sleeping soundly.

And so the light of dawn fell on hundreds of people who
were to meet their end as a result of this day. They did not
all die because they took an active part in the attempt to
eliminate Hitler. Many of them did so because of a few chance
remarks, others because they had given refuge to wanted men,
and quite a few because, unbeknown to them, their names appeared on some list or other. One indiscreet doodle was enough
to snuff out a human life, but perhaps the most comprehensive
set of documents covering the coup d'état reposed in a briefcase in a small room on the third floor of No. 13 Schifferdamm.

Elisabeth and Konstantin were still lying side by side, staring
up at the pale ceiling which seemed to enclose them like a
protective dome.

" Aren't you asleep?" Elisabeth asked softly.

" I can't sleep," Konstantin said, " —not here beside you."

They turned and looked at each other. Their faces had
the faint luminosity of silver in dim candlelight, and their deep
breathing caressed each other's cheeks like timid fingers.

"Elisabeth," he said in an almost inaudible voice.

"Yes?"

Somewhere downstairs a door slammed violently. There was the sound of a lavatory being flushed, and cautious footsteps shuffled down the passage. Silence fell once more, to be broken by a woman's piercing scream. It seemed to come from far away, and it was suddenly cut short as if someone had stifled it with a pillow.

Elisabeth and Konstantin heard nothing of this as they groped blindly for each other.

"I love you," Konstantin said.

"Yes." Elisabeth closed her eyes as though to shut out the daylight which was creeping through the curtains, and resigned herself to what had to be. "Yes . . ."

"I really envy you, you know," said Corporal Lehmann.

The playwright seemed amused. "Why—because of the nice young things who keep me company at nights?" He indicated the two girls, who were still asleep in the far corner of the basement.

"Of course!" Lehmann replied with a chuckle. "I haven't felt so young in heart for a long time."

They spoke in low voices. The candle had been extinguished for some time now, and enough light came in through the blacked-out window for the playwright to write his notes in its vicinity.

"You can have that any night," he said.

Lehmann smiled. "No, you know why I really envy you? Because you've a good conscience. You can tell yourself you've done something positive."

The playwright looked embarrassed. "Don't credit us with something we don't deserve," he said hurriedly. "We do this because we can't help ourselves, that's all."

"Are there more of your sort?"

"Hundreds of them. There are two groups based in this street alone. Then there's a disabled 1914-18 veteran living near Alexanderplatz who writes postcards denouncing Hitler and the war—in block capitals. He posts one every day. An electrician in Metzerstrasse keeps us supplied with torches, bulbs and batteries. The other night, three separate slogans were chalked up in Luxemburgerplatz by three separate groups, not including ours."

Lehmann wagged his head. "We don't know enough about each other, and that's a fact."

"But you guessed that people like us existed, didn't you?"

"No," Lehmann admitted sadly. He suddenly looked older than his years. "I suppose we don't get together enough."

"But we not only think the same way—sometimes we act the same way as well, even though it's not a concerted effort. That's a promising sign, isn't it?"

The daylight had now crept into the far corner of the cellar. The girls stood up, rubbing their eyes sleepily. They straightened their clothes, patted their hair into place, smiled at the two men and came over. Their youthful skin looked fresh and unlined in the morning light.

"When are we going to see you again?" one of them asked Lehmann.

"It's difficult to say," Lehmann replied. "Maybe tonight—maybe not at all."

"You're welcome any time," the blonde girl said cordially. "We can use people like you."

"This may be our last meeting—I hope it is, in a way, though you can't be expected to understand why. Who knows what'll have happened by tomorrow? I won't forget you, anyway."

"The same goes for us."

Lehmann hugged them spontaneously in turn, experiencing an involuntary tingle of pleasure as their lips brushed his homely cheek. He slapped the playwright on the back and said: "It's good to know there are people like you around. If Stauffenberg realised that, he'd find things a lot easier."

The bulging briefcase which Captain von Brackwede had entrusted to his brother stood beside the bed, near Konstantin's boots. A woman's flimsy slip lay draped across it.

The owner of the flat, Frau Wallner, was a war-widow whose husband—a major—had fallen " for Fuehrer and Greater Germany." Her status had not exempted her from a compulsory billeting-order, but she welcomed Elisabeth Oldenburg-Quentin as someone who would not disturb her "lodger."

At this moment, Frau Wallner was addressing her "lodger" in a fierce whisper. He had, it seemed, made too much noise going down the passage. Furthermore, he had forgotten to close the bathroom door before pulling the chain. "People will start suspecting things if you're not careful, and then we'll be in real trouble!"

The timid little man with the wrinkled, emaciated face

begged her forgiveness. He looked abject. " I didn't mean to, my dear lady. I do my utmost to observe the rules, please believe me . . ."

Frau Wallner interrupted him angrily. " I don't want your apologies! I'm the one who should apologise to you for having to accommodate you in such a wretched fashion."

The " lodger " gave a grateful bow. He was a Jewish doctor named Grunefeld, and he had been living in Frau Wallner's back room for two years. He had saved the late Major Wallner's life twice, once on the Western Front during the First World War and a second time after a road accident in Berlin. He had been unable to save him from a hero's death in 1941.

" I'm afraid I give you a lot of trouble," he said.

" The war will be over one day," Frau Wallner replied grimly. " When that day comes, at least I'll be able to say I put one over on *him*!"

In the flat next door, Erika Elster, described by her identity card as an actress, slumbered on in unaccustomed solitude. Erika enjoyed the patronage of certain influential figures, one of her specially favoured guests being the Police President of Berlin. It was he who had secured the flat for her and ensured that she could live there alone, uninconvenienced by billeting orders.

The remaining flat on the third floor was occupied by Johann Wolfgang Scheumer and family. Apart from an invalid wife, Scheumer's family included two patriotic daughters, one a nurse and the other a member of the women's auxiliary corps. Both were away from home at the moment. Time had been hanging rather heavily on Scheumer's hands since his school was bombed, but he did his best to put it to good use. He had dedicated the past few days to a re-examination of the German philosophers, notably Hegel and Hitler, in an endeavour to prove that the latter complemented the former. At the moment, however, he was prudently devoting himself to the rather less exalted task of drafting a form of written deposition. This was to the effect that he had caught and detained an alien worker employed in the house (surname unknown, commonly addressed as " Maria ") whom he had suspected of trying to escape. He had duly handed her over to the custody of SS-Scharfuehrer Jodler, who had duly taken charge of her. The statement concluded by giving details of place, time and date.

On the second floor, Frau Breitstrasser had finally succumbed to sleep, her mind seething with confused impressions. Her lips moved soundlessly as the morning sunlight illuminated her wizened lemon of a face.

Down on the ground floor, in the right-hand flat, SS. Scharfuehrer Jodler was lying on his back, stark naked. His mouth hung open and he was breathing with the stertorous abandon of a man recovering from strenuous physical exercise. Beside him lay Maria, also naked. She had rolled herself into a ball, like a frightened dog.

The left-hand flat on the ground floor was deserted. Local Group-Leader Jodler, its usual occupant, was down in the cellar. He was dead.

Colonel von Stauffenberg's 'plane taxied punctually on to the runway at Rangsdorf, its wings vibrated as the pilot, a reliable and experienced man, warmed up the engine and checked his instruments.

The machine—a Heinkel—had been placed at Stauffenberg's disposal by General of Artillery Eduard Wagner, First Quartermaster-General of the Army. It was a slow, safe and carefully maintained means of transportation, but, like many transport 'planes, it was not equipped with radio.

Just before 7 a.m. Colonel von Stauffenberg's car drew up at the edge of the airfield and Stauffenberg dismounted with his brother and Lieutenant von Haeften. They were met by Major-General Helmuth Stieff, another of the initiates, who had also been summoned to the Fuehrer's Headquarters on official business. The officers exchanged salutes in a friendly way which transcended any differences in rank, and Stauffenberg patted one of the briefcases carried by his aide as though to say: " This time we'll make it!"

The four men's faces shone with perspiration as the heat of the early morning sun beat down on them, wrapping them in a cocoon of warm, humid air, but Stauffenberg's voice sounded brisk and cheerful.

" How are you feeling, General?"

" Pretty well," Stieff replied, smiling. "Who wouldn't feel optimistic, looking at you!" Almost in the same breath, he added: " But apart from your personal part in this, are you sure everything will go according to plan this time?" There was no doubt or anxiety in his tone, merely the staff officer's insistence on precise planning.

"There's no such thing as a hundred-per-cent certainty," Stauffenberg conceded with a touch of reluctance. "However, all our arrangements have been double-checked with the utmost care."

Lieutenant von Haeften extended the two briefcases. "We've taken out double insurance this time, sir. If one charge doesn't work, we'll have a second shot."

"Have you got enough cotton wool for your eye?" Berthold asked his brother anxiously.

Stauffenberg nodded.

Major-General Stieff looked pensive. He had already seen too many well-laid plans go awry to be able to forget the fact. "This time, the whole thing may hinge upon how well our communications network functions—it's a damned complicated business."

"Then it ought to be simplified, sir," Lieutenant von Haeften said firmly. "However, we've got to produce a *fait accompli* first."

Von Haeften and other young officers of his circle were all in favour of the "radical" solution. General Beck and the army leaders were thinkers and Olbricht, Stauffenberg and Brackwede were planners who had been driven to act, but the younger conspirators were more daredevil in their approach. To them, there was only one way of dealing with a Gordian knot, and that was to cut it.

"The time for theorising is past," Stauffenberg said. "Another few hours and we'll know where we stand."

He bowed his head as though obeying some self-imposed command. Then he straightened up, gave his brother a single nod and climbed into the waiting 'plane.

The pilot revved his engine. The wind-sock dangled limply against a cloudless sky. Permission to take off was given at 0700, almost to the second. The machine lumbered along the runway, became air-borne and began to climb.

Berthold von Stauffenberg stared after it for a long time, until it was only a speck suspended above the shimmering horizon. His face remained impassive, but his eyes were moist.

The cellar of No. 13 Schifferdamm was subdivided into storage compartments for the benefit of tenants. Here, enclosed by roughly carpentered partitions, their meagre stocks of putrefying potatoes and cabbages scented the warm summer air. Old jars of preserved fruit stood on the shelves, and suitcases and trunks crammed with treasured possessions lined the walls from floor to ceiling. The central passage had been converted into a makeshift air-raid shelter.

Here lay the body of Joachim A. Jodler, erstwhile caretaker and Local Group-Leader. He was sprawled across two benches with a rust-red patch the size of a man's palm staining his open shirt. He had been shot through the chest, and his expression was positively peaceful.

Frau Wallner, who had decided to give herself and her "lodger" a treat after their disturbed night by fetching a tin of corned beef from the cellar, was the first person to see Jodler's corpse.

Her immediate reaction was to recoil sharply and cast a fearful glance round the cellar to satisfy herself that she was alone. Then she examined the body more closely. "Just the way I imagined him in my dreams," she muttered.

Deciding that temporary blindness was the best policy, she turned and hurried up the steps to the ground floor.

In the hall she met Scheumer, who greeted her with a sweeping gesture which came half-way between a chivalrous flourish of the hat and a Nazi salute. Scheumer was well-versed in the art of compromise.

"Going out already?" he inquired with neighbourly courtesy. "A little morning stroll, eh? I must say, I feel an urge to take the air myself."

"If you happen to go to the cellar first," Frau Wallner said brightly, "you might take a look at my padlock. I'm not sure I remembered to lock it properly, and I can't be bothered to go down there again."

Scheumer's eyes shone with love of humanity as he volunteered to visit the cellar straight away. He turned and trotted downstairs on winged feet.

Two minutes later he reappeared, looking pale. His reaction on seeing Jodler had been to exclaim "Oh God!"—a spontaneous appeal to the deity in whom, as an enlightened philosopher, he did not believe.

After prolonged and intense reflection, he decided that he had not seen anything either.

"Heil Hitler, People's Comrade Schulz!" Captain von Brackwede called sardonically. "Cleared away all the rubbish we produced yesterday?"

The cleaning-woman's eyes twinkled. "Good morning, sir. You look cheerful today."

Brackwede's eyes were keen and alert despite his lack of sleep. "Ma" Schulz was one of his protégés. She had been passed on to him by a friend when the Gestapo started to take an interest in her activities, and was now doing her war-work in the Bendlerstrasse.

Brackwede invited her to sit down and have a cup of coffee with him. He treated her like a favoured guest—which she was. "Ma" Schulz was a mine of information on the habits of Bendlerstrasse inhabitants, particularly those who were on night-duty there.

"Most of them sleep like tops. They must have good consciences, that's all I can say!"

According to "Ma" Schulz's observations, no one in the building seemed to be a glutton for work except Captain von Brackwede's friends. "As for that Colonel Mertz—anyone'd think he was chained to his desk!"

Brackwede valued these snippets of information because they made it easier for him to gauge the general tone of the Bendlerstrasse atmosphere.

"What about Lieutenant Herbert?" he inquired.

"Is he one of your friends?" demanded "Ma" Schulz. "He acts like it, I'll say that, but I wouldn't trust him as far as I could throw him."

Brackwede looked amused. "Why not?"

"Because he never laughs. He looks as if it hurts him to smile, even. I wouldn't use him as a nutcracker, I tell you straight."

"You ought to join the women's police," Brackwede said. "I'll transfer you as soon as I get a chance."

He strolled down the imitation marble staircase which led from the third floor to the second floor of 11-13 Bendlerstrasse. The daily hum of activity had not reached full volume yet, since most of the officers employed in the building behaved like civil servants: they had their hours of duty and they stuck to them religiously.

General Olbricht was already in his office with Colonel Mertz von Quirnheim at his side, poring over a pile of operational schedules.

Captain von Brackwede joined them in a leisurely fashion. Without any formal greeting he bent his aquiline nose over their papers and asked: "Are you looking for possible sources of confusion?"

"Our schedules have been checked down to the last detail,"

Olbricht assured him. " As soon as we receive confirmation that Stauffenberg has done his job successfully, the balloon will go up."

Mertz nodded. " And this time we'll go all out. Instead of proceeding by stages we'll operate on a broad front and use all the resources at our command—a policy after your own heart, I imagine!" he added with a smile.

" Unfortunately, I've got a head as well as a heart," Brackwede drawled amiably. " It asks awkward questions sometimes—for instance, what happens if everything goes haywire?"

" If it does," Olbricht replied simply, " we're done for."

" Completely?" Brackwede's tone was unrelenting. " I thought staff officers were taught to allow for every contingency, defeat included. I mean, when you embark on a battle, shouldn't you leave the door open for a strategic withdrawal rather than accept total annihilation?"

Mertz von Quirnheim raised his balding, scholarly head. " You're thinking of taking out some form of insurance?"

" Let's say I'm in favour of taking precautionary measures."

" What, for instance?"

" Well, for one thing, there's far too much bumf on the premises. Most of it ought to be burned in case it falls into the wrong hands. Had you thought of that?"

" Of course," Olbricht replied. " We've provided for measures of that sort—should anything go wrong. However, you've got to bear in mind that certain documents possess what might be termed historical value . . ."

" Gentlemen!" Brackwede exclaimed sarcastically. " There'll be plenty of time to worry about posterity after this is all over. For the moment, today's needs are all that matter. My advice to you is to make a clean sweep here. Burn everything that isn't absolutely essential and transfer the rest to a place of safety. I've already done that in my department."

The briefcase still stood beside the bed, and the strong sunlight was now forcing its way through the drawn curtains of Elisabeth's room.

" I love you," Konstantin murmured with his mouth against her neck. " I love you."

" Yes," said Elisabeth, as she had done many times in the past few hours.

The ceiling with its pale grey moulding of ornamental roses

seemed to descend upon them like a coffin-lid. They clung to each other with closed eyes.

To Konstantin, it was as if he were plummeting into an endless abyss, only to be caught and borne up by her soft arms and feverishly quivering body. "Do you love me too?" he asked breathlessly.

"Yes," she repeated in a low, urgent voice. Her fingers dug into his back. "Always remember I love you—never forget that."

She buried her face in his chest to shut out the harsh glare of the morning sun and trembled with fear and joy.

No. 13 Schifferdamm seemed to soar away on the crest of a towering, irresistible billow of foam. The world around them dissolved, leaving them utterly alone. Elisabeth's cry of ecstasy faded and died.

A shaft of sunlight illuminated the briefcase, and the glossy brown leather glowed like a warning beacon.

At 10.15 a.m., after a three-hour flight, the Heinkel landed at Rastenburg in East Prussia. Colonel von Stauffenberg was the first to get out, followed by General Stieff and Lieutenant von Haeften. Their figures etched sharp shadows in the trampled earth.

Von Haeften told the pilot: "Hold yourself in readiness for the return flight from midday onwards. You must be prepared to take off within a few minutes."

The pilot wiped the sweat from his brow and nodded. As a military pilot, he received orders and carried them out like any other soldier. The men in the Bendlerstrasse were banking on this—indeed, the whole of Valkyrie was based upon that assumption. Orders, once given, were implemented. This was Germany.

Colonel von Stauffenberg glanced around him keenly. Everything was going according to plan. They had touched down within a minute or two of their scheduled arrival time. Their 'plane had proved itself airworthy and would be waiting for them precisely when they needed it.

The German equivalent of a jeep, sent to fetch them by the camp commandant of the Fuehrer's Headquarters, lumbered slowly towards them and stopped. Stieff and Stauffenberg got in without speaking and Haeften, after exchanging a few words with the driver, followed suit. He cradled the two briefcases tenderly on his lap.

"Do you want me to step on it, sir?" the driver inquired, eager to please.

Stauffenberg shook his head. "No, keep to the usual speed limit." At that rate, the trip would take twenty-five to thirty minutes—exactly as planned.

They drove through a blue-black forest of giant pines, their branches closely entwined like the fingers of men in prayer. A few minutes later they were surrounded by a sea of pale and effervescent green—birches, mostly, with silvery-white trunks. Warm gusts of humid air buffeted their faces.

Claus von Stauffenberg breathed in the scent of steaming earth, damp moss and oozing resin, remembering the forests of his childhood, his walks with Berthold and the lines of poetry which had illuminated their hours of solitude like shafts of magical light. His companions saw him smile suddenly.

Lieutenant von Haeften gingerly fingered his briefcases while General Stieff stared ahead at the pot-holed road with dark, thoughtful eyes. He felt oppressed by the memory of the interminable series of failures that had gone before—untested explosives, malfunctioning detonators—Hitler's unpredictability. Practical experiments with bombs had yielded the most extraordinary results. A light curtain flapping in the breeze could protect a room as effectively as a concrete wall. Whole housefronts collapsed under the impact of a severe explosion, whereas plaster figures in the immediate vicinity could escape completely unscathed.

Stauffenberg suddenly leant across to Stieff. "Do you know what I find most remarkable?" he said with an engaging smile. "I'm used to planning things down to the last detail—that's what I've done this time—but I've always been aware that nothing is entirely predictable—human nature, nations, the age we live in, the thing we like to call destiny—nothing."

"In fact we're just pawns?"

"No, not pawns—we're *part* of destiny, that's all. As I see it, all we can do to influence the course of events is to come to terms with ourselves. That's the only thing that matters."

They reached the Fuehrer's Headquarters at approximately 10.45 a.m.

Almost at the same time, Corporal Lehmann reappeared in the Bendlerstrasse. To accord with his new identity as a cranedriver from Westhafen—exempted from work by a doctor's certificate—he had donned a set of blue dungarees.

"Want anything repaired?" he inquired brightly.

Captain von Brackwede ushered him into the inner office. "You can take it easy for the time being," he said. "We won't be setting up shop for a few hours yet. Besides, you look as if you could do with a rest."

"You shouldn't go by looks," Lehmann assured him with a grin. "I know I haven't been getting my Bendlerstrasse grub —not to mention my extra rations from Herbert—but I'm feeling fresh as a daisy. I spent last night with two young ladies from the university—quite an experience, I can tell you!"

He glanced meaningfully at the filing cabinet where the cognac was kept. Brackwede produced a bottle and two glasses and demanded further details.

"Just think of it," Lehmann said gravely. "While you sit here planning, a lot of people you've never heard of are risking their necks night after night. I tear around carrying messages and you do paper-work, but they cover walls with slogans and shelter fugitives from the Gestapo."

Brackwede nodded. "I'm aware of that. We're far stronger than we thought we were at one time."

"What we need is a bit more co-ordination," Lehmann insisted. "There ought to be more contact between the top brass and the rank and file. Your union is a closed shop."

"It is in a way," Brackwede admitted. "Take Lieutenant Colonel von Hofacker, for instance. He's not only a relative of Stauffenberg's; he was one of the witnesses at my wedding and he's a personal friend of a dozen other officers in our group. One of our staunchest members is General Olbricht's son-in-law. My father was a close friend of General Beck and General von Stuelpnagel—they often visited our house. Hoepner used to be Stauffenberg's divisional commander and Eugen G. knows masses of churchmen. Julius Leber can count on the support of a whole host of former political associates and Goerdeler is backed by a number of industrialists. It may be a closed shop, but it has its advantages."

"I know what you mean," Lehmann said. "You have to be able to trust each other."

"Precisely, and in times like these you can only do that if you know someone really well. There's more involved here than mutual affection or common likes and dislikes—it's a matter of life and death."

"All the same," mused Lehmann, "we ought to have spared

a thought for the people who weren't related to us—people who weren't personal friends or members of the same regiment."

"I've been trying to remedy my errors and omissions for years, Lehmann," Brackwede sighed. "Don't you start on the same tack now! I can't say I feel particularly pleased with myself, but the atmosphere in this great age of ours makes breathing difficult. We ought to thank God we've survived long enough to see this day."

Lehmann grinned impishly. "It's not over yet."

The corpse in the air-raid shelter in No. 13 Schifferdamm was officially discovered by Erika Elster. There was nothing complex about her reaction: she merely inspected Jodler senior and established that he was dead.

Glancing at her wrist-watch, which said 11.15, she climbed the steps to the ground floor and rang the doorbell of Jodler senior's flat. When no one answered she rang the bell of the flat opposite. The door was opened by the scantily-clad figure of Jodler junior. He grinned broadly.

"Looking for me, sweetheart? I was just having a kip, but if you've got the time I've got the inclination . . ."

The circumstances were too inauspicious for Erika to indulge in repartee. "Just at the moment," she said, running an appraising eye over his luxuriantly hirsute chest, which would have done credit to a gorilla, "I think you ought to take a look at your father—he's down in the cellar."

"Drunk?" inquired Jodler junior.

"No." Erika did not hesitate to tell the truth—indeed, she awaited his reaction to it with some curiosity. "He's dead."

Josef Jodler knit his brows in silence for several seconds but betrayed no other sign of emotion. Eventually he said: "An accident or something, eh? No?—I'll go and take a look anyway."

He descended into the cellar with Erika at his heels. Her curiosity increased. Free spectacles of any form or description always fascinated her. She watched the son bend over his father's corpse with a professional air which betokened that dead bodies were all in a day's work to him.

The expert straightened up again. "Shot," he said judicially. "Know who it was?" He eyed Erika. "Wasn't you, was it?"

"Certainly not—and that's all I do know."

Josef Jodler remained entirely unmoved. If he was aiming

at a display of self-control he was succeeding admirably. "Well," he said, "these things happen in war-time. Berlin's lousy with foreign scum. Could be an accident, of course—or suicide." He stood there thinking laboriously. "What's the best thing to do?"

"Well, the police ought to be notified for a start." Jodler junior's sang-froid was beginning to impress Erika despite herself. "I expect they'll want to make inquiries."

"You don't say!" Jodler junior seemed surprised. "Do they still bother with that sort of thing after five years of war? The air-raids must leave thousands of stiffs lying round Berlin every night."

"Yes, but your father was a Local Group-Leader, don't forget. That makes him a special case."

"Fair enough," Jodler said eventually. "We'll turn out the guard, and if I find out who did my old man in I'll take him apart, so help me!"

Colonel von Stauffenberg could already see the third and final gate that separated him from Hitler. He was still in the area enclosed by the first and second cordons surrounding the Fuehrer's Headquarters. After breakfasting with the camp commandant's aide he had been summoned into the presence of Field Marshal Keitel.

Wilhelm Keitel, Chief of the Armed Forces High Command, gave the one-eyed colonel a markedly cordial reception. To him, as to many others, Stauffenberg exemplified the gravely wounded officer who soldiered on regardless—ostensibly for the greater glory of Fuehrer and Reich. After a few friendly preliminaries, he got down to his business.

"What we're mainly interested in is the formation of these new replacement divisions."

"They're to be placed under the command of the Reichs-fuehrer-SS, aren't they?" Stauffenberg inquired point-blank.

Keitel smiled with the studious, brother-officerly heartiness so characteristic of him. "If they are, I'm not aware of it," he lied without hesitation, even though he could easily have supplied Stauffenberg with a precise answer to his question. "The first step is to organise these supplementary divisions. As to how they're employed—well, the final decision naturally rests with the Fuehrer."

Stauffenberg's tone and manner remained unchangingly courteous, but the three fingers of his left hand tightened on the handle of his briefcase. " If it really is intended to place army units under SS jurisdiction, sir, I'd much prefer to know in advance. It would save unnecessary complications."

Keitel gave another urbane smile. " Don't worry your head about it, Stauffenberg—trust the Fuehrer's judgment. Concentrate on the idea that we must mobilise every last ounce of strength. How and where we deploy it will be decided in due course."

It was only a few hundred yards from Keitel's concrete hut to Hitler's bunkers, but it was no simple matter to cover the distance between them. An elaborate system of controls, security precautions, camouflage and double and treble checkpoints transformed the Wolfsschanze, or Wolf's Lair, into a Tartar chieftain's stronghold, bristling with armed men.

After the first gate came a mined and fortified area about two miles across. This was guarded by pickets, traversed by patrols and occupied by detachments of motorised infantry. The second gate gave access to the administrative area of the Fuehrer's Headquarters proper. This was where his staff officers worked under the supervision of security units whose nucleus was formed by the so-called " Officers' Guard."

" When you report to the Fuehrer, kindly confine yourself to essentials," Keitel urged. " We're extremely pressed for time today, so one or two changes in the day's schedule will be unavoidable."

Stauffenberg betrayed none of the concern he felt at this news. The conspirators' plans had more than once been thrown out of joint by last-minute alterations.

" Substantial changes, sir?"

" The Fuehrer's daily conference will not take place at the usual time of 2.30 p.m.," Keitel told him. " The Duce is due at that hour, so all prior commitments have had to be curtailed or brought forward. The staff conference is now scheduled for 12.30." Keitel glanced nervously at his list of engagements. He was an exceedingly busy man. " Kindly make a note of that."

" Duly noted, sir," said Stauffenberg. He stared through the open window at a vista of tall, dark-stemmed trees and slab-shaped concrete buildings camouflaged in blurred shades of green and brown. On this side of the nine-foot electrified barbed wire fence, sentries were mechanically patrolling their beats and harassed-looking officers hurried to and fro, armed with briefcases, memorandum pads and bundles of documents.

It was exactly 12 noon.

"What a glorious day!" Konstantin exclaimed happily, pulling the curtains a little to one side. Blackened rubble and gutted buildings could be glimpsed against a backcloth formed by the wharves, warehouses and coal-dumps of Westhafen, but the bright sunlight coated the scene with a film of dull gold.

"Don't open the curtains—not yet," Elisabeth pleaded. "I want to be alone with you. I don't want to see anything or anyone but you."

Konstantin turned and looked at her. "You're beautiful—did you know that?"

"Come here," Elisabeth said. She held out her arms to him. As he hurried across to her he tripped over the briefcase, which was still standing beside the bed. He kicked it aside and it fell against the chair laden with their clothes, knocking it over. They both burst out laughing, and Elisabeth told him to put it in the far corner "—between the window and the waste-paper basket, where I can't see it."

"I'll chuck it out of the window if you like," he said gaily.

She shook her head. Lying down beside her, he took her hands in his and drew her close. Gently, he kissed her forehead and tried to see his reflection in the eyes that looked back at him with such mysterious tenderness.

"It ought to be like this always," he murmured.

Elisabeth smiled. "We'll have to get up sometime, I suppose."

"I don't want to think that far ahead."

"We've got the whole of today to ourselves, anyway."

"Today and every day from now on!"

Elisabeth's presence was not required at the Bendlerstrasse and Konstantin had his pass. Thanks to Captain von Brackwede, the future seemed to be lost in a rosy haze.

"Oh, Konstantin," she murmured. "I don't think I ever knew what happiness was before. I'm happy now and I want to go on being happy for as long as I possibly can."

"Pixie" Lehmann, a corporal once more, had made himself at home in Captain von Brackwede's office. He was carefully manicuring his nails with a file taken from his crane-driver's tool-kit, but this activity did not prevent him from keeping a wary eye on Brackwede.

The captain was standing motionless by the window, uniform tunic unbuttoned at the neck and hands deep in his trousers pockets. Only the aggressive tilt of his head hinted at his hidden impatience.

"I've recruited a little posse of N.C.O.s," Lehmann announced. "Only three besides myself for the moment, but all good lads who know how to keep their eyes open and their mouths shut."

"Excellent." Brackwede gave an approving nod. He left the window and came over to Lehmann. "We've got to be prepared for any eventuality, however unlikely. I suggest we fortify ourselves a little first. How does that appeal to you?"

Lehmann's expression brightened. "Been robbing your wife's larder again, sir?"

Brackwede opened the briefcase lying on his desk and produced a salami sausage as long as a wine-bottle. Lehmann grunted contentedly and opened a jack-knife. They cut off a number of thick slices and began to eat with single-minded concentration.

"First-class!" Lehmann commented with his mouth full. "Tell me, sir," he asked abruptly, "do you ever feel guilty —about the Fuehrer, I mean? You used to be quite a fan of his once upon a time, didn't you?"

"True," Brackwede admitted, chewing vigorously. "I joined the Party before it came to power—from personal conviction."

"How long did that last?"

"Oh, years . . . I found the combination of nationalism and Socialism irresistible. I still do today, for that matter, but only up to a point."

"Not with this mob in charge, you mean?"

"I was a public servant for years, Lehmann—I even became Deputy-President of the Berlin police, as you know. Throughout that time I tried to do my duty like a good Prussian, but then I joined the army."

"And that's when you saw the light?"

"I began to have misgivings as early as nineteen-thirty-three. Solemn promises were broken, and remarks which I hadn't taken seriously turned out to have been made in deadly earnest. The nation became stupefied by barefaced lies, and National Socialism turned into political bossism." Brackwede shook his head wryly, for once at himself. "I tried to make the best of a bad job, even then, but it wasn't any use. You can't come to terms with criminals and there's no conceivable excuse for doing so except total ignorance of the real nature of their crimes—and that doesn't apply to people like you and me."

"This salami is grand, anyway," Lehmann said, carving himself a fourth slice. "I'm just beginning to see what's at the bottom of this. The way you and Beck and a lot of other people look at it, that lunatic with the toothbrush moustache has let you down. You made the mistake of thinking that a loud-mouthed, bloodthirsty fanatic was a sort of German Messiah, and you can't forgive him for showing you up."

"No," Brackwede said quietly, "I can't forgive him for that."

Field Marshal Keitel stood fidgeting in front of his hut. "Get a move on Stauffenberg!" he called impatiently. General Buhle, the Army representative at Supreme Headquarters, glanced at his watch and saw that it was almost time for the daily conference.

"Coming, sir!" Stauffenberg called back. "I'm just fetching my briefcase."

Alone in the ante-room, he swiftly took his cap and belt from a coat-hook and laid them out on a small table. Then he opened his briefcase, pushed the papers concealing the bomb to one side and removed the pliers from his left-hand trousers pocket. Grasping them firmly between three fingers and palm, he nipped the acid capsule. There was a faint noise like an ice-cube tinkling against a glass, and Stauffenberg knew that the explosion would occur within fifteen minutes.

"Take the Colonel's briefcase," Keitel called to his A.D.C. as Stauffenberg re-emerged. The young officer hurried forward to compy but Stauffenberg politely declined his assistance. Field Marshal Keitel, who was hastening Fuehrer-wards, did not even turn to look.

They exchanged a few casual remarks as they approached the third gate, which was flung wide by an SS sentry. Before them lay Hitler's private bunker, his guest-house, the conference hut and the kennel reserved for the Fuehrer's Alsatian bitch.

SS-Fuehrer Rattenhuber materialised promptly as was his custom. His sharp eyes seemed to search everyone he encountered for concealed weapons, but he grinned broadly at Keitel and allowed him and his companions to pass without closer inspection.

Stauffenberg forced himself to maintain a steady pace.

On entering the ante-room of the conference hut he walked over to the sergeant-major on duty at the switchboard and warned him that he was expecting an urgent call from Berlin.

Keitel and his A.D.C. heard the conversation distinctly. They also heard the colonel say: " I need some information to complete my report for the Fuehrer."

They entered the conference room, where proceedings were already in full swing. General Heusinger was presenting a report on the state of the Russian front.

Two dozen men were grouped round Hitler in an oblong room measuring roughly fifteen feet by thirty. The walls and ceiling were faced with greyish-white pith-board, and in the centre stood a heavy oak table constructed of four-inch planks. Its dimensions were eighteen feet by five, and it was supported by two massive wooden socles.

Hitler's chair was situated on the side nearest the door, with General Staff maps neatly stacked in front of it in the correct sequence. The Fuehrer's carefully polished spectacles lay ready to hand.

The room had ten windows, all of which were open because of the sultry heat. Stauffenberg, who had anticipated this, took in the situation at a brief glance.

Hitler looked up from his map, nodded at Keitel and acknowledged Stauffenberg's salute. Never able to resist playing the role of a warlord greeting one of his wounded warriors, he shook the colonel warmly by the hand.

" I'll hear your report later, Stauffenberg. For the moment: the general situation."

General Heusinger immediately resumed his dissertation. All those present, Hitler included, bent over their maps again with an air of keen attention and profound concentration—all, that is, except Colonel Claus von Stauffenberg. Having deposited his briefcase beneath the map-table a bare six feet from Hitler's legs, he waited a few moments and then slipped out of the room.

The time was 12.37.

In the Bendlerstrasse, Captain von Brackwede was roaming up and down the corridors and poking his aquiline nose into one office after another. He did so less as a form of distraction than because it was one of his favourite and well-established party-games.

The traditional response to his opening gambit—" How's

the battle going"—was: "What battle?" This, in turn, evoked the reply: "The one we're losing, of course!" followed by one of Brackwede's grimmer witticisms.

Although his essays at morale-boosting met with some success, Brackwede felt a trifle off-form—possibly, he told himself, because of the muggy weather.

Still in quest of entertainment, he made for Lieutenant Herbert's office. As he had expected, the Fuehrer's faithful soldier and servant was in full spate. Brackwede found him on the 'phone, eagerly pestering some Party official for crates of propaganda literature for the new replacement divisions which Stauffenberg was organising.

"You've really got the bit between your teeth, I see." Brackwede dropped into a chair with an air of amusement. He nodded at Molly Ziesemann, who was now the lieutenant's personal assistant as well as his girl-friend, having been promoted from the switchboard downstairs. "What are you doing—planning for the next war?"

Herbert felt flattered by the implication that his department was forging ahead. His fuel consumption was gradually over-taking Stauffenberg's—and that was saying something!

"I'm afraid things aren't going as smoothly as they might," he said regretfully. "It's not my fault, though. The switch-board isn't functioning with its usual efficiency."

Brackwede pricked up his ears. "Not functioning?"

"Not a hundred per cent."

"Why not?"

"It's change-over day, that's why not," Molly Ziesemann remarked in professional tones. She had not worked in the Bendlerstrasse's communications centre for nothing. "They're switching the exchange over."

Brackwede showed perceptible interest at this news and pressed Molly for further details. It appeared that—on this day of all days—the Supreme Headquarters exchange was being transferred from Rastenburg in East Prussia to Zossen on the outskirts of Berlin. This meant that the conspirators might not be able to exercise full control over what was probably their most vital communications network.

Brackwede rose abruptly. With an encouraging "Keep up the good work!" he hurried downstairs and burst into Mertz von Quirnheim's office. He found the colonel lovingly sorting out the contents of his safe. The operational schedules were once more spread out on his desk, neatly arranged in convenient piles. "We're only waiting for the word," he said, looking up.

"What if you never receive it?" demanded Brackwede. "Did you know that it's change-over day today?"

The bespectacled colonel looked thoughtful for a moment. Then he picked up the 'phone and asked to be put through to an officer in Signals.

The signals expert, who was another of the initiates, confirmed Brackwede's information. "It's not a good day for controlling the network, sir," he said gloomily, "in fact, you could hardly have chosen a worse one. It all depends how far they've got with the job of switching the circuits round."

"Well?" Brackwede's eyes glinted angrily. "Did you allow for that in your schedule?"

"We were reckoning on all kinds of difficulties and complications," Mertz replied, twitching his glasses into place. "Don't worry, we'll take any unpleasant surprises in our stride."

"The unpleasant surprises have started rather early on—don't you agree, my dear fellow? How are you going to conduct a military revolt by telephone if the lines are out of order?"

Mertz von Quirnheim looked slightly put out. "I shall ensure that the problem is dealt with by Signals, of course." He gave a sudden chuckle. "Don't stop trying to put the fear of God into us, my friend—that's what you're here for, and I'm sure you've no intention of neglecting your duties. Tell me," he said, changing the subject, "what are our colleagues at police headquarters doing?"

"Hanging around, like most of their opposite numbers in the Bendlerstrasse. They don't know how lucky they are—yet."

The police station responsible for maintaining law and order in the Schifferdamm area despatched two of its myrmidons to No. 13. A sergeant named Kopisch set off for the house accompanied by a constable, a species of human watch-dog who came to heel promptly when called but could be relied on not to take independent action.

Kopisch, whose grizzled head testified to long years of loyal service in peace and war, was a man who went by the book. He inspected the scene of the crime and jotted down some preliminary notes with an expression of stolid dignity on his weather-beaten face.

"You are the son of the deceased?" he inquired.

Josef Jodler introduced himself, giving his name and rank and hinting at the nature of his duties. Sergeant Kopisch noted his martial bearing with approval and treated him with the respect he deserved. No difficulties need be expected from a man with such an obvious respect for authority.

"And you?" he demanded, pointing at Erika with his pencil. "What's your connection with this?"

"I found the body," said Erika.

Sergeant Kopisch took an immediate and profound dislike to her. He detested plump, firm-fleshed females because they reminded him irresistibly of all the things he had missed in life. He had been compelled to pay a high price for the irreproachability of his private life.

"You occupy a flat all to yourself?" Kopisch eyed her with deep suspicion. "Here, in this area, in the fifth year of the war?"

"I bet that surprises you, doesn't it?" Erika felt that she had been challenged, and she was determined to hit back with maximum effect. "I've got connections, you see."

Sergeant Kopisch brushed the remark aside. Lots of people claimed to have connections but few of them amounted to anything. "Don't tell me you're friendly with a Minister," he said, mildly amused.

"No—just the Police President of Berlin," Erika replied casually. "Is that good enough for you?"

Kopisch looked up from his notes with an air of incredulity.

"We're very good friends," Erika pursued, "—in fact you might almost say we're engaged."

The sergeant shut his mouth and his notebook with a simultaneous snap and murmured a few words which might have been construed as an apology. Then, instructing his watch-dog to stay behind, he vanished.

"You're a marvel!" Jodler said admiringly. "You told him where he got off all right—but then I always did think a lot of you. I reckon you could get away with anything."

Erika produced her stage laugh—a silvery trill with dark, aluring undertones. It seldom failed her. "*C'est la vie*," she said coquettishly. "Life's full of surprises, isn't it?"

Meanwhile, Sergeant Kopisch had doubled to the nearest telephone-box and was submitting a hasty report to his immediate superior.

"It looks like a tough one," he concluded, "—could be really awkward. Better send for someone from the Gestapo—

147

preferably from headquarters, in case of accidents. In the meantime, I'll sew the place up good and tight."

The bomb in the Fuehrer's Headquarters exploded at approximately 12.42 p.m.

General Heusinger was in the middle of his report. "The Russians are pushing northwards in strength. If our army group round Lake Peipus is not immediately withdrawn, a catastrophe . . ."

At that moment the conference hut seemed to shudder under the impact of a gigantic thunderbolt. A sheet of flame enveloped its occupants in fiery devastation and the room filled with dense clouds of suffocating blue-black smoke. There was a deathly hush, followed by a confused babble of cries.

Colonel von Stauffenberg was standing two hundred yards from the centre of the holocaust. His face betrayed no form of emotion when he saw the hut erupt into flame. He hesitated for a fraction of a second and then turned to Lieutenant von Haeften, who was waiting beside the car.

"To the air-field," he said, getting in.

Fifty yards further on, at the gate leading to the central zone of the Fuehrer's Headquarters, they were flagged down. The duty officer apologised, but insisted that he could not let them through. Stauffenberg climbed out with apparent calm and asked for permission to telephone. He dialled a number, spoke a few words into the mouthpiece, hung up, and said in a clear, steady voice: "Lieutenant, I am allowed to pass."

He had not spoken to anyone, but his iron composure carried the requisite conviction. The entry in the logbook read: "12.44—Colonel Stauffenberg passed through."

At 12.45 a general alarm was issued.

Three or four minutes later the colonel's car approached Outer Guard-post South. Here, barriers had been lowered and all sentries doubled.

With unruffled calm, Stauffenberg climbed out of the car once more. The guard-commander, a stolid and imperturbable sergeant-major named Kolbe, said tersely: "Sorry, sir—no one's allowed through."

"Except me," Stauffenberg said. "Let me use your 'phone."

On this occasion Stauffenberg instinctively refrained from any attempt to bluff. Instead, he called the camp commandant's adjutant and said: "Colonel Stauffenberg here, speaking from Outer Guard-post South. The guard-commander won't let me through because of the explosion, but I'm in a hurry. General Fromm is waiting for me at the air-field."

Up to this time—roughly 12.49—no details of what had happened were circulating in the Fuehrer's Headquarters. All the camp adjutant knew was that an explosion had occurred. In view of this, he said simply: "You can pass, sir."

Stauffenberg replaced the receiver with crisp precision and said: "You heard, Sergeant-Major, I'm allowed through." The lean face and lofty brow remained unalterably serene. Lieutenant von Haeften watched his colonel with bated breath, exulting in the man's iron nerve.

Sergeant-Major Kolbe had not noticed anything out of the ordinary, but his own instincts prompted him to insist on receiving a direct order. Winding the handle of his field telephone, he asked to be put through to the camp adjutant. Stauffenberg resigned himself to this time-wasting and perilous display of punctilio without flinching. Seconds crawled by in agonising inactivity before Sergeant-Major Kolbe signalled to his men to raise the barrier.

"You can pass, sir."

A white table-cloth had been spread on the floor beside the bed, and on it reposed an open tin of sardines and two slices of bread. While Elisabeth and Konstantin were eating, someone tapped gently at the door.

"It's wonderful to be here with you like this," Elisabeth said happily.

He leant across and drew her towards him.

The tapping slightly increased in volume. This time they noticed it. Elisabeth raised her head without taking her hands from Konstantin's shoulders and said to the closed door: "Not now, please—I'm busy!"

"It won't take a minute," Frau Wallner called in a hoarse, agitated whisper. "I must speak to you—it's urgent!"

"I can't talk to you now, really I can't—don't you understand?"

"Of course I understand!" Frau Wallner mumbled indignantly. "I'm not deaf!"

"All the better—I'll have a word with you later."

She laid her head against Konstantin's chest and he cradled it in his hands. Their skin gleamed softly in the subdued light. They gazed into each other's eyes and sighed.

Frau Wallner's voice was heard again, louder and more agitated than before. "I'm sorry to have to disturb you, but something has happened—something serious!"

"It's nothing to do with us," Elisabeth said in an abstracted voice. She sank slowly back on the pillow. "Nothing!" she repeated, adding, in a whisper: "Just what happens to us, Konstantin—that's all that matters."

An army car drew up at the Bendlerstrasse and a man got out. He was dressed in a nondescript civilian suit and carried a leather suitcase. A sentry approached him.

"It's all right," the driver said. "General Olbricht is expecting this gentleman."

The sentry saluted casually. The man in civilian clothes made no particular impression on him—he might almost have been a travelling salesman from his appearance—but when he spoke there was a brusque, incisive quality in his voice which stamped him as a man accustomed to giving orders. "No need to escort me," he said curtly. "I think I can still remember my way around here."

"Whatever you say," the sentry replied with a shrug. He could not be expected to know that he was speaking to General Fromm's prospective successor. He pushed open the door leading to the appropriate wing and the man with the suitcase marched up the steps.

He did not, in fact, find the way immediately. The Bendler block resembled a rabbit-warren. There were a number of main entrances—1, 1a, 2, and so on—as well as a door leading to the guardroom, the C.-in-C.'s private entrance and several rear entrances for the use of supply personnel. The building was criss-crossed by a labyrinth of interconnected passages, side corridors and staircases which ran parallel to the street above the main entrance, transversely into the wings of the building and up and down to the intermediate floors. There were several hundred offices in the block.

The man with the suitcase started to perspire gently, and his lean, lined face turned pale pink, but he marched onwards with head erect.

"Well, here I am!" he announced, when he finally reached General Olbricht's office. He put his suitcase down and froze into statuesque immobility for some seconds. "I hope I'm not too late."

The insignificant civilian had the satisfaction of seeing General Olbricht jump up with an exclamation of delight.

Mertz von Quirnheim, too, shook his hand, and even Captain von Brackwede rose to his feet. Admittedly, Brackwede's manner was somewhat casual, but the man with the suitcase knew better than to expect anything else.

"Welcome, General!" cried Olbricht, and General Erich Hoepner, Stauffenberg's former divisional commander and the man who had been "dishonourably discharged" from the Wehrmacht in 1942 for withdrawing troops on his own responsibility, beamed with pleasure.

Brackwede relieved Hoepner of his suitcase and weighed it in his hand. "I hope you haven't got any papers in here, sir—we're knee-deep in them as it is."

Olbricht's embarrassed laugh conveyed that he found Brackwede's attempt at humour misplaced. "The captain's hipped on that subject. He's afraid we're going to get tangled up in our own red tape."

"He has a point," Hoepner said with grudging approval. "Precise orders required no detailed explanation. However," he continued, indicating his suitcase, "all I've got in there is my uniform. When the time comes, I'll put it on."

"I look forward to that moment, General," Brackwede remarked, grinning. "I hope I won't have to wait too long."

No one in the Bendlerstrasse yet knew whether or not the bomb had exploded, since no definite information had been received. To pass the time, Olbricht invited Hoepner to join him for lunch.

"*Bon appétit!*" said Brackwede. "While you're at it, I'll indulge in my favourite pastime and do some telephoning."

At about 12.43 p.m., shortly after the explosion at the Fuehrer's Headquarters, two figures emerged from the smoking ruins like a pair of spirits from the nether regions. Adolf Hitler, anxiously supported by Field Marshal Keitel, tottered into the open air.

Hitler stumbled across to his living quarters without a word. He was visibly shaken but not badly hurt, as his personal physician, who rushed to the scene, soon ascertained. His hair was singed, his right leg scorched, one of his ear-drums punctured and his back lacerated by fragments from the fallen ceiling.

"It's a miracle!" Keitel exclaimed, employing a term which always sprang readily to the lips of Hitler and his entourage. It later turned out that the man responsible for the "miracle" was a Colonel Heinz Brandt. Finding Stauffenberg's brief-case in his way, he had picked it up and transferred it to the other side of one of the massive wooden supports on which the heavy oak table rested—the side furthest from Hitler. This action had saved his Fuehrer's life but not his own.

Hitler re-emerged from his private lair and stared dumbly at the ruins of the conference hut, now a bizarre heap of shattered planks, jagged lumps of concrete and smoking rubble.

"The Fuehrer is alive!" Keitel shouted encouragingly. "More alive than ever!"

Bowed and shaking, Hitler nervously eyed the survivors and first-aid parties, but their universal air of loyal solicitude reassured him. Eventually he said: "It may have been a low-level attack by enemy fighter-bombers. I demand a thorough investigation!" he added brusquely.

In response to Rattenhuber's parade-ground bellowings, the inner zone was hermetically sealed. Alarm Phase I was put into operation, effectively cutting everyone off from access to the outer world and vice versa. Medical officers and orderlies bustled to and fro, first-aid kits were unpacked and stretchers transported to the scene—all of which proceedings were supervised by SS guards brandishing tommy-guns. Barely half an hour after the explosion, the first ambulance moved off in the direction of Rastenburg.

The survivors hung around looking anxious. General Jodl, Chief of Operations to the Armed Forces High Command and second only to Keitel in his blind devotion to the Fuehrer, blamed the Todt Organisation for using foreign labour to build the conference hut. He was convinced that some alien worker had secreted a time-bomb in the building—apparently beneath the floor, as a gaping hole three feet deep seemed to indicate.

At once, the wildest rumours began to circulate in the Fuehrer's Headquarters. With the dead, dying and wounded cleared away, the survivors gave free rein to their imagination, conjuring up pictures of subversive foreign labourers, British Secret Service agents, Russian Commandos, American gangsters on a special mission. Bormann even evolved the idea that a Jewish terrorist organisation might have been at work, but Hitler, with a certain prescience, remarked:

"It is conceivable that there may be creatures in our own ranks who wish to destroy me—and, through me, Germany!"

Initially, no shadow of suspicion fell on Claus von Stauffenberg, and the "one-eyed colonel" did not become a potential suspect until two hours later. It was at first assumed that he might have landed behind the Russian lines in the interval.

The preliminary balance-sheet was as follows: of the twenty-five persons attending the conference, four were dead, five dying and six gravely injured. The only man to escape completely unscathed was Field Marshal Keitel, but the Fuehrer, anxious to maintain his reputation as an invulnerable national symbol, gave strict instructions that no details of his own injuries must be allowed to leak out.

No. 13 Schifferdamm gave an impression of greyness and neglect. The patched windows looked opaque and the fissures in the outer walls resembled the tracks of monstrous, sluggishly moving worms which were slowly eating the house away, ignored by its occupants.

" My name's Voglbronner," announced the short man who had just arrived. He folded his hands neatly, like a model schoolboy. " I've been instructed to carry out the necessary inquiries here."

" The old man's dead," observed Josef Jodler. " There's no doubt about that, anyway."

" No, no doubt about that." Voglbronner studied him with mild eyes which seemed to apologise for the very fact of his existence. " On the other hand, this isn't an ordinary death. The deceased was no ordinary man."

" You can say that again ! " Jodler said staunchly. It occurred to him that Voglbronner might be expecting him to play the Greater German warrior, and he had no intention of disappointing him. " He was a Party member."

" Can I go now ? " Erika demanded with visible impatience. " I don't see where I come into all this." Voglbronner's appearance on the scene displeased her. She scented complications.

" Please don't misunderstand my position," Voglbronner entreated. " I'm not here solely on account of a dead body—they're a common enough phenomenon these days. My duty is to safeguard the interests of the Party and State—with your assistance, of course."

" That's what I like to hear ! " Jodler said with approval. " You've got the right idea there."

" Just make sure you don't go treading on anyone's corns, that's all," Erika remarked pertly. Her voice contained a note of warning.

" You, my dear lady," the Gestapo man assured her gallantly, " are under my personal protection." He had taken the precaution of making inquiries about her, and the particulars supplied by Sergeant Kopisch appeared to have some foundation. She certainly owed her flat to the good offices of the Berlin Police President, Count Helldorf, who maintained four other similar establishments as well as a suite in the Hotel Exzelsior. "You can rely on me to look after your interests."

"What about me?" Jodler inquired eagerly. "What do you want me to do?"

"I propose to enlist your active support and assistance."

Sergeant Kopisch had provided Voglbronner with a roll-call of the occupants of No. 13 Schifferdamm. It listed an air force lieutenant named Brackwede, which was why Maier's department—in the temporary absence of the Sturmbann-fuehrer himself—had gone into action.

"Let's start by putting the other members of the household through the mill," Voglbronner continued. "I look forward to seeing what comes out at the other end."

At this stage—*circa* 1 p.m.—Colonel von Stauffenberg was still on the way to the air-field at Rastenburg, accompanied by his aide, Werner von Haeften.

Their car bounced madly along the worn and pot-holed highway as the driver skilfully manipulated his wheel in an effort to keep the vehicle on an even keel. He later stated: "There was nothing unusual about the trip. The officers behaved like all the others I've ever driven to the air-field."

Stauffenberg and Haeften sat there without speaking, their faces drained of tension. They were convinced that it had happened at last: Hitler had ceased to exist, and so had the diabolical oath of personal allegiance which still inspired so many patriots to proceed with caution.

"There was a jet of flame," Stauffenberg told his friends later that day. "It was as though the place had been hit by a 155 millimetre shell. No one could have survived." He was as certain of this as he was unaware of what the consequences of his absolute certainty would be. According to one rumour, Stauffenberg had actually seen Hitler's body hurled from the exploding hut, and General Fellgiebel had watched the Fuehrer "sailing through the air like a bat." Others, again, swore that Fellgiebel had said: "Something terrible has happened —the Fuehrer is still alive. Shut everything down." By shutting everything down, the Signals chief meant blocking the main communications centre in the Fuehrer's Headquarters, which was under his control, thereby cutting the link with the Bendlerstrasse as well.

Unfortunately, this was not the only switchboard in the Rastenburg area. Himmler's headquarters, which were in the neighbourhood, possessed their own facilities, and Reichsleiter Bormann hit upon the simple idea of using the normal post office net work. The result was that Hitler's henchmen were already telephoning busily while Stauffenberg and Haeften were still on their way to the air-field. Meanwhile, the Bendlerstrasse remained without any clear and conclusive information. Only Quartermaster-General Wagner at Zossen received any news, and this was an imprecise message, timed 1.15 p.m., to the effect that there had been an attempt on Hitler's life, but that it had " probably " failed.

During the drive to the air-field Lieutenant von Haeften jettisoned the bomb which had been held in reserve. It fell into the ditch beside the road with a dull thud. After all that had happened, it was merely ballast.

This incident did not escape the notice of the driver, who later reported it. Historians of the day in question have been unanimous in describing Haeften's actions as peculiar—but was it really so peculiar? Travellers in a hurry generally avoid carrying superfluous baggage.

"Everything's going according to plan," Haeften said confidentially when he saw the Heinkel warming up its engines on the air-field at Rastenburg.

The 'plane took off a few minutes later. Almost three hours would have to elapse before it reached Berlin, but Stauffenberg consoled himself with the thought that Hitler was dead and the coup d'état under way.

TWO

The broad, slab-like building in Bendlerstrasse lay baking in the early afternoon sunlight like a brick in a kiln. The narrow windows looked as if they had been barred up, and the central drive-in resembled the entrance of a dark cavern.

Brackwede was back in General Olbricht's office again. Olbricht had finished his snack and was sitting there with Hoepner and Mertz von Quirnheim, waiting for news.

"Perhaps we ought to take a little siesta," Brackwede suggested. "The whole building seems to be asleep—why not us?"

Olbricht looked faintly astonished. "Could you really sleep now?"

"I could if I wanted to, but I don't," Brackwede replied, sitting down uninvited.

"Worried?" inquired General Hoepner, who liked to play the sympathetic superior. He magnanimously overlooked the strange captain's nonchalantly civilian ways, notably his habit of wearing his uniform tunic open like a sports coat.

"I'm worried even if he's not," Mertz said, "especially after that vague 'phone call."

"We must keep our nerve," Hoepner said. "We've got to sit tight until we receive definite news."

Brackwede looked up sharply. The seemingly imperturbable self-assurance of this general in civilian clothes was beginning to irritate him. "What telephone call are you talking about?"

Hoepner waved the question aside. In his view, semi-civilian officers below field rank were not entitled to full information, but Mertz, in response to an almost imperceptible nod from Olbricht, reported that a few minutes before—at about 13.15—a brief message had been received via General Thiele, the Army Signals chief. According to him, the attempt had taken place but must be presumed to have failed.

"Vague, imprecise and virtually meaningless," declared Hoepner.

Brackwede frowned. "Wasn't the daily conference at headquarters scheduled for 2.30?"

" Yes, but it was unexpectedly changed to 12.30."

Brackwede leant forward, pale blue eyes alight with eagerness. " In that case, what are we waiting for?"

" For definite confirmation, of course," Hoepner said reprovingly.

" Are we in touch with the Fuehrer's Headquarters?"

" No." Mertz's manner might have been deliberately designed to fan the flames of Brackwede's impatience. " There's no reply from the switchboard—it seems to be out of commission."

" Then the whole thing's clear as daylight!" Brackwede explained, jumping to his feet. " The fact that the Fuehrer's Headquarters has been cut off proves that Stauffenberg has done his job."

" Precipitated action must be avoided at all costs," Olbricht interjected. " We can't afford to issue code-word Valkyrie prematurely, as we did last Saturday. This time we've got to be absolutely certain."

" Starting the operation too early might be rash," Brackwede said fiercely. " Starting it too late would be suicidal."

Hoepner cleared his throat warningly. " Let's keep our heads, gentlemen. We must be sure of our ground, as anyone with a proper sense of responsibility will agree."

Mertz von Quirnheim glanced silently at Brackwede. He removed his glasses, and the cold grey of his eyes turned to sparkling blue.

Brackwede said: " We've got to act now, one way or the other. There are two alternatives: either we start the ball rolling at once or we try to hush the whole thing up. Either way, we've got very little time—approximately three hours, in my estimation—so we'd better decide at once."

" I agree with Brackwede," Mertz said quietly.

Olbricht looked worried. " General Beck has repeatedly warned us against being over-hasty," he said, glancing across at Hoepner.

Hoepner appeared to meditate for a moment or two. Then he announced: " I think we ought to sit it out. Don't let's rush into anything blindly."

Berlin simmered like a cauldron as the mercury crept slowly towards the ninety mark.

On the ground floor of No. 13 Schifferdamm, Voglbronner's pallid face remained as dry as parchment. He did not seem to notice the heat—in contrast to the Gestapo stenographer, who was melting like a wax candle. Thick beads gathered on the man's brow as he bent industriously over his notebook.

"The death of the Local Group-Leader," dictated Voglbronner, "appears, on the basis of preliminary inquiries, to have occurred between three and six a.m. A revolver bullet has been found and is currently being subjected to laboratory tests." He broke off. "You see, Herr Jodler, we go about these things methodically. One of my first questions to every occupant of this house will have to be: Where were you during the hours in question? Well, where were you?"

The Scharfuehrer grinned. "I was in bed."

"Alone?" Voglbronner inquired in a mild voice.

"My wife's away, if you really want to know," Jodler leered. "She's making her contribution to the war-effort. Very right and proper too, but I'm only human and I've just got back from a tough tour of duty. Get me?"

"I understand," the Gestapo man assured him amiably. "All right—who was it?"

Jodler junior named Maria, adding a plea for discretion. "She happened to be handy, if you know what I mean. You wouldn't begrudge me a bit of fun, would you?"

Voglbronner refrained from passing judgment. He asked Sergeant Kopisch to fetch Maria, and Maria appeared promptly. She stood there with her head bowed, trembling and crimson-faced, while Jodler plied her with words of encouragement.

"She's a bit slow," he explained to his new-found Gestapo friend, "—doesn't speak much German, so you'll have to make allowances for her. All the same, she's willing."

Maria substantiated the last remark by eagerly confirming every detail of Jodler junior's statement, stammering as she searched for the right words. At least two people in the house seemed to have an alibi for the period in question.

Voglbronner gave an understanding smile. "Tell me," he asked casually, "is this girl employed in your household or your father's?"

"The old man had first call on her, in a manner of speaking, but she gets around."

"Gets around?" Voglbronner raised his eyebrows.

"Well, yes," Jodler confided. "I'll give you a tip, if you like. Take a dekko at the tenants on the third floor—it might pay you."

When Corporal Lehmann walked into Brackwede's office he

found the captain ensconced in his chair with a book propped on the desk in front of him.

"Reading?" Lehmann asked.

"That's what books are for."

Brackwede was thumbing through an edition of Georg Christoph Lichtenberg, whose aphorisms he found particularly comforting at moments of stress. He had underlined a number of them and was re-reading them with a certain degree of satisfaction. One such—" Human frailties no longer harm us once we recognise them"—struck him as particularly apt.

"Any news of the Colonel?" inquired Lehmann.

"Not a word."

"Is that good?"

"I don't know."

The corporal shook his head disapprovingly. "You must have a pretty lousy communications set-up. Doesn't anyone know what he's doing at the moment? Is he still waiting to do the job, or has he started back already?"

"Not a clue, Lehmann."

"I don't like the sound of that—it sounds like a proper cock-up to me. If I was Olbricht I'd be ringing up every quarter of an hour to see how far Stauffenberg has got."

"But you're not a member of the General Staff, Lehmann."

The corporal grinned. "No, worse luck. By the way, I've got my little squad organised. There's me and Beckerath and Klimsch, and I've also recruited one of the mess waiters and Fromm's batman. Beckerath's hanging round the main entrance and the others are patrolling the corridors. My headquarters is here."

"Excellent," said Brackwede. "You've built up quite a spy-ring from the sound of it."

"I was bored, that's all. I don't like sitting around twiddling my thumbs."

"Have you told your men what it's all about?"

"What do you think! " Lehmann looked quite shocked. "In the first place I've worked with you too long to do a thing like that, and in the second place I operate on the Stauffenberg principle: everyone has to know just enough to be able to do his job and no more. I shouldn't think more than one man in five realises what's really going on in this place."

"One in ten," Brackwede amended with a smile.

"All the better. The main thing is to keep the engine

running at full revs. All I told my people was: keep your eyes and ears open, and if anything strikes you as unusual, tip me the wink sharpish. We'll see what they come up with."

A dense fog of uncertainty still shrouded much of what was to happen before the day was out. It was as though the muggy heat had stultified people's reactions, both in Berlin and—several hundred kilometres or a three-hour 'plane-trip away—in the "Wolf's Lair" at Rastenburg in East Prussia, the Fuehrer's Headquarters.

Adolf Hitler, who had already changed his clothes, was examining the trousers he had been wearing during the explosion. Grouped round him were a personal aide, a secretary, an SS officer and one of his personal body-guards, all staring at the garment in awe. One leg looked as if it had been cut with a sharp knife.

The Fuehrer, Chancellor and Supreme Commander of the Armed Forces, found the sight both symbolic and indicative—symbolic of yet another brush with "destiny" and indicative that he had been spared to perform still greater works.

The trousers at once became a show-piece. Reichsleiter Bormann inspected them and spoke of "Providence," and Field Marshal Keitel hastened to point out that he had said the same thing immediate after the explosion.

Reich Marshal Goering also appeared on the scene, brimming with boisterous high spirits. He noisily congratulated the Fuehrer on his escape and proceeded, in his turn, to invoke the sacred name of Providence.

Hitler was still at a loss to find the right words to describe the enormity of what had occurred. His silence was at once impressive and awe-inspiring. All he said was: "How could it have happened? I want this business cleared up."

Heinrich Himmler, the Reichsfuehrer-SS, was already busying himself with this problem at his own headquarters, where the switchboard was still working. His first call reached the Central State Security Bureau in Berlin a few minutes after 1 p.m. He asked to be put through to Kaltenbrunner.

"There's been some dirty work here," he said. "Get a 'plane-load of your best men together—investigators and explosives experts—and pack them off to Rastenburg as quickly as you can."

"Certainly," replied Kaltenbrunner. "Anything else, Reichsfuehrer?"

"Not for the moment, but keep on your toes. Things will

sort themselves out in due course. I can't say anything for certain yet."

The world at large was equally ignorant of the details of what had actually happened.

Colonel von Stauffenberg and Lieutenant von Haeften still sat in their 'plane with the East German landscape crawling by beneath them—a dark blanket of largely uniform forest pierced by lakes like pale sightless orbs.

They did not speak. Stauffenberg, who had closed his single eye, looked relaxed, and there was a relaxed smile on the lieutenant's lips. The pilot surveyed his instrument panel with an air of boredom. The engines of the radio-less 'plane droned with monotonous regularity, and the two officers wondered what was happening in the Bendlerstrasse.

The short answer was: nothing. Hoepner, Olbricht and Mertz continued to wait for " definite " news, occasionally raising a glass to their mutual success. Captain von Brackwede tried to put through a call to General Fellgiebel at the Fuehrer's headquarters, but failed.

Erich Fellgiebel had done what was expected of him. He had closed down the switchboard at the Wolf's Lair, and closed it down with a thoroughness which could hardly have been bettered. As a result, not even the Bendlerstrasse could establish contact with the Fuehrer's Headquarters.

Having done this, Fellgiebel sat with his officers around him and waited with stoical calm for the inevitable. It came quickly, in the shape of a summons to report to Keitel.

Fellgiebel rose, straightened his uniform, tossed his last cigar out of the window and told his silent companions: " If we believed in a world hereafter, gentlemen, this would be the time to say *au revoir*!"

At approximately 2.30 p.m. a call from Zossen to Colonel Eberhard Finckh in Paris informed him that " the exercise was under way," a cryptic phrase signifying that the attempt on Hitler's life had been carried out. German troops stationed in the Greater Paris area were immediately alerted—far earlier than their counterparts in Greater Berlin. Nothing, even now, was happening in the Bendlerstrasse.

At this stage a minor character wandered unwittingly into the arena in the person of Lieutenant Dr. Hans Hagen.

Hagen, a fresh-complexioned, amiable-looking young man whose uniform sat incongruously on his boyish frame, was walking down the Friedrichstrasse, meditating on a lecture which he was about to deliver to the officers of the Berlin guard battalion. Its theme was "National Socialist Guidance Questions"—a subject which merited effective presentation. As a National Socialist Guidance officer, Hans Hagen was well-equipped to give it the treatment it deserved. Before entering the army he had worked as an official of the Propaganda Ministry, where he had been treated with unfailing benevolence by "the Chief" himself, Dr. Josef Goebbels. Hans Hagen counted for something!

And so Hagen strolled down the Friedrichstrasse, devising effective turns of phrase for incorporation in his lecture—"no sacrifice can be too great when true greatness is at stake," for example, or: "patriotism thrives on adversity," or possibly: "nothing in life is free; every achievement has its price."

As he reached the vicinity of the Winter Garden, a variety theatre, a staff car drove past with a man in general's uniform sitting in the back seat. There was nothing unusual in this, except that the man in general's uniform looked like Field Marshal von Brauchitsch, and Field Marshal von Brauchitsch was currently in disgrace. The Fuehrer had personally removed him from the active list. Consequently, he ought not to have been wearing uniform anywhere, let alone in Berlin.

According to his subsequent testimony, Lieutenant Dr. Hans Hagen's initial reaction to the sight was one of amusement. He did not deem it necessary to expend further thought on the incident and continued on his way, murmuring —to the best of his recollection—"How odd!"

It so happened that Field Marshal Walter von Brauchitsch, who had been Commander-in-Chief of the Army until 1941, was on his estate in East Prussia that day, so Hagen could not possibly have seen him.

This, however, was unimportant. Hagen had seen something which began to prey upon his mind, at first subconsciously, until his delusion became one of the factors which unleashed a tragedy without parallel.

The sky was cloudless, the air breathlessly still, the shade-temperature in the low nineties and still rising, the situation on the battle fronts unchanged. There were no bomber formations in the area of Greater Berlin.

Voglbronner took his time, knowing instinctively that No.

13 Schifferdamm was full of possibilities. He was aware that, sooner or later, he would encounter a lieutenant named Brackwede on the third floor. He had not yet worked out what his approach to the encounter ought to be.

He could not know, either, that the room occupied by Lieutenant von Brackwede contained a briefcase whose contents were quite as explosive as any time-bomb. His only concern was to steer as devious and skilful a course as possible between the interests of legality, the State, and his immediate superiors.

It was about 3 p.m. when he climbed the stairs to the third floor.

At about 3 p.m. Keitel came to Hitler and asked permission to lift the " communications shut-down " because of urgent calls from the fighting fronts.

The Fuehrer regarded his loyal henchman with astonishment. "Who said anything about closing down communications? I know nothing about this. Who gave the order?"

Keitel cleared his throat and looked embarrassed. "General Fellgiebel must have misinterpreted your remark, my Fuehrer —deliberately misinterpreted it."

"What remark?" Hitler demanded with an undertone of menace.

"If you remember, my Fuehrer, you said that nothing must leak out."

"What! You mean to say someone shut down the whole network because of that!" Hitler's voice rose to an infuriated bellow. "This is sabotage! Who was responsible? Arrest the man immediately!"

"I have already taken the precaution of apprehending General Fellgiebel, my Fuehrer."

At about 3 p.m. Colonel Finckh put a call through from Paris to the Commander-in-Chief, West. The telephone was answered by the C.-in-C.'s Chief of Staff, General von Speidel, who informed Finckh that Field Marshal von Kluge was not at his headquarters.

"Then you must contact him at once," Finckh insisted. "Hitler is dead."

General von Speidel did not reply for some seconds. He was overwhelmed by the news but not unduly surprised. Although he did not know the full details of the conspirators'

163

plans, he was in their confidence. At last he said: " I can't reach the Field Marshal for the moment. He's up at the front, discussing the situation with divisional commanders."

There was no need for further comment. Both men knew that Field Marshal von Kluge occupied a key-position. Only he could initiate the "Western solution" and so start the avalanche which would carry the entire Wehrmacht with it.

" When is the Field Marshal due back?" Finckh asked, restraining his impatience with an effort.

" It's hard to say. Possibly not before late evening."

" And until then?"

" We'll have to wait."

Nothing, even now, was happening in the Bendlerstrasse.

Lieutenant Dr. Hans Hagen spent the period between 3 p.m. and 4 p.m. addressing the officers of the Berlin guard battalion. His flowers of rhetoric appeared to be taking root, judging by his listeners' air of absorption.

In the audience was the unit's commanding officer, Major Otto Ernst Remer, a somewhat coarse-featured but soldierly figure who listened attentively, giving an occasional nod of approval. It was plain to see that Major Remer was a faithful servant of the Fuehrer, on duty or off.

Hagen spoke of unswerving loyalty and the Greater German nation's Germanic Reich, sprinkling his address liberally with quotations from the Edda, Nietzsche and Rosenberg. Not even Goethe was spared.

" In these hours, the greatest which it has fallen to the lot of our nation to witness . . ."

Colonel von Stauffenberg's 'plane flew on towards Berlin.

Adolf Hitler stood on the platform of the temporary station near his headquarters, waiting to greet Benito Mussolini.

Major Remer said to Hans Hagen: " Don't go yet. I'd like to explore some of the points you raised in greater detail."

On the Bendlerstrasse front, all was quiet. Total inactivity still reigned there, as it had done for the past three hours.

Shortly before 4 p.m. the grey-black official saloon belonging to SS-Sturmbannfuehrer Maier turned out of Luetzowplatz into Bendlerstrasse. Replacement Army H.Q. was not difficult to spot. It stood almost isolated in a dusty sea of rubble.

Maier, wearing a dark and inconspicuous civilian suit, got

out in leisurely fashion and ordered his driver to wait in the empty side-street across the way. Then, with an air of curiosity, he approached the massive concrete building. The sentry saluted casually and did not bother to check his credentials. Maier's irritation was succeeded by a faint sense of anxiety. His pace quickened as he steered an unerring course through the labyrinth of corridors, whose lay-out was familiar to him from the accurate ground-plans which he kept in his office. His anxiety mounted. Instead of the turmoil and hectic activity he had been expecting, he found the Bendlerstrasse going about its daily business in an apparently normal way.

"What are you all up to?" he demanded, charging into Brackwede's office like an angry bull. "The place looks fast asleep."

Brackwede looked up from his book with an expression of surprise.

"I thought things would be humming by now," Maier pursued in an aggrieved tone. "What are you playing at? Don't you realise what's been happening, or don't you care?"

Brackwede feigned indifference, but a gleam of interest crept into his eye. "What are you so excited about?"

Maier snorted indignantly. "You're a great disappointment, I must say. What's the matter with you—getting cold feet? I'll tell you this much—all hell's broken loose at Rastenburg. Himmler has asked Kaltenbrunner for a whole 'plane-load of detectives and explosives experts—they're already en route for the Fuehrer's Headquarters. What are you doing about it?"

"Waiting."

"I can see that, blast it—but what for?"

Brackwede failed to produce an answer to this question. He merely said: "Things haven't started moving here yet, but don't let that worry you. I promise you one thing: as soon as the balloon goes up I'll let you know straight away. That was part of our bargain."

"Aren't you going to give me any details?"

"Not yet. Besides, with your contacts and natural intelligence you'll find out all you need to know soon enough."

"Listen," said Maier. "If you hang around much longer you'll miss the boat—and then you'll be in real trouble. I won't hesitate to wring your necks one by one, and when I do a job I do it properly. Is that clear?"

Brackwede nodded. "I know, that's another of the terms of

our agreement. However, our account isn't closed yet. All I can tell you for certain is that we won't be in each other's debt by the time it's settled. Be patient."

At No. 13 Schifferdamm, Voglbronner had been ambushed by Frau Breitstrasser.

She was standing, arms akimbo, outside her door on the dimly-lit second-floor landing, enveloped in a heavy, rancid odour compounded of cooking smells and stale perspiration.

Voglbronner knew what to expect of her even before she opened her mouth.

"When it comes to morals and decency," she announced, "nothing can stop me speaking my mind."

Leaving Josef Jodler, his faithful companion, on the landing, Voglbronner followed his budding witness for the prosecution into her apartment, where he spent a full half hour in her company. He emerged looking smug.

"Well, my friend," he told the Scharfuehrer, "much as I appreciate the value of your services, I'm compelled to inform you that your own position looks shaky, to say the least."

"What's that!" Jodler expostulated. "I suppose that decrepit old windbag has been slandering me because I'm a man with blood in my veins! All right, so what? At least I'm not a randy old goat like that schoolmaster upstairs. Why don't you take a look at him—or that Wallner woman and her shady bunch of lodgers—and don't forget that snooty bitch of a Countess. She only opens her legs for members of the aristocracy, from what I can see."

"That sounds promising," Voglbronner said indulgently. "However, all the inquiries I've made so far point in one direction—you."

Jodler gasped like a stranded fish and a moustache of perspiration formed on his upper lip. "That's utter crap!" he bellowed hoarsely. "Are you suggesting I killed my own father?"

"It's happened before now." Voglbronner's favourite hobby was the training of human bloodhounds, and he was engaging in it now. "Don't worry, though—I've no intention of incriminating you. We're in the same line of business, after all."

Jodler emitted a noisy sigh of relief. "Just what I was thinking myself."

"Which is why I'm going to give you every opportunity to clear this business up in your own way—in our way, if you prefer. Do you follow me?"

Jodler thought he did. Voglbronner's methods resembled those of his own department. As soon as a suitable scapegoat presented himself, everyone else was automatically exempt from suspicion. "Leave it to me!" he said grimly.

"Fine," said Voglbronner. Having temporarily postponed his encounter with Lieutenant von Brackwede, he could use the respite to cover himself as carefully as possible. "I'm relying on you to do a thorough job," he went on. "Personally, I'm going off to have a cup of coffee before I do anything else."

Shortly before 4 p.m. the Heinkel landed at Rangsdorf, near Berlin, with Colonel von Stauffenberg and Lieutenant von Haeften on board.

Haeften leapt out and hurried off to find the nearest telephone. Stauffenberg stared across the parched and faded grass of the runway towards the control tower. When he realised that no one—not even a squad of SS men—was waiting for him, he drew a deep breath and strode on after von Haeften.

Meanwhile, the lieutenant had succeeded in getting a connection to the Bendlerstrasse. A few moments later he heard the calm, sonorous voice of General Olbricht.

"We've just landed, sir," he reported.

"At last!" Olbricht exclaimed with a mixture of relief and suspense. "Well, what happened?"

"What happened?" Lieutenant von Haeften repeated incredulously. He glanced at Stauffenberg, who took the receiver from him.

"Am I speaking to General Olbricht?" he asked, but any idea that von Haeften might have been put through to the wrong office was quickly dispelled by the familiar voice at the other end of the line. "Well, how are things shaping at your end?"

"We've been on tenterhooks, Stauffenberg, waiting for you to call."

Stauffenberg felt almost certain that he had misheard. "How far have you got?" he demanded. "Are you making good progress?"

"Did you bring it off, then?" asked Olbricht.

His question was followed by long seconds of numb and horrified silence. Lieutenant von Haeften, who was listening in, shook his head helplessly.

"Then you haven't started Valkyrie yet," Stauffenberg said in a flat voice.

"How could we, without receiving definite news."

167

" Hitler is dead!"

" Are you positive?"

" I saw the explosion with my own eyes—it was like a direct hit by a 155 millimetre shell. No one could have survived."

" Damnation!" growled von Haeften. " Three full hours and they've done absolutely nothing—three hours, when every minute counts!"

" Operation Valkyrie must be put into effect at once,"

From that moment onwards, 20 July 1944 became *his* day.

The first man in the Bendlerstrasse to react was Colonel Mertz von Quirnheim. Without uttering a word or displaying any excitement he opened the operational schedule that lay beside him on the desk. The first orders began to go out a few minutes later, at 4.12 p.m. precisely.

General Olbricht was reporting on the situation to General Beck, who had since arrived and was standing near the window, dressed in a civilian suit. He had deliberately refrained from wearing uniform " in order to emphasise the civilian element of the resistance movement."

" Stauffenberg is convinced that Hitler is dead," Olbricht said.

" If Stauffenberg says so," Beck replied, " he must be."

" He also insists that we put Valkyrie into effect at once."

" Then do it, in God's name!" Beck's voice rang with emotion. " I'm ready."

General Hoepner nodded approvingly several times but did not speak. Olbricht hurried into the office next door, where Mertz von Quirnheim—in Stauffenberg's view the finest backroom strategist in the Bendlerstrasse—was hard at work. His telephoned instructions were crisp, cool and concise. It was as though a high-precision machine had been set in motion and was functioning at maximum speed.

His favourite preamble—" You are instructed to . . ."—only rarely had to be supplemented by the words: " That is an order!"

The commonest response was a simple affirmative.

Captain von Brackwede, his aquiline nose at a belligerent angle, pushed open the office door and strode over to Corporal Lehmann, who was seated behind his desk. He halted, leant forward with both hands spread flat on the desk-top and fixed Lehmann with a quizzical stare. The face which so often irritated people by its seeming air of condescension suddenly broke into a broad grin.

Lehmann interpreted it at once. "So we're in business? I should hope so too, after all the work we've put in!"

Brackwede gave a brief chuckle and picked up the telephone. A minute later he was speaking to Count Helldorf, the Police President of Berlin. On being told that Hitler was dead, Helldorf assured Brackwede that he would put all pre-arranged measures into effect without delay and announced that he would be calling at the Bendlerstrasse in person.

Meanwhile, Lehmann had opened the centre drawer of the desk and taken out a box of cigars. He proffered it to Brackwede. They were the captain's favourite brand—choice specimens reserved for very special occasions—and there were only three left.

"Two of these are going to be smoked today," Brackwede said, taking the box. "This one's for you, my friend. I'd have smoked one of the others in any case—it's my wife's birthday."

The corporal accepted his cigar as if it were a decoration for bravery. As he held a match for Brackwede he remarked thoughtfully: "You don't seem too happy."

"What makes you say that?"

"It's just a feeling. Something's worrying you, isn't it?"

Brackwede puffed pleasurably at his cigar. "You've got a head on your shoulders, Lehmann. When you heard that it had happened, there was one point you might have asked me about."

Lehmann smoked in silence for a moment. Then his eyebrows rose. "The timing, you mean?"

Brackwede nodded. "Precisely."

"Well, when did it go off?"

"About four hours ago."

"You must be joking!" Lehmann exclaimed. "Where's the Colonel now?"

"On his way here from Rangsdorf. He landed there at about four. It's a forty-five minute run from the airfield." Brackwede glanced at his watch. "Another ten minutes and things will really start to hum."

General Olbricht, taking turns with Colonel Mertz, divided his time between the operational schedules, the telephone and the outer office, where two secretaries were busily banging away at their typewriters. Relays of orderlies scurried off to deliver pre-drafted orders to individual departments and the communications centre in the basement.

The duty personnel in the communications room set to work with speed and efficiency. Calls were put through promptly and teleprinters began to chatter. Within a few minutes the basement had transformed itself into a human ant-hill.

" Something to do at last! " the Signal Corps sergeant-major observed, relishing the sight of his staff at full stretch.

The duty signals officer was more restrained in his enthusiasm. He took the messages as they were handed to him, checked them and passed them on in the routine way. His sole comment was: " Rather a lot of stuff all at once, isn't it? "

The signals officer, a Lieutenant Roehrig, owed his presence in the basement to the duty roster. This was purely fortuitous. His place might have been taken by any one of five or six other officers, but it so happened that he was next in line.

Roehrig was a keen, serious-minded young man who had studied music and belonged to the League of National Socialist Students—not that this rendered him in any way exceptional.

Holding the text of a teleprinter message in his hand, he examined it with a look of faint surprise. The sergeant-major, who was standing beside him, already had his hand poised to take it from him.

" Something wrong, sir? " he inquired.

" There are a couple of irregularities about the form of this message," Roehrig replied cautiously.

The sergeant-major raised his eyebrows. " I'm sure it's all right, sir. These orders have come direct from General Olbricht—there's his signature."

" I know, I know," Roehrig conceded hastily. " But they're written on plain paper. They don't carry any classification or priority stamp."

" It happens sometimes," said the sergeant-major, " —especially when signals are as urgent as these seem to be." He gave a worried frown. " Do you want me to send them back upstairs? "

" No, of course not." Lieutenant Roehrig hurriedly handed the forms over. " I'm a bit surprised, that's all. I like to do things by the book, and when something isn't quite in order it makes me sit up and take notice. However, our first job is to keep traffic moving as fast as possible. You'd better carry on."

Lieutenant Roehrig of the Bendlerstrasse communications centre had sat up and taken notice. That was as far as it went for the moment, and the first signals duly left the building.

Nevertheless, one young officer in the basement had become suspicious.

"Let's have a celebration," Elisabeth cried gaily, " —a really enormous celebration! What do you think, Konstantin?"

Konstantin gazed at her rapturously, as he had done, almost without interruption, for hours on end. He gave a smiling nod of agreement.

"I'll use up all my stores—all of them!" Elisabeth went on, looking round eagerly. "Let's pretend that tomorrow doesn't exist—that we've got to pack a whole lifetime into a single day. Do you know what I mean?"

Konstantin's incomprehension did not prevent him from nodding vigorously. Whatever Elisabeth said sounded marvellous. He hurried towards her, stumbling over the omnipresent briefcase.

Elisabeth clung to him for a moment and then broke away quickly, almost shyly. "I've still got some coffee beans— enough for a whole pot. I've also got half a cake and a tin of caviare and two packets of crispbread and a little jar of goose-dripping."

"We'll never manage it all," Konstantin exclaimed happily.

"Then we'll invite some guests. We can't have a party without guests. I'll ask Frau Wallner and her lodger."

Konstantin fell in with every suggestion she made. Having loaded the table with all the food in the flat, they flung the door wide.

"Frau Wallner," Elisabeth called, " —the pleasure of your company is requested!"

Frau Wallner had evidently been lurking outside in the dark, furniture-encumbered passage. Her snow-white hair gleamed in the light from the open door, but the face beneath it looked drained of expression.

"We've put together all the food we've got left," Elisabeth told her. "We'd like you to share it with us—you and your lodger."

The landlady shook her head. "Don't do that," she replied quietly. "Enjoy your privacy—don't worry about me, let alone my lodger."

"He's a Jewish refugee, isn't he?" Elisabeth seemed to accept the fact without question. "I've known for a long time. It's good to know that people like you still exist."

Konstantin took several seconds to digest this revelation, but his surprise and incredulity were swamped by the compassion which Frau Wallner's seamed and careworn face aroused in him. Besides, whatever Elisabeth said or did was all right.

"Lock your door," Frau Wallner urged, "even if it only gains you a few minutes. Old Jodler was murdered last night and the house is swarming with policemen and Gestapo, looking for someone to pin it on. They're bound to go though the place with a tooth-comb, God help us!"

The light on her white hair died as she withdrew into the shadows. She stretched out her arm to close the door with a gesture like a drowning woman and tiptoed silently away down the passage.

"I don't see what this has got to do with us," Konstantin protested.

"You seem to have forgotten about your brother's brief-case."

"I don't understand, Fritz's briefcase is one thing—we're another. We're a world in ourselves."

Elisabeth's head drooped. "You really don't understand," she said, almost inaudibly, "—do you?"

At approximately 4 p.m. General Olbricht went to see General Fromm. As usual, he found the Commander-in-Chief entrenched behind his massive desk as though it were a ferroconcrete bastion. Fromm believed in keeping his distance.

Olbricht opened the conversation. "Hitler has been assassinated," he announced without preamble.

General Fromm did not speak for some seconds, and his fleshy, arrogant face set in a mask of intense concentration. He stared down at the highly polished parquet floor of his office, not at Olbricht.

"Where did you hear this?" he asked slowly.

Olbricht refrained from telling Fromm that the source of his information was Stauffenberg himself. The C.-in-C. would have to be broken in gently. "The news of Hitler's death came direct from the Fuehrer's Headquarters. Apparently, there has been a successful attempt on his life."

"Who can vouch for that?"

"General Fellgiebel."

"Who else? Have you received any official confirmation?"

"Hardly, sir, since Hitler isn't there any longer to give it."
Olbricht did his best to convey unshakable conviction. "How-

ever, similar reports have reached the Quartermaster-General's office at Zossen. I'm afraid there's only one thing to do—we must launch Operation Valkyrie. I request permission to issue the order at once, sir."

General Fromm gave a snort of agitation and resentment, like a horse confronted by a blazing hedge. His blood-pressure had been abnormally high of late, and he felt his cheeks growing hot.

"You baffle me, Olbricht," he said, retaining his composure with an effort. "On the basis of an ill-confirmed report received at third-hand you come rushing in here and urge me to take a step which could have the gravest possible repercussions. Aren't you being a trifle hasty? Have you double-checked thoroughly? No? Well, I don't propose to get involved in any hare-brained scheme myself, believe me."

"This has got nothing to do with hare-brained schemes, General. On the contrary, there's a crucial decision to be made."

Fromm propped his heavy chin on one hand and regarded Olbricht through narrowed eyes. "Are you certain of this?" he demanded.

"Absolutely positive!"

"I'm not wholly unaware of the convictions and aspirations shared by you and your friends, my dear Olbricht," Fromm said deliberately, "—indeed, I view them with a degree of understanding. On the other hand, I'm sure you'll agree that I can't afford to lend myself to any form of rash or irresponsible action. I bear a heavy responsibility, and no one can divest me of it."

Olbricht at once realised that Fromm was—as usual—trying to cover himself. He was so sure of his facts that he could even sympathise with the man's dilemma. Picking up the telephone, he asked the exchange to call the Fuehrer's Headquarters, confident that there would be no reply. He handed the receiver to Fromm and waited.

The "Wolf's Lair" answered with such speed that even Fromm was taken aback. A few moments later he was speaking to Field Marshal Keitel.

Fromm frequently referred to Keitel as a boot-licker and Keitel described Fromm as a malcontent, but no one could have told from their tone that they shared a mutual wish to eliminate each other. Fromm's voice carried a note of comradely warmth.

"Tell me," he said with as much casualness as he could

muster, "what's been happening at Supreme Headquarters? Berlin is seething with the wildest rumours."

"There's no need for serious concern," Keitel assured him.

"They say there's been an attempt on the Fuehrer's life. Is that correct?"

"Certainly there was an attempt on the Fuehrer's life, but it failed, I'm happy to say. The Fuehrer is alive and only slightly injured." Almost in the same breath Keitel added: "By the way, where's your Chief of Staff, Colonel von Stauffenberg?"

"He hasn't arrived back yet."

That was all—no further reference to Stauffenberg, not the slightest hint that a dangerous situation had arisen. On the contrary, the prevailing impression was that the Fuehrer had once more come through with flying colours.

"There you are—a lot of fuss about nothing," Fromm told Olbricht. "Absolutely no necessity to issue code-word Valkyrie, just as I suspected. You see? The Fuehrer isn't so easy to dispose of after all, so calm down!"

At No. 13 Schifferdamm, SS-Scharfuehrer Jodler—now in full uniform—was carrying out his threat to take the initiative.

No one disturbed him at his work. Voglbronner had gone off for his promised cup of coffee, the police constable was barring the front door like a pillar, and Sergeant Kopisch, engulfed in a huge leather arm-chair belonging to the deceased, was enjoying a belated afternoon nap. Waves of heat flowed up the stairs like an invisible cloud of gas as the house relapsed into a state of semi-torpor.

Josef Jodler's determination to avoid half-measures sprang from two interrelated motives: a wish to divert suspicion from himself and an equally fervent desire to pin it on somebody else.

His first port of call was the second floor, where he systematically went to work on Frau Breitstrasser. Confident that he knew how to deal with her type, he began by slapping her hard in the face, twice. After this introductory treatment he promised her a reduction in rent, a larger share of the cellar and the prospect of a flat on the first floor.

Frau Breitstrasser declared herself ready to amend her original statement if Herr Jodler would be kind enough to offer some alternative suggestions. Herr Jodler graciously consented. From then on, Frau Breitstrasser was prepared to swear to anything the Scharfuehrer thought right and proper.

Jodler's next stop was at Johann Wolfgang Scheumer's flat. In his case, Jodler decided to start by beating a brief but vigorous tattoo on the patriotic drum. He appealed to the schoolmaster's public spirit and devotion to the war-effort, but with only moderate success.

Becoming more explicit, Jodler grasped him by the coat-collar and hurled him against the wall. Scheumer gasped for air and stared at his interlocutor with terror written on his pallid face. " Please," he panted, " what exactly do you want?"

" I want to help you. I always thought you were a good National Socialist, but I'm not so sure now, judging by your behaviour. My old man often warned me against you. That's it! Perhaps you're an enemy of the people—perhaps you murdered my old man!"

Scheumer threw up his hands in supplication and begged to be allowed to dispel any such misconceptions. Not only was his plea granted, but, since he was a man of literary bent, he was commissioned to write a comprehensive report embodying references to the Scharfuehrer's good character and hints as to the identity of the potential killer.

Next, Jodler betook himself to Erika Elster's flat. Here he met with a highly cordial reception which he was too pressed for time to exploit to the full.

" Can I trust you?" he demanded. " I mean, can I trust you to say the right thing?"

" Of course. I can think of any number of reasons why I wouldn't want them to take you away."

" Thanks," he said gratefully. " As soon as I wrap this up we'll have a little party—just the two of us."

And then Jodler encountered an unexpected obstacle. Frau Wallner's door remained obstinately shut. He hammered it with his fists and drove his boot into the panelling, but Frau Wallner refused to open up.

" I'll count three!" Jodler panted. " If this door isn't open by then, you'll regret it!"

Captain von Brackwede had screwed a monocle into his left eye and was standing beside a window, staring into the street. The afternoon sun beat down on his balding head, but no trace of perspiration was visible on his face, which now wore an expression of almost ungovernable impatience.

" At last!" he exclaimed, as Stauffenberg's car drew up outside.

He crossed the room in three strides, flung open the door

and, leaving it ajar, hurried down the corridor to the landing.

Stauffenberg's feet clattered dully on the stone stairs as he raced up them like a man storming a mountainside. It was 4.40 p.m.

"Is Valkyrie under way?" he called to Brackwede.

"Thank God you're here!" Brackwede said. He pushed open the door leading to General Olbricht's offices. "You'll find everything as you expected."

"Thanks," Stauffenberg replied breathlessly. "It's good to see you, Fritz."

Their eyes met for a fraction of a second and they exchanged a fleeting handshake before hurrying inside.

Olbricht's office was dominated by the figure of General Beck, serene as a stone monument. The silent group around him turned to stare at Stauffenberg expectantly. Mertz von Quirnheim was the only person who did not interrupt his activities. He merely raised one hand in greeting and continued to pass orders by telephone with mechanical precision.

"Hitler is dead," announced Stauffenberg.

"Supreme Headquarters allege otherwise," Beck said in measured tones.

"As far as it is humanly possible to judge," Stauffenberg pursued, undeterred, "Hitler must be dead. I saw the explosion myself."

Beck raised his hand, but Brackwede intervened before he could speak. "Whether he's dead or not, we must act—and act on the former assumption. I suggest we regard Keitel's statement as a smoke-screen."

"Very well," Beck said firmly, "as far as I'm concerned, the man is dead, and I shall base my future actions on that belief. Having once taken this line, gentlemen, we must stick to it."

From then on, no further uncertainty prevailed in the Bendlerstrasse, at least on this particular point. Olbricht inclined his head in assent, Hoepner looked martial, Brackwede nodded at Stauffenberg and the more junior officers in the room looked momentarily as though they were attending church parade in the garrison chapel at Potsdam.

"The units at Krampnitz, Gross-Glienicke, Doeberitz and Potsdam have already been alerted," Mertz informed Stauffenberg. "All instructions are being confirmed."

"Good," replied Stauffenberg, making for the nearest telephone. "Have you been in touch with G.O.C. Berlin District?"

"General von Hase's unit commanders are assembling for a briefing session at this moment."

"Any news from elsewhere?"

"Vienna reports a state of readiness. Prague has only confirmed receipt of our orders so far, but Paris has already started operations."

Stauffenberg gave Brackwede a meaningful glance. He had expected no less of Paris, where Caesar von Hofacker must be hard at work by now.

"Where is Field Marshal Witzleben?"

Erwin von Witzleben, the prospective Commander-in-Chief of the Armed Forces, was another of Hitler's avowed opponents —and not merely because the Fuehrer had removed him from his post in 1942. He was a great admirer of Beck and a close friend of General von Brackwede. In his stated view, Hitler was an "emetic."

In fact, Field Marshal von Witzleben had already put in an appearance, not at the Bendlerstrasse but some twenty miles away at the Quartermaster-General's headquarters in Zossen, where there was nothing vital for him to do.

"Where is the Field Marshal?" Stauffenberg repeated. "We need him here."

"He'll come," Brackwede observed. "He can leave it as late as he likes, as long as he doesn't leave it too late."

Stauffenberg and Mertz embarked on a series of fierce telephone battles, each working from a carefully prepared list so as to ensure an effective division of labour.

Beck and Hoepner, who realised that virtually nothing was likely to arise which would necessitate their personal intervention in the next few minutes or even hours, resigned themselves to a long wait.

Meanwhile, a few officers had gathered in the corridor on the second floor and were exchanging remarks in subdued voices. Some of them looked pale and haggard, others merely perplexed.

"Keep smiling, gentlemen!" Brackwede called as he hurried past. "If there's going to be a funeral, let's make it a cheerful one."

"He can't behave like that!" Konstantin von Brackwede declared indignantly. He stationed himself beside Frau Wallner, who was fluttering her hands in desperation. "It's plain trespassing, trying to break in like this."

Josef Jodler was still pounding the door like a drum. The wood groaned under the impact of his boot. "Open up, damn you! This is the SS!"

Elisabeth looked apprehensive. "We'd better have a word with him, Konstantin," she urged, "—but please, no violence. There must be some other way."

"Maybe, but this has got to stop," Konstantin snapped. He had been too rudely awakened from his idyll to feel anything but belligerent. "The man needs a lesson."

"I won't let him into this flat—ever!" Frau Wallner cried, trembling with anger. "If he comes in, it'll be over my dead body!" She sounded in earnest.

"Please don't worry," Konstantin told her gallantly. "There's still some law and order in this country. After all," he added unnecessarily, "that's one of the things we're fighting for."

Frau Wallner looked dumbfounded for a moment and Elisabeth's lips twisted in an involuntary smile. Whether or not he heard the remark, even Jodler seemed to have interrupted his drumming in astonishment.

"All right, that's it!" he shouted. "I've been patient long enough!"

"Me too," said Konstantin. He strode resolutely down the passage, buttoning up his uniform tunic.

"Please be careful!"

"I will."

"Try to be tactful. Don't provoke him unnecessarily or you'll endanger us all. My God, Konstantin, I don't think you realise what people are capable of in this country."

Konstantin ignored her warning. Going to the door, he opened it wide. Jodler hurtled through the gap like a battering-ram and into Konstantin's waiting arms.

"Steady!" Konstantin said, braking hard. "Not so fast, my friend, unless you're determined to commit suicide."

The officers of the Greater Berlin guard battalion clustered round their commanding officer, Major Remer, as he chatted with his guest, Lieutenant Dr. Hans Hagen.

"A really first-class lecture—edifying, stimulating, topical . . ."

Hagen bowed gratefully. Glancing round, he noted that the other officers appeared to share their C.O.'s opinion. They, too, looked as if they had just passed an instructive afternoon.

While they were still exchanging amicable remarks, Major Remer was called away by his adjutant. "An urgent telephone call, sir. They asked for you personally."

It was 4.15 p.m.

Remer picked up the 'phone and listened. The adjutant, who was standing beside him, saw him turn deathly pale. "Yes, sir," he said, "I understand. At once, sir!" He replaced the receiver gloomily, squared his shoulders and returned to the hall.

"Gentlemen!" he called, injecting a note of command into his harsh voice. "The Fuehrer has been assassinated. The Armed Forces have taken over the government."

There was a shocked and bewildered silence as the officers strove to preserve their martial poise. One or two of them looked aghast, but the majority waited for the inevitable follow-up: an order. Only an order would clarify the situation —until the advent of further orders.

"Operation Valkyrie will now be put into effect," Remer announced. "Our task will be to occupy the government quarter and cordon it off. So much for the first stage of the proceedings. I propose to brief you on your various assignments at once, in so far as you're not already aware of them after the last practice alert."

While Remer was issuing his preliminary orders to an attentive and unquestioning audience, Lieutenant Hagen found himself edged into the background. As he stood there thinking, the memory of what he thought he had seen a couple of hours before flashed through his mind: a retired field marshal driving down Friedrichstrasse in full uniform.

Turning to the officers in his vicinity, Hagen whispered: "Gentlemen, there's something funny going on!"

The man who had been shown into Captain von Brackwede's office exuded a certain mannered elegance. He bowed not only to the captain but, a shade less deferentially, to Corporal Lehmann, who was manifestly delighted.

"I don't think you two gentlemen know each other," said Brackwede. He gestured theatrically at Lehmann. "Allow me to introduce one of my most trusted associates."

The visitor vowed again. "Police President Count Helldorf."

"Corporal 'Pixie' Lehmann," the corporal replied with a grin. "Pleased to meet you."

Helldorf was momentarily taken aback until he heard Brackwede burst out laughing.

"I ought to have been prepared for one of your little jokes, Brackwede," Helldorf said, joining in the laughter as he shook the corporal's hand. "However, I hardly thought that on a day like this . . ."

"A perfect day for a joke," Brackwede interposed. "Tell me, have you taken all the measures we agreed on?"

"We're all ready to go, but I just wanted to check personally that . . ."

"What! Haven't you started yet?" Brackwede spoke with quiet courtesy, but there was a sharp edge to his voice. "Come with me," he said firmly. "You're going to see Stauffenberg at work and have a word with Beck."

Stauffenberg was on the telephone when they reached Olbricht's office.

"Hitler's dead!" he called to Count Helldorf, cupping his hand over the receiver before resuming his conversation.

"That's that, then," Helldorf murmured, looking relieved. He exchanged formal handshakes with the other men in the room while Brackwede hovered impatiently at his elbow.

"What are you waiting for? You must put our prearranged plans into effect straight away."

"I only have to give a code-word."

"Then kindly give it!" Brackwede started to shepherd Helldorf into the office next door, and Helldorf seemed disposed to comply.

At that moment General Beck spoke. His voice sounded calm, assured, impressive. "In the interests of honesty," he said, "I feel we ought to inform Count Helldorf that certain reports which have reached us from Supreme Headquarters suggested that Hitler may not be dead."

Stauffenberg paused in the middle of his telephoning, Hoepner turned away and stared out of the window, and Mertz von Quirnheim looked up from his papers with an air of incredulity, but Olbricht cried passionately: "Keitel's lying—he's lying, I tell you!"

"I can only call it a dispensation of providence," Field Marshal Keitel repeated for the umpteenth time. "Nothing else can possibly account for what happened."

Keitel was conducting the Fuehrer and his guest, Benito Mussolini, to the scene of the disaster. Hitler's Alsatian bitch had been confined to her kennel for the duration of the State visit and was howling piteously.

"It was just like the Front in '14-'18," Hitler reminisced, warming to one of his favourite topics. "I remember when a mine went up and buried me and my men in débris. Today was much the same."

The Duce raised his massive head jerkily and stared at the pile of rubble which had been the conference hut. His once vigorous-looking face resembled a shapeless lump of bleached rubber. Slowly, he picked his way across shattered beams to the spot where, so he was assured, Hitler's chair had been standing.

The Fuehrer did not begrudge Mussolini his sight-seeing tour because it absolved him from the necessity of making conversation. However, he was not destined to enjoy his moment of leisure for long. From behind him, Keitel whispered: "I spoke to Fromm on the telephone. He was extremely uneasy, but I managed to calm him down."

Another whisper, this time from Himmler, on the Fuehrer's right: "Investigations carried out so far seem to point to Colonel Stauffenberg." With suppressed triumph, he added to Keitel: "*Your* Stauffenberg, Field Marshal!"

"He's not *my* Stauffenberg," Keitel parried hastily. "I hardly know the man. Of course, if you're in possession of incontrovertible evidence . . ."

"Not yet, but I shall be soon."

Hitler was becoming restive. He was keenly aware of the conflicting undercurrents of ambition in his immediate circle. He not only tolerated them but encouraged them. Today, however, he found the idea of court intrigue repugnant. He wanted results, and results achieved by a united team.

"The man who brings me the culprit can count on my gratitude and appreciation," he said harshly. "I want him, whoever he is."

Benito Mussolini clambered back over the rubble in the direction of his fellow-dictator and comrade-in-arms. Two specially picked photographers fired off their flash-bulbs reverently, confident that they were capturing an historic moment for posterity. Few subjects could have been more photogenic.

The Duce descended from the pile of rubble and squared his shoulders—click! He advanced on Hitler with arms extended—click! Hitler and Mussolini exchanged a fervent handshake—click! They gazed into each other's eyes, radiant with faith in final victory—click!

And Mussolini, evidently with an eye to such organs of the world press as were still accessible to him, declared—according to the stenographic record: "After seeing this, I am convinced that it was a sign from Heaven!"

"You don't know me, except possibly by name. My name is

Maier. I'm a friend of Count von Brackwede—we have certain interests in common. Were you aware of that?"

"No," replied Julius Leber. It was only a short walk down the corridor from his cell to Maier's subterranean interrogation-room, but his weakened legs and crippled feet were still throbbing from the exertion.

"I know all about you," Maier pursued, waving Leber into a chair which stood ready. "I hope, for your sake, that you know something about me."

"Nothing," Leber said.

The Sturmbannfuehrer betrayed neither disappointment nor exasperation. Although he knew that he was up against one of the toughest nuts in the resistance movement, he had not abandoned hope of cracking the man's shell.

"It's no good trying to hoodwink you, Herr Leber—I realise that. No one has managed to break you down yet, and even I feel no temptation to try my hand. On the contrary, I'm anxious to co-operate with you, just as I do with Count von Brackwede."

There was something impressive about Leber's bulky frame, even now. His body might be twisted in secret pain, but he held his craggy head erect and there was a gleam of sardonic humour in his eye.

"What has happened?" he asked.

"You may have guessed already, Herr Leber," Maier replied suavely.

Julius Leber's sole reaction was to close his eyes. The Sturmbannfuehrer watched him with a twinge of admiration —a sentiment which in his case possessed rarity value. "Would you be prepared to take me into your confidence—provide me with some definite suggestion as to what to do?"

"No," Leber said simply. "Why should I?"

Maier felt as though the walls were closing in on him, but for the moment he saw no means of escape. Leber had with-stood every conceivable form of torture. Not even Inspector Habecker, the most eminent and successful of Gestapo inter-rogation experts, had succeeded in getting the man to talk. Leber's indestructible toughness had been a legend even before the Nazis came to power in 1933. He had more than once battered his way through a knife-wielding mob with a chair-leg, and had routed a gang of brown-shirts single-handed. One of them had died, two lay where they had fallen, severely injured, and the rest had taken to their heels.

"I can't afford to remain aloof," Maier said. "I don't want to sit here doing nothing—can you understand that?"

"Perfectly. You want to jump on the band-wagon."

"Call it what you like." The Sturmbannfuehrer ran a finger round the inside of his collar, which seemed to have become too tight. "I'm ready to make any kind of concession. Just give me something to work on."

"Ask Count von Brackwede."

At that moment Maier awoke fully to the dangers of the game he was playing. Leber knew that if everything went well he would be a free man; if not, he would be no worse off than before. There was no need for him to yield an inch of ground.

The Sturmbannfuehrer's face shone with sweat.

At approximately 4.40 p.m. Lieutenant Dr. Hans Hagen asked Major Remer for a word "in confidence," and the C.O. of the Berlin guard battalion readily consented.

The briefing session was over, the officers were already hurrying back to their men and the first alarm whistles were shrilling in the distance. Major Remer stood facing Hagen in full battle order.

"You bear a grave responsibility, Major," Hagen began tentatively.

"I know."

"I find this business slightly disturbing," Hagen admitted.

"So do I."

So far, unanimity reigned.

"Major," Hagen said, taking the bit between his teeth. "What if we are the victims of a misunderstanding?"

"That would be regrettable. However, an order is an order —and I'm a soldier."

"A National Socialist as well?"

"A National Socialist soldier, an officer of the Fuehrer . . ." Here the major hesitated. He seemed surprised at himself. "But if the Fuehrer no longer . . ."

He came to a full stop, and a look of bewilderment crossed his face. He wanted to display courage, discipline and initiative simultaneously, but was clearly at a loss how to combine the three.

"Major," Hagen suggested, "why don't you allow me to go and see Minister Goebbels. I'm sure he's better informed about this than we are."

"Operation Valkyrie stipulates that I have to take the

Minister for Popular Enlightenment and Propaganda into protective custody—which means in practical terms that I have to arrest him."

"Does that accord with your conscience—your personal convictions?" Lieutenant Hagen demanded fervently. He saw Remer begin to vacillate. "Put a motor-cycle at my disposal and let me clarify the situation for you. Another hour at most, Major, and you'll have a fuller picture."

Remer hesitated. "All right, it can't do any harm. Carry on, Lieutenant."

"Do you mind!" exclaimed Josef Jodler, rebounding off the air force lieutenant who had perversely got in his way. He regarded him with some perplexity. "You're not trying to stop me entering this flat, are you?"

"Yes," Konstantin said resolutely, "I am."

Jodler's eyes wandered to the young officer's Knight's Cross, which could hardly be ignored. It counselled caution, but not surrender. This was a state of emergency, and he had right on his side. Apart from that, he belonged to the élite who determined what methods were to prevail in the Third Reich.

"All right, Lieutenant," he said, as one old soldier to another, "I won't ask you what you're doing here. You obviously have your reasons and I don't begrudge you them, but that doesn't alter the fact that I want access to this flat. Someone killed my old man last night and I've taken over his job."

"I can't help that," Konstantin retorted. "Frau Wallner is the occupant of this flat, and she has asked me not to let anyone in."

"I only want to take a look round and have a little chat with Frau Wallner."

"No!" shouted the trembling woman in the background. "I won't have him in here!"

"Why shouldn't we meet Herr Jodler half-way?" Elisabeth suggested in a conciliatory tone. "There's no reason why he shouldn't take a look round, and he can always have a word with us if he wants to."

"No!" Frau Wallner cried shrilly.

"You won't?" demanded Jodler.

"No!" The black-clad figure with the mane of white hair shuffled off down the passage and disappeared into the kitchen, slamming the door.

"I'm sorry. You heard what she said." Konstantin sounded polite but firm. "I'm afraid you'll have to resign yourself to not coming in."

Elisabeth had also slipped away leaving the two men alone together. Konstantin looked calm, composed and—though he would never have guessed it—surprisingly like his brother.

Jodler felt obliged to strike what he hoped was an emotional but effective note. "I'm acting in the interests of the Party and the State. You've no objection to that I suppose?"

"None whatsoever—that's why I don't want to see you overstep the mark. This is Germany, after all."

"But that's just what I'm trying to tell you, Lieutenant—can't you understand?"

Elisabeth had hurried to her room and was staring round in desperation. Snatching up the bedspread, she threw it over the rumpled bed. Then she picked up the briefcase, which was standing by the window, and hastily concealed it at the bottom of her chest of drawers.

"My God," she said to herself in a breathless, almost inaudible whisper, "the world's gone mad. If only I knew what to do!"

"I'm afraid it's high time we told General Fromm the facts of life," Olbricht said firmly.

Hoepner shrugged. "As long as he doesn't notice what's going on here, why not leave him in peace?"

"We mustn't underestimate Fromm. He has a pretty fair idea of what's afoot but he won't acknowledge it."

Hoepner shrugged again. "That's all right by us, surely?"

"Fromm is anything but a naïve man," Beck put in. "I shouldn't care to have him as an enemy. He has the same sort of cold-bloodedness as Hammerstein without Hammerstein's scruples. The thought of someone like him hovering uncommitted in the background doesn't appeal to me either."

"I suggest we hold a pistol to his head," Brackwede said "—and I don't mean that symbolically! Either he joins us, or . . ."

Beck gave the captain a look of reprimand. "I'm firmly opposed to any methods of that kind."

"The sentiment does you credit, sir," Brackwede replied, unimpressed. "However, you may be making a big mistake. We're not dealing with erring but respectable popular leaders. These people are utterly ruthless. The only way to stop them is by force."

Beck shook his head disapprovingly and Hoepner frowned.

"For all that," Olbricht persisted, "we ought to settle the question of Fromm as quickly as possible."

"Very well," Hoepner said after a pause, "you deal with it."

"I'm quite prepared to," Olbricht rejoined. He turned to Beck. "Would you care to accompany me, General?"

Beck hesitated for a moment. "I'd sooner not intervene until later. For the time being, we must do everything possible to avoid any suggestion of coercion. Fromm must be allowed to decide of his own free will."

Brackwede gave an exclamation of impatience. "With respect, General, this is a pure waste of time, as you'll no doubt discover in due course."

"You may well be right, Brackwede," Olbricht conceded. "On the other hand, it's equally possible that Fromm will react favourably. He's capable of jumping in either direction, which is why we ought to give him the benefit of the doubt."

"Don't expect him to fall into your arms, anyway," said Brackwede. "By all means be prepared to celebrate with him over a bottle of good burgundy, but post a couple of reliable subalterns outside the door—youngsters who aren't easily over-awed, even by a man like Fromm."

"A good idea," Olbricht replied. "What's more, I think it would be better if I didn't approach Fromm alone. I may need a witness—someone to back me up." He looked round the room. "May I ask which of you gentlemen will accompany me?"

"I will—with pleasure!" called Brackwede.

Before anyone else had time to object, Colonel von Stauffenberg sprang to his feet. "No, I'll come with you. I'm the logical person."

Eugen G. hurried towards the main entrance of the Bendler block, dressed in a light summer sports suit. His keen eyes surveyed the exterior of the building carefully, but he could see none of the signs he had been expecting—no bustling figures, no concentration of vehicles of troops. The grey walls seemed to stare back at him with total indifference.

A young captain emerged from a door on the left and came to meet him. His manner was studiously calm and correct. "Can I help you?" he inquired.

The thick-set but athletic figure of the "Doctor" hardly

reached the tall young officer's shoulders. Looking up at him, he said in a low voice: "The password is Homeland."

The captain's expression remained as politely non-committal as before, but his right hand went to his cap in a regulation salute. "Welcome, sir," he said simply. Then, turning to the sentry, he called: "This gentleman can pass."

Eugen G. felt vaguely encouraged. Despite the prevailing air of somnolence, someone in the building seemed to be awake. This impression gained strength as he hurried up the mock-marble steps and along the second-floor corridor. A number of doors stood open, and he could hear animated voices issuing from inside. Little knots of officers stood around, apparently deep in conversation.

"Fritz!" Eugen G. exclaimed joyfully as he caught sight of Brackwede. He hurried towards him. "Fancy running into you, of all people!"

"Good God, man!" cried the captain. "What the devil are you doing here!"

"How are things?" Eugen G. shook Brackwede warmly by the hand. "How far have you got? Is everything going all right?"

Brackwede drew his friend to a window overlooking the inner courtyard of the Bendler block—flagstones, a patch of dusty grass, a solitary vehicle and two men standing motionless side by side—not a hint of hectic revolutionary activity.

"What are you doing here, Eugen?" Brackwede repeated.

Eugen G. dismissed the question. He studied his friend's face with mounting anxiety. "You don't look too happy."

"Happy! I'm extremely annoyed to see you here. Have you been given a job to do—a message to deliver? No, nothing of the sort—but you're here all the same. Why, in God's name?"

"I ask you, Fritz, where else should I be at this time?"

Brackwede flung an arm round Eugen G.'s broad shoulders and hugged him affectionately. Then he held him at arm's length and regarded him with mock severity. "What a strange lot we are, Eugen! God-fearing folk who threw up everything to follow an insane Pied Piper, rabid revolutionaries who still cherish a sentimental attachment to the land of their birth. A man like you ought to be down on his knees praying for us, not trying to join us. Where will it end, my dear fellow, where will it end?"

"Ah, there you are at last, Stauffenberg," said Fromm.

"Fuehrer's Headquarters have been inquiring about you—any idea why?"

Olbricht, who had taken the precaution of posting two officers in the outer office and had sent a third to get a room ready for use as an emergency detention-centre, said: "We've come on a matter of the utmost importance, General."

"That may be your view, Olbricht. It remains to be seen whether I share it." The Commander-in-Chief of Replacement Army sat back and drummed his fingers on the desk. "Well, what's so special—in your opinion?"

"Hitler is dead, and Colonel von Stauffenberg can confirm the fact."

Fromm gave a condescending smile. "Colonel von Stauffenberg must be mistaken," he said deliberately. "I spoke to Field Marshal Keitel on the 'phone a short while ago, as you know, and he assured me that the reverse was true."

"Keitel was lying, as usual," Stauffenberg observed.

The Commander-in-Chief dropped his eyes and fidgeted with a paper-knife, his hands betraying barely controlled agitation. And then, to cap it all, he heard General Olbricht say: "All prearranged measures against internal unrest are already under way. Code-word Valkyrie has been issued."

Fromm flinched as though he had been stung by a bee. His chair crashed to the floor as he leapt to his feet. "This is rank insubordination!" he bellowed furiously, pounding the desk with his fist. "Who had the effrontery to issue such an order?"

Olbricht accepted full responsibiity, but Fromm declared himself dissatisfied with this "gentleman's solution," as he termed it.

"Mertz von Quirnheim put his signature to the order," he shouted. "Tell him to report to me immediately."

Under the circumstances, Fromm felt sure that this was a skilful gambit. Mertz was too cool, calculating and realistic to indulge in a piece of spontaneous stupidity. Almost hopefully, he watched the door.

Mertz von Quirnheim appeared a minute or two later. He returned Fromm's gaze with stoical calm.

"Mertz," said the Commander-in-Chief, "I can't imagine that you would be rash enough to issue orders in my name without consulting me first."

"On this occasion, sir," the colonel replied serenely, "yes."

"I don't believe it—I can't believe it! You wouldn't be such a fool, Mertz!"

"I merely acted in the light of the facts, General, and the salient fact is that Hitler is dead."

"Nonsense!" Fromm burst out. "The creature—I mean, the Fuehrer—is alive! I'm satisfied that he is, and I'll put anyone who refuses to act on that assumption under close arrest, regardless of rank. That applies to all of you!"

Mertz remained unmoved. He merely took a step backwards so that he stood shoulder to shoulder with Olbricht and Stauffenberg. Fromm felt as if he were hemmed in by a human wall.

Stauffenberg said: "I detonated the bomb myself."

Fromm swayed fractionally but recovered himself. "If that is so, Count von Stauffenberg," he said in a harsh voice, "you must shoot yourself at once—you have no alternative. The attempt has failed."

The colonel gave a mocking bow, and a lock of dark hair fell across his high-domed forehead, which was damp with sweat. He brushed it casually aside.

"I hereby declare you under close arrest—all three of you!" Fromm said in a hoarse voice.

"You deceive yourself, General," said Olbricht. "You can't arrest us—we are arresting you."

"You wouldn't dare!" Fromm advanced on Olbricht as though he meant to hurl himself at him, but Stauffenberg stepped between them. The C.-in-C. buried his hands in his Chief of Staff's uniform jacket, only to be thrust aside. He staggered slightly and clung to the desk, shaking with impotent rage.

"You can't do this," he muttered.

"You leave us no choice, General," replied Olbricht. "Please resign yourself to the inevitable and look on this as a purely provisional measure. If your attitude changes in the meantime you have only to let us know."

"You'll regret it!" fumed the C.-in-C.

Stauffenberg opened the door and two officers entered. They invited the Commander-in-Chief, Replacement Army, to accompany them and he complied mechanically.

He was confined in a neighbouring room.

Time: 5.15 p.m.

On the third floor of No. 13 Schifferdamm, Konstantin von Brackwede was having a disconcerting time. Despite his conviction that he had acted correctly, he was not meeting with the approval he had hoped for.

"I don't understand," he said, looking hurt. "I only did what anyone would have done."

"You've put us all in jeopardy," Elisabeth replied bitterly.

She stared out of the open window. Leaden-grey clouds had veiled the sky above Berlin and blotted out the sun, but the air was still as hot and sultry. It was hard to breathe.

"There are a lot of things I don't understand," Konstantin pursued, "but one thing I have learned in the past few days is that it never pays to generalise. Every rule has its exceptions —I realise that now."

Elisabeth walked round to the other side of the little table and leant against the window-frame. She seemed to be avoiding him.

Konstantin sensed that this was more than a physical withdrawal. He longed to see her smile again. "Does it worry you, my being here?"

"It's not that." She glanced at the chest of drawers where she had hidden the briefcase. "We must stop them searching the house, but it won't be easy. We're dealing with the Gestapo. Have you any idea what that means?"

Konstantin smiled confidently. "But the Gestapo are always popping in and out of your office. I know Sturmbannfuehrer Maier personally, and my brother is supposed to be a friend of the head of the Berlin police. There's no reason why we shouldn't have a word with them, is there?"

"Then do it!" Elisabeth urged. "Speak to them at once, before it's too late."

"Everything's back to normal in Zone A, my Fuehrer," Rattenhuber reported eagerly. "The dead have been removed and the wounded hospitalised. The site is being guarded by two of my most reliable men until the special investigation team arrives from Berlin. They should be here at any moment."

"Very well," Bormann told him in a subdued voice. The Fuehrer was meditating and must not be disturbed. He made a gesture of dismissal and Rattenhuber withdrew, looking faintly resentful.

Bormann never let slip any opportunity to reinforce his own position, and the most effective way of doing this was to run down, denigrate or cast suspicion on others. Hitler usually rose like a fish, but he was not, Bormann noted with regret, doing so now.

Pregnant with thought, the Fuehrer sat hunched in his

personal bunker surrounded by a scaled-down version of the amenities he enjoyed in the Berlin Chancellery—capacious arm-chairs, oriental rugs, damask curtains and sombre-hued Flemish paintings in heavy gilt frames.

Various high-ranking dignitaries had gathered in the bunker, among them the lean and taciturn figure of Grand Admiral Doenitz, who had flown to the scene immediately on receiving vague tidings of an attempted assassination. The sight of Hitler virtually uninjured had prompted him to extol God, the Reich and the virtues of unswerving loyalty in moving terms. Now he sat with martial rigidity in a privileged position on the Fuehrer's right, maintaining as pregnant a silence as his supreme war-lord.

Reich Marshal Goering, who had been fortifying himself with alcohol, improved the shining hour by embarking on a lengthy tirade against the army. "Those army generals are in this up to their lily-white necks, take it from me!"

Keitel, himself a soldier, did not make any immediate response. He glanced at Hitler, but the Fuehrer still sat huddled in his chair.

"On this point," said Grand Admiral Doenitz, abruptly coming to life, "I second the opinion of the Reich Marshal. The Army has indeed failed to come up to expectations, but the Air Force has also failed—and lamentably so."

"I utterly reject that!" snapped Goering. "It's a complete generalisation."

"It also happens to be my opinion, and I stand by it," Doenitz said with restraint. Having clearly implied: "Only the Navy . . ." he looked hopefully at the Fuehrer.

Hitler, however, remained as silent as before. Opposite him sat Benito Mussolini, now scarcely more than the Gauleiter of Lombardy, looking like a time-worn effigy of his former self. He had carefully refrained from joining in the heated discussion, and no one spared him a glance.

Keitel looked conciliatory, Bormann and Himmler whispered in the background, Goering drained his glass and refilled it at once. Suddenly, Foreign Minister Ribbentrop leant forward.

"To me," he observed with unwonted boldness, "the Grand Admiral's views seem to carry a certain amount of weight."

"Shut your damned mouth, you dirty little champagne salesman!" Goering roared.

Ribbentrop relapsed into aggrieved silence. The Duce pretended to count the flowers on the patterned carpet. The Fuehrer, whose hearing seemed to have suffered as a result of the explosion, still remained disconcertingly mute.

Martin Bormann decided that it was time to jolt Hitler out of his reverie, a lethargic state of mind which was partly attributable to the fact that he had missed his afternoon rest. Leaning forward, he said deliberately: " This revolt—if it really is one—reminds me of nineteen-thirty-four."

This was a shrewd reference to the year in which Ernst Roehm, the SA Chief of Staff, had tried to engineer a putsch against Hitler. He and his supporters and a number of other troublesome individuals had been liquidated at Hitler's personal behest. Goering and Himmler had handled most of the dirty work with considerable efficiency.

Bormann's bolt went home. Hatred bubbled up in Hitler like a mountain spring. " I'll exterminate them—the whole brood of them!" he gurgled. " They'll die like the rats they are!"

He stumbled across the room to Himmler. " Shoot them!" he screamed. " Shoot anyone who had anything to do with it!"

" Well, how goes it?" Sturmbannfuehrer Maier inquired pleasantly. " What do you think, my dear fellow—are your people going to pull it off?"

Brackwede looked optimistic. " We've certainly got away to a good start—not, of course, that we can't use all the help we can get."

They were sitting in a corner of the Café Roehr, ten minutes from the Bendlerstrasse. No one appeared to be taking any notice of them.

" You don't feel that the whole project is doomed, then?" The Sturmbannfuehrer paused for a moment, then added: " No, of course you don't. Knowing you, I don't suppose you'd deliberately back a loser."

To Maier, the main thing was that they were not only " in business," but conducting it on semi-neutral territory. If the revolt failed, nobody would be able to prove that he had visited the Bendlerstrasse at this inauspicious juncture.

" All right, let's get down to cases," Brackwede said. " You want to cover yourself and I intend to make the most of the fact, so let's proceed stage by stage. To begin with, I want to be kept up to date on planned counter-measures."

"All right," replied Maier, "here's my first offering: Standartenfuehrer Piffraeder will be turning up at the Bendlerstrasse within the next half-hour—for the moment without any specific instructions. He's merely been told to nose around a bit."

"Good," said Brackwede. "That's not bad for a start. Your next job will be to make available certain detainees whom we may need urgently."

"Julius Leber, for instance?"

Brackwede blinked at the speed of Maier's reaction. "We can go into personalities later," he said quickly. "For the time being, all I want is your agreement in principle."

"Granted—subject to one proviso."

"I know. If things go wrong, the matter was never raised and you'll take full advantage of everything I've told you. All right, I accept that. To use the language of your trade, I'm risking my neck."

"Not only that," Maier told him, unabashed. "You'll have to take it for granted that I'll put you through the mangle—you and your whole crowd."

Lieutenant von Brackwede descended the stairs of No. 13 Schifferdamm, dressed in his uniform, and asked to speak to the "man in charge." He was directed to Voglbronner.

"I've come to lodge a complaint," he said briskly. "I take strong exception to the behaviour of Herr Jodler, who claims to be acting on higher authority—presumably yours."

"I'm sincerely sorry to hear that," Voglbronner assured him, "—always provided that your complaint is justified."

The Gestapo official gave vent to some fashionable clichés, e.g., one had to take the rough with the smooth, there was a shortage of well-trained personnel, this was war-time, and, finally, willing co-operation with the authorities was a mark of confidence in the rulers of the Third Reich. "I trust you share that confidence, Lieutenant?"

"I do," Konstantin declared promptly. "That's just why I object to methods of this kind."

Voglbronner felt certain that his first impression had been correct. The young man was an unadulterated idealist and, as such, to be handled with kid-gloves. "What was your name again?" he inquired evasively.

"I'm sorry, I forgot to introduce myself." Konstantin stated his name and rank.

"Brackwede?" Voglbronner feigned surprise. "I know a captain of that name. He used to be Deputy Police President of Berlin."

"My brother," Konstantin said proudly.

Voglbronner rose. Making his way round the table behind which he had entrenched himself, he proffered his hand. "Why didn't you say so straight away!"

Further demonstrations of goodwill were drowned by a noise like an avalanche rumbling down the stairs. A moment later the door burst open to reveal Scharfuehrer Jodler, purple in the face with triumph.

"I caught him!" he announced. "He was trying to sneak into a cupboard, but I'm an old hand at that sort of game. I can smell 'em a mile off!"

Voglbronner frowned. "What are you talking about?"

"A Jew!" Jodler trumpeted. "A dirty Jewish swine! That Wallner woman had him hidden in her flat. Now I know why the old bitch wouldn't let me in!" The Scharfuehrer gazed about him like a victorious general. "It speaks for itself, doesn't it?"

"This alters the whole picture, of course," Voglbronner said. "It's hard to say what the repercussions will be, but I'll tell you this much: they could be considerable!"

When Captain von Brackwede re-entered the Bendler block on his return from the Café Roehr he was met by Lieutenant Herbert. The lieutenant, who appeared to have been lying in wait for him, wore a solemn expression.

"Captain von Brackwede," he began in well-rehearsed tones, "I'm in a quandary."

"Really?" replied Brackwede, who was itching to get back to Stauffenberg, "What sort of quandary?"

"If the report of the Fuehrer's death is true . . ."

"You can take that for granted. What then?"

"In that case, I intend to act accordingly." Herbert seemed to sense the imminence, or at least the likelihood, of a momentous decision. He gave a rapid conspiratorial glance round but no one appeared to be listening. Then he pointed to the eagle and swastika on his chest. "I'm prepared to rip that off, and so are one or two of my friends, if you think it's advisable."

"My advice is to wait and see."

"But what do you really think?" Herbert insisted. "I mean, do you think it would pay? Is it time to decide now? I trust your judgment implicitly, Captain."

"An unmerited honour," Brackwede observed dryly.

"What ought we to do—I and my friends, I mean?" Herbert shot Brackwede a look of entreaty. "We'd welcome any suggestion."

"Keep out of the line of fire," recommended Brackwede. "That's the best advice I can give you and your kind. If the Fuehrer's alive, doing nothing now may turn out to be as good as having done a great deal. If he's dead, you can always pin your faith on God—and the big battalions, of course."

He hurried upstairs to see Stauffenberg, leaving Herbert free to return to the small group of like-minded individuals who had nervously congregated in his office.

"Everything's still in the air," he announced. "Captain von Brackwede says so, and he should know. I suggest we wait and see—unless anyone's got a better idea?"

"I think we ought to cover ourselves."

The speaker was a major named Heythe, who regardetd himself as a person of some importance and had taken umbrage at the fact that he had not been initiated into the conspiracy.

Three other officers had assembled in Herbert's room apart from Heythe, and not solely on account of the lieutenant's ample stocks of liquor. One, a former Hitler Youth leader, had been driven there by political conviction, another was a lieutenant employed in Major Heythe's department and the third was a member of Molly Ziesemann's intimate circle and the Nazi Party.

"I'm naturally in favour of covering ourselves," Herbert agreed. "The question is, how?"

"We must get hold of some arms," said Heythe.

The officer who was also a Party member looked bewildered. "For use against whom?"

"An ill-phrased question," Major Heythe amended poitely. "We need them for a specific purpose. Its exact nature still remains to be determined, but the important thing is to be prepared."

"Quite right," agreed the former Hitler Youth leader. "Service revolvers won't be much use if it comes to a show-down. We need something that packs a heavier punch."

"There's masses of stuff in the Berlin armoury," Heythe said knowledgeably. "All we have to do is indent for it, and I suggest we do so at once."

"I second that!" cried Herbert. "Let's not stand around

doing nothing. We must show people they can rely on us—in every respect."

Major Heythe nodded approvingly and reached for the telephone. Glancing at his watch, Herbert saw that it was 5.15 p.m.

"There's a man called Piffraeder on his way up," one of Lehmann's watchdogs announced over the guardroom 'phone, "—a real live SS brass-hat in full uniform."

Lehmann passed the information to Brackwede, who nodded. "Have him shown into Colonel von Stauffenberg's office."

Brackwede hurried downstairs to the first floor. More than a dozen people had congregated in Olbricht's office, among them Eugen G., who was sitting in the general's chair. No one seemed very talkative.

"Still bright and cheery?" Brackwede inquired.

"Just waiting," Eugen G. replied.

There was a newspaper lying on the desk in front of him. Intrigued by the slight bulge in it, Brackwede picked it up, to reveal a cocked automatic with the safety catch on.

"Does this hardware belong to you, Eugen?"

"Naturally."

"Congratulations!" exclaimed Brackwede. "Person manqué complete with automatic pistol—quite a sight!"

Eugen G. grinned. "What could be more fashionable?"

Brackwede slapped him on the back and walked into the outer office, where Stauffenberg was still telephoning.

"There's a visitor for you, Claus. Standartenfuehrer Piffraeder will be knocking on your door at any moment."

"Who's he and what does he want?"

"You don't know Piffraeder? He's one of the most successful men in his field—got about two hundred thousand Jews to his credit in the Balkans alone. As to your second point—I don't think he's been given any precise instructions. He'll probably try to sound you out."

Stauffenberg made a grimace of repugnance. "What do you expect me to do with him?" he demanded.

"Shooting would be as good an idea as any."

"I know how you feel, Fritz," Stauffenberg said quietly. "We've decided on an extreme course and I realise that half-measures are undesirable. However, I can't follow your advice, if only for General Beck's sake."

"In that case, don't worry about it. Leave that sort of thing to me. One of us has to do the dirty work. This isn't

196

a drawing-room squabble, Claus—it's a matter of life or death for millions of people, not just us."

"No," Stauffenberg said gently. "I like and respect you far too much to allow that. It's quite enough that I have blood on my hands."

Meanwhile, SS-Standartenfuehrer Piffraeder had arrived in the ante-room leading to the Commander-in-Chief's office. He was there, as he stressed with lofty condescension, on behalf of Reichsfuehrer Himmler. Three young officers—Kleist, Fritsche and Hammerstein—encircled him with expressions of polite but watchful interest. Not that the Standartenfuehrer was aware of it, their job was to arrest him if it became necessary.

Almost at once, Colonel von Stauffenberg appeared in the doorway. "What do you want?" he asked curtly.

"Merely to ask you a few questions, Colonel."

"Permission refused."

"Your refusal may have grave consequences."

"Not for me, Herr Piffraeder."

"But I insist."

Piffraeder, Germanically blond and blue-eyed, stood there looking stern, self-assured and toughly virile, like a cartoonist's impression of an SS leader.

"You are under arrest," said Stauffenberg.

"Piffraeder and Fromm make two," Lieutenant von Hammerstein remarked to his fellow-subalterns. "It looks as if number three's on his way."

General von Kortzfleisch, commander of the Berlin garrison, was a man who believed that National Socialism and loyalty to the Fuehrer were fundamental to the German character. He arrived at the Bendlerstrasse a prey to the gravest misgivings.

Having asked for Fromm, he was conducted instead to Olbricht's office, where the first person he caught sight of was General Beck.

"I demand an explanation of what is going on here," he said, planting his legs firmly apart.

"There has been a complete change in the political situation," Beck replied. As one officer to another, he added: "We all know you to be a good, reliable soldier, Kortzfleisch. You must be prepared to do your duty like a man."

Kortzfleisch dismissed the implication. "I swore an oath and I intend to keep it."

"An oath of allegiance sworn to a man who has broken his own word is not binding."

"I'm unaware of any evidence to warrant such a statement," Kortzfleisch declared, edging backwards. "Quite apart from that, I'm satisfied that you're making a disastrous, if not criminal, blunder. General Fromm is still my immediate superior. I take my orders from him alone."

"I appeal to your conscience, General!"

For a moment Kortzfleisch seemed to waver, and a look of indecision flitted across his face. He had never served under Beck but he was familiar with the general's almost legendary reputation, which painted him as the reincarnation of Schlieffen and Moltke combined. As against this, there was Adolf Hitler, who had frequently favoured him with tokens of his goodwill.

"No," he said.

Beck turned away with a look of distress, leaving the decision to Stauffenberg.

"Arrest him!" he ordered.

"Number three," murmured Lieutenant von Hammerstein.

"It's a start," said Brackwede, who was quickly informed of the incident. "But only a start," he added.

Voglbronner had now reached a point where he could afford to sit back, leave things in the air, make no firm commitments, devise as many loopholes as possible. He donned an air of profound meditation to conceal the fact that he was playing for time.

"I've shut the Jew up in the cellar for the moment," Jodler reported happily, secure in the knowledge that he had earned universal esteem.

The Jew was a fact which had to be accepted, as Voglbronner was well aware. The Jew himself was done for—there was no doubt about that—but what inferences could be drawn from his presence in the house?

"It's nothing to do with me," Konstantin said stiffly.

Although this was merely an assertion, any assertion made by a von Brackwede merited more than passing notice. Voglbronner was already juggling with at least two balls at once, but he could perform far more elaborate tricks when need arose.

"The Wallner woman's under surveillance," Jodler continued. "I've told the schoolmaster, Party Member Scheumer, not to let the old bitch out of his sight."

"I sincerely hope that my fiancée, Countess Oldenburg,

hasn't been subjected to any inconvenience," Konstantin said with barely suppressed anger.

Jodler grinned. "Well, what do you know! So she's your fiancée, is she? I aways thought your brother had a finger in her little pie!"

"Kindly keep your foul insinuations to yourself!" Konstantin shouted furiously. He gave Jodler a withering glance and turned to Voglbronner. "I trust you'll put a stop to remarks of that sort."

Voglbronner busied himself with his notes for some time before looking up.

"Don't let me detain you gentlemen," he said impassively. "I propose to continue my investigations."

When Konstantin and Jodler had left the room, Voglbronner picked up the telephone and called the Prinz Albrecht-strasse. Sturmbannfuehrer Maier, who seemed to have nothing better to do than wait for telephone calls, answered promptly.

Voglbronner reported that he had been summoned to No. 13 Schifferdamm on a purely routine case, presumed to be murder. Among those directly or indirectly concerned were a Party functionary, an SS N.C.O. and an air force officer. The presence of military personnel was the sole reason why their department had been called in. So far, so good, but . . .

"But then I discovered that the air force officer was Lieutenant von Brackwede—the captain's brother. What would you like me to do with him?"

"Can you pin anything on him?" Maier asked.

"A couple of things, if necessary." Voglbronner went on to explain that Lieutenant von Brackwede had laid himself open to a possible charge of complicity, since he had spent the entire night with his alleged fiancée, Countess Oldenburg, under the same roof as a Jewish refugee. "We might make something out of that, sir, if you want to."

"Keep things on the boil," Maier ordained after a short pause. "But avoid complications at all costs. Simmer the stew but don't burn it—get me?"

"Yes, sir," replied Voglbronner.

The only thing he had " got " was that Maier had passed the buck to him yet again. Worse still, he had no idea what to do with it.

It was 5.25 p.m.

Lieutenant Dr. Hans Hagen had reached the Ministry of Popular Enlightenment and Propaganda and succeeded in penetrating as far as Goebbels's ante-room. He cleared this hurdle too, by insisting that he had come on a matter of the highest moment.

Naumann, Goebbels's Secretary of State, knew Hagen's reputation for reliability. He also knew his Minister's predilection for useful contacts. Barely a quarter of an hour elapsed before Hagen was admitted to Goebbels's presence.

"Well, my dear Dr. Hagen, and what brings you here?" Goebbels inquired with an affable smile. He was dressed in a well-worn but tasteful lounge suit tailored in choice English cloth—pearl-grey with a fine blue dot. "Out with it!"

"I gave a lecture to the Greater Berlin guard battalion this afternoon," the lieutenant began, hurriedly but with characteristic attention to detail. "Just after I'd finished, a Valkyrie alert was announced."

Goebbels sat hunched behind his desk like a dwarf on a throne, his manner conveying that he always had time to spare for fellow-believers. He had pulled a pad towards him and was, as usual, making notes.

"The government quarter is being sealed off by the guard battalion at this very minute," Hagen announced.

Goebbels seemed to freeze for a fraction of a second. "But that's impossible!"

Hagen gazed at the Minister with awe. He relished seeing the great man so impressed, but it would have been rash to savour the moment too long. "The troops have been issued with their orders," he continued hastily. "In default of effective counter-orders, it must be assumed that they will carry them out."

Goebbels flinched at this revelation as though he had been kicked. Throwing down his pencil and pushing the note-pad aside, he rose abruptly to his feet and limped to the window like a mechanical doll.

Looking out, he saw a convoy of trucks packed with heavily armed soldiers moving down the street. An armoured car rolled past, its gun-barrel swaying menacingly. To Goebbels, it was almost as if the gunner were aiming at him. Involuntarily, he recoiled a step.

A dull roar of engines rose to the overcast sky as the vehicles filed past No. 20 Hermann Goering Strasse. The fact that Goebbels's official residence should be located in a street which bore the name of the "rubber lion," as the fat Reich Marshal was secretly christened, had often moved the Propaganda Minister to ironic mirth. Now, however, his professional smile seemed to have been extinguished like a torch. He stood there in silence for several seconds.

Then he asked: "What sort of man is this Major Remer?"

"Reliable, I'd say," Hagen replied. "The Major is a good National Socialist—I'm convinced of it."

"Fetch him here," Goebbels decreed. "Tell him to come and see me at once. I want a word with him.'

"Take a look at those." Lieutenant Roehrig of the Bendlerstrasse communications centre pushed a bunch of teleprinter messages across to his sergeant-major. "What do you make of them?"

"They're top priority."

"I know that—everything seems to be top priority at the moment." The lieutenant tapped two or three lines of text with his forefinger. "But I'm beginning to wonder more and more what sort of stuff we're sending out of here."

"The contents of messages isn't our business, is it?" the sergeant-major observed cautiously.

"Not in the normal way," Roehrig conceded, "but this is different. Take a look at what's written here and tell me if you don't agree."

The sergeant-major read:

To Command H.Q.s i-xiii, xvii, xviii, xx, xxi, Gen. Gov. Bohemia-Moravia.

. . . *all Gauleiters, Reich governors, ministers, police commissioners, senior SS and police officers, Gestapo and SS departmental heads, heads of propaganda bureaux and district administrators to be removed from their posts forthwith and placed in solitary confinement.*

"Well," said the sergeant-major, "that sounds a bit rich, I must say."

"Read on!" urged Lieutenant Roehrig. "Read this bit here!" He pointed to a passage which ran:

Units of the Armed SS whose unqualified compliance is in doubt are to be disarmed at all costs. Vigorous action must be undertaken in overwhelming strength so as to prevent major bloodshed.

Now it was the sergeant-major's turn to look worried.

"That's going too far! It gives me the shudders to think of it, but what can we do?"

"These orders are supposed to be signed by General Fromm and Colonel von Stauffenberg, but Fromm hasn't answered his 'phone for nearly an hour. Whenever anyone asks for him, Stauffenberg takes the call."

The basement rooms were filled with the incessant chatter of teleprinters and the harried voices of female telephone operators as they struggled to keep pace with demand. The muted bells on their switchboards never stopped ringing.

"Maybe we ought to tap one or two lines," hazarded the sergeant-major.

"Which ones do you suggest?"

"Stauffenberg's, Olbricht's and Mertz's, for a start."

"An excellent idea," Roehrig agreed. He sounded relieved that the sergeant-major had followed his train of thought so readily. "See to it, would you?"

"What about these teleprinter messages here?"

"They can wait a while, in spite of their priority rating. I'll have to check them carefully first, and that's going to take me some time—hours, maybe. What do you think?"

"I'm with you all the way, Lieutenant. It's a pity there isn't someone we could have a quiet chat to, though."

"Don't worry," Roehrig said optimistically. "We're doing the right thing—being methodical and not rushing into anything blindly. That's all we can do for the moment."

Lehmann's private army was going into action with increasing rapidity. The corridor scout told of cautious gatherings of officers, Fromm's batman reported on the incarceration of his general, and the man in the ground-floor guardroom criticised the lax way in which entries and exits were being checked.

The corporal transmitted all these reports to Captain von Brackwede. "This place needs tightening up."

"No doubt," Brackwede replied, "but errors and omissions are inevitable."

"Herbert's mob are spending their whole time on the 'phone to the armoury," Lehmann went on. "They've indented for arms."

"Good, they may come in handy."

"The indent has been approved already."

"Never mind, it'll be hours before the consignment arrives, judging by past experience." Brackwede was right. Four hours were to elapse before it did. "Any news of Fromm?"

"Yes, hot from the press." Lehmann grinned. "The General has asked to be allowed to go to his private quarters."

"It doesn't really matter where he goes, provided he's kept on ice."

"He's promised to behave like a good boy—even gave his word of honour."

"I don't like the sound of that. You can't play games with a man like Fromm. His word of honour may just be a blind. It won't prevent him from trying to dish us at the first opportunity. I'd better go and see Stauffenberg straight away."

"Bear one thing in mind while you're about it," advised Lehmann. "This building's riddled with emergency exists and Fromm probably knows them like the back of his hand. There's only one person who knows the geography of the place better, and that's Lieutenant von Hammerstein. His old man used to live here when he was C.-in-C. The lieutenant was only a boy, but boys are fond of exploring."

"Thanks for the hint. Anything else?"

"Yes, double up the guard on the gate. There's only an officer wandering around there at the moment, and the rest are half asleep. This place is like a bleeding hen-coop, with everyone popping in and out just as they please. I always thought you were going to pull up the draw-bridge when the time came."

"I expect action—swift and ruthess action!"

Hitler's instructions travelled via Himmler to Kaltenbrunner and from Kaltenbrunner to Mueller.

SS-Obergruppenfuehrer Heinrich Mueller, head of the Gestapo, originally hailed from the German C.I.D. and had once been an acknowledged expert on crimes of violence. He now devoted his energies, as he had done for the past ten years, to the detention and extermination of so-called "antiState elements."

"The Fuehrer demands that the swine should be apprehended," Kaltenbrunner told him. "Put your best men on to it straight away."

"Leave it to me!" Mueller promised.

Mueller was a master of his profession, and the honorific nickname "Corpse" Mueller owed nothing to dramatic exaggeration. He was a punctilious accountant of death. The immediate impression he gave was of a conscientious and unassuming civil servant who occasionally indulged in modest jokes, but nothing could have been further from the truth.

Many had paid for such a misapprehension with their lives, including some of his own associates.

Mueller knew precisely where to apply pressure. He summoned the man who had been semi-officially entrusted with keeping an eye on the armed forces—Sturmbannfuehrer Maier —and read him the riot act.

" There's been some dirty work, Maier, and from the sound of it you're completely out of touch. One or two of those military gentlemen you've been keeping under such close surveillance have obviously been plotting to their hearts' content. What have you got to say for yourself?"

" I did hear a few vague rumours . . ."

" What! And you stand there doing nothing? Put a squib under your people and get cracking yourself. The Fuehrer wants results and so do I—in double-quick time."

" Certainly, sir," Maier said with outward humility. He had delivered too many similar pep-talks in his time not to admire Mueller's technique.

The Gestapo chief wasted no further thought on his subordinate. Maier would come to heel all right. Picking up the 'phone, he asked for the State Security Service.

" Where's SS-Hauptsturmfuehrer Skorzeny?"

" On the train to Vienna."

" Then intercept him. He's to report to Berlin at once—to the head of the Reich Security Bureau. That's right, Kaltenbrunner wants him in person. Yes, man—stop the train. I don't care if the time-table does go up the spout. That's an order from the Fuehrer—and me."

Next on Heinrich Mueller's list was Count Helldorf. Without preamble, he instructed the Police President to note the following points: one, a military putsch appeared to be in progress: two, the Fuehrer was in good health; three, until further notice, police headquarters were directly subordinated to the Central State Security Bureau; four, Helldorf would therefore take his orders only from Kaltenbrunner or Mueller himself, who would be representing Kaltenbrunner while he was at the Fuehrer's Headquarters; and, five, SS units were already converging on Berlin.

Not all this information was strictly accurate, but this was a matter of total indifference to SS-Obergruppenfuehrer Mueller. He was solely concerned with the effect of his words, nor was he disappointed. Count Helldorf gulped several times and seemed to be at a loss for words. The Gestapo chief gave a satisfied smirk.

At length Helldorf said: "I have heard quite a different story . . ."

"From whom, may I ask?" Mueller snapped. "Are you in receipt of orders which conflict with what I've just told you? No? Very well! I sincerely hope you won't give credence to wild and subversive rumours. If in doubt, be guided by me. Any other course would be most unwise. I could only conclude that you'd suddenly grown tired of living, but that seems improbable. After all, who'd look after your harem?"

Situated in the Hotel Majestic in the Avenue Kléber, Paris, were the headquarters of the Military Governor of France, General of Infantry Karl Heinrich von Stuelpnagel, a man with the sharp features of a fighting soldier and eyes which normally regarded the world with paternal benevolence.

"I've spoken to Stauffenberg in person," reported Air Force Lieutenant-Colonel Caesar von Hofacker. "All prearranged measures have been initiated in Berlin." With evident satisfaction, he added: "We seem to have a head start on them. General von Boineburg-Lengsfeld has already sent troops to take over all the SS, Gestapo and SD establishments in our area."

An almost imperceptible nod indicated that General von Stuelpnagel accepted this news as a matter of course. He had issued the order to arrest and detain the SS without hesitation.

"Any resistance must be overcome by force, Hofacker. Summary courts martial are to be set up, as planned."

Stuelpnagel was fully in control of the situation in Paris. Every unit under his command could be relied upon and numerous members of his staff were lending him their unqualified support, but his expression as he surveyed his fellow-conspirators was pensive.

"I spoke to General Beck on the telephone," he announced. "I assured him that he could rely on us to play our part to the full. However, when he inquired about Field Marshal von Kluge I couldn't give him a definite answer."

"The Field Marshal can't stand aside any longer," Hofacker said briskly. "This die is cast now, and Kluge knows that the ultimate decision rests with him. One direct order from Kluge and the armies in the West will join us, followed by the rest of the armed forces."

"General Beck shares your view," Stuelpnagel observed thoughtfully.

"Then he must speak to Kluge himself."

"That's what I told him."

"And did he?" Hofacker's tense face glowed with excitement. "What luck did he have, General?"

Stuelpnagel looked vaguely resentful. "I don't know. All I know is that Field Marshal von Kluge has instructed me to report to Army Group H.Q. at eight this evening with my Chief of Staff—i.e., you, Hofacker—for an important conference."

"That sounds fairly hopeful," Hofacker said cheerfully, "typical of Kluge, too. He doesn't say yes or no—just postpones the decision. Still, it's only for a few hours."

"What if Kluge does say no?" someone inquired.

Stuelpnagel made no response. He merely glanced at Hofacker, who said with infectious optimism: "The Field Marshal is an exceedingly cautious man, I know—circumstances have made him so—but he's also capable of clear and rational thought. He'll be guided by the realities of the situation."

"What if the right realities don't materialise?"

"Then we must create them!" Hofacker cried. "If he refuses to act unless he's handed the facts on a plate, that's what we'll give him. If Hitler's assassination isn't good enough, we'll present him with all the Party, SS and Gestapo officials we can lay our hands on. That ought to convince him!"

"Well, how did you get on?" Elisabeth demanded anxiously, when Konstantin returned. "Are they going to leave us alone?"

"I hope so. The official I spoke to seemed a pretty reasonable type." He sat down on a chair near the door. "The situation's rather complicated, of course."

"You mean they may search the flat after all—this room included?"

"I doubt it."

"Is it out of the question?"

"No, I wouldn't say that, but you mustn't worry. I'm pretty positive the man in charge won't allow any miscarriage of justice. I told you—he seems a decent sort."

"They often do!" Elisabeth said bitterly. "They look the soul of kindness, even when they're reaching for their guns." She was standing by the window drawing in deep breaths of the sultry air. The undiminished heat of the late afternoon oppressed her.

"You mean—this business with the Jew?"

"Yes!" she said with sudden vehemence. "They treated him like an animal."

Konstantin looked distressed. "I'm afraid people exceed their authority sometimes. I'll lodge a complaint."

"Shut up!" Elisabeth snapped. "Don't talk so glibly about things you're totally ignorant of. Ask your brother about the Gestapo."

"All right, I will," Konstantin replied soothingly. He went over and tried to put his arms round her, but she eluded him.

"And the briefcase?" she asked. "What about the briefcase!"

Konstantin frowned as he tried, unsuccessfully, to follow her train of thought. "I don't see what it's got to do with us. My brother asked me to keep it for him—that's all there is to it."

"What if the Gestapo come to search the room and insist on taking the briefcase away with them?"

"But that's absurd, Elisabeth."

"No, I'm afraid it isn't. They're bound to take an interest in it, and if they got an inkling of its contents wild horses wouldn't hold them—believe me, Konstantin!"

"What's the matter with Doeberitz?" Stauffenberg demanded impatiently. "Why don't they answer?"

"I'm just checking," replied Mertz von Quirnheim.

Brackwede pricked up his ears. He had been putting his head round the door every half-hour or so to see how things were progressing. Normally, he retired again without disturbing his friends, but this time he lingered.

"I thought we had a particularly reliable man in charge at Doeberitz."

"Three," replied Stauffenberg, interrupting his telephone warfare long enough to accept a cigar from Brackwede.

"Haven't the radio stations been occupied yet?" Brackwede inquired as he held a match for him. Being familiar with Operation Valkyrie, he knew that the School of Infantry at Doeberitz had been given one of the day's most vital assignments. Reliable troops from the school were to have taken over the Masurenallee Building and the Deutschlandsender at Koenigswusterhausen, undamaged and ready to broadcast.

"Nothing's happened so far," Stauffenberg said with a frown of annoyance.

Further conversation was interrupted by the appearance of General Hoepner, who had since changed into his uniform in one of the wash-rooms on the half-landing. Brackwede eyed him with gratified surprise. Contrary to his expectations, the man still exuded a certain martial magnificence.

" Fromm is pestering us every two minutes," Hoepner complained. " He's asking for food now."

" What's that?" exclaimed Brackwede. " What does he think we're doing—reorganising the mess catering?"

General Hoepner refrained from descending to the pugnacious captain's level. His manner clearly conveyed that he intended to negotiate with Stauffenberg alone. " Beck, Olbricht and I are of the opinion that Fromm should be treated with the courtesy due to his rank. He ought to be allowed some sandwiches and a bottle of wine."

" Why fatten him up?" Brackwede demanded grimly. " We're running a military revolt, not a meal-service."

" Please do as you think fit, General," Stauffenberg said curtly. With a slight look of irritation, he added under his breath: " We've got more important things to worry about at the moment." He glanced across at Mertz von Quirnheim. " Well?"

" General Hitzfeld, the School Commandant, is attending a family funeral in Baden," Mertz reported.

" Today of all days!" groaned Brackwede.

" No need to worry," Stauffenberg said briskly. " There's always his second-in-command, Colonel Mueller. He's one of us, too. What about him?"

" Colonel Mueller is also away," Mertz replied. " He's giving a series of lectures in the neighbourhood and won't be back until about eight-thirty."

" That's late, by God," Brackwede interjected, " —far too late."

" Our third man at Doeberitz is the adjutant. He informs me that the troops are standing-to and ready to move off, but the officers are divided among themselves. They've discussed the situation and decided by a majority vote to hold fire for the time being."

The so-called " General Order " or proclamation of martial law was not sent down to the Bendlerstrasse communications centre until about 6 p.m.

Although a rough draft of this all-important document had existed in the Valkyrie file for some time, it had taken hours to produce the final version. Margarethe von Owen and Erika von Tresckow, the wife of the general, had been working on it without a break, filling the C.-in-C.'s ante-room with the unceasing clatter of their typewriters.

Carefully edited, corrected and adorned with linguistic refinements, the General Order percolated to the communications centre, where it inevitably fell into the hands of Lieutenant Roehrig.

"They're getting more and more outspoken upstairs," Roehrig observed to the Signals Corps sergeant-major. "I really don't think I can pass this stuff for transmission."

"Perhaps we ought to make a few alterations," the sergeant-major suggested casually. He had not only grasped the lieutenant's drift from the start but had joined in without hesitation. If things went wrong, Roehrig would bear full responsibility. If not, he, the sergeant-major, would share the jack-pot.

By now, Roehrig and his sergeant-major were as well-informed as anyone in the Bendlerstrasse. They tapped Stauffenberg's and Mertz's 'phones, blocked incoming calls and either garbled the messages that were passed to them or simply ignored them—at least provisionally. Their record delay to date stood at two hundred and twenty minutes.

"We ought to get in touch with a few people ourselves," mused Roehrig. "What about going over to the offensive?"

The idea grew on them. Being aware of SS-Sturmbannfuehrer Maier's function in life, they tried to contact him by 'phone but were politely informed by his aide that the Sturmbannfuehrer had been summoned away on a matter of extreme importance.

"How about getting in touch with the State Security Bureau direct?" ventured the sergeant-major. "You could ask to speak to Kaltenbrunner or Mueller in person."

"Not for the moment," Roehrig replied cautiously. "I don't think we've reached that stage yet."

As he spoke, a colonel named Hassel was standing around idly on the second floor. Hassel, who was a staunch member of the resistance, had reported to Olbricht promptly, only to be informed that the situation was still "fluid." Everything was going according to plan, but for the moment it was a question of waiting, being patient and keeping one's nerve.

Colonel Hassel happened to be one of the leading signals experts in the German Army. He was also a man of integrity, determination and ingenuity, but he stood around idly, only two floors from the communications centre where he might have done invaluable service.

After chatting to a few officers and being puzzled by their apparent uneasiness and indecision, he paid another visit to Olbricht's office. For some moments he stood in the doorway, noting the hectic activity that prevailed inside, but no one paid any attention to him.

So, with a shrug, he left the building and drove home.

Shortly after 6 p.m. Lehmann's corridor scout reported that there were three generals in the C.-in-C.'s outer office.

Lehmann informed Captain von Brackwede, who greeted the news with raised eyebrows.

"What do they want?"

"They're carrying briefcases and they want to see General Fromm. They say that he's expecting them."

Brackwede hurried off to the nerve-centre of the revolt and surveyed the scene keenly. The two colonels were still telephoning, the generals conferring and the other members of the group standing about, talking in subdued voices.

Brackwede sat down on the chair in front of Stauffenberg's desk, and Stauffenberg beckoned his aide across.

"What can we do for you, Captain?" asked von Haeften.

"I hear there are some visitors for Fromm," Brackwede said.

The lieutenant gave a lighthearted laugh. His boyish face beamed with pleasure as though he found the whole situation great fun. "I know," he replied, "they were due to attend a routine conference with the C.-in-C. at 6 p.m. I told them Fromm wasn't available for the moment, but they said they'd wait until he was."

"Aren't you worried?"

"Why on earth? They can wait."

With an inquiring glance at Stauffenberg, who nodded back, Brackwede rose and made his way into the ante-room. The three generals subjected him to a searching stare. Fromm never kept them waiting for more than a quarter of an hour without sending word, and they were clearly becoming restive.

"What's going on here?" demanded one of the generals. "Have you any idea?"

Brackwede firmly denied all knowledge of anything unusual.

"Where's the Commander-in-Chief?"

"I'm afraid I can't tell you that either."

There was a brief consultation. One general said: "Let's

wait another fifteen minutes." The second said: " I suggest we go back to our offices. If the C.-in-C. wants us he'll send for us." The third member of the party was more circumspect. " Fromm either keeps his appointments or cancels them in good time," he said. " If he couldn't see us now he'd tell us so in person. I'm very much afraid there's something wrong here, gentlemen."

Fromm's three departmental chiefs were trustworthy and experienced desk-strategists, blooded in battle, Staff-College-trained and hand-picked by Fromm himself. They trod the straight and narrow path prescribed for them with conscientious docility. They would never lend themselves to anything " underhand," as Brackwede was quick to realise. He went back to Stauffenberg.

" I'm afraid they won't be dislodged, Claus."

" Perhaps they're debating whether to join us or not," von Haeften said hopefully. " What about enlightening them?"

Brackwede shook his head and turned his attention to some notes which Stauffenberg pushed across the desk towards him. After a couple of minutes he was interrupted by raised voices in the ante-room, where the three generals were waxing indignant.

" They're asking to be taken to General Fromm immediately," von Haeften reported.

" All right," murmured Brackwede, " if they insist, I think their request ought to be granted."

" Very well," Stauffenberg decreed. " Arrest them."

The posse of subalterns, who were rapidly acquiring experience in arresting generals, did so firmly but politely, ignoring threats and turning a deaf ear to violent protests.

" Kindly follow us, gentlemen," said Lieutenant von Hammerstein. He might have been inviting them to a mess dance.

" Still no radio announcement?" Hitler demanded impatiently.

" I'm afraid not," Bormann replied, looking deliberately lugubrious. " I can't understand it either, my Fuehrer," he added meaningfully. " Goebbels is usually quicker off the mark."

Unfortunately, Hitler did not have a chance to take in the primitive cunning of Bormann's tribute-cum-innuendo. It was time to bid farewell to his guest, Benito Mussolini.

The two dictators were standing on the platform of the makeshift station which served the Fuehrer's Headquarters near Rastenburg. Tall pines surrounded them like gargantuan sentinels, and the evening sun bathed them in its gentle radiance.

" I shall never forget this day," declared the Duce.

" That you should have been here today of all days is a fact of profound and symbolic importance," Hitler replied.

Clasping hands, they gazed into each other's weary eyes with well-gauged solemnity. Then they parted, never to meet again.

Hitler hurried back to the bunker and huddled in his arm-chair again, wary as a wild beast sensing a trap. " I have a feeling that all is not as well as some of you seem to imagine." He wagged a trembling forefinger. " There's something brewing, I know it. The bomb was not the whole story."

Keitel announced that he had tried to contact Olbricht but failed to get through.

" Complete calm prevails in the Foreign Office," said Ribbentrop. " No one has reported anything unusual."

" The Central State Security Bureau is in full operation," Himmler declared. " My men are ready to step in immediately if a threatening situation develops."

" For all that," Bormann said, " the Fuehrer ought to address the German people—purely as a precautionary measure."

" I'm only too ready to do so," Hitler replied eagerly. " How can it be arranged?"

Bormann gave a deprecating cough. " I'm afraid no direct radio link has been provided for the Fuehrer—in my view, a grave omission. It seems almost incredible that the Propaganda Minister should have overlooked such a contingency."

Hitler demanded to be put through to Goebbels, who came to the 'phone at once. There was something almost suspect about the unemotional way in which he delivered his bomb-shell.

" Armoured units have moved into the government quarter, my Fuehrer. I can see three tanks and several platoons of motorised infantry from the window of my office."

Hitler's whole body started to shake with feverish intensity, but his voice remained as harsh and commanding as ever.

" What does it mean, Goebbels?"

" A military putsch, presumably." The Propaganda Minister's tone was wholly phlegmatic. His nerves appeared to be intact. " I am already taking counter-measures, however, and shall hope to have some more definite news for you shortly."

This brief conversation unleashed a storm of misgiving in

the Fuehrer's Headquarters. "As I thought!" cried Bormann. "The swine!" Himmler muttered gloomily. Only Field Marshal Keitel preserved an optimistic front. "It may be a mistake," he said. "German officers would never lend themselves to such a thing."

Hitler sipped tea. Goering sank into a semi-alcoholic stupor. Ribbentrop congratulated himself on having kept both himself and the Foreign Office out of this "foul affair." One of Hitler's secretaries broke down and wept.

The Fuehrer retired to a corner of the room, leant against the cool surface of the bomb-proof wall and beckoned Bormann and Himmler to his side.

"Could it be," he inquired nervously of his two trusty henchmen, "that Goebbels himself has defected?"

Himmler gave a noncommittal shrug. His eyes were expressionless. Bormann bowed his head as though accepting the inevitable. "I have always regarded Doctor Goebbels as utterly loyal and I still do. However, recent events compel one to acknowledge that virtually nothing is impossible in this world of ours."

Almost at that precise moment, Colonel von Stauffenberg was assuring someone on the telephone that reports of Hitler's escape from death were deliberately misleading.

The teleprinter messages emanating from the Bendlerstrasse —in so far as Lieutenant Roehrig had not delayed, amended or completely re-drafted them—were signed variously "General Fromm/Colonel Stauffenberg," "General Hoepner, Commander-in-Chief, Replacement Army," and finally, even, "Field Marshal von Witzleben, Supreme Commander, Armed Forces."

Prague reported "routine progress," Vienna announced that prearranged plans were being put into effect, and news was received from Paris that tanks were already on the move there.

At approximately 6.30 p.m. it was reported that No. 3 Company of the Berlin guard battalion had cordoned off the government quarter as instructed. No one, from generals and ministers downwards, was to be allowed across the line.

"We're over the hill!" Stauffenberg announced.

Brackwede shook his head. "You can't have a wake without a corpse."

Elisabeth had taken out the briefcase and placed it in the middle of the table. She opened the catch and pushed it towards Konstantin.

"Please look inside. You've got to know what this is all about."

Konstantin shook his head. "I'm not interested in knowing what's inside."

"Don't you care?"

They eyed each other warily. Burgeoning mistrust seemed to have extinguished every spark of mutual affection. They stood staring at each other for several seconds like total strangers.

"This briefcase has nothing to do with me. It belongs to my brother."

"What would you say if I told you that it contained documentary evidence of an anti-Hitler resistance movement? What if it contained detailed plans for a revolt against your beloved Fuehrer, detailed plans for his elimination—his assassination? What would you say then?"

Konstantin froze for a moment and the light went out of his eyes. He shrugged defiantly, but it was some time before he spoke. When he did so, it was with unconstrained simplicity.

"Even if what you said were true, Elisabeth, what would it add up to? I trust Fritz completely. Even if his briefcase does contain the material you suspect, he may have been collecting it in order to protect the Fuehrer."

"My God," she said dully. "These pieces of paper could cost the lives of several hundred people—don't you realise that?"

At 6.35 p.m. Major Ernst Otto Remer was standing in Goebbels's office with Lieutenant Hagen at his elbow.

Goebbels played what he had always found to be his most effective card: he smiled. It was a warm, engaging smile which skilfully concealed his malicious delight in the unusual.

"Welcome, Major," he said. "I appreciate your faith in me and reciprocate it to the full."

He invited the two men to sit down in a tone which conveyed that they were old friends for whom he had unlimited time.

Remer's sun-tanned face wore an expression of disciplined humility, a sight which Goebbels found infinitely gratifying. He was dealing with an officer in the Prussian tradition who also happened to be a loyal National Socialist—and there were few more promising combinations.

"I think we understand each other," the Minister said

briskly, " so we can waive any time-wasting preliminaries and come straight to the point. Have you received orders to arrest me?"

" Yes, sir," Remer admitted, looking shamefaced. " That's what I'm supposed to do."

Goebbels restrained an urge to question Remer more closely on the exact procedure he had intended to adopt. Instead, he said: " I fully sympathise with your position, Major, nor do I expect you to be influenced by me in any way—provided, of course, that you believe the Fuehrer to be dead."

" I find it hard to believe, sir, but I've been told so on good authority."

" Then your problem couldn't be more straightforward." Goebbels picked up the telephone. " Connect me with the Fuehrer's Headquarters, please."

The " Wolf's Lair " answered almost at once. Bormann snatched the 'phone from Keitel, and within a few seconds Hitler was at the other end of the line.

" My Fuehrer," Goebbels announced gleefully, " With me at this moment is the Commanding Officer of the Berlin guard battalion, Major Remer. Major Remer has instructions to seal off the government quarter and take all ministers and other senior officials into custody. May I ask you to express your views on the subject?"

There was a sound of muffled breathing. Then Hitler said: " Let me speak to the major."

Remer reported his presence. The greatness of the hour threatened to overwhelm him, but the Minister's encouraging smile prevented him from losing his poise.

" Major Remer," said Adolf Hitler. " Do you recognise me? Do you recognise my voice?"

" Yes, my Fuehrer," Remer replied, moved to the core.

Goebbels nodded benevolently at Lieutenant Hagen, and Hagen blushed with pride at the realisation that promotion, if not an even greater reward, was in store for him.

" Major Remer," Hitler pursued. " I am addressing you now as Supreme Commander of the German Armed Forces. As of this moment, consider yourself under my personal command. From now on, you are to act on my behalf. I rely on you to do so."

" Yes, sir!" barked Remer.

" I am entrusting you, Remer, with the task of smashing all opposition. Work in conjunction with Dr. Goebbels, but contact me immediately if you are uncertain on any point. In the meantime, act with the utmost resolution. Be absolutely ruthless! Always remember that what is at stake is Greater Germany, the Third Reich, our nation . . ."

He sounded as if he were on the verge of adding " and me!" —but he did not.

This telephone conversation seemed to inject new life into Adolf Hitler. Realising that the long hours of silent and brooding apathy were over, Bormann heaved a sigh of relief.

In the Bendlerstrasse, Stauffenberg was telephoning to his friend and cousin, Lieutenant-Colonel von Hofacker, in Paris. "Everything's fine here," Hofacker assured him. " Stuelpnagel is reacting splendidly. We're off to see Field Marshal von Kluge in a few minutes—he'll join us, don't worry!"

General Beck sent for the latest reports and read them through carefully. They looked promising. He nodded encouragingly at Hoepner and Olbricht.

Brackwede was chatting with Lehmann's private army, whose prevailing mood was one of cheerful unconcern. "Whatever happens," Lehmann said, " I know at least three escape routes now—one through the back courtyard, one via the canteen and another across the roofs."

Lieutenant Herbert sat, mute and motionless as a tin soldier, surrounded by his fellow-believers. They afforded him neither hope nor consolation. Uncertainty reigned, the consignment of automatic weapons from the armoury had still not arrived, and Molly's attempts to raise his spirits were fruitless.

In the government quarter, Major Remer assembled his officers and instructed them to carry out an orderly withdrawal in the direction of the Bendlerstrasse. " Our first step will be to regroup," he told them. " Long live the Fuehrer!"

SS-Sturmbannfuehrer Maier was " not available." There was no sign of life at the State Security Bureau. No interrogations had taken place at Prinz Albrechtstrasse for several hours. Obergruppenfuehrer Mueller paced his office like a caged lion.

At No. 13 Schifferdamm, Voglbronner yawned and vegetated. The Jewish refugee crouched silently in one corner of the cellar. Frau Breitstrasser feigned prayer. Jodler junior groped idly for Maria. Erika Elster lay on her back, daydreaming. Scheumer pretended to seek consolation in Goethe. Frau Wallner wept. Elisabeth and Konstantin stared at each other, as through a glass, darkly. The briefcase still stood between them like an insurmountable obstacle.

Elsewhere, troops were on the move. They converged on Berlin, concentrated in Paris, marched through the outskirts of Vienna, Prague and Munich. The soldiers stared stolidly ahead, unaware of what was expected of them.

"I've never trusted the army!" Hitler proclaimed to his entourage. "The generals have always been in league against me."

Himmler sidled up to him. "In this hour of national emergency . . ." he began. Then he placed a sheet of paper on the desk. It was a prepared document appointing the Reichsfuehrer-SS to replace General Fromm as Commander-in-Chief, Replacement Army. Hitler signed it on the spot.

"Shoot anyone who resists!" he adjured him. "The fate of the nation is at stake!"

"My Fuehrer," Himmler replied thankfully, "wherever and under whatever circumstances enemies of the State still exist, we shall eliminate them. That is what we live for. No true German could think otherwise."

THREE

The radio which Captain von Brackwede had switched on in his office was blaring out the usual succession of cheerful melodies designed to stimulate the flagging spirits of a war-weary population.

Corporal Lehmann poked his head round the door. "What's the matter—bored?"

"Just curious, that's all," Brackwede replied, and went on telephoning above the din.

Instead of waiting for his contacts to call him, Brackwede was plying them with doses of encouragement at disturbingly regular intervals. The more these pep-talks irritated his fellow-conspirators, the more cheerful Brackwede became.

"My dear fellow," he said in tones of friendly exhortation, "you sound as if I've just interrupted your afternoon nap."

The man at the other end of the line—a major of police—sounded more worried than somnolent. "The situation's so confused . . ."

"Does that surprise you? It'll go on being confused until people like you stop wavering and take the plunge."

"I'm sorry, but until I know something more definite . . ."

"What!" Brackwede expostulated. "There'd never be a revolt at all if everyone insisted on a written guarantee in advance!"

Lehmann, who had listened in on the last conversation, stood grinning in the doorway. "Sounds as if some of them are getting cold feet already."

"It infuriates me, Lehmann." Brackwede spoke quietly, but his jaw was set in a belligerent line. "I can understand some people not joining us in the first place. But to talk big, swear solemn vows, burble about the real Germany and then sneak away at the last minute—that makes me want to vomit!"

"Talking about that, my scouts tell me there's quite a crowd of officers in the mess—probably fortifying themselves before making up their minds which way to jump."

"What's on the menu this evening?"

"Fresh plaice. I told my mess-waiter friend to put some aside for you."

" Thanks." Brackwede attached a measure of importance to food and drink, not so much because he enjoyed it as because it was an old soldier's rule never to pass up any form of sustenance. One could never tell where the next meal was coming from.

Shortly afterwards Lieutenant Herbert rang to request an interview. Lehmann went to ground just before the lieutenant walked in, looking worried.

" My friends and I are becoming more and more convinced that something ought to be done," he began.

" A reasonable assumption."

" We ought to come to a decision, I suppose."

" I agree."

" The question is, what decision?"

" That's quite simple, Herbert," Brackwede drawled, "—either shoot Stauffenberg or shoot someone Stauffenberg wants shot. That would make your position perfectly clear."

Lieutenant Herbert did not appreciate pleasantries of this sort, but he summoned up a dutiful smile.

" May I take the liberty of asking what you are going to do, sir? I'd be glad to be guided by you."

" I'm going down to the mess. They've reserved some plaice for me."

Herbert thanked him deferentially and hurried back to his friends. He was greeted by an expectant silence.

" That man Brackwede is a sly dog," Herbert announced. "Do you know what he's doing?—Listening to the radio. And do you know what his future plans are?—A quiet supper in the mess. I wish I had his nerve!"

Having racked their brains as to the possible significance of this behaviour, Herbert's friends came to the conclusion that Brackwede, who kept his ear close to the ground, was deliberately keeping out of the line of fire.

Herbert summed up the general view by an appeal for the utmost caution. His friends seconded this, adding a rider to the effect that vigilance was also indicated and that a discreet word with the Party authorities would do no harm.

At that moment—6.40 p.m.—the monotonous blare of the radio was suddenly interrupted. Turning up the volume, Captain von Brackwede heard the following announcement broadcast over the Deutschlandsender:

" Today, a bomb-attempt was carried out on the Fuehrer's

life . . . The Fuehrer himself suffered no injuries apart from slight burns and bruises. He immediately resumed his work . . ."

The announcement, which took well under a minute to read, gave the names of those who had been gravely or slightly injured. It also referred to the Duce and Reich Marshal Goering, but no one else. No definite suspicions were voiced.

Lehmann eyed Brackwede inquiringly, but he merely turned the radio off and sat there in silence for some moments. Then, his footsteps gradually increasing in tempo, he went off to see Colonel von Stauffenberg.

The same announcement was also heard by Konstantin von Brackwede, who had idly switched on the " people's receiver " in Elisabeth Oldenburg-Quentin's room.

"Who would be capable of doing such a thing!" he murmured in a shocked voice, and went on listening.

The voice of the announcer suddenly died as Elisabeth wrenched the plug out of the wall.

"That's secondary," she said curtly. "We've got other things to think about."

Konstantin looked bemused. " But he was talking about the Fuehrer!"

"So what? He's still alive—allegedly." Elisabeth walked to the door and paused for a moment, listening. "What's going on in this house is far more important from our point of view. We're trapped—that's all you should be worrying about now."

Konstantin shook his head and stared sadly round the room. Everything seemed to have changed. The white walls looked grubby, the blue curtains faded, the furniture worn and shabby. The brown paint of the door was scuffed and chipped, and the bed was just a bed like a thousand others.

There was a discreet knock. Opening the door, Elisabeth found herself confronted by a mild, almost schoolboyish face.

The little man said: "Allow me to introduce myself. Voglbronner's the name. I'm conducting the investigations here."

"If you're thinking of searching this room," Elisabeth said firmly, "allow me to point out that you'll need a special warrant—isn't that so, Konstantin?"

Konstantin stationed himself beside her. "It certainly is."

Hurt though he was at being so grossly underestimated, Voglbronner intensified his smile. " I've no intention of putting you to any inconvenience. I fully realise who I'm dealing with. What's more, I cherish the deepest respect for Captain von Brackwede. He's a remarkable man."

"And Countess Oldenburg works in his department," Konstantin added with what he considered to be a justifiable sense of relief.

"I'm aware of that." Voglbronner's manner was positively deferential. "I'm extremely well-informed," he went on. Then, quick as a snake, he asked: "Why are you so afraid I might search this room? What do you think I might find if I did?"

"This radio announcement is no concern of ours," General Beck said loftily. He knew what value to attach to propaganda in a country where false news reports had been commonplace for years. As a man of integrity, he was revolted by sharp practice.

"It may be no concern of ours," Brackwede persisted, "but the fact remains that it was broadcast—and it was only broadcast because Valkyrie isn't functioning properly. The station should have been occupied at least an hour ago."

"An unpalatable truth," Beck conceded with an approving nod in Brackwede's direction. "It was high time someone said so frankly."

As though bent on demonstrating that he was what Brackwede believed him to be—an old lion who had not yet lost his teeth—Beck marched ponderously across the room and came to a halt in front of Olbricht.

"I'm not satisfied," he announced angrily. "Where's Witzleben?"

"The Field Marshal is on his way here from Zossen. I'm afraid he seems to have been delayed."

"He should have been here by now," growled Beck. "Point number two: where's General Lindemann? I thought he was supposed to be making a radio announcement?"

"He's nowhere to be found, I'm afraid."

"And the text of his address?"

"He has it with him."

Beck glanced grimly at Brackwede. Words were superfluous. The next question followed immediately: "Why isn't General Wagner answering his 'phone?"

"He's not the only one," Brackwede interposed. "I can't say I'm altogether surprised. The general situation isn't clear enough, and people are bound to react accordingly. Some of them are playing for time and others are simply running out on us."

Beck walked over to Brackwede. His steel-grey eyes appraised him, half-critically, half-hopefully, as though he were some newly invented secret weapon. Brackwede's expression did not alter, but his beaky nose jutted at a characteristically provocative angle.

"We won't get very far on high-minded sentiments alone, General," he said with a meaningful glance at Stauffenberg, who was standing twenty yards away in Fromm's office, separated from them by the half-open glass door. He was still telephoning incessantly, still repeating, over and over again: "Keitel's lying . . . Hitler is dead . . . Operations are continuing!"

Beck turned to Brackwede and said in a low voice: "If only they were all like him." He looked across at Hoepner.

Hoepner said resentfully: "Those troops you alerted haven't turned up yet."

"Nor have the SS," Brackwede observed with faint irony.

Stauffenberg was saying: "Who cares about propaganda announcements on the radio? It's all lies, I tell you! The facts are as follows: operations are proceeding according to plan in Paris, and here in Berlin the main administrative buildings in the government quarter have been sealed off by units of the guard battalion. The first tanks have reached the city centre."

"And when will the first shot be fired?" mused Brackwede.

At the Fuehrer's Headquarters, the special Gestapo team flown in by Kaltenbrunner—explosives experts, arson specialists and trained detectives—was hard at work.

The Gestapo men operated in accordance with firmly established rules of procedure. Cautiously, they surrounded the scene of the explosion and converged on it in an ever-decreasing circle, like entomologists closing in on some exotic beetle.

Their preliminary findings were as follows: dimensions of the site of the explosion or, more precisely, the conference hut, 41 feet by 16.4 feet; in the centre, a map-table; on the right, a small round table; on the left, a desk and bookcase; room and entire contents severely damaged; on the right of the entrance, a hole in the floor, radius 21.6 inches.

A mere fifty yards away, Hitler was rampaging through his living quarters. His female stenographers, who were normally treated with comparative gallantry, had fled in dismay. Only Bormann withstood the tornado.

"I demand to speak to the German people!" roared the Fuehrer. "Why am I still unable to?"

"A recording and relay van is on the way from Koenigsberg, my Fuehrer."

"And when will it be here, Bormann?"

The Reichsleiter spread his hands in a gesture of regret. He knew that several hours might elapse before the actual broadcast, but he refrained from saying so. "I am doing my best to expedite matters. Of course, if broadcasting facilities had been arranged in the first place . . ."

In and around the ruined conference hut, the experts from the State Security Bureau laboured on, drawing diagrams, taking measurements and filling in pro-formas. Their investigation of the crater in the floor revealed that the explosive charge had been detonated above ground-level. The downward blast had blown a hole in the floor while the upward blast had found its way out through the windows, door and inner wall.

"My Fuehrer," announced Bormann, brightening visibly, "the recording team from the radio station at Koenigsberg have arrived. They will be ready for you in about fifteen minutes' time."

The radio technicians set to work with grim determination. They installed a microphone, ran out cables, checked tonal quality and tested the recording apparatus, perspiring copiously as they did so. They were less overawed by the greatness of the moment than oppressed by the knowledge that their future hung in the balance.

"All set to go, my Fuehrer," said Bormann, pulling up a chair.

The sheets of paper in Hitler's hand fluttered as he took his seat.

"Silence!" Bormann called. "Recording in progress!"

Hitler had put his glasses on, but he was still forced to bend forward in order to read the centimetre-high script produced by the typewriter which had been specially made for him. His voice sounded muffled and almost inaudible.

"Turn up the volume!" Bormann whispered to the technicians.

Hoarsely, gratingly, the inimitable voice ground out the words of the prepared speech. ". . . A very small clique of ambitious, irresponsible and, at the same time, senseless and foolish officers . . . a gang of criminal elements which will be destroyed without mercy . . . this crew of usurpers . . ."

Fifty yards away, a handful of Gestapo experts were earnestly indulging in what appeared to be a child's game. They were sifting sand—or, in official terminolgy, "conducting an examination of débris." This process brought to light fragments of metal and leather, together with the remains of a pair of steel pliers.

The metal fragments belonged to a bomb-case, identifiable as being of British manufacture. The detonator employed had evidently been of the chemico-mechanical type Finally, the fragments of leather had formed part of a briefcase, and this was identified, with the aid of witnesses, as having belonged to Colonel Count von Stauffenberg.

" . . . This time we shall settle accounts with them in the manner to which we National Socialists are accustomed." Hitler laboriously concluded his proclamation and looked up.

"Have that broadcast immediately!" Hitler commanded. "Broadcast it at once and have it repeated several times."

It was shortly after 7 p.m. when Hitler rose from his chair, looking pleased with himself.

"Most impressive, my Fuehrer," Bormann assured him.

"Hard-hitting words," Keitel chimed in.

The chief technician heaved a sigh of relief and reported: "Recording satisfactorily."

Reich Marshal Goering and Grand Admiral Doenitz, both of whom had prepared equally impressive pronouncements, took their place at the microphone in turn. Bormann supervised their utterances with zealous care.

"How soon can you get that on the air?" he demanded.

"At the earliest possible moment," declared the broadcasting supervisor.

This hopeful statement elicited not only words of appreciation but an extravagant display of hospitality in the form of real coffee, sausage and cream-cake. Bormann eyed the technicians optimistically.

"That should do the trick!" he whispered to Keitel.

As it turned out, five hours were to elapse before the speeches could be broadcast.

But, late as they went out, they did not go out too late.

Konstantin von Brackwede drew himself erect. "As far as I'm concerned, you're welcome to search this room."

"Really?" Voglbronner inquired with gentle menace.

"Of course. We haven't got anything to hide—have we, Elisabeth?"

She shook her head, concentrating desperately on Voglbronner's face to prevent her eyes from straying to the bottom drawer where Captain von Brackwede's briefcase was again concealed.

"Ah, well," sighed Voglbronner, "why should we confuse the picture when it seems to be clear enough already? We have a confession, after all."

"A confession?" Elisabeth said sharply. "From whom?"

"The Jew, of course," Voglbronner sighed again—it was impossible to tell whether he was pleased or the reverse. "He has admitted to shooting the Local Group-Leader. Herr Jodler saw to that."

"But that's utter nonsense!" Elisabeth burst out.

"I don't think it's any of your business," Konstantin said with a warning frown.

Voglbronner smiled. "I like to be thorough," he observed mildly, "nor am I in the habit of rushing matters. May I assume, just for the record, that you were both unaware of this Jew's presence in the house?"

"You can assume one thing," Elisabeth said resolutely, "Frau Wallner's lodger can't possibly have been responsible because there was no way he could have left the flat last night. We always double-lock the front door from the inside, and there are only two keys. One hangs downstairs in the caretaker's flat—Jodler's—in case of fire, and the other was on my bedside table all night—Frau Wallner lent it to me. I can swear to that if necessary."

"Have you carefully considered the implications of that statement?" Voglbronner inquired.

"There's nothing to consider!"

Voglbronner glanced briefly at his watch, welcoming the prospect of distraction. In the continuing absence of definite instructions from SS-Sturmbannfuehrer Maier he could afford to mark time.

"In that case," he said, "perhaps you won't have any objection to accompanying me downstairs . . ."

"I'll come too," Konstantin volunteered.

"It's none of your business—you said so yourself," Elisabeth replied brusquely. "Kindly allow me to handle this on my own."

Konstantin stared after her, feeling forlorn and misunderstood. A yawning chasm seemed to have opened between them. Tormented by the thought, he stared absently at the small velvet-brown Bokhara rug beneath his feet. Then, as though drawn by magic, his eyes went to the spot where he knew his brother's briefcase was hidden. The fading daylight scarcely penetrated to the chest of drawers in the corner of the room, but Konstantin advanced on it with slow and unerring steps.

" I'm worried, my dear Brackwede," General Beck confessed. " I have a feeling things aren't going as they should."

" That's an understatement," the captain replied.

Beck drew him into a window embrasure. He had known Brackwede's father well, and he was beginning to realise that the captain resembled him more than he had once imagined. His defiantly casual manner was probably a deliberate veneer. Beck sensed that he could speak to him freely.

" What are we doing wrong, Brackwede?"

" Treating rats like domestic animals, General," Brackwede rejoined with unhesitating candour. " We ought to force certain of our so-called brother officers—irrespective of rank —to make a definite choice between two alternatives: honour or degradation."

Beck paced restlessly up and down the room. Making brutal demands on people was alien to his nature. He yearned for an atmosphere of mutual trust, but unfortunately it was not forthcoming, or not in sufficient measure.

" I've never felt lonelier than I do now," he muttered.

" I find that quite understandable, General."

Impulsively, Beck put out a hand and patted the captain's shoulder. He had seldom made such a gesture of spontaneous warmth in his life before, but he felt a sudden wave of paternal affection for the son of his dead friend.

" What can I do to put things back on the right lines?"

" Ring Field Marshal von Kluge," urged Brackwede. " Try to squeeze a decision out of him."

" And if he backs down?"

" At least we'll know more than we do know."

Beck nodded, and Brackwede asked the exchange for a line to the Commander-in-Chief, West. The call came through within a few minutes.

" How do things stand?" Kluge asked quickly.

Beck embarked on an accurate but circumstantial account of the situation. He endeavoured to explain how the present state of affairs ought—in his opinion—to be interpreted.

Brackwede, who was listening in, whispered: "Cut out the preliminaries, General. Kluge only reacts to hard facts."

Beck knit his brow. "I'm going to ask you a straight question, Kluge: are you in agreement with the steps now being taken and will you place yourself under my authority?"

Kluge did not speak for some moments. Finally, he said: "This is an unforeseen situation, General. I don't need to tell you that my approach to a certain subject hasn't altered, but I need time to consider."

"Ask him how long he wants," Brackwede hissed.

Beck stood there stiffly. He looked a little pale but showed no other sign of emotion. In a matter-of-fact voice, he put the question.

"I'll call you back in half an hour," Kluge replied. His eagerness to terminate the conversation was only too apparent.

"That's Kluge for you!" Beck commented bitterly. There was no more to be said.

Having carefully gone into retreat, Sturmbannfuehrer Maier was now engaged in covering himself from every possible angle. He had transferred his headquarters to the home of a lady of his acquaintance. He knew quite a few such ladies, but this one recommended herself to him on this particular occasion because her apartment was conveniently situated halfway between Bendlerstrasse and Prinz Albrechtstrasse.

Maier was engaged in the fashionable activity of the day. He lay stretched out on a sofa luxuriously upholstered in wine-red plush, telephoning. The principal items of his clothing had been removed—not only, it may be added, on account of the heat.

"I'd like you to switch off one of your five highly developed senses," he told his willing hostess. "Don't listen—find something else to do."

Maier's telephone technique consisted in calling people up continually but never being called up himself. He deliberately omitted to inform them where he could be reached and always signed off with the words: "Just on my way out."

First, he rang Voglbronner and inquired about the state of affairs at No. 13 Schifferdamm. Voglbronner reported that it offered scope for development in any desired direction. He was again instructed to mark time.

"And don't let's have any slip-ups, my friend! If things go wrong you'll take the can back on your own."

Maier's next call was to Captain von Brackwede, with whom he adopted a tone of silken intimacy. "Well, my dear fellow, and how fares the day?"

"Come over here and see for yourself," Brackwede said cheerfully. "We've already got half a dozen generals under lock and key."

"You don't say! Don't tell me you've arrested SS-Gruppen-fuehrer Piffraeder?" Maier's surprise gave way to something like respect when his question was answered in the affirmative. "I suppose you'd like to add me to your collection, too—just for safety's sake."

"I could do with your advice, that's all."

"You can have it, but only by telephone." Maier gave a raucous laugh. "You know I'll be the first to congratulate you—or stick you up against the nearest wall, whichever applies. I'm sure we understand each other, don't we?"

There was no doubt about their mutual understanding. The Sturmbannfuehrer found this conversation as satisfactory as the first. Idly caressing his hostess's posterior with one hand, he picked up the 'phone with the other and put a second call through to the Bendlerstrasse, this time to Lieutenant Herbert. If he was going to cover himself effectively, Herbert was the ideal person to help him.

"What, still in the land of the living?" he inquired jocularly. "—Still at large, I mean?"

Herbert gave a faint groan. "We're in complete chaos here," he mumbled. "I wish you'd tell me what to do."

"With pleasure," Maier said briskly. "In the first place, lay off the drink—you sound as if you've got a mouthful of wet flannel. In the second place, keep a clear head and do your duty, that's all."

"I know, I know, but where does my duty lie, Sturmbann-fuehrer?"

Maier's gratification increased. "I should have thought that was obvious. When the time comes, I hope you'll remember that it was I who appealed to your conscience. For the moment, I can do no more than remind you that the survival of Germany is at stake. Bear that in mind!"

Having concluded this inspiring conversation, the Sturmbannfuehrer telephoned his own office. The call was taken by one of his chief assistants, a Sturmfuehrer.

"Glad to hear your voice at last, sir. Your 'phone hasn't stopped ringing."

"What I'm doing at the moment takes priority over everything else. I'm on the track of something really big. It seems fairly certain that we're dealing with a large-scale conspiracy. Inform Reichsfuehrer Himmler immediately, and tell the rest of my department to pull their fingers out and get on with the job."

What the job was he did not divulge, but he felt satisfied that he had now covered himself against every eventuality. The next fifteen minutes—if not more—could be devoted to the lady of his choice.

The sentries on duty at the Bendlerstrasse block, who were drawn from the Greater Berlin guard battalion, continued to check visitors' credentials in the routine way. No special orders reached them—only reinforcements in the person of a lone captain who had turned up at the guardroom shortly after 4 p.m. He took a personal interest in the identity of those who requested admittance, but his usual verdict was a terse " Let him through."

The first captain was relieved by a second, and the second by a third. Their manner was polite, reserved and firm, and they were assisted in their duties by one or two junior N.C.O.s. There was nothing unusual about their presence. Extra officers were often posted at the entrance when the C.-in-C. was holding receptions or special conferences.

At 6.50 p.m. a staff car drove up to the gate. The captain on duty saluted and gave a stereotyped " Pass!" The sentry raised the barrier, the captain turned to the corporal beside him and said " Colonel Glaesemer," the corporal rang Lehmann, Lehmann informed Captain von Brackwede, and Brackwede reported to General Olbricht that the C.O. of Tank School No. 2 at Krampnitz was on his way up.

" What's Colonel Glaesemer doing there?" General Hoepner asked, raising his eyebrows. " I thought he was supposed to be somewhere else at this time."

" We'll see him at once," Beck said, and the words rang out like a command.

Colonel Glaesemer paused in the doorway and surveyed the imposing assembly with suppressed astonishment. He looked every inch the professional soldier—stern, upstanding and energetic.

Catching sight of Beck, he gave a respectful bow but did not address him personally. Instead, he marched up to Olbricht and asked if he might speak to the Commander-in-Chief on a matter of urgency.

Olbricht politely declined his request. "General Fromm is not available at the moment, but you can speak to me."

"Very well, sir," Glaesemer replied. "The point is, I've received orders to carry out the steps laid down in the Valkyrie plan."

"Quite so," said Olbricht, "and I trust that you've carried them out to the letter."

"No, sir."

Glaesemer's laconic announcement came like a bolt from the blue. Murmurs of indignation were heard, and even Olbricht failed to hide his consternation. Only General Beck seemed totally unmoved. Walking over to the tank school commandant, he asked: "Why not, Colonel?"

"Because I don't like this business!" Glaesemer replied fiercely. "I won't have any part of it."

"Not even if I give you my personal assurance that compliance with the orders you have been given would do nothing to violate your professional integrity?"

Glaesemer was undeterred. "No, sir."

"Then you'll have to take the consequences," warned Olbricht.

Glaesemer stood silently to attention. He had disobeyed an order at the bidding of his conscience, and he had openly flouted that order in the presence of those who had given it. There was no more he could say.

"A mistaken but honourable decision," Beck declared with characteristic magnanimity. "I sympathise with the Colonel's attitude."

"Nevertheless," said Olbricht, "it leaves us with no choice." He glanced across at Lieutenant von Haeften, who nodded. The group of subalterns moved forward.

"I protest," said Glaesemer.

"Your protest is duly noted and will be recorded in writing," Olbricht told him. "You can refer to it later, if need be."

Colonel Glaesemer was led away and confined on the fourth floor. The Bendler block was gradually transforming itself into a provisional detention centre. Fromm and four other generals were already incarcerated there, together with SS-Oberfuehrer Piffraeder and—now—the tank school commandant.

Stauffenberg's reaction to the news was swift and unhesitating.

"The second-in-command at Krampnitz must carry out Operation Valkyrie instead—and that applies to all similar cases from now on. If someone drops out, someone else must take his place. Germany can't be quite as hard up for men of initiative as some people here seem to fear!"

Konstantin von Brackwede knelt in front of the chest of drawers with the dun-coloured light of early evening falling obliquely on his tense face. Cautiously, almost hesitantly, he grasped the ornamental brass handles and pulled.

The briefcase was lying there, lock uppermost. Konstantin lifted it out and began to pull it towards him, but as he did so one or two postcard-sized pieces of paper which had got caught up in the leather flap fluttered to the ground. He went to pick them up, intending to replace them with the other papers which filled the drawer to the brim.

Then his arm froze in mid-air. The pieces of paper were photographs, and staring up at him from each one was Elisabeth. She was not alone. Grouped round her were familiar figures—Count von Moltke, Caesar von Hofacker, jaunty and debonair, Claus von Stauffenberg, wearing a grave and preoccupied expression, his brother's relaxed and smiling face, Julius Leber, tough as an old oak, and a paternal-looking General Beck.

"She knows them all but she never told me," Konstantin muttered. "Why not?"

Laboriously, he came to the conclusion that the photographs were no concern of his, but they still intrigued him. He put them back with reluctance.

The whole drawer seemed to be full of photographs. The briefcase had only compressed them temporarily, with the result that they were now spilling over the edge. As Konstantin was pushing them back into place he caught sight of an envelope lying on top of the photos. He recognised it immediately as the letter his brother had asked him to deliver to Elisabeth barely twenty-four hours before.

His fingers reached for it mechanically. The look of brooding curiosity on his face yielded to one of dawning uneasiness. Resolutely, he withdrew the letter from its envelope.

With mounting agitation, he read:

"*The time has come . . . I'm sending you this briefcase and my brother . . . take care of them both . . . twenty-four hours at least . . . I know I can rely on you—in every respect . . .*"

He dropped his arms, and the sheet of paper fell to the floor. Everything around him looked suddenly drained of colour, like an over-exposed negative—the floor he was still kneeling on, the letter beside him and the slowly fading square of daylight in the window.

Clenching his fist, he drove it into the briefcase. It toppled on to its side and burst open.

In the Bendlerstrasse, General Olbricht was addressing the members of his staff. Thirty-five or forty officers stood around him, listening in silence.

" This undertaking could be of immeasurable importance," Olbricht declared. " I am not in a position to supply you with full details, gentlemen, but this much I can tell you: the outcome may well lie in your hands. I am relying on you!"

" We won't let you down, sir!" a colonel called out. One or two officers nodded, but the vast majority preserved an impassive silence. Olbricht talked on and on, directing his remarks at the latter.

" You ought to take a breather, sir," Lehmann told Stauffenberg. He offered him a cigar appropriated from mess stores and the colonel accepted it gratefully. It was the last cigar he ever smoked.

" Aren't you getting tired?" the corporal asked anxiously. " Judging by the last three 'phone-calls, more and more people are crying off."

" You get used to anything in time," Stauffenberg replied. With a smile, he added: " I am prepared for this, anyway. I'd probably have felt uneasy if everything had gone too smoothly."

In the office next door, General Beck had just put through a call to the Russian front at Brackwede's instigation. He asked for the Commander-in-Chief, Army Group North, but was informed that the C.-in-C. was not available.

" So he's opted out too," Beck commented.

" The bastards!" exclaimed Brackwede, dropping his supercilious pose for the first time.

Beck called for a stenographer and dictated a memorandum. In measured tones, he put it on record that he had tried to give Army Group North an opportunity to defend the soil of East Prussia in a manner that was militarily practicable. His intention had been to safeguard German soldiers against further orders of an insane nature, but he had unfortunately failed.

" Time: 7.30 p.m.," Beck concluded.

It was the only written statement he made during the course of that day. He signed it not as " Colonel-General "

Beck but simply as " General " Beck, disdaining to use the rank with which Hitler had once invested him.

What he really thought at that moment he revealed to no one. He uttered no word of reproach—simply stated a fact, and one which must have cut him to the quick.

" The old man's firm as a rock," Brackwede told Stauffenberg and Mertz. He perched on the edge of the C.-in-C.'s desk while Lehmann took over Stauffenberg's telephone. " It's a noble but harrowing spectacle, my friends—like watching a thoroughbred stallion confronting a pack of wolves with no one lifting a finger to help."

" General von Hase reports that he can't get through to the guard battalion," announced Lehmann.

" It may mean they're on the move at last."

" Either that or the line isn't functioning properly any more," Lehmann said.

Even Brackwede failed to explore this line of thought because at that moment Lieutenant von Haeften appeared.

" Field Marshal von Witzleben has arrived," he called excitedly. " At last!"

" I did it," the huddled figure blurted out. " I shot him with a pistol. I couldn't help myself. It was—it was a sudden impulse. I can't remember the exact details."

" He can't have done it," Elisabeth said firmly. " He didn't leave the flat all night."

" You keep out of this!" Jodler growled. " It's bugger-all business of yours—unless, of course, you're claiming the Jew as your personal property."

Voglbronner gave a placatory smile. The situation was developing in an extremely promising fashion. The Jew was a physical wreck and ready to make any statement required of him. Young Jodler was still behaving like a human battering-ram and could be launched in any given direction. Finally, the Oldenburg girl's obstinacy was proving simply invaluable, since it enabled him to spin out the proceedings to his heart's content.

" I don't get it!" Jodler shouted angrily. " I bring you the guilty party on a plate and he sings like a canary, but you're still not satisfied."

" Because his story happens to be completely untrue," replied Elisabeth.

The crouching figure gave her a look of entreaty. " Please don't—you'll only harm yourself. I'm done for anyway."

"No," Elisabeth said resolutely, "this is a murderous injustice and I won't be a party to it."

"Ugh!" ejaculated Jodler. "A fine way for a German woman to talk, I must say!"

Voglbronner suppressed an urge to yawn. How seriously these drivelling fools took themselves! What was the Jew, after all? Just one more candidate for the gas-ovens. And what did a corpse amount to, even when it happened, for a change, to be that of a local Party functionary? And what were truth and honour and justice? Just verbal manure designed to boost the harvests of the State.

Voglbronner's urge to yawn finally overcame him. Ordering the Jew to be taken back to the cellar, he told Elisabeth to hold herself available in her room and went to work on Jodler.

"With all due deference to your concentration-camp methods," he said, "you're not just dealing with a Jew, you know. Things are a bit more complicated than that."

"What do you mean?" Jodler demanded. "Don't tell me you take any notice of what that stuck-up bitch says?"

It irked Voglbronner to know everything—the nature of the crime and the identity of the criminal—and not to be able to make use of his knowledge. He felt entitled to a modest little diversion.

"Countess Oldenburg states, and plausibly so, that the Jew can't have left the flat because the key was in her possession. It won't be easy to disprove that—unless, of course, the Jew was seen outside the flat during the time in question by another witness. Chew that one over."

Scharfuehrer Jodler snapped at the bait and swallowed it whole. "What about the Breitstrasser woman? She's reliable enough—she'd swear to anything . . ."

Voglbroner cautiously applied the brakes. Jodler's solution would have been too quick, too easy, too lacking in entertainment value. "Possibly," he said, "but a garrulous old washerwoman won't tip the scales against a thoroughbred filly like the Countess. You'll have to find a more impressive specimen—and no more half-measures, if you don't mind."

"Fair enough, I'll do a proper job this time," promised Jodler. In a low growl, not directed at Voglbronner, he added: "I don't know what things are coming to in this country!"

"A fine how-do-you-do, I must say!" Field Marshal von Witzleben rumbled ominously.

Captain von Brackwede grinned with delight, and even the corporal beside him gave a covert smile. " Now perhaps things'll get off the ground at last," he murmured.

Erwin von Witzleben had arrived in full uniform, complete with marshal's baton. His face was beetroot-red with anger, and his " fine how-do-you-do " took precedence over any more conventional form of salutation.

Only then did he appear to notice General Beck. He marched up to him with something akin to a parade-ground strut, clicked his heels respectfully and said in more subdued tones: " At your service, General."

There ensued a solemn handshake—no reproaches from Beck, no query as to why Witzleben had taken so long to put in an appearance. The onlookers breathed more easily.

" I feel it my duty to state . . ." the field marshal began in a booming voice, but Beck politely cut him short.

" There's no need, Witzleben."

The field marshal fell silent and gave a little bow. It was not an unfamiliar spectacle to some of those present. Almost all the senior serving officers in the German army had been instructed by Beck at one time or another, and they remained his pupils still. No one who had worked under him ever ceased to admire him.

Brackwede leant across to Lehmann. " Let's hope they cut out the formalities," he whispered. " We can't afford the time, especially at this stage." Lehmann hurried over to the door leading into the C.-in-C.'s office and held it open invitingly. The Supreme Commander designate plunged into Fromm's former abode and stalked up to Stauffenberg, breathing fire.

" Hell and damnation!" he fumed, banging his fist on the desk. " What the devil have you been doing all this time?"

No one was spared during the tirade that followed. Witzleben berated everyone in sight, not excluding Olbricht. Hoepner came in for a special ration of abuse. Stauffenberg abandoned his telephone for some minutes and listened to the volcanic outburst with grave attention.

" A fine how-do-you-do!" the field marshal reiterated. " Nothing seems to be going right here—nothing!"

Mertz von Quirnheim was concerned to see a look of growing gloom settle on Stauffenberg's face. He leapt into the breach.

" We were expecting difficulties from the outset, Field Marshal."

"I'm not interested in difficulties," thundered Witzleben. "What successes have you had?"

"Successes take time, sir."

"But you haven't got any time!"

"Things are shaping very well in individual areas," Mertz hazarded. "The latest reports seem to confirm . . ."

"I want facts!" Witzleben drummed excitedly on the desk with his field marshal's baton. "What government offices have been occupied, what ministers have been arrested, which radio stations are in our hands, when is Kluge going to make up his mind, what response have you had from the Russian front, how far have you got with the job of putting SS units out of commission? Well?"

"It's too early to expect any really tangible results yet."

"Too early? It's eight hours since the bomb went off, gentlemen. According to our calculations, the first four hours were to be decisive."

"We lost three hours."

"That's a statement of fact, not an excuse. No, gentlemen, count me out. No one could expect me to associate myself with a half-baked venture of this sort."

No one did, it seemed. Stauffenberg remained silent, Mertz von Quirnheim stared helplessly at nothing in particular and Lieutenant von Haeften stood pale-faced and motionless by the door.

"I'm extremely sorry," Witzleben told Beck in a strained voice, "but under the circumstances . . ."

"I'm sorry too," Beck replied, turning away.

Erwin von Witzleben left the Bendlerstrasse with his head held high. His performance had lasted little more than half an hour. Shortly after 8 p.m. he climbed into his Mercedes and told his chauffeur to drive him to his country house, thirty miles from Berlin.

He was arrested there next day.

Stauffenberg gazed moodily after the departing field marshal and then joined Brackwede at his post in a window embrasure. Together, they stared down at the Bendlerstrasse. It looked utterly dead. No one came or went, and the accumulated heat of the day still rose from the surrounding ruins.

"I know what you're going to say, Fritz." Stauffenberg sounded thoughtful. "I know all your arguments backwards and I sympathise with them—I've even prepared, now, to believe they're sound. However, I still refuse to take the sort of measures you think are necessary. I set my sights on one man's life—Hitler's. I refuse to sacrifice any more."

He stared across at the fortress-like tower of the Matthaei-kirche, about three-quarters of a mile away, which had been exposed to view by a night of bombing which had blasted away the adjacent buildings. Nestling close to the church was a small cemetery.

Brackwede said: "We must all come to terms with this situation in our own way. Personally, I've always paddled my own canoe and I'm not dropping the habit at this stage. You needn't feel in any way responsible for my future actions. From now on, I'm forming my own resistance movement."

Stauffenberg grinned at him. "You're worth a dozen generals, Fritz."

"Only a dozen?" Brackwede's grey-blue eyes twinkled. "I always thought you had a high opinion of me!"

Two teleprinter messages were lying on Field Marshal von Kluge's desk. One had originated in the Fuehrer's Head-quarters and was signed by Field Marshal Keitel; the other bore Field Marshal von Witzleben's name and came from the Bendlerstrasse. The first was in complete contradiction to the second.

"What are you going to do, sir?" inquired his chief of staff.

"For the time being," said Kluge, "I'm going to have some dinner."

"What happens meanwhile?"

"The situation remains unchanged."

Those who had been invited to dine with the Commander-in-Chief, West, at La Roche-Guyon gathered there just before 8 p.m. They included General von Stuelpnagel, Lieutenant-Colonel Caesar von Hofacker, General Speidel and General Blumentritt. The formalities proper to such an occasion were observed to the letter.

Before they retired to the dining-room, Caesar von Hofacker spoke for about fifteen minutes. Suppressing his excitement, he tried to summarise all the factors which rendered a military insurrection so urgently necessary—Hitler's subhuman be-haviour, the military situation, the soldier's code of honour, the dictates of conscience, burning concern over the fate of Germany . . .

Field Marshal Kluge did not interrupt Hofacker. Instead, he listened with outward attention, evincing neither agreement nor the reverse. He did not speak, and his silence hung over the room like a dead weight.

Eventually, he said: "Well, gentlemen, the attempt has failed."

Caesar von Hofacker regarded the Commander-in-Chief with appalled incomprehension and General von Stuelpnagel paled visibly. The rest of the men in the room avoided each other's eyes. Only Kluge seemed unperturbed.

"Shall we go in now, gentlemen?" he said.

They filed into the dining-room and silently took their places—"as if they were sitting in a house visited by death," Speidel recalled later.

"Lehmann, old lad," said Captain von Brackwede, "I intend to take a short trip."

"How do you propose to do that?"

"Quite simple—I just climb into a car and drive to H.Q. Berlin District. Someone ought to put a squib under the place, and I fancy the idea of doing it myself."

"You want me to raise a car for you, I suppose?" With a worried frown, Lehmann went on to report that groups of heavily armed infantry and isolated tanks had already been sighted in the streets south of the Tiergarten. "It looks as if they've abandoned the government quarter and started moving in on the Bendlerstrasse."

"So what?" exclaimed Brackwede. "All the more reason to get cracking at once."

"Well—if you're really set on the idea . . ."

Lehmann left the sentence unfinished and picked up the telephone. He looked preoccupied. After three minutes he announced that there were no cars available.

"But that's impossible!"

"Strange but true, sir. There are only six duty cars and they're all in use. No one seems to know when one'll be available."

"Blast!" Brackwede said succinctly.

"Don't say that," Lehmann exhorted him. "This way we don't lose you. Beside, you never know what you might miss—the show's only just starting."

"Well, how goes the backstairs battle?" Sturmbannfuehrer Maier inquired cheerfully. His jovial mood was not inspired solely by the lady-friend who had provided him with his temporary headquarters. All his contacts had functioned admirably so far, so there was no need to commit himself yet.

"Everything's going fine," Voglbronner assured him.

"What makes you so sure?"

"I can supply you with almost anything you need, Sturmbannfuehrer—within limits, of course."

"How do you know what I need, Voglbronner?"

"Because it doesn't matter what you're after, sir. I've got a complete range of goods here."

Maier pricked up his ears. "All right, let's have a sample."

"Very well. In the first place, there's a dead Local Group-Leader—murdered, beyond a shadow of a doubt."

"By whom?"

"Probably by his son, a Scharfuehrer serving with one of the SS Special Action Squads."

"Not bad," Maier said. Here was an item for potential use in the State Security Bureau's system of interdepartmental barter. "Go on."

"Well, there's a schoolmaster and a talkative old woman—but they're just make-weights. On the other hand, I can offer you one of the Police President's girl-friends—or so she claims."

"You don't say!" Maier said admiringly. "What have you got on her?"

"It's not beyond the bounds of possibility that she's been having an affair with the son of the murdered man—i.e., the murderer. We might be able to build her up into an accessory after the fact."

"I take my hat off to you, Voglbronner. Just tell me you can pin something on young Brackwede and Countess Oldenburg and my cup of joy will be complete."

"I'll say I can pin something on them! There was a Jew hidden in the flat where they spent the night together. That could lay them open to charges of collusion, conspiracy, harbouring, suspected perjury—why, sir, we might even get them for anti-State activities!"

"Do your turtle-doves have any idea what they're in for?"

"Not a clue, sir. They don't know they're born, those two."

"Then don't disillusion them yet. Let them stew in their own juice for a while—the whole household, that is—until you receive direct orders from me. And by the way, my dear

Voglbronner, take a pat on the back. Keep your nose clean, and you can bank on a spot of promotion—like me."

Lieutenant Herbert made his way downstairs, bound for the basement and a confidential talk with Lieutenant Roehrig of the Signals Corps. The subject for discussion, so he had been informed in advance, was a "potential pooling of resources."

Herbert did his best to assume an air of innocent probity in the hope that it would render him inconspicuous. He threaded his way unnoticed through the knots of officers who were still standing around in the corridors, scarcely speaking now. More groups had gathered on the landings and in the courtyard outside. The majority were still amenable to the idea of a radical change, but warning voices were already to be heard.

Lieutenant Roehrig greeted Herbert cordially, and the two men withdrew to the far corner of the teleprinter room, assuring each other how much they welcomed the opportunity for a private chat.

The person responsible for bringing them together was Molly Ziesemann, who thus played a modest but not inconsiderable part in shaping the outcome of a momentous day. The current girl-friend and personal assistant of Lieutenant Herbert had once worked in the Bendlerstrasse communications centre, to which she was still bound by sentimental ties. Hence she came to form a vital link between the two groups.

"I only hope you're better-informed about things than we are," Herbert said. "We're working in the dark upstairs."

"Are you for or against the Fuehrer?" demanded Roehrig.

"What a question!" Herbert's eyes flashed with righteous indignation. "I'd remind you that I'm responsible for National Socialist propaganda in this building. Of course I'm loyal to the Fuehrer!" Without pausing for breath, he added in a confidential whisper: "But the situation is a bit obscure. They say the Fuehrer's dead."

"The Fuehrer is alive, and what's going on upstairs is high treason."

"Good heavens, man—are you sure?"

"Absolutely positive."

Herbert reeled under an invisible blow. His face glistened with sweat and he wiped his damp forehead on his sleeve.

"Well, what do you intend to do about it?" asked Roehrig.

"I'm not completely unprepared, of course," Herbert replied

ponderously. "I took the precaution of ordering some weapons from the armoury."

"I know—but that was hours ago, and they still haven't arrived. How do you propose to use them when the time comes?"

"You know about that, do you? Excellent! In that case, you can testify to it later." Herbert squared his shoulders. "As soon as the arms arrive we'll clean the place up. Are you really certain that Hitler's alive?"

"We've been acting on that assumption for hours."

The counter-revolutionary activities of the Bendlerstrasse communications centre had been considerably stepped up in the interval. Lieutenant Roehrig, his sergeant-major and sundry loyal signals personnel, male and female, were doing yeoman service. They had already started to countermand earlier teleprinter messages, all telephone calls made by Stauffenberg and his associates were being monitored, and a permanent link had been established with the State Security Bureau.

Lieutenant Herbert's response to this information was: "At last I know where my duty lies."

"I request permission to go to my private quarters," said Fromm. "I should like to lie down."

He was sitting comfortably in an arm-chair, having eaten his sandwiches and drunk his bottle of red wine. The three departmental chiefs who had also been detained sat round him in a silent circle. They too had been regaled at mess expense.

"I'm prepared to give my word of honour—in any desired form—that I shall observe the conditions of my arrest for as long as they remain in force."

The officer guarding the captive generals conveyed this offer to Olbricht, Hoepner and Beck, who held a short consultation. Beck expressed no view on the matter and Olbricht disclaimed responsibility, but Hoepner said: "At least it's one way of getting rid of him. It isn't a pleasant sensation, having the man breathing down our necks the whole time."

"Very well," Olbricht said reluctantly.

With that, Fromm's parole was accepted and he was permitted to retire to the living quarters which led off his suite of offices. He rose without a word, invited his three generals to accompany him, nodded not unbenignly at the officer on duty, and disappeared.

General Fromm was now at liberty in his own lair, which he knew far better than his captors.

"Well, gentlemen," he told his companions, "now we can get down to work."

The three departmental chiefs stood there mutely, overwhelmed by the enormity of what had happened to them.

"I shall remain at my post," Fromm pursued. "Not because of a parole which I virtually didn't give—a parole given to traitors isn't binding, anyway—but because I propose to stay here until I regain complete freedom of action." Heartened by their obvious approval of his line of conduct, he went on: "You, gentlemen, will alert the Berlin garrison."

Beckoning to them to follow him, he hurried them down some back stairs to an emergency exit on the right of the main entrance—a small glass-panelled door to which only he had a key. It was unguarded.

"I expect prompt and ruthless action, gentlemen. You have full authority to act on my behalf, so let me see some results!"

"Captain!" cried Herbert, storming into Brackwede's office. "There's a treasonable conspiracy going on—I've just heard!"

Brackwede screwed his monocle into his eye. "Where did you get that from?"

"A reliable source."

"In that case it must be true." Brackwede's tone was almost gay. "I'm only surprised it took you so long to find out."

"You knew?" Herbert gasped, looking bemused.

"Of course."

"But I don't understand! Why aren't you doing something about it?"

"What, for instance?"

"Well, force is the only way to deal with this sort of thing —don't you agree?"

Brackwede smiled indulgently. "Your enthusiasm does you credit, my dear Herbert, and I'm positively touched by your faith in me. However, don't allow your finer feelings to override your common sense."

"What do you mean, sir?"

"What I say. Examine the following hypothesis: assume that a revolt, a coup d'état, an insurrection—call it what you will—is actually in progress. What if it succeeds?"

Herbert looked as if he had run full tilt into a brick wall. He stood there stupefied, staring at his guide, philosopher and friend with an almost beseeching expression.

" Let us assume that the revolt is a flash in the pan," Brackwede continued. " All right, at least we'll know exactly who's been indulging in high treason. If it succeeds, on the other hand, there'll automatically be another brand of traitor. Do you want to qualify for membership?"

Lieutenant Herbert mechanically shook his head. No, he certainly did not! His brain reeled with bewilderment. "What do you think I ought to do, then?"

" Sit tight, my dear fellow—what else?"

So saying, Brackwede again put the Herbert fraternity out of commission, at least for the next hour. At the end of that time the weapons arrived from the armoury.

Towards 9 p.m. Field Marshal Keitel issued the following signal from the Fuehrer's Headquarters. It was addressed to " all commanders."

" The Fuehrer has appointed Reichsfuehrer Himmler to command the Replacement Army with effect from now . . . All orders issued by Fromm, Witzleben or Hoepner are invalid."

" Should we give this top priority?" inquired the Signal Corps sergeant-major.

" Of course," Lieutenant Roehrig told him. " Retransmit it to everyone you can think of."

" And the signals from upstairs?" The sergeant-major jerked a thumb in the rough direction of Olbricht, Stauffenberg and Mertz. " What do we do with them?"

" From now on," said Lieutenant Roehrig, " we simply disregard them."

Candles illumined the table at which Field Marshal Kluge was sitting with his guests, among them General von Stuelpnagel and Lieutenant-Colonel Caesar von Hofacker. The latter ate in silence—to quote Speidel again—" as though turned to stone."

Kluge's chief of staff reported that fierce fighting was taking place round St. Lô and Caen. Reinforcements had been urgently requested but no more reserves of any kind were available. The front was bound to collapse.

The Commander-in-Chief did not appear to absorb this information. The candlelight flickered restlessly over his meditative face as he sipped his coffee. To the men round him it seemed as if, even at this late stage, his mind was not finally made up.

"May I have a word with you in private, sir?" asked General von Stuelpnagel.

When they had retired to the room next door, Stuelpnagel said: "In Paris at this moment, the SD, SS and Gestapo are being arrested, disarmed and brought before courts martial."

"No," Kluge said tonelessly, "you wouldn't dare."

"I went ahead, sir—I couldn't do otherwise. You'll have to accept the fact, I'm afraid."

"I should have been notified in advance!" Kluge burst out furiously. "I refuse to be involved in this." Quickly he added: "You are removed from your command."

The field marshal controlled himself with an effort. He strode to the door, paused there for some moments and then turned back. When he spoke, there was sympathy in his voice as well as anger. "You must go into hiding, Stuelpnagel. Try to get away."

"I can't, sir."

"But it's your only hope!"

"Not if you obey your conscience."

"I am accountable for the lives of several hundred thousand men," Kluge said earnestly. "No one can absolve me of that responsibility."

"Try to think in wider terms, sir—think of Germany."

"I refuse to associate myself with your hare-brained scheme, and that's my last word on the subject. You have my deepest sympathy, but as to my approval—no, certainly not. Must I be more explicit?"

"No," Stuelpnagel replied, turning away.

"If only the swine were dead!" Kluge muttered fiercely.

Shortly afterwards, Field Marshal Kluge sent his Supreme Commander a loyal message of congratulations: ". . . the base and murderous attempt on your life, my Fuehrer, has failed thanks to a kindly dispensation of Providence . . . I felicitate you and assure you, my Fuehrer, of my unswerving loyalty, come what may . . ."

Elisabeth Oldenburg-Quentin saw the open briefcase standing on the table. She also saw the open drawer and the photographs inside, but she seemed reluctant to acknowledge the presence of Konstantin von Brackwede.

Closing the door behind her, she walked over to a chair, dropped into it wearily and closed her eyes. There was a bitter smile on her lips.

Konstantin said slowly: "I'm not going to reproach you, you know."

"Why should you?" Elisabeth retorted with surprising vehemence. She opened her eyes and looked at him as if she were seeing him for the first time.

He was standing in the middle of the room, his Knight's Cross glinting faintly in the fading daylight. The contours of his boyish face had taken on the sharp angularity of a much older man. She felt a sudden wave of pity for him.

"You've no cause to reproach me, really you haven't," she said in a brittle voice. "Please—what's worrying you?"

"Nothing," Konstantin replied harshly.

Elisabeth put out her hands to him and then dropped them limply. She sank back in her chair.

"Is it the photographs?" she asked.

"No. They're your business, not mine."

She looked slightly relieved. "What is it, then? Is it what's inside the briefcase?"

"No," he said in the same mechanical tone as before. "The briefcase is nothing to do with me, and my brother's connection with it is his own concern. Besides, I'm still convinced that he's a man of integrity . . ."

Elisabeth sat up. "Who said he wasn't?"

The setting sun had painted dull red streaks on the darkening sky, filling the little room with dusky pink light. Konstantin's face seemed to be burning with fever.

He held out his brother's letter in a trembling hand.

"Is that it?" she asked.

"Yes." When she made no move to take it, he let it fall on to the table beside the briefcase.

"That was yesterday," Elisabeth said gently. "A lot of things have happened since then, Konstantin. Can't you understand?"

"I asked you in here," Brackwede told Eugen G., "to offer you a piece of advice—you and Lehmann."

They were sitting in Brackwede's office. The radio was still churning out a non-stop stream of cheerful music provided by light orchestras, dance bands, military bands and folk ensembles.

"I always get suspicious when you start making suggestions, Captain," Lehmann said. "Perhaps it'd be best if you gave it us straight."

"Very well. I suggest you take a little stroll."

" Without you? "

Eugen G. raised his eyebrows. " You want us to make ourselves scarce? "

" More or less," Brackwede agreed. " Let's say we're putting you into cold storage for the time being. Lehmann will show you how to get out of here, won't you, Lehmann? "

" With pleasure. What about you, Captain? "

" I'll catch you up later. "

" No," Eugen G. said firmly. " Either we go together or not at all. "

Brackwede got up and walked over to the radio, which had suddenly gone silent. He turned and surveyed his friends with an indecipherable expression. " I could make it an order, Lehmann . . . "

" You can't give orders to a civilian. I'm a crane-driver from Westhafen, and I've got papers to prove it. "

" You're incorrigible," Brackwede said with a wry smile. " As for you, Eugen, what good are you doing by staying here? What function are you supposed to be performing? None. What do you hope to achieve by staying here? Nothing. So why stay? "

Eugen G. looked faintly embarrassed. " I'm here, that's all, and I wouldn't wish to be anywhere else at this time. "

Brackwede turned to the radio. An announcement proclaimed that the Fuehrer would address the German people very shortly over the national broadcasting network. The announcement was repeated several times.

" It's just after nine," said Lehmann, glancing at his watch.

" Well? " Brackwede demanded sharply. " Want any more reasons why you ought to take that little stroll I mentioned? "

" It's time we made a move," Lehmann replied with a grin, " —me to the canteen and you to the mess, otherwise that nice fish I reserved for you will be spoilt. "

" That was my alternative suggestion," Brackwede said.

" I never felt less hungry in my life," observed Eugen G., " but if that's your alternative suggestion I accept it. "

" Let's go, then." Brackwede headed for the door. " As far as your appetite's concerned, Eugen, don't worry—I'll be happy to eat your share. "

" Why no news yet? " Hitler's agitated voice rang round the walls of his command bunker. " We ought to have heard long ago! Am I completely surrounded by traitors and incompetents? "

The Fuehrer's intoxicating sense of having been spared by Providence yet again had quickly worn off, dispelling his renewed faith in final victory and leaving him morose and apathetic. A cloud of gloom enveloped him.

"To think of all I've done for those generals," he brooded "—and what thanks do I get?"

"The Party is sound as a bell," Bormann assured him.

"As for the armed forces," Keitel declared soothingly, "the group involved is extremely small. It will soon be eliminated."

Adolf Hitler was alone with the Reichleiter and the Field Marshal. The others had withdrawn to the neighbouring rooms, which were humming with feverish activity.

"Why doesn't Fromm call? Get through to him at once—I want to speak to him."

"We've tried to establish contact with General Fromm," Keitel reported, "—so far without success."

"That infernal Bendlerstrasse, that hotbed of treachery!" Hitler's voice rose to a shriek. "I want it put out of action! Why hasn't that been done yet? Aren't there any tanks on the way? They can raze the place to the ground for all I care!"

"All SS units in the Greater Berlin area have already been alerted, my Fuehrer," Bormann announced. "Obergruppen-fuehrer Mueller of the Gestapo is directing the operation in person. Skorzeny has arrived too, as instructed. He will be taking over command at the Bendlerstrasse on Himmler's behalf."

"But when—when?" Hitler drummed on his desk. "And what's Remer doing? Does he know I've promoted him?"

"He does," Keitel said. "According to latest reports, the guard battalion has been withdrawn from the government quarter and is moving in on the Bendlerstrasse. Colonel Remer has arrested the head of the Berlin Kommandantur, General von Hase."

"Did he put the swine up against a wall?"

"He handed him over to Minister Goebbels, who is keeping him in custody." Keitel hurried on to the remainder of his report. "General Herfurth, Chief of Staff to General Kortz-fleisch, has telephoned to say that a military putsch is definitely in progress, but that he has everything well under control."

The Fuehrer stared stiffly into space. He was tempted to inquire exactly who Herfurth was, but this would have cast doubt upon the "phenomenal memory" for which he was so widely renowned. In fact, Major-General Otto Herfurth was privy to the conspiracy but had decided that the time had come to don protective camouflage. Numerous others followed his example, but their last-minute change of face did not save their lives.

"Is Remer big enough to handle the situation?"

Keitel was able to banish the Fuehrer's doubts on this point. "I've placed Colonel Remer under the command of General Reinecke, my Fuehrer." This was a wise choice, Reinecke being a dutiful ultimate-victory enthusiast in the best Third-Reich tradition. "Reinecke is supervising the job of sealing off the Bendlerstrasse."

"Good, good!" Hitler said impatiently. "Tell Reinecke to be quick about it—thorough, too—but tell him I want the ringleaders alive. I want to watch them die."

"That seems to be that." Wolf Heinrich, Count von Helldorf, Police President of Berlin, sounded bitter but resigned. "We've obviously reached the end of the road." His friend Hans Gisevius acted as a sort of globe-trotter for the anti-Hitler resistance. A born conspirator who maintained important contacts with the outside world, he had been stimulating and galvanising the opponents of National Socialism for the past eleven years. Now, he stubbornly refused to give up. Too much time had been invested in this day, too many risks run and hopes cherished for him to surrender without a struggle.

"But it's been twelve years, Wolf!"

"It's hopeless, you can see it is."

"Give it an hour," Gisevius pleaded. "—just an hour!"

Helldorf slumped back in his chair, looking exhausted. "It's hopeless, I tell you."

Gisevius leant forward with an air of supplication. The fire in his eyes had died, but he appealed fervently to Helldorf's faith in Germany—or the remains of it.

"Don't delude yourself," Helldorf retorted. "The generals have been letting us down for years. They've promised us the earth and done absolutely nothing. What happened today is typical."

The corpse of Local Group-Leader Jodler still reposed in the cellar of No. 13 Schifferdamm. The once vigorous body lay there limply with the prostrate figure of the "lodger" from the third floor huddled beside it, moaning softly.

Voglbronner was lounging in an arm-chair on the ground floor with a policeman stationed outside the door, awaiting instructions. In a neighbouring room, Maria lay stretched out on the bare floor-boards, fast asleep.

The first-floor tenants did their best to escape notice. Frau Breitstrasser flitted about on the second floor, poisoned arrows at the ready. On the third floor, schoolmaster Scheumer had helped his invalid wife to another liberal dose of sedatives and was sitting with a copy of his beloved *Faust* open on his knee. He was not reading, however, but listening for noises from next door.

The first thing he heard was a loud but unintelligible duologue, evidently of a light-hearted nature. Next came a high-pitched tittering, followed after an interval by a medley of animal grunts and moans. Scheumer was no stranger to these acoustic offerings from the flat next door. The men might change but the noises remained the same.

"You're a bit of all right," Erika murmured. "Just say the word if there's anything I can do for you and I'll do it."

"Fine," said Jodler. "In that case, what about a nice alibi? I could use one." He winked. "I'm always ready to return favours in kind."

In the other flat on the third floor, Konstantin and Elisabeth were still staring down at the briefcase and the letter on the table between them. Their heads were bowed, and neither of them seemed willing to break the silence.

Finally, Elisabeth said in a clipped voice: "Why won't you believe me?"

"I don't know," Konstantin replied quietly. "Perhaps I've forgotten how to."

Shortly after 10 p.m. a fifteen hundredweight truck drove through the gateway of the Bendler block and pulled up in the inner courtyard. No one flagged the vehicle down or checked its authorisation. No one took any notice of it at all.

The accompanying N.C.O. climbed out and sauntered idly over to the guardroom on the left of the drive-in. It was a scene of frenzied but unsystematic turmoil. At least two separate factions were squabbling over their respective spheres of responsibility.

The transport N.C.O., a sturdy Pomeranian peasant, wagged his head wonderingly at the sight and picked up the nearest telephone. "Is there a Lieutenant Herbert in this dump?" he inquired. "If so, you might put me through to him."

The men in the guardroom were grouped round two officers, each of whom announced his intention of taking over the job of duty officer. A third, who was equally reluctant to be dislodged, sat waiting in a chair while the rank and file whispered among themselves. There was a sudden hush as one of the officers drew his pistol and rapped it on the guardroom table.

The transport N.C.O., whose stolid demeanour suggested that he had merely come to deliver a few crates of beer, seized his opportunity.

" Got a consignment of tommy-guns and ammo for you," he said into the 'phone. " They're outside Entrance 2a. If someone doesn't turn up soon I'll cart the whole lot back again."

He replaced the receiver on the hook and looked round expectantly. Almost everyone in the room heard what he had just said, but no one seemed unduly interested. They all had their own worries. Instinctively, they observed the old soldier's golden rule and steered clear of trouble.

Emerging from the guardroom, the transport N.C.O. found his truck already surrounded by six willing arms-bearers, Lieutenant Herbert at their head. As soon as he had handed over the consignment—but not before it had been carefully checked and signed for—the boxes and cases were eagerly manhandled upstairs to Herbert's third-floor office. On the second-floor landing, Herbert was greeted by Captain von Brackwede.

" Any help needed?" inquired Brackwede, who had been informed of the latest development by one of Lehmann's scouts. Apart from Herbert and his friends, he was the only person in the Bendlerstrasse to have taken any interest in the delivery of arms.

" Thank you, sir, I can manage." Herbert's response was polite and unsuspecting. He rested a case containing two sub-machine-guns on the banisters and assumed an attitude of respectful attention.

" Have you worked out who you're going to use those things on?"

" It's just a precautionary measure," Herbert assured him hastily, " —unless you can put forward some suggestions, that is."

" One or two. How about shooting our five captive generals —Fromm included?"

" But Hitler's alive!"

" I know, but for how long?"

Herbert grimly lugged his tommy-gun up the next flight of stairs, gnawed by doubt. The sweat running down his youthful face was not a product of physical exertion alone.

"Now we're ready for anything," he announced to his friends, quickly adding, in admonitory tones: "All the same, we must think things out carefully first."

Their deliberations took some time—to be precise, nearly an hour.

Sturmbannfuehrer Maier thoughtfully buttoned the jacket of his SS uniform. It was time to take leave of his lady-friend. What was more, to judge by the information he had just culled from a further series of telephone conversations speed was of the essence.

One particularly alarming feature from Maier's point of view was that he had been unable to reach Captain von Brackwede. This implied either that Brackwede had opted out or that he was no longer in a position to answer the 'phone. Whatever the truth, Maier decided to accelerate his movements.

Before leaving, he fired a few parting shots. First, he called Voglbronner and inquired after Lieutenant von Brackwede. He was informed that the lieutenant insisted on being allowed to leave the house, ostensibly because he wanted to speak to his brother without delay.

"Perfect!" Maier exclaimed in high delight. "Just what I was about to suggest myself. Tell the lieutenant I'll give him a lift there—out of the goodness of my heart, you understand."

Maier's second call was to Lieutenant Herbert.

"I hope all your preparations are complete, Herbert. I'm sending Lieutenant von Brackwede to you. He'll be at the Bendlerstrasse in fifteen minutes' time, complete with instructions from me. Meet him at the entrance."

Finally, Maier called his office.

"Existence of military putsch clearly established. All available personnel to rendezvous with me at the southern end of Bendlerstrasse, by the Spree Canal."

Bidding a hasty farewell to his hostess, Maier hurried out and whistled his car over from the shadow of a neighbouring pile of rubble. "Thirteen Schifferdamm—and step on it!" called the Sturmbannfuehrer, jumping in.

At approximately 10.30 p.m. General Olbricht assembled the members of his staff for the third time that day and informed them that the Berlin guard battalion, normally responsible for guarding the Bendlerstrasse block, had just instructed the sentries still on duty there to leave their posts.

"We shall now organise an officers' guard to take care of our own security."

"Why only now?" complained a major, and an anonymous lieutenant called sharply: "Just what is going on round here?"

Olbricht's face stiffened angrily. In a strained voice, he said: "Your fears and misgivings are of no interest to me, gentlemen—I am asking for volunteers."

Out of thirty-six officers, only six stepped forward, of whom four had already taken an active part in the events of the day, the remainder left the room, most of them without saluting.

General Olbricht looked shaken. "Is that all?"

Lieutenant von Brackwede stood waiting outside No. 13 Schifferdamm, flanked by Voglbronner and Sergeant Kopisch. His belt was buckled, his cap on his head, his hands begloved and the briefcase tucked under his left arm.

"Quick, quick, my friend—get in!" Maier called. "Something frightful's happened—we must get to the Bendlerstrasse at once!"

Konstantin climbed in and the car roared off. The Sturmbannfuehrer shook hands and asked: "Did you hear the news on the radio? There's been an attempt on the Fuehrer's life."

"I know, but he only received slight cuts and bruises . . ."

"Yes, but did you also know that a military putsch is in progress? That tanks are on the move? That generals have been locked up? That the would-be assassin is hiding in the Bendlerstrasse at this moment and that the army's morale is being systematically undermined from there with the avowed intention of overthrowing the Fuehrer?"

Konstantin did not know. His face went grey.

"Lieutenant," Maier went on, "can I rely on you—on your loyalty to the Fuehrer?"

"To the limit!" Konstantin assured him.

"Good." The Sturmbannfuehrer leant back against the cushions with a satisfied expression and rested his hand on the briefcase between them. "I can't enter the Bendlerstrasse myself, I'm afraid—not without risking my neck, and I'm rather attached to that. You, on the other hand, can get in without any difficulty. Lieutenant Herbert will be waiting for you at the entrance."

"And my brother?" asked Konstantin. "What about my brother?"

"I was in continuous touch with him until a short while ago," Maier told him, relishing this unwonted excursion into the realm of truth. "However, I can't get through any longer. It's a bad sign, I'm afraid. You may have to fight your way through to him, my boy. That's why you'll need the help of Herbert and his friends."

For the rest of the trip, Maier retailed his instructions with a professionalism which was soon to be vindicated in practice.

Nocturnal Berlin seemed to glide past them on a conveyer belt—a frieze of dark house-fronts, grotesque mountains of rubble, withered avenues of trees which appeared to dissect the purple sky with their sharply outlined branches.

About two hundred yards from the Bendler block the car halted beside a waiting armoured car.

"Right, lad," Maier called encouragingly, "go to it!"

"I need written authorisation—urgently!"

The colonel who had just burst into the C.-in-C.'s office found himself confronted by a silent group of men who might have been mistaken for a congregation of calm but grief-stricken mourners. Olbricht came to meet him, striving to conceal his surprise.

"What did you say?"

"Some of my officers are undecided and others frankly hostile, sir. I need a written order—a form of authority. Then I can occupy the radio stations at once, as planned."

"Colonel Wolfgang Mueller from the School of Infantry at Doeberitz," whispered Mertz von Quirnheim.

Olbricht digested the information. Of course, he remembered now: the commandant, General Hitzfeld, was out of town atending a funeral and his second-in-command, Colonel Mueller, had been away on a lecture tour. Now he had returned, only to request confirmation of an order which should have been carried out seven hours ago.

"We're grateful to you, Colonel," he said with a touch of emotion.

Even Brackwede lost his poise for a moment. Then, with an oblique smile at Eugen G., he asked: "Sure there isn't anything else you'd like, Colonel?"

"Thank you," Mueller replied. "The authorisation is all I'm interested in."

Mertz von Quirnheim dictated it impassively and General Olbricht signed it. The last written order issued by the conspirators was timed 10.40 p.m. Colonel Mueller pocketed it with a sigh of relief.

Brackwede described a small bow. "I'll get one of my men to show the Colonel out," he said. "There are a few holes in this rabbit-warren which not even Fromm knows about."

"Good-bye, Colonel, and thank you," Olbricht said quietly. "It's people like you who make our efforts worthwhile."

"In here!" hissed Lieutenant Herbert, who was lurking in one of the entrances to the inner courtyard, so shrouded in shadow that only his beckoning arm was visible. "And watch your step!" he added.

He groped for Konstantin's free hand and shook it warmly, drawing him into the doorway as he did so. "Well, what have you got for us? Have you really come straight from Sturmbannfuehrer Maier?"

"He drove me here himself. What's going on?"

"God knows—the place is in a turmoil. Everyone's spying on everyone else, everyone suspects everyone else, and no one knows exactly why. What does the Sturmbannfuehrer want us to do?"

"Where's my brother? Is he all right?"

"I've no idea. He isn't in his office—I wanted to tell him you were coming but I couldn't get through. What does Maier want?"

They paused on a landing, slightly out of breath. Konstantin was still clutching his briefcase. Herbert peered over the banisters in quest of potential eavesdroppers.

"Can you get hold of a few reliable men?" Konstantin asked, adhering to Maier's instructions.

"There's a whole bunch of them in my office."

"Are you armed?"

"Come with me!" With many a backward glance, Herbert hurried Konstantin upstairs to his office. Flinging open the door he made a sweeping gesture which took in the whole room and said triumphantly: "Well, what do you say to that?"

Konstantin said nothing. At his feet, fully assembled and ready for use, lay a machine-gun, several sub-machine-guns, carbines, some obsolete army revolvers and two Very pistols. Behind them were ranked the members of Herbert's group, later known, out of deference to the senior officer present, as the Heythe group: a major, two captains, a lieutenant, two second-lieutenants, three N.C.O.s and four privates.

"Our friend here," Herbert announced, indicating Konstantin, "has brought us some instructions from the State Security Bureau."

Konstantin, who wanted to go and find his brother, seemed to be in a hurry to discharge his mission.

"Sturmbannfuehrer Maier's instructions are as follows: certain officers in the Bendlerstrasse are engaging in high treason, so this is a matter of life and death. Armed counter-measures must be undertaken at once. All offices are to be searched and their occupants challenged to say whether they're for or against the Fuehrer."

"Does that include everyone?" asked Major Heythe.

"Everyone, irrespective of rank."

"What if someone refuses to co-operate?"

"Anyone who doesn't make his position absolutely clear must be arrested—that's what the Sturmbannfuehrer says. All those who are loyal to the Fuehrer must join in the operation immediately."

"Do I understand you to say that we must take action against general officers, too, if necessary?"

"In Maier's view—yes. He told me to tell you that for all practical purposes anyone who takes part in this operation will be acting directly on the Fuehrer's behalf."

"Well, what are we waiting for?" cried Lieutenant Herbert, seizing a sub-machine-gun.

Major Heythe stepped forward. "Don't let's go off at half-cock," he said, following suit. "We must organise this thing properly. Raiding-parties must be formed, runners detailed, a provisional detention-centre set up . . ."

Herbert scented competition. "I'll go on ahead!" he announced, brandishing his tommy-gun. Beckoning to the two young subalterns, he said: "You come with me. As far as I'm concerned, Major, you can organise the rest."

He charged out of the room, obviously forgetting all about Konstantin. Konstantin did not resent the fact. He settled the briefcase under his arm and went off in search of his brother.

"Have you got a cigarette left, Fritz?" asked Stauffenberg.

"I'm afraid not," Brackwede replied with a wry smile. "You see, even my talent for organisation has its limits." He was disturbed to note that Stauffenberg had been off the telephone for the last few minutes. " Getting tired, old friend?" he asked gently.

Stauffenberg shook his head. " Just waiting for a call to Paris, that's all."

" You'll never give up, will you?"

" No." Almost off-hand, he added: " Will you do something for me, Fritz? Tell the others that no one else must be coerced or talked into joining us. On the contrary, those who can still jump off the band-wagon should do so, if they want to. I insist on shouldering as much of the responsibility as I can. Above all, I want you to get away from here—you must testify to what has happened."

" Certainly, Claus," Brackwede replied with equal calm. " However, I hope you'll allow me to sit in for a while longer."

" I can only tell you what I told General Beck a few minutes ago. Please leave me to do what still remains to be done."

" What did Beck say to that?"

" He said he'd taken up his post and he didn't intend to abandon it now."

" That goes for me too, Claus."

The 'phone rang. Stauffenberg picked it up and listened intently, his face glowing like candlelit bronze.

" That was Paris," he said. " Operations against the SD, SS and Gestapo have been completed. They're all under lock and key—the whole crew. Paris is firmly in our hands."

" Highly commendable," Brackwede observed without a trace of sarcasm. " However, we happen to be in Berlin. I'm going to take the initiative and try to organise a couple of cigars for us."

Lieutenant Herbert and his companions began by combing the third floor. The procedure was as follows: an N.C.O. flung open the door of a room and Herbert stormed in, tommy-gun at the ready, flanked by his two second-lieutenants. Complying with instructions, he called:

" There are traitors in this building! State whether you're for or against the Fuehrer!"

In most cases he was tilting at windmills. True, majors and colonels raised their hands obediently—to Herbert's eyes an edifying enough sight in itself—but they almost invariably declared for the Fuehrer in the same breath.

" Then join us!" Herbert adjured them, drunk with zeal.

"Make your position absolutely clear or you'll regret it, I assure you. Long live the Fuehrer!"

He employed the same formula more than a dozen times, almost word for word, rapidly acquiring practice as he went. Staff officers assured him of their unwavering loyalty, generals expressed their approval and subalterns drew their service revolvers and followed him. Before long, he found himself at the head of a milling throng of eager loyalists. Herbert told himself happily that things were shaping well.

Ten minutes of diligent research with sub-machine-guns went by without a shot being fired. One major had to be jabbed hard in the ribs with a gun-barrel before he professed his devotion for the Fuehrer, but the only person who declined to make any declaration at all was a solitary captain. He was led away, silent and crimson-faced.

These professions of faith came to an abrupt end when Herbert's happy band charged downstairs to the second floor. Several officers who had been standing in the corridor took to their heels, disregarding Herbert's cries of "Halt!" He couldn't bring himself to add: "Or I fire!"

Then, some distance away, he heard a series of shots. Someone was emptying the magazine of a tommy-gun. "What the devil's that?" demanded Herbert, panting hard.

A runner enlightened him.

"It's the other raiding-party, sir—Major Heythe's. He made straight for the C.-in-C.'s office."

Herbert was outraged. He had been good enough to enlist Heythe in his group, and now the man was trying to steal his thunder. Somehow, he had to forestall him.

He raced forward, tripped and fell headlong, banging his forehead on the floor. When he staggered to his feet again he saw an officer strolling towards him along the deserted corridor. "For or against the Fuehrer?" Herbert yelled.

"Got any cigars?" the figure rejoined politely.

Herbert saw that it was Captain von Brackwede. He tried to summon a comradely grin. "I'm just mopping up, sir—care to join me?"

"No, thanks," Brackwede replied, adjusting his monocle, "I'm otherwise engaged for the moment. I'm looking for some cigars, preferably with a Havana wrapper."

"We're to be spared nothing, I see," General Beck remarked grimly as he heard the sound of shots coming closer. He walked over to the window, deliberately avoiding the others' gaze.

His companions stood around silently with mask-like faces. They might have been posing in small, formal groups for the benefit of a painter. The only one to make any move was Eugen G., who was sitting behind Olbricht's desk. He pushed the newspaper aside and picked up the pistol that had been lying beneath it. Looking at his hand, he saw that it was steady. He smiled in surprise because he was afraid.

A moment later the door opposite him was kicked open and Major Heythe burst in, only to be brought up short by the heavy door of the safe in which the Valkyrie plans had been kept.

Eugen G. could only see Heythe's feet and his astonished face from the tip of his nose upwards. The rest of him was obscured by the safe. The spectacle was not without its comic side, but, suppressing an urge to laugh, he took aim.

"Don't shoot, Doctor," General Olbricht's deep voice said behind him, "don't shoot."

At that moment the second door burst open and Lieutenant Herbert rushed in. The tommy-gun in his trembling hands described a wide arc.

"Where's General Fromm?" he demanded.

There was no response. The men in the room stared through Herbert as if he were made of glass. His tight forefinger tightened round the trigger at this mark of silent contempt.

"General Olbricht," he said harshly, "I demand an explanation."

"I owe you no explanation whatsoever."

"In that case I declare you under arrest—all of you."

Major Heythe shouldered his way forward. Now was the time to display some initiative or Lieutenant Herbert would eclipse him altogether. Herbert had undoubtedly shown a certain amount of spirit, but he, the Major, was the better organiser.

"All conversation is forbidden," he commanded. "These gentlemen will be isolated. Resistance is quite pointless and will be suppressed without mercy. I call on you to observe our instructions to the letter."

"Or we shoot!" Herbert roared. "We're giving the orders now—in the name of the Fuehrer!"

"Thank God you're alive!" cried Konstantin.

The look in Captain von Brackwede's eyes as he entered his office and saw him standing there killed Konstantin's urge to fling his arms round his brother's neck and bombard him with questions.

"How did you get here?" Brackwede demanded incredulously.

"Sturmbannfuehrer Maier gave me a lift."

Brackwede slammed the door behind him with his foot. "You really are incorrigible, aren't you?" he said bitterly. "How much longer is it going to be before you realise what human beings are capable of?"

"There's been a treasonable conspiracy," Konstantin said, eager to defend himself. "I know it's nothing to do with you, of course."

"Good God!" Brackwede exclaimed in near desperation. "If you believe that, why aren't you running amok with those patriotic friends of yours, popping off at everything in sight?"

Konstantin frowned. "I couldn't bring myself to, somehow."

"You're not very consistent, are you?" Brackwede said sarcastically. He gave a shrug of dismissal. "Enough of that, though, there isn't time. Tell me what you did with that briefcase I gave you."

"I brought it along. It's over there on your desk."

If anyone had ever seen Count Fritz-Wilhelm von Brackwede completely at a loss for words, that person was his brother and the moment was now. The captain's face stiffened, and he gulped several times.

"What's the matter?" Konstantin asked anxiously. "Are you ill?"

Brackwede averted his face. "No, not ill—dead."

The armed mob swept on, through General Olbricht's offices and beyond.

With cries of mutual encouragement, the officers burst through the three glass doors leading to the Commander-in-Chief's ante-room. Jack-boots thudded across the parquet and a tommy-gun chattered in the direction of a wall, criss-crossing a portrait of the Fuehrer with bullet-holes.

"Hands up and stay where you are!" yelled Herbert.

The tall colonel with the black patch over his eye jumped to his feet as the field-grey wolves poured hungrily into the room. An officer raised his pistol and fired six shots. Two appeared to find their mark, one in the upper arm and another in the back, but the nature and extent of the wounds was never precisely established.

Leaving a trail of blood behind him, Stauffenberg staggered into the Commander-in-Chief's office.

"Let's finish him off!" shouted one of the mob. "Let's finish them all off, the dirty swine!"

"No," Herbert commanded, heedful of Maier's instructions, "we must free General Fromm first."

General Fromm was awaiting his liberators in the drawing-room of his private apartment. He was sitting in a dark brown leather arm-chair when they burst in. His eyes lit up when he saw them, but his fleshy face did not change expression. "And about time too, gentlemen!" he said curtly.

Rising, he continued: "All suspects are to be detained until further notice. Anyone who tries to escape or makes trouble is to be shot. I want a thorough job done!"

Konstantin von Brackwede had retired behind the desk on which his brother's briefcase lay, clearly reluctant to hand it over.

"Are you mixed up in this crazy business?" he insisted.

Brackwede looked impatiently. "What's it to do with you?"

"Did you take part in this putsch? Tell me, Fritz, I beg of you!"

His brother gave a short laugh. "I haven't much time left and I don't propose to waste it here with you. I've got to get out of here before they seal off all the exits."

"So it's true," Konstantin said.

Brackwede grasped the handle of the briefcase and picked it up. "I've always lived my own life," he said, endeavouring to smile. "Try to do the same. Under present circumstances— and with your political convictions—it may pay off hand-somely."

He opened the briefcase and glanced keenly at its contents. The light of the desk-lamp fell full on his face, emphasising the beaky nose and high-domed forehead.

"Fritz," Konstantin said softly, "what am I to do now?"

"I told you—survive," Brackwede replied, shutting the briefcase with a snap, "—and remember occasionally that you're a Brackwede."

"I'm devoted to you, Fritz—you know that."

"Yes, I know that." The note of restrained affection

vanished from Brackwede's voice abruptly, as though a door had been slammed. " But don't let it stop you going your own way, even if it leads over my dead body. Fratricide is a mere bagatelle in a great age like ours."

A few minutes later—shortly after 11.15 p.m.—General Fromm was reinstated behind his desk, flanked by officers toting sub-machine-guns. Four N.C.O.s armed with rifles and hand-grenades guarded the doors.

In the centre of the room stood three generals: Beck, Olbricht and Hoepner; two colonels: Stauffenberg and Mertz; and one lieutenant, von Haeften. None of them spoke.

Fromm did not look at the six men. "Well, gentlemen," he said coldly, " I am now going to treat you as you treated me this afternoon." He waved the pistol which one of his rescuers had handed him. " Lay down your arms!"

All the conspirators were unarmed. None of them made any response except General Beck.

" I left my pistol next door," he said simply. " I should like to retain it for personal reasons."

" Do that." Fromm grasped the implication at once. He looked relieved. " But do it at once."

Beck started to say a few words about " the old days," evidently unwilling to end his life without a last attempt to win sympathy for his attitude, even from a man like Fromm, but Fromm brusquely waved him away.

" We don't want to hear that stuff now. Kindly stop talking and do something!"

Germany's most consistent army officer and Prussia's last philosopher in uniform went to fetch his pistol. Placing it to his head, he fired. He slumped in his chair with the blood oozing from his white hair and trickling down his face, but the bullet had only grazed him.

" Help the old man," Fromm told one of the officers beside him.

Beck was handed another loaded pistol. Holding the muzzle to his head with both hands, he fired a second time. His head jerked to one side and his body arched convulsively, but he failed to kill himself outright.

On Fromm's orders, a sergeant-major dragged the gravely wounded man into a neighbouring room and gave him the *coup de grâce*.

The Bendler block was now surrounded by tanks, armoured

cars and units of motorised infantry under the command of General Hermann Reinecke.

General Reinecke had been instructed to maintain "the closest co-operation" with SS-Hauptsturmfuehrer Otto Skorzeny throughout the course of the operation. He had further been informed that, until the arrival of Kaltenbrunner or Himmler, Skorzeny was to take over the duties of Commander-in-Chief, Replacement Army. This meant that ultimate control rested with the Hauptsturmfuehrer, and Skorzeny, who was well aware of the strength of his position, ordered the general about in his best swashbuckling manner.

Not even the head of the Gestapo, SS-Obergruppenfuehrer Heinrich Mueller, had much of a say in the operation. Skorzeny reiterated several times that he was acting "on direct orders from the Fuehrer," and Mueller was shrewd enough not to intervene in anything which did not directly concern his own department. The idea of functioning as a raiding-party commander did not appeal to him.

Instead, he reviewed his special task-force of five Gestapo teams, checked the arrival of police units as they moved in and—in complete silence—listened to Sturmbannfuehrer Maier's personal report.

"May I have a final word with you?" asked Skorzeny.

He, Mueller, Maier and General Reinecke were standing at the southern end of the Bendlerstrasse. The soldiers round them sat silently in their trucks, and the occasional gleam of a torch pierced the gloom.

"All units are ready to move in," reported General Reinecke. "The Bendler block has been completely sealed off. Tanks will cover the exits, ready to open fire in the event of opposition. All other prearranged details have been taken care of."

"Good," replied Skorzeny. "When the time comes, get in there and give them hell."

"The Gestapo is concerned with two points," Mueller said, "the preservation of documents and the detention of suspects."

Sturmbannfuehrer Maier coughed discreetly. "I've taken the liberty of preparing a comprehensive list, sir, but judging by my latest information I'm afraid it's far from complete."

"The safest plan would be to arrest the whole lot," Skorzeny said.

"Not my contacts," Maier interjected hastily.

Mueller turned and looked at him. "Trying to cover someone, Maier—yourself, perhaps?"

"I've merely taken certain precautions, sir."

"Pretty late in the day, it seems to me." The Obergruppen-fuehrer smiled thinly. "At the eleventh hour, one might almost say."

"Better late than never, Obergruppenfuehrer."

Skorzeny followed the drift of the conversation perfectly. Mueller and Maier were playing an elaborate game designed to reinforce their respective positions. Anxious to prevent their verbal skirmish from developing into a time-wasting duel, he said: "I suggest that your Gestapo teams carry out the requisite arrests while Maier and his department secure all the incriminating evidence they can lay hands on. We ought to make a move straight away."

"There's no hurry," Maier replied. "Give it another half-hour or so, and the place will drop into our laps like a ripe plum without a shot being fired."

"What makes you so sure?" Mueller asked warily.

Maier produced a self-assured chuckle. "Those precautions I mentioned. I've been in touch with reliable elements in the Bendlerstrasse for several hours. I not only organised counter-measures by 'phone but managed to introduce some reinforce-ments into the building as well. You'll see—my puppets always perform as they should."

Obergruppenfuehrer Mueller looked sceptical. "I sincerely hope so."

"They're welcome to massacre each other as far as I'm concerned," Skorzeny said. "Heads are going to roll one way or another, so a few more or less won't matter."

"As long as no one escapes," observed the Gestapo chief, glancing at Maier.

"Lehmann, old friend," Captain von Brackwede said, gripping the corporal by the arm, "how does the idea of a moonlight flit appeal to you?"

Lehmann eyed him curiously. "You're not planning to quit after all, are you?"

"Yes. Can you arrange it?"

"Of course. I was just going to say goodbye to the place myself, but I didn't think I'd have the honour of your company. What changed your mind?"

"I've got to get a briefcase out of here."

"Where to?"

"Anywhere—it doesn't matter where."

" Well, perhaps we'd better get that settled first." Lehmann perched on the captain's desk, ruminating. " You obviously can't hide out with any of your friends. The Gestapo will be knocking at their door before the night's out. On the other hand, if you were prepared to come down the social scale a bit—say to the level of my new friends in the slogan-writing business—I could give you a couple of useful addresses."

" Cut out the chit-chat," Brackwede said impatiently. " This building could be occupied at any moment."

" That's just the moment I'm waiting for, Captain."

Brackwede didn't know whether to feel exasperated or amused. Lehmann cut a small cigar in two and presented him with the slightly longer piece.

" I suggest we take Lieutenant von Hammerstein's route," he continued. " He's studied all the alternatives, and the best one goes like this: over the roofs, down a drain-pipe, through the basements of two bombed-out buildings, across a wall and along a disused sewer for thirty feet. Then we can spit in the Spree."

" All right, let's go! I'm curious to meet your friends, especially those girl students. What are we waiting for?"

Lehmann squinted at the smoke from his cigar. " The tighter they draw the net, the better for us. We can slip under their guard at the last moment. Our safest bet is to watch the show from the roof. As soon as they're inside, all we have to do is take a little stroll."

" He's dead, sir," reported the sergeant-major.

Fromm nodded. His gloomy but determined expression conveyed that Beck's death was a regrettable necessity. " Next!" he snapped.

General Hoepner stepped forward. He declared that he could prove his innocence and politely requested that he should be treated accordingly.

" My conduct was prompted by honourable motives, and I sincerely deplore . . ."

" Perhaps, but you'll have to take the consequences!" Fromm said sharply.

Hoepner inclined his head. " I realise that."

Fromm greeted this statement with relief. Obviously, Hoepner would do him no personal harm. " Take him away!" he called with a curt wave of the hand.

An N.C.O. and a private soldier stepped forward. Hoepner

followed them with a dignity which was lost on the rest of the room.

Fromm drew a deep breath. His gaze travelled swiftly over the figures of General Olbricht, Colonel von Stauffenberg, Colonel Mertz von Quirnheim and Lieutenant von Haeften.

"What about you, gentlemen?" he asked, avoiding their eyes.

There was a disdainful silence. After some moments, Fromm rose. "I take it you've no illusions about your fate. I must do my duty. I'll give you another few minutes to write your farewell letters—five minutes, let's say."

Ordering writing materials to be put at their disposal, he left the room. Half a dozen soldiers stood guard with guns at the ready. The writing-material remained untouched. No one moved.

Five minutes later Fromm reappeared.

"In the name of the Fuehrer," he announced, "a court martial convened by me has duly taken place."

No one ever succeeded in proving whether such a court martial was actually held. Its membership remained anonymous, the accused were given no hearing and no record of indictment or sentence was ever found. Everything was swallowed up in the sanguinary confusion that shrouded the dying hours of the day.

"The court martial has passed sentence of death on the following:" Fromm continued, "Colonel of the General Staff Mertz, General of Infantry Olbricht, this colonel whose name I no longer know——" he pointed in Stauffenberg's direction without looking at him " —and this lieutenant."

Silence fell once more.

Fromm waited for some angry word or gesture, some cry of protest, but in vain. All he received was a look of bitter contempt.

"These sentences are to be carried out forthwith," he concluded hastily. He turned to a young officer who was standing in the background, sub-machine-gun at the ready. "Take a few men and execute them in the courtyard."

"Yes, sir," the anonymous lieutenant replied promptly.

The hands of the clock moved toward midnight.

The headlights of the army truck in the courtyard of the Bendler block blazed up as the black-out visors were removed, casting jagged shadows on the matt grey wall. The rectangular piles of sandbags stacked against it had been put there as a protection against bombing. Now they were to intercept the bullets of a firing-squad.

The four condemned men marched down the echoing stone stairs to the courtyard, escorted by eight privates, officers and N.C.O.s. No one spoke.

They stationed themselves side by side on the left of the courtyard, barely twenty yards from the main entrance. The firing-squad formed up opposite them, a line of figures which moved with the mechanical stiffness of marionettes.

"Safety-catches off—load!" ordered the lieutenant.

There was a rattle as each man worked his bolt backwards and forwards, forcing a round into the breech. An expectant silence fell.

"Take aim!" called the lieutenant.

The place of execution was cramped—a bare seven or eight feet of wall-space between two windows. The condemned men stood crowded together with their shoulders touching. The last thing they saw was the glare of the headlamps and the distorted shadows surrounding them. The purple dome of the night sky seemed to hang low overhead.

Eugen G. was leaning against a wall with a fellow-prisoner on either side of him. Facing him were three guards, one of whom, armed with a pistol, was supervising the other two, whose sub-machine-guns were trained on the three prisoners opposite them.

"No false moves!" one of the guards said warningly.

Eugen G. gazed about him, searching for a possible means of escape. He weighed up the chances of launching himself successfully at one of the tommy-gunners but decided that they were zero.

"I knew this would happen," said the fellow-prisoner on his right.

"Shut your trap or else!" shouted the N.C.O. in charge.

The man on Eugen G.'s right was Count Helmuth James von Moltke, adviser on martial and international law to the Armed Forces High Command. His face wore a faint smile of resignation, but there was something stiff and frozen about it.

The man on Eugen G.'s left was Count Berthold von Stauffenberg, the colonel's brother. He stood there, motionless and unspeaking.

Suddenly they heard a voice they knew—Stauffenberg's voice. It seemed to come from infinitely far away.

" . . . Germany!" was all they managed to distinguish. Then the cry was blotted out by a fierce volley of shots like hailstones rattling on a tin roof.

In later years a number of self-styled eye-witnesses came forward almost all of whom contradicted one another. According to one version the firing-squad was commanded by a Lieutenant Schady, according to another by a Lieutenant Schlee.

Major Remer asserted that he had nothing to do with the executions. Kaltenbrunner, strongly supported by Mueller, Maier and Skorzeny, stated that by the time his men had succeeded in occupying the Bendler block everything was over.

All that seems certain is that the lieutenant in charge ordered his men to fire, and they duly did so.

Lieutenant von Haeften reared up and collapsed. General Olbricht crashed to the ground like a felled tree. Colonel Mertz von Quirnheim tried to shield Stauffenberg with his body.

And Stauffenberg, just before he died, called out: " Long live our sacred Germany!"

PART THREE

THE DAYS AFTER

*" To stake one's life is a fitting price
to pay for such a just and worthy cause."*
Julius Leber

ONE

At a few minutes past midnight the courtyard of the Bendler block resounded to a triple " *Sieg Heil!*" General Fromm, who had supervised the proceedings in person, led the cheering, and the firing-squad and spectators, their faces looking like dirty grey smudges in the gloom, joined in with a will. Their voices rang out lustily over the four dead bodies on the ground and re-echoed from the bare wall above them. With an upward glance at the warm night sky, which seemed to be trembling with exhaustion, Fromm turned on his heel.

His officers made way for him as he left the courtyard. Silence hung over the scene like a mute question, broken only by a harsh scrape of boots on stone.

" A teleprinter message to the Fuehrer," Fromm said, when he re-entered his office. He dropped wearily into a chair. Most of the men round him were new to his entourage. They looked blank and uncommunicative, and he avoided their eye.

" Attempted putsch quelled," he dictated, as though drafting a routine report. " All ringleaders shot . . . in unswerving loyalty . . ."

Almost simultaneously the occupation of the Bendlerstrasse began. Troops and tanks moved in according to plan without encountering any resistance.

The officer on duty in the guardroom saluted as Skorzeny shouldered his way in, accompanied by two SS men and followed by Sturmbannfuehrer Maier.

Skorzeny waved his automatic pistol. " I'm taking charge here."

" Yes, sir," replied the officer, saluting again. " We've been expecting you."

At this point a reception committee appeared in the persons of Major Heythe and Lieutenant Herbert, who pressed forward in high excitement. Skorzeny eyed them suspiciously.

"We've made a clean sweep," Herbert announced.

"Yes," Heythe chimed in, "all the rebels have either been liquidated or taken into custody."

General Reinecke appeared. "All exits are blocked," he told Skorzeny. "My men have met no resistance of any kind. They're still sealing off the side and rear wings, but the front of the building is at your disposal."

Skorzeny turned to Major Heythe. "Take me to General Fromm."

"Where's Captain von Brackwede?" Maier asked Herbert.

"In his office, I imagine—he'll be waiting for us." Herbert glowed with martial pride, confident that he had risen magnificently to the challenge of an historic hour. "Your suggestions were enormously helpful, Sturmbannfuehrer, and I can assure you that . . ."

"Later," Maier said, looking round uneasily. "I want Brackwede first—take me to him."

They hurried upstairs. No one attempted to stop them. The few officers they met stood politely aside, some of them with their arms raised in the Nazi salute. Maier merely noted this in passing but did not return the compliment.

"What about Brackwede?" he demanded, forging ahead. "Has his behaviour been suspicious in any way?"

"Captain von Brackwede suspicious?" Herbert registered astonishment. "Quite the reverse: He gave us a lot of invaluable advice."

"That sounds like him," commented Maier. "I only hope he'll be as helpful to me."

"General," said SS-Hauptsturmfuehrer Skorzeny, "I have been instructed to relieve you of your post until further notice."

"If those are your instructions," Fromm replied in measured tones, "far be it from me to stand in your way. I assume that you're acting on orders from the Fuehrer?"

"On direct orders from the Fuehrer."

The general vacated his chair and the Haupsturmfuehrer installed himself in it. The take-over ceremony was accompanied by an exchange of bows, but neither party considered it necessary to seal it with a handshake.

"I had the traitors shot in accordance with court martial procedure," Fromm said.

"I trust you weighed your decision carefully," drawled Skorzeny. "I've no doubt you'll be called upon to justify it."

Fromm drew himself up. "Naturally! I only did my duty."

"What do you propose to do now?"

"I intend to submit a full report to Reich Minister Goebbels. Have you any objection?"

"None whatsoever," Skorzeny replied, reaching for the telephone. He did not favour the general with a second glance.

Stiffly, Fromm stalked out of the office which he had occupied for so long, never to return.

General von Stuelpnagel stood silently in the foyer of the Hotel Raphael in Paris. Loudspeakers were blaring forth military band music, and from the erstwhile hotel dining-room—now the mess—came the sound of officers' voices raised in heated discussion.

Lieutenant-Colonel Caesar von Hofacker, who was standing beside him, said morosely: "That man Kluge! Even so, there's still a chance. If we shoot all the SS leaders we've arrested . . ."

Stuelpnagel did not reply. He gritted his teeth and closed his weary eyes, watched sympathetically by his army driver. Without any change of expression, he listened to the latest items of news: Admiral Krancke had alerted all naval units stationed in Paris; SS-General Sepp Dietrich had issued an ultimatum, namely, that he would order his armoured corps to advance on Paris if the SS leaders were not freed immediately; finally, General Blumentritt would soon be arriving to relieve Stuelpnagel of his duties at Kluge's behest.

"Results," Hofacker said desperately, "—we must produce results!"

Stuelpnagel regarded his companions sadly and then stared at the floor. All at once, the martial music ceased and the silence was broken by the voice of a radio announcer.

"Stay tuned! The Fuehrer will shortly be addressing the German people."

"We'll wait another half-hour," Stuelpnagel said in a flat voice. "I must have time to think."

"We've done too much thinking," Hofacker said inaudibly. With sudden vehemence, he added: "Why don't we act!"

"Everything's going according to plan," Skorzeny told Kaltenbrunner. "Fromm has disposed of the ringleaders and the rest of them are coming to heel splendidly."

The head of the Central State Security Bureau, who had

just arrived in the Bendlerstrasse with his potent-looking body-guard, frowned.

"Aren't things going a bit too smoothly? I find it suspicious."

"Not at all," Skorzeny replied confidently. "Orders are still obeyed in this country, as long as they're uttered with sufficient conviction."

"Did you have to shoot anyone out of hand?"

"Our army friends saved us the trouble by doing most of the dirty work before we got here. General Reinecke is mopping up after them now."

General Hermann Reinecke was currently engaged in combing the first and second floors of the building, assisted by reliable members of the Bendlerstrasse staff. Reinecke, too, was enjoying a rare moment of glory, and he had no intention of squandering it. He was gradually transforming the Bendler block into a remand centre, employing the standard phrase: "Gentlemen, you are under arrest. Judgment will be passed on you by the Fuehrer himself!"

"I still think it's much too simple," commented the chief of the State Security Bureau. "This can't be the final solution. A lot of people in this building were seriously determined to bring about the Fuehrer's death. Where are they all now?"

"Still here, of course—behaving like loyal subordinates."

"I hope you're right, Skorzeny." Kaltenbrunner paced up and down the spacious office as though he found it too constricted for him. "Men were killed today, ruthlessly killed. It was an attempt on the life of the Fuehrer—the Head of State —planned by senior army officers. This is a unique occurrence in German history."

The sexton of the Matthaeikirche, the church with the fortress-like tower which Colonel von Stauffenberg used to be able to see from his office window, was a patient and long-suffering man. When someone knocked at his door in the middle of the night he climbed into his trousers without a murmur and sleepily went to open it.

He found himself confronted by a sergeant-major of equally worthy and reliable appearance. They might have been brothers. Both had learned to accept what was decreed, the one by God and the other by his more immediate superiors.

"We've got to dig a grave," the sergeant-major announced, "—a big one. I've brought five bodies along with me, but we may have to reckon with another couple of dozen."

271

The sexton refrained from asking any questions. He merely nodded, hitched up his trousers and followed the sergeant-major outside. In front of the church he saw the light-weight army truck. Dimly visible in the murk, the members of a fatigue party were carrying bodies into the churchyard and lining them up beside the wall.

"Right, let's get started!" The sergeant-major spat on his hands and reached for a spade. "Come on," he called to his companions. "Move!"

The sexton withdrew, looking apprehensive. Reluctant to accept sole responsibility for a nocturnal and highly un-Christian burial, he telephoned the local police station.

Shortly afterwards, the station sergeant and two constables arrived. They played their torches over the corpses: a general, two colonels, a lieutenant and the civilian-clad body of General Beck.

"Well, what do you know!" exclaimed one of the constables.

"You there!" the perspiring sergeant-major called indignantly. "Don't stand around with your mouths open—lend us a hand instead! This is government business. Nothing must come out—direct orders from the Fuehrer!"

The constables propped their torches on a tombstone, picked up a pair of spades and began to dig industriously. The torchlight shone on their perspiring faces and the five elongated bundles in the background.

"Where's your brother?" demanded Sturmbannfuehrer Maier, pouncing on Konstantin von Brackwede like a hawk.

Konstantin was alone in his brother's office, standing near the window. He looked pale and uneasy.

"Are you feeling ill?" Maier persisted. He took hold of Konstantin's arm and shook it. "What's the matter—suffering from shock? I asked you a question."

"I don't know where my brother is and I don't care," Konstantin replied in a flat voice.

"Come, come, that's no way to talk! I've got to have a word with him straight away—we need him urgently."

The overhead light fell on Konstantin's tense face, turning it into a chalk-white mask and bleaching his fair hair ashen-grey. "Are you planning to arrest him?"

"What makes you think that?" Maier exclaimed. "Don't jump to conclusions, my boy—not unless you're convinced that he was involved in this business, of course."

"I don't know," Konstantin said, throwing up his hands

in desperation. "I don't know what to think any more."

The Sturmbannfuehrer breathed a sigh of relief. "Your best policy is to stop thinking and await developments. You can sit back with an easy mind—I give you my personal guarantee. You did a first-class job, passing on my orders and suggestions to Herbert and his friends."

"But what's this all about, and where do I come into it? Why are you so anxious to find my brother?"

"There you go again! Don't bother your head about me or your brother. We've got some business to settle, that's all. The only point is, where's he gone?"

"I really can't tell you, but I imagine he'll be back soon."

"When did you see him last?"

"About half an hour ago."

Maier looked relieved. "Then he must be somewhere in the building."

Konstantin nodded. "I hope so, but he seemed to be in a tremendous hurry. He hardly spoke to me, and I couldn't understand what he said when he did. He just took the brief-case and vanished."

"What briefcase?" Maier demanded, pricking up his ears.

"The one he gave me to keep for him yesterday—no, the day before yesterday."

"He gave you a briefcase to keep? What was in it?"

"A lot of papers. It was the one I had with me when we drove over here together, don't you remember? You handed it to me when I got out."

The Sturmbannfuehrer gaped helplessly at Konstantin, panting like a hound who sees his quarry vanish under his very nose. "God help us!" he said with an effort. "We'll have to do something about this quickly if we don't want to end up in the same boat—all three of us."

Shortly after 1 a.m. Adolf Hitler, Fuehrer, Reich Chancellor and Supreme Commander of the Armed Forces, addressed the German people. His voice, which sounded hoarse and barely controlled, carried an undertone of wolfish fury.

"My German comrades! If I speak to you today, it is for two reasons: first, so that you should hear my voice and know that I am uninjured and well, and, secondly, so that you should be acquainted with the details of a crime unparalleled in German history."

Colonel von Stauffenberg's body was dumped into the common grave like a sack of coals. Fromm sought out

273

Goebbels and greeted him with a ringing "Heil Hitler!" In Paris, Stuelpnagel decided to capitulate. In Berlin, Captain von Brackwede hurried northwards in the direction of Schiffer-damm, keeping to the shadows and clutching his briefcase.

"A very small clique of ambitious, unscrupulous and criminally stupid officers concocted a plot to eliminate me . . ."

General Beck was thrown on top of Stauffenberg. Their faces brushed together and earth trickled over their lips. Lieutenant Herbert eyed his girl-friend with joyful anticipation and uncorked the wherewithal for a toast to final victory. Field Marshal von Kluge regarded his radio set with contempt, like a man looking in a mirror.

". . . a very small group which believed that it could deal us a dagger-blow in the back, as in nineteen-eighteen . . . a gang of criminal elements which will now be annihilated without mercy."

Countess Elisabeth von Oldenburg-Quentin lay on her bed, heard this, and wept. Two floors down, Jodler junior growled: "Liquidate them, the bastards." In the churchyard of the Matthaeikirche, Lieutenant von Haeften was the last to be thrown into the grave. Goebbels said to Fromm: "You seem to have been in a great hurry to dispose of awkward witnesses, General!"

". . . it is impossible that hundreds of thousands and millions of brave men should give of their best at the front while, at home, a little gang of criminal, ambitious and pitiable creatures should persistently attempt to undermine their morale . . . This time we shall settle accounts in the manner to which we National Socialists are accustomed . . ."

"God bless our beloved Fuehrer!" Frau Breitstrasser mumbled devoutly—taking her eye off the landing at the precise moment when Captain von Brackwede was tiptoeing past. Sturmbannfuehrer Maier telephoned the Prinz Albrechtstrasse and told his minions to clear as many cells as possible.

The streets of Berlin were empty. Few of the city's in-habitants bothered to listen to Hitler. Most of them were sound asleep, subconsciously thanking their Maker that no Allied bombers had come for the second night in succession.

Corporal "Pixie" Lehmann met his new friends at their usual rendezvous. "Here I am again!" he called. "Ready and willing to paint for my country! We must think up some really powerful slogans tonight—like DON'T LET THEM FOOL you! or words to that effect. We may be getting a new recruit—a real live Count, but one of the best."

When the Fuehrer had finished the Badenweiler March rang out. Then Reich Marshal Goering's voice came over the air. Speaking with deliberate emphasis, he began: "*An unspeakably vile murder-attempt was today carried out by a Colonel Count Stauffenberg . . .*"

Earth fell on Stauffenberg and hid him from view. Fromm drank wine from Goebbels's cellar. Hofacker had tears in his eyes.

At the Fuehrer's Headquarters, Himmler reported that the revolt had been suppressed. "Berlin is quiet. Numerous arrests have been made and there are more to come."

The strains of another sprightly march died away, and Grand Admiral Doenitz came to the microphone. He fired off his sentences like broadsides, surpassing both the previous speakers in his mastery of Third-Reich rhetoric.

"*Terrible wrath and boundless fury overwhelm us at the criminal attack which was to have robbed our beloved Fuehrer of his life . . . A small and insane clique of generals, who have nothing in common with our brave army, did, in their craven disloyalty, instigate this murder . . .*"

The announcer concluded: "The conspiracy has totally collapsed . . . Some of the ringleaders . . . have committed suicide. The remaining culprits will be called to account."

Sitting huddled in his living quarters, Hitler nodded repeatedly as he heard himself speak. "I want to see them hanged," he muttered, "—that's what I want to see!"

"Why look so shocked, my dear?" Captain von Brackwede gave Elisabeth a cheerful smile and sank into an arm-chair. "I always hoped you'd welcome a visit from me in the middle of the night."

Elisabeth stared at him in a bemused fashion. Automatically, as though she felt cold, she drew her dressing-gown tighter around her. "My God, how did you get here—here, of all places?"

"Are you frightened?"

"Yes, for you." She switched off the centre light, leaving the room dimly lit by the pinkish glow from her bedside-lamp, and hurried to the window. Lifting one corner of the black-out curtain with a trembling hand, she peered out.

"Don't worry, I shan't stay long," Brackwede told her.

" However, before I go to ground I'd like to know what you've done to my brother—the boy's an emotional wreck. What happened?"

" The Gestapo were here nearly all day," Elisabeth replied. She froze suddenly. " I think that's them again!"

Brackwede leapt to his feet and hurried to the window. A dark-grey saloon purred silently along the street and halted at the kerb. Voglbronner got out and stood squinting up at the third floor.

" Congratulations!" Brackwede said. " That man Maier certainly knows his job. I didn't think he was subtle enough to believe I could be so stupid. Where can I hide?"

He was hustled, complete with briefcase, into a small windowless chamber between the kitchen and the lavatory—the same room which had served Frau Wallner's Jewish lodger as a hiding-place for so long.

" What do you want?" Elisabeth asked Voglbronner. " Have you come to arrest me? If so, here I am."

The Gestapo man made a deprecating gesture. " Please! I only came to give you a message in the hope that you'll pass it on as quickly as possible. The message is: Captain von Brackwede's presence is urgently required at headquarters. Sturmbannfuehrer Maier would appreciate his co-operation, and the sooner he gets it the better—for all of us, with the possible inclusion of yourself. Do you understand, or must I spell it out for you?"

The official residence of the Reich Minister for Popular Enlightenment and Propaganda had been transformed into a provisional detention centre. The master of the establishment, now satisfied that he had the situation well under control, was revelling in his victims' humiliation.

" Call these people conspirators!" he exulted, having bagged one general after another without encountering any resistance whatsoever. " They can't even set off a bomb properly—no wonder we haven't won the war yet!"

Fromm had been shut up in the smoking-room with a bottle of wine. Count Helldorf was in the music-room. General von Hase of the Berlin Kommandantur was confined in one of the smaller reception rooms, also with a bottle of wine. When he asked for another, Goebbels said indulgently: " He can have one more, but I'm not going to have my cellar drunk dry!"

"A revolution by 'phone!" he observed contemptuously to Himmler. His eyes narrowed slightly as he added: "Just a couple of well-aimed rifle-shots, and who knows where we'd be by now . . ." Then he chuckled again.

In Paris, General von Stuelpnagel had resigned himself to the inevitable. He gave orders to liberate the SS, SD and Gestapo men in his sphere of command, almost all of whom had been taken into custody. He further instructed that this should be done in a gentlemanly manner and with expressions of regret.

"Perhaps we ought to hold a party to celebrate the reconciliation," Caesar von Hofacker observed bitterly.

The general did not reply, but his intermediary, Lieutenant-General Hans von Boineburg-Lengsfeld, arbitrarily staged a macabre comedy of his own. Seeking out the incarcerated SS leaders, he informed them, with polished courtesy, that there had been a "regrettable error" and graciously invited them to join him in a glass of champagne at the Hotel Raphael. His invitation was accepted with alacrity.

At the Hotel Raphael, General von Stuelpnagel greeted the ex-captives in person. Polite smiles were exchanged. SS-Obergruppenfuehrer Oberg, known as "the Butcher of Paris," took the glass of champagne which offered him and raised it to his host, who was as good as dead.

A weird orgy began. Army and SS officers drank together in an atmosphere of hysterical relief. Cases of champagne were emptied, the babble of voices increased in volume, and there were moving scenes of fraternisation.

Lieutenant-Colonel Caesar von Hofacker did not participate. He silently withdrew to his room, where he stood lost in thought for several minutes. Then he began to burn the remnants of his papers.

Meanwhile, General von Stuelpnagel and SS-Gruppenfuehrer Oberg had retired into a corner with Otto Abetz, the German Ambassador in Paris, who was doing his best to mediate between them.

A euphemistic formula was devised, according to which a "practice alert"—nothing more—had been held with the prior agreement of senior SS leaders. All troops and Party officials were to be informed of this at the earliest possible moment.

"Well," said the ambassador, "don't you think that's the best solution, under the circumstances?"

"Agreed," replied Gruppenfuehrer Oberg. Raising his champagne glass to Stuelpnagel he added confidentially, in a low voice not intended for other ears: "You don't seriously think you'll get away with it, do you?"

Stuelpnagel shrugged. "We shall see."

"This time, General," the SS leader said with a smile, "I'm afraid you've staked far too much on the wrong horse."

An equally exalted mood prevailed in the Bendlerstrasse.

Sturmbannfuehrer Maier had made his first important find in General Olbricht's office—a list embodying about a hundred names. Kaltenbrunner and Skorzeny took charge of it. Gestapo chief Heinrich Mueller had already conveyed three dozen suspects to the Prinz Albrechtstrasse and entertained high hopes of doubling that number in due course.

Herbert Herbert was making free with his remaining stocks of food and drink, doling them out to comrades-in-arms, sending consignments down to the communications centre and lavishly entertaining the unit-commanders of the occupying troops. Now that the preliminary tokens of the Fuehrer's gratitude and appreciation had been received, there were more than sufficient grounds for celebration.

Major Remer had been promoted colonel and three staff officers had been invested with the same rank. Signal Corps Lieutenant Roehrig was now a captain, and his erstwhile sergeant-major greeted the dawn as a newly-fledged officer.

"It paid off!" Herbert babbled, uncorking another bottle with the aid of his girl-friend. Herbert, whose apple-cheeks looked as if they had been polished with a duster, was a major now!

However, not even that exhausted the cornucopia of Hitler's gratitude. The hero of the Bendlerstrasse revolt was additionally invested with the Iron Cross First Class—an order normally awarded for "outstanding gallantry in the face of the enemy."

"Where's my friend Konstantin?" cried the new major and national hero, swaying on his feet. "I must give him a hug! And where's good old Brackwede, bless him? I'd like to clasp him to my bosom!"

"Ladies and gentlemen," said Corporal "Pixie" Lehmann, a Westhafen crane-driver once more, "permit me to introduce the newest member of our club. —He's a friend of Julius Leber," he added, as though no further qualification were needed.

Lehmann pointed to Brackwede, who was standing in the basement doorway with his briefcase under his arm. His monocle sparkled provocatively as he surveyed the gathering with a look of curiosity.

"You're looking at a bunch of traitors," Lehmann informed him.

"Splendid," said Brackwede, "I couldn't feel more at home."

The two girl students showed a lively interest in Brackwede, but Lehmann restrained their enthusiasm. "The Count is a happily married man, girls, so don't get any ideas."

There was something comforting about the cheerful laughter that followed Lehmann's sally. Brackwede put his briefcase down with a sense of relief.

"I ought to warn you—I'm a dangerous person to have around. Sheltering me could cost you your lives."

"You won't impress anyone round here with that sort of talk," Lehmann said, grinning.

"I need somewhere to stay for an indefinite period," Brackwede said. "Luxuries don't matter. I'm only interested in one thing—a stove which'll burn efficiently. I've got to dispose of the contents of this briefcase."

He promptly received six offers of accommodation.

"Think it over and take your time," Lehmann said. "You've got to spend the next few days with us anyway, so you may as well make the most of it."

Shortly after 4 a.m. Goebbels gave a contented yawn and announced: "Gentlemen, the putsch is over."

He headed for his private quarters, accompanied by Neumann, his Secretary of State. As they strolled along the corridor they passed an alcove containing a bust of the Fuehrer. Goebbels paused by it and rested his hand on the bronze lock of hair draped across the forehead.

"That's the sixth putsch against the Fuehrer I've lived through." He laughed suddenly. "This was the most dangerous of the lot, but none of them took such a short time to put down."

The urge for sleep deserted him. The Fuehrer's bust emitted a hollow, booming sound as he tapped it absently. Sitting down at a small table beside it, he swung his short legs and began to wax sarcastic at the expense of the conspirators.

After a while he relapsed into a brooding reverie. His shrewd gallows-bird face looked pensive. Quietly, as though to himself, he said: "The whole business would be utterly ludicrous if it weren't for one thing. Do you know what I'm talking about?"

Neumann admitted that he did not. He stood waiting patiently, red-eyed with fatigue.

"Stauffenberg, of course!" said Goebbels. "What a man! What coldbloodedness, and intelligence, what iron nerves!" He shook his head ruefully. "How he got mixed up with that bunch of cretins surpasses my comprehension!"

At dawn, the sexton of the Matthaeikirche was again roused from his bed, this time by a Gestapo squad.

"We've come for the bodies," announced the man in charge.

"They're buried already."

"No trouble—we'll dig 'em up again." The Gestapo agents looked faintly amused. A heap of earth was no obstacle to the likes of them, and spades were standard churchyard equipment. "The records office wants some photographs."

The bodies of Lieutenant von Haeften. Colonels Mertz and Stauffenberg, General Olbricht and General Beck were disinterred, thrown into the back of a truck and driven off. They ended up in an incinerator and their ashes, so Himmler announced later, were "scattered in the fields."

Major-General Henning von Tresckow had no inkling of what had happened in Berlin. He was fast asleep on his camp-bed after yet another exhausting day at the Russian front, where the situation was catastrophic.

He was woken by Lieutenant Fabian von Schlabrendorff, his aide and personal friend. Tresckow got up at once. He was so used to being roused at all hours that no Job's messenger could have shaken his composure.

The general listened to Schlabrendorff's report with an impassive face. He paced deliberately up and down the sparsely furnished room for a moment or two, then paused, deep in thought. At last he said simply: "They will try to make me divulge the names of our friends. In order to prevent that, I shall take my own life."

Schlabrendorff was struck dumb by Tresckow's unaffectedly businesslike tone. His eyes wandered round the room, absently noting the rotten, disintegrating plank walls, the General Staff maps and organisation charts, the dog-eared books lying scattered around like cast-off clothing. The night air was stiflingly close.

"Everyone will turn and rend us now," the general continued, "but it doesn't alter my firm conviction that we did the right thing."

Tresckow had once declared that a man's moral worth did not amount to anything unless he was prepared to sacrifice his life for his convictions. He was nothing if not consistent. Ordering his driver to take him to the front, he climbed out and walked alone through the German lines into no-man's-land. Here he emptied his pistol into the air to simulate an exchange of shots and blew his head off with a hand-grenade.

It was reported that Major-General Henning von Tresckow had died "in action."

Early on the morning of Friday, 21 July 1944, a corporal approached the building whose postal address was 11-13 Bendlerstrasse. His name was unimportant and his mission equally so. He had simply come to deliver an envelope.

The corporal knew nothing of what had happened. He had not heard any radio announcements nor been enlightened on the situation by his superiors. He had enjoyed a good night's sleep, and now he was carrying out an order.

In response to a subsequent inquiry as to whether he had noticed anything special, he merely said: "It was bloody hot and my shirt was sticking to my back. The street was empty. Some troops marched out of the gateway of the Bendler block—about a company strong. They were carrying their sub-machine-guns and rifles slung, and they were singing. That was all."

Nothing exceptional seemed to have occurred. Sentries guarded the entrances and people came and went as usual. The soldiers' singing faded into the distance. There were no obvious signs of what they had been doing there.

"Everything looked quite normal," was the corporal's verdict.

"No one will get away," SS-Sturmbannfuehrer Maier said firmly. "Our system is infallible—we'll round them all up sooner or later."

Konstantin von Brackwede looked noncommittal. "Is that so?"

"Yes, and you ought to bear it in mind, if only for your brother's sake. The sooner he gives himself up—makes himself available, I mean—the better for us all."

Konstantin had been asked to report to Maier at the Prinz

Albrechtstrasse headquarters, where he found the Sturmbann-fuehrer wading through a pile of warrants and progress reports. The Gestapo dungeons now contained more than a hundred detainees and the first interrogations had already taken place.

Kaltenbrunner, who was directing the operation in person, had begun by setting up three sub-departments. The most important of these, which covered Bendlerstrasse military personnel, had been entrusted to Maier. " The Fuehrer wants prompt results," Kaltenbrunner informed him, " and so do I. You were told to keep an eye on these people in the first place, so you ought to be able to produce the goods in double-quick time."

This was a threat rather than a statement. Maier's tentative objection that the main witnesses had already been eliminated was dismissed with a curt wave of the hand. " There must be others. You'll find them."

There were indeed others—or one, anyway, and that was Captain Count Fritz-Wilhelm von Brackwede, perhaps the last man alive with a detailed knowledge of the Stauffenberg circle. He simply had to be found.

" Your brother can't escape," Maier told Konstantin, who sat opposite him looking unco-operative. " He'd need special authorisation to fly anywhere by 'plane. Car journeys call for a travel permit and petrol. Double and treble checks are being held at all stations and in trains. It would be pointless for him to try and escape on foot—we've alerted the civil police and sent out additional patrols. No one can get across the frontiers—they're all sewn up tight. So, your brother must still be in Berlin."

" Quite possibly. I wouldn't know."

" For the moment, just listen to what I have to say," Maier replied with a touch of impatience. " I want to impress upon you how hopeless it is for him to try and escape or hide. Take the question of food, for a start. Ration cards only last a month and no hotel or country inn will give anyone more than three nights' accommodation. Every village is swarming with evacuees. Finally, anyone who harbours a wanted man risks the death penalty. Your brother knows the rules as well as I do."

" Then it's up to him," Konstantin said doggedly.

" Have a bit of sense, man!" Maier burst out, thumping the papers on his desk with a clenched fist. " I'm not asking you to turn your brother in. I'm asking you to assist me—to further the ends of justice, if you prefer. Do that, and you may save him from the gallows. Can't you see?"

Konstantin remained pale and silent. His mouth and jaw were set in a stubborn line, but there was helpless bewilderment in his eyes.

"Very well," Maier continued, with an undertone of regret. He picked up a warrant. "In that case, we shall have to take every possible precaution. Since we don't have your brother, we must make do with his personal assistant."

"Countess Oldenburg has nothing to do with this," Konstantin said quickly, " —nothing at all."

"You could be right," Maier replied. "We shall see. For the time being we'll simply take her into custody. Don't worry, my boy—it's merely a precautionary measure. We shan't touch a hair of the girl's head—not for the present, anyway—and as soon as your brother turns up we'll let her go. That's a promise."

"But I've no idea where he is."

"I believe you, but the situation may change rapidly. He may get in touch with you at any moment." Maier donned an air of commiseration. "Believe me, my dear fellow, I'm deeply attached to you and your brother. I only hope our suspicions about him turn out to be unfounded."

"You mean it isn't certain . . .?"

"Certain? What is, in this life?" Maier came over to Konstantin with the warrant in his hand. "Here, take this. Just to demonstrate my good faith, I'll let you inform the Countess yourself that I'm unfortunately compelled to arrest her. Take your time about it. You can have an hour—two, if you like. I'm sure you'll find something to say to each other."

On 21 July, General Karl Heinrich von Stuelpnagel received orders to " report " to Berlin. He knew what this meant. Pale but smiling, he bade farewell to the members of his staff in a clear, serene voice.

"It was inevitable," he said. "I accept full responsibility for all that has happened, and I ask each of you to behave accordingly." Then he climbed into his car and drove off.

Towards evening the general and his party reached Verdun. He told his driver to make a short detour via Sedan, where he had fought as a young officer in the First World War. For the first time that day, the others noticed a certain tenseness in his manner. When the car pulled up in a side road he got out, saying that he was going to take a short walk, alone.

283

Stuelpnagel's slim, erect figure vanished from sight as though the horizon had swallowed him up.

Several minutes later his travelling-companions heard two or three revolver-shots. They stared at each other in dismay and ran to see what had happened. It was some time before they found him. He was lying face-upwards in a canal with his hands clutching his throat, breathing stertorously. When they pulled him out they saw that his cap and belt had disappeared, together with his Knight's Cross, which he seemed to have ripped off. Stuelpnagel lay there on the ground, pale and gasping. He had shot himself in the right temple. The bullet had destroyed one eye and badly damaged the other, blinding him.

The gravely wounded general was conveyed to the field hospital at Verdun, operated on and carefully nursed until he was able to think, speak and stand upright. Then he was brought before a court, sentenced to death and hanged.

He died without a word.

Ex-Corporal Lehmann and ex-Captain von Brackwede found themselves with time on their hands. Circumstances had wrought a change in their respective roles, transforming Lehmann into the staff officer and Brackwede into his aide.

" How's your memory these days?" inquired Lehmann.

" Lousy, when I want it to be. If necessary, I could forget I'd ever seen you."

" I've already ordered some identity cards for us, and our ration books will be arriving tomorrow. I've also laid on half a dozen special travel permits, as well as tram and underground season tickets."

" You're planning some large-scale artistic projects, too, from what I can gather."

" Oh, that!" Lehmann said airily. " That's only a side-line. I'm cooking up a lot of other schemes beside that."

" Is that why you asked about the state of my memory?"

Lehmann nodded. " Slogan-painting's all right at night, but I don't propose to sit around in other people's homes all day, doing nothing. I'm looking for an enjoyable way of occupying my spare time."

They were spending 21 July, a Friday, in the playwright's flat. Brackwede had fallen on their host's library and carried off six books to his post beside the balcony door. Lehmann, having put a new washer on the kitchen tap and falsified the reading on the electricity meter with the aid of a magnet, was on the look-out for fresh distractions.

"You know what I'd really like to do, sir? A little home handiwork."

Brackwede put his book down and regarded the corporal's impish face with astonishment. "You're not thinking of taking up your favourite hobby again?"

"Yes—just to keep my hand in."

"Good God, man, haven't you done enough? Your last bomb only went off yesterday!"

"I know, but why waste time? There must be some explosives around somewhere and I'd like to get my paws on some—that's all."

Brackwede shook his head wonderingly. "Why?"

"Because. After all, you never know when something like that won't come in handy."

"So that's why you asked about my memory! You want me to supply you with an address."

"That's right, and the sooner the better, otherwise the Gestapo'll beat me to it."

Brackwede gave Lehmann an approving nod. "Not a bad idea. Who knows, we may be doing someone a favour by taking the stuff off their hands." He scribbled an address on a slip of paper. "Here, try and cash that."

Ernst Kaltenbrunner, head of the Central State Security Bureau, was appointed "Chairman of the Special Commission for 20 July" on the day after the revolt. The Fuehrer ordered him to submit detailed and comprehensive reports in writing every day.

The Special Commission soon embraced eleven sub-sections and employed the services of approximately four hundred Gestapo personnel. They interviewed almost seven thousand people, of whom more than a thousand were detained and several hundreds executed.

On 22 July the Reichsfuehrer-SS, Heinrich Himmler, arrived at the Bendlerstrasse to inaugurate his reign as C.-in-C. Replacement Army. Those of the staff who were not already dead, incarcerated or on the run, assembled to greet him. Himmler gave a speech in which he appealed to their integrity, loyalty and sense of responsibility. He concluded his address by leading a triple "*Sieg Heil!*" in the Fuehrer's honour, and the officers of his new command joined in enthusiastically.

Shortly afterwards, Dr. Josef Goebbels was appointed "Pleni-potentiary-General for total War-Effort." He at once went into action with one of his well-tried radio harangues.

There followed a frenzied and extravagant torrent of abuse. Reich Marshal Goering called the 20 July plotters "a miserable clique of former generals who had to be removed because of their incompetent and cowardly leadership." Grand Admiral Doenitz spoke of "scoundrels and lackeys of the enemy." Himmler described the officers who participated in the revolt as "saboteurs of the war-effort" and "confederates of hostile foreign powers."

Reichsleiter Bormann, Hitler's closest confidant, poured fuel on the flames by talking of a clandestine attempt to make peace with Moscow—a bugbear of the first order. General Jodl attempted to outdo him. He propagated the view that the conspirators had been "in with the Jesuits," and declared that they should be classified as "even more despicable than the vilest professional criminal."

Spurred on by his colleagues' patriotic zeal, Foreign Minister Ribbentrop described Stauffenberg as "a mentally inferior creature in colonel's uniform," and Reichsleiter Ley, drunk with hatred, mouthed demands for total extermination.

This was going too far. In view of the fact that some members of the much-reviled "aristocratic officers' clique" were still needed to help to run the war, Hitler personally issued a confidential directive which prohibited phrases of this kind.

Goebbels, shrewd and unscrupulous as ever, struck a far more appropriate note in his broadcast address. He referred unblushingly to Stauffenberg as "an evil and degenerate form of life" and spoke of a plot which had been "hatched in the enemy camp." The explosives had come from England, the money from America, the inspiration from Soviet Russia. That said, he too launched into a fanfare of trumpets: "If the Fuehrer's deliverance from mortal danger was not a miracle, miracles no longer exist . . ." Then, for the benefit of those believers who uttered the name of Hitler and God Almighty in the same breath, he proceeded to pull out all the stops of his emotional organ. "We can rest assured," he cried, "that the Almighty could not have manifested himself to us more plainly than through the Fuehrer's miraculous preservation."

Women sobbed, soldiers wept unashamedly, and hampers full of congratulatory telegrams arrived. Some clergymen even intoned prayers of thanksgiving.

Goebbels grinned with delight and told his intimates that "a bomb under Hitler's arse" was one way of making him listen to reason.

"Elisabeth," Konstantin said softly, "what's happened to us?"

He longed to go up and put his arms round her. Instead, he stood there stiffly, unable to move—unable to find the words that would express what he felt.

Elisabeth's face was a pallid mask. "Go on, then—arrest me. What's one more arrest? Just a drop in the ocean."

"Not to me!" Konstantin cried desperately. "You're everything to me!"

He sank down on a chair. It was the chair his clothes had been draped on a few hours before, but nothing could have been further from his mind.

"You must try to forget," Elisabeth said. "People can't live their own lives at a time like this. We tried it, but it didn't work. It's your brother we ought to be thinking about now—he's the one that matters."

"He's got no right to demand such sacrifices!" Konstantin put out a hand towards her and then withdrew it. "He wouldn't ask it of you, I know he wouldn't. If only I could talk to him . . ."

"Konstantin," Elisabeth said in a low, urgent voice, "they're trying to play you off against him—don't you realise that? Don't you realise your brother's potential value to these people? They'd stop at nothing to get their hands on him."

"What's the matter with him?" Konstantin complained. "He's my brother, isn't he? Why hasn't he ever been completely frank with me? Whatever he's done, he must know that I'm devoted to him. Even if I couldn't understand his motives—even if he were guilty of the most heinous crime—it wouldn't change my love for him." He paused. "The same applies to you."

"So you do accept the possibility that he may have been involved in the bomb plot?"

"Yes."

"Does that mean you sympathise with the motives behind it?"

"I can't answer that question, Elisabeth—not yet. All I know is, the Fuehrer and Germany have always been one to me. I was ready to die for Hitler, but if men like Beck, Stauffenberg and my brother are so unalterably opposed to him they must have a very good reason."

"Good," Elisabeth said quietly. After a moment's hesitation, she added: "I agree—you must talk to your brother. It might be managed. We made arrangements in advance, just in case things went wrong. Be in the booking-hall of the Zoo Station as soon as possible after eight this evening. Wait beside the news-stand at the foot of the subway—but please be careful."

"I'd do anything to help you—him, all of us."

"We'd better go now," she said unemotionally. She put her cool, firm hand in his and drew him toward the door. "And please—don't worry about me more than you need. I'm almost happy to be joining the others, believe me."

The two men who arrived at the Fuehrer's Headquarters were clad in formal black and comported themselves with dignity. Hitler received them at once.

"Gentlemen," he declared, regarding them with favour, "you have a great task ahead of you. Rest assured that I have the fullest confidence in your abilities."

He extended his hand as he would have done to a pair of friendly Heads of State and ushered them to a sofa, where they all sat down: the Fuehrer, the President of the People's Court and the public executioner of Greater Berlin.

The President of the People's Court, Roland Freisler, was a lean man with a voice like a saw-edged knife. The executioner resembled a conscientious post-office clerk. Both men gazed at the Fuehrer with humble reverence, obviously sensible of the high honour that was being bestowed on them.

"Let us get down to details, gentlemen," Hitler continued. "I take it that we are under no illusions as to the vile rabble we're dealing with?"

"The scum of the earth!" Freisler assured him. "If it were left to me I'd dispense with a trial altogether—there can't be any doubt about the verdict. However, I assume that the conventions must be observed."

"Of course," Hitler replied. "We're a constitutional State, even if we don't allow ourselves to be swayed by sentimentality."

Freisler grasped Hitler's implication at once. "I shall proceed with the utmost despatch, my Fuehrer. I never tolerate long-winded speeches in my court. Any digressions will be nipped in the bud."

"Excellent. How many cases will you handle per day?"

"Between six and eight, I should imagine."

Hitler turned to the executioner. "Will you be able to keep pace?"

"I shall do my utmost. My present daily capacity is three or four—roughly thirty per cent more than that of my colleagues in Koenigsberg and Munich. However, I estimate that my output could be stepped up by a hundred per cent, provided that sufficient materials were allocated to enable me to extend my facilities."

"They will be," said Hitler.

They sipped their tea, a pleasantly bitter brew served in delicate egg-shell porcelain cups. Plates of cakes had also been set out on the table in front of them.

"The enormity of this crime demands atonement of an unparalleled kind," Hitler declared. "Deterrence must be absolute. I expect the trials to be brief but impressive, the judgments to be concise and to the point, and the executions to be carried out instantly. A man sentenced in the morning must hang the same afternoon."

"It will be done," promised Freisler.

"We'll manage," said the executioner.

"No shooting!" Hitler warned. "Don't waste ammunition on the swine—our men at the front need all they can get. They must hang."

"Death by hanging is the normal method," Freisler said judicially.

"How long does it take?"

"Ten to fifteen seconds," the public executioner replied, "—depending on the strength of my assistants and the constitution of the condemned man."

"Can't it be prolonged?"

"Certainly, my Fuehrer. If piano strings are used in place of a thin wire noose, the time can be extended to several minutes."

"I want to see it," Hitler insisted. "I want it filmed in full—the court proceedings as well. Sound-recordings will do for the less important passages."

In the background, Bormann jotted down a memorandum for Goebbels, whose ministry was responsible for films and broadcasting. The tea-cups were refilled.

The President of the People's Court leant forward confidentially. "If armed forces personnel are to be removed from military jurisdiction, my Fuehrer, certain legal formalities will have to be gone through first."

"It's all settled," Bormann interposed. "We're convening a Court of Honour. That ought to dispose of any possible objections."

The Court of Honour of the Greater German Wehrmacht met for the first time on 4 August 1944. Field Marshal Gerd von Rundstedt took the chair.

"In the name of the Fuehrer," he began, and went on to read out a preliminary list of twenty-two names, among them those of a field marshal and eight generals "These men have forfeited the right to wear the uniform of this nation."

None of those present dissented. They included Field Marshal Keitel and Generals Burgdorf, Haisel, Schroth, Specht and Kriekel. General Guderian's name also appeared on the list of participants, but the successful tank specialist later claimed that he had attended no more than two or three sessions, and then only under protest. He characteristised the proceedings as "repulsive and tragic," but he voted with the rest.

"Creatures who have raised their hand against our Head of State," Field Marshal von Rundstedt declared, "no longer merit a place in our ranks."

Roughly a hundred officers were duly discharged "with ignominy." In practical terms, this meant that no military tribunal was now competent to try them and they could be legally consigned to the tender mercies of the Gestapo and the People's Court.

"Much as some of us may regret it," continued the President of the Court of Honour, "we cannot fail to reach the only possible decision. We owe it to Germany and our Leader."

The Gestapo spread its net still wider, urged on by Himmler in person. Kaltenbrunner needed material for his daily reports to the Fuehrer, and Sturmbannfuehrer Maier proved to be his main supplier. His men, and Voglbronner in particular, promptly discovered further treasure troves of evidence. A "government list" belonging to the conspirators was found in the Bendler block, together with a form of log-book written in a coded shorthand which experts deciphered without difficulty.

Another important cache of documents was found at the Quartermaster-General's office in Zossen Further material arrived from Obergruppenfuehrer Oberg in Paris, and members of the Bendlerstrasse Signals personnel swore affidavits on the subject of their telephone-tapping activities.

"Not bad at all," Maier said confidently.

"Not bad for a start," Kaltenbrunner amended. "However, it's nothing like enough. You'll have to bring up some heavier artillery if you really want to carry conviction."

The Sturmbannfuehrer requested reinforcements and was granted them on the spot. He then concentrated his attentions on the last remaining aces in the pack. Beck and Stauffenberg no longer existed and Leber had been taken out of service in the nick of time, but Goerdeler was still at large.

Maier's efforts to track him down remained unavailing, even though he assigned nearly a hundred Gestapo agents to the job. Their inquiries did, however, bear some fruit.

Two Gestapo men paid a routine visit to the Temperance Hostel where Goerdeler had occasionally spent the night. They found that recent bombing had reduced it to a heap of rubble, but the ruins were still administered by a caretaker. The latter, a haggard but helpful individual, informed them that Herr Goerdeler was known at the hostel but had not stayed there for some time.

The Gestapo men shrugged and turned away, but the caretaker hurried after them.

"All we've got is a big envelope belonging to Herr Goerdeler. He left it with us and we put it in our safe."

The envelope was relayed, via the Gestapo agents and Voglbronner, to Maier, who handed it to Kaltenbrunner with an air of triumph.

"Some of the memoranda in there are sheer treason, sir."

"What else did you expect from a man like Goerdeler?"

"He quotes names—about a hundred of them."

The chief of the State Security Bureau nodded. "That's a bit better. However, what we need is an over-all picture of the conspiracy, and we still haven't got one."

"There's probably only one man who can provide that, and that's Count von Brackwede."

"Where is he?"

"I'm not sure at the moment."

"Then you'd better find him, Maier. We're relying on you to supply the best possible evidence in the shortest possible time. Why do you think you were given this assignment in the first place? If you fall down on the job now, I don't have to tell you what the consequences will be—or do I?"

"Don't turn round," said a low voice behind Konstantin's back. "Eyes front, and keep that innocent look on your face."

Konstantin was standing in the booking-hall of the Zoo Station, covertly watching the crowds who jostled him. He had bought several newspapers and tucked them under his arm.

"Open one of those papers," the voice said quietly. "Pretend to read it—then we can talk without giving the game away."

Konstantin did as he was told. He opened the *Voelkischer Beobachter*, and its large format conveniently hid his face, his Knight's Cross and almost all his distinguishing features. In a subdued voice, he asked: "Is that you, Lehmann?"

"Yes, but don't mention any names and don't go throwing your arms round my neck, either. Try to look as casual as possible."

Lehmann was standing beside and slightly to the rear of him, pretending to examine a display of picture-postcards. He bought one—a reproduction of a Third Reich work of art depicting Adolf Hitler in shining armour. He was mounted on a charger and held a fluttering swastika banner in his hand.

"Follow me," Lehmann said, "—and don't be too obvious about it. Keep five or ten yards between us."

Konstantin picked up the rules of the game with surprising speed. He folded his newspaper in a leisurely fashion, glancing at Lehmann as he did so. The corporal, who was dressed in a well-worn civilian suit, looked like a worker on the way home from day-shift at an armaments factory.

There followed a zig-zag promenade through the central districts of Berlin. It led from the Zoo Station to Nollendorfplatz, from there to Gleisdreieck, and from there back to Buelowstrasse and Wittenbergplatz. It ended, provisionally, in Uhlandstrasse, where Lehmann vanished into a doorway. Konstantin sauntered after him like a man out for an evening stroll.

"You're making progress, Lieutenant," Lehmann said. He tipped his blue cap to the back of his head and regarded Konstantin with approval. "Anyone'd think you were one of us."

Konstantin took his hand and shook it warmly. "How are you?"

"Fine—like your brother," Lehmann replied with a grin. "That's what you really wanted to know, was it? We're pretty cheerful, all things considered."

"Are we there yet?"

"You must be joking—of course not! We've got any amount of back-tracking to do yet." Lehmann wiped his damp forehead on his sleeve.

Konstantin produced a handkerchief and followed suit. The weather was still as sultry as it had been on the day of the bomb. There had been a downpour on the Tuesday following, but the air had now regained the consistency of treacle.

"You think we've been followed?"

Lehmann shrugged. "I don't think so, but I like to be thorough. I'm not a great believer in luck, Lieutenant—method's more in my line. That's why we've been taking all these detours."

"You look as if you enjoy this sort of thing."

"There isn't much scope for amusement in Germany these days. I grab any opportunity that comes along."

Konstantin shook his head ruefully. "This is a strange country to live in," he said on impulse.

"It's a hard country to survive in, I know that." Lehmann tugged the peak of his cap down over his sweating face. "That's why we've got to reckon with the possibility that there's someone waiting for us round the next corner who believes that our Adolf is the ever-loving daddy of his people. I tell you, Lieutenant, honest men are fair game in this country."

Carl Friedrich Goerdeler had not witnessed the events of 20 July at first hand. He was on the run from the Gestapo, and the organisers of the revolt did not seek to involve him directly.

He had, however, heard the speeches and announcements on the German radio as he flitted from one hide-out to the next, totally isolated from his fellow-conspirators.

"The Fuehrer is alive, then."

"So it appears," Goerdeler replied, as he took leave of one of his numerous hosts, an official who worked in the Ministry of State Economics.

"Alive and in full control of the situation."

The man murmured a few words of regret but escorted him to the door with obvious relief. Goerdeler vanished into the night.

He changed his abode daily now. Ceaseless flight from his pursuers had become the regular pattern of his existence, but for the moment he remained in Berlin, where, on 31 July, he celebrated his sixtieth birthday.

He passed the day in the flat of an office-clerk named Labetzki. To Goerdeler, he was merely one more name on a seemingly interminable list, but the fleeting nature of Labetzki's acquaintance with the former mayor of Leipzig did not prevent him from giving him food and accommodation with simple-hearted generosity. Goerdeler asked for some writing-paper, and Labetzki watched him as he sat in a corner, hunched and silent, drafting yet another of his monographs. This one was shorter than most.

Some days later, while he was on the way to yet another hide-out by Underground, Goerdeler met a female acquaintance. Adopting the itinerant preacher's tone so characteristic of him, he murmured: "Thou shalt not kill!"—implying that he regarded Stauffenberg's tragic failure as a divine judgment.

Goerdeler's face and name stared back at him from every hoarding and newspaper kiosk, on the underground railway and outside theatres, on walls and wooden fences, in every newspaper he opened. There was a price of a million marks on his head now—the largest sum ever offered for "information leading to the arrest of a criminal" and one which was destined to be paid in the near future.

Those who sheltered Goerdeler risked their lives, and many of them later died merely because he had eaten at their table or slept in their home. He roamed from one place of refuge to the next, leaving a trail of death behind him.

On 8 August he left Berlin and made for his home in West Prussia. His ultimate objective was Marienwerder and his parents' grave. He took two days and nights to get there, shunning his fellow human beings like a leprous beggar.

When he reached the grave he knelt and prayed. Then he stretched out, exhausted, with his head pillowed on the ground.

Goerdeler did not linger there long. Quickly, he hurried onwards. He slept in the fields, in a barn, in a station waiting-room, fed himself on stolen turnips, begged bread from a farm labourer, lapped water like an animal.

On 12 August, at the end of his resources, he walked into a country inn at a place called Konradswalde. Here he was recognised by a member of the Women's Air Force Auxiliary, detained by her two male companions, and handed over to the Gestapo.

This was not the end of Goerdeler's Calvary. His brain, crammed with names and data, was tapped assiduously for months on end—long after he had been sentenced to death.

Captain von Brackwede looked his brother up and down. "What an edifying sight you are, Konstantin! Why did you come?"

"To see you, Fritz."

"All right—you've seen me."

Brackwede was lolling on a sofa, smoking a cigar. His latest refuge was situated near Savignyplatz and belonged to an employee of Leber's coal-merchanting business.

"I've got to talk to you, Fritz. They've arrested Elisabeth."

Brackwede closed his eyes. "It was only to be expected. However, I don't think she's in any danger. She's an extremely bright girl, as you've probably gathered. Besides, she's got guts."

"But she's far too good a person to be sacrificed like this!"

Brackwede made no response. Almost casually, he asked: "Any news from home?"

"Yes, your wife's worried sick."

"Women who marry people like me often are," Brackwede said quietly.

"Your children are asking for you, too."

Brackwede raised himself on one elbow. "Listen, Konstantin," he said harshly, "a man and his family sometimes have to live in two separate worlds—don't you realise that?"

Konstantin eyed his brother angrily. "You obviously don't know what you've started, Fritz. Your wife and children are out of their minds with worry, the Gestapo are after you, and Maier wants to speak to you urgently. Apart from that, I want to know the true facts. The most important thing now is to help Elisabeth!"

"Moving house—that's the most important item on my agenda at the moment." Brackwede got to his feet. "Look, I don't care if it's the family or the Fatherland you're worried about, Konstantin. Just stop peddling your emotions round the place."

"But frightful things have happened, Fritz!"

"You may call them frightful—I call them inevitable."

"What was your connection with this affair—tell me!"

Brackwede smiled as he pulled on his socks. The room had a wide Berlin window and the furniture was early Biedermeier, elaborately ornamented but beautiful in its delicacy. The air filled with silvery sound as the clock on the mantelpiece struck the hour.

"The world's chock-full of idealists," Brackwede said, reaching for his shoes, "—you can call them fools, too, depending on circumstances. Whichever they are, I'm sick of the lot of them."

"I can't make up my mind what you are, Fritz."

"Don't bother to try." Brackwede fumbled with his laces. "I'm neither a martyr nor a stool-pigeon—nor am I a fool. My sole aim is to survive. I hope that answers your question."

Konstantin was standing with his head bowed, staring at the floor. His hands twitched nervously as though seeking something. Brackwede looked up at him with sudden affection.

"If I've destroyed any of your illusions, Konstantin, I'm glad."

"But I want to come with you—don't you understand?"

"Where to?"

"Anywhere you say."

"No," Brackwede said firmly. "I intend to go my own way, and you can tell anyone who expresses an interest in me —it doesn't matter who—that they've got to dismiss me from their minds altogether."

"You misjudge us, Fritz!" Konstantin burst out.

"I wish I did, my boy. Tell my wife to carry on with her life as though I had never existed, and make it clear to Elisabeth Oldenburg that she must cope with the situation on her own—tell her to behave as if saving her own skin were all that mattered."

"You can't expect it of them, Fritz!"

Brackwede straightened up. He buttoned his uniform jacket, perfunctorily as ever, omitting to fasten the collar. "One more thing: you can tell our mutual friend Maier that I'm not doing any more deals with him."

"I have been asked to hand you a communication from the Fuehrer," announced Field Marshal Model.

Field Marshal Kluge hesitated before picking up the envelope which Model pushed across to him. "Am I relieved of my command?" he asked dully.

Model's cool, bland features did not change expression, but he inclined his head. "Much as I personally regret being

296

the bearer of this news, I am acting on direct orders. I cannot evade my duty."

"Are you taking over from me?" Kluge asked.

Model shrugged. "Someone has to."

Hitler's letter instructed Kluge to report to Berlin at once in order to clarify certain "doubtful points." The significance of this was not lost on him: interrogations, presumably conducted by the Gestapo, lay ahead. He sat there for some time in stupefied silence.

"My conscience is clear," he said at length. His voice sounded strained and unnatural.

"Far be it from me to judge," Model replied politely.

With that, Field Marshal Model became Commander-in-Chief, West—the zenith of his military career. A few months later he shot himself with his service revolver in a small wood near Essen, but that day was yet to come.

Kluge's request for time to write a few letters was graciously acceded to, and while his staff car was being prepared for the journey he wrote to his son. He had always done his duty, he said, and if he were to die it would be in the execution of that duty. He then wrote to his Supreme Commander:

I have always admired your greatness, my Fuehrer . . .
You have waged a great and honourable struggle . . .
History will bear witness . . .

This done, the field marshal emerged from his headquarters, settled himself in his staff car and drove off, taking a minimum of luggage with him.

Kluge's driver reported later that he had conducted loud but intelligible conversations with himself in the back seat. After hours of monotonous driving, by which time they had reached the neighbourhood of Verdun, the field marshal announced that he would like a rest and told him to pull up.

He got out, stiff-legged, and looked round for a suitable spot. The driver spread a rug in the shade of some old chestnut-trees and withdrew. Kluge thanked him in a weary voice, lay down on the rug and bit into a capsule of poison which he had been carrying around with him for months.

Death came to him speedily and silently, only a few miles from the spot where General von Stuelpnagel had blinded himself.

Hitler, the honourable warrior of Kluge's farewell letter, survived the twentieth of July by only nine months and ten days.

Then he shot himself. His body was soaked with petrol and burnt, and his ashes, like those of Colonel von Stauffenberg, were scattered to the four winds.

"I could have you taken apart if I wanted to," said Sturmbann-fuehrer Maier.

Lehmann ventured a cautious grin. "But you don't want to, is that it?"

"Why grill a sausage when I can roast a whole ox?"

Lehmann had been arrested near the Zoo Station at noon that day, while out on one of his foraging expeditions. All he had noticed at first was that someone was following him. This did not perturb him unduly. He made a few rapid diversionary manoeuvres and felt certain that he had shaken off at least three or four pursuers. He could not be expected to know that there were more than two dozen men on his trail.

"Sausage or no sausage," he said tentatively, "you seem to think I'm worth something. Why, I wonder? All this fuss is beginning to put the wind up me. I hope you don't think I'm a sort of poor man's Stauffenberg."

Maier could not hide his amusement, as Lehmann was quick to note. They eyed each other warily for a few moments. Then the corporal pulled up a chair and sat down.

"You're a joker, I see," Maier said, following suit. "What's more, you're a lot craftier than I thought."

"Which makes me a man after your own heart, eh?"

Lehmann could afford to indulge in this double-edged form of flattery because they were alone in the room. After a pause, during which he appeared to be thinking deeply, the Sturmbannfuehrer pushed a cigar-box across to the corporal and made a gesture of invitation.

"The whole lot?" Lehmann inquired brazenly.

Maier's booming laugh rang out again. "I envy your sense of humour, young man! I suppose you realise that I could have you flayed alive for what you've done."

"You don't know the half of it." Lehmann opened the cigar-box and expertly sniffed its contents. "I'd like three of these—one for now, one for the road and one for a friend—you know who."

The Sturmbannfuehrer nodded. Something akin to respect dawned in his eyes. "What the hell are you doing with that bunch of broken reeds? A smart lad like you ought to be in our mob."

"We might discuss it sometime," Lehmann replied airily

298

" However, we've both got other worries at the moment. I want to get out of here in one piece and you're pining for a sight of Captain von Brackwede—isn't that so?"

" More or less," Maier conceded, " and I'm relying on your active co-operation."

" Why not?" Lehmann lit one of his cigars, thinking swiftly. " It won't be as easy as all that, of course, but I don't need to tell you that. I notice you haven't asked me for the Captain's address—I couldn't give it to you, either, because I don't know it. I'll do my best to find him, of course, but he hops around the whole time."

" Come off it!" Maier said impatiently. " You don't have to go through that rigmarole for my benefit—it's an insult to my intelligence."

" No offence meant," Lehmann assured him. " Can I get lost, then? You won't put any of your bloodhounds on my tail, will you?"

Maier shook his head. " You go back to Brackwede. I'll find you again when I want you—and I will want you sooner or later. We'll find Brackwede too, in due course, take it from me."

" But you need to see him right away and you're willing to pay for the privilege. Am I right?"

" I'm ready to pay a high price, and that includes the loss of your company."

" I'm supposed to take him a message from you, is that it?"

" You've caught my meaning perfectly." The Sturmbannfuehrer leant forward. " Tell him this: he's welcome to throw his brother and Countess Oldenburg to the wolves if he wants to. On the other hand, he's got a wife and children as well—three or four, if I remember rightly. I'll rope them all in—all of them—unless he gives himself up without delay. Pass that on, and be quick about it."

Lehmann registered no surprise. He was familiar with Gestapo methods and the current price of human life. " What security are you offering?"

" If he accepts my suggestion I'll get his wife and children out of the country. They can be in Switzerland inside twentyfour hours. Details like passports, travel permits and tickets have already been taken care of, but an hour after his dependants cross the frontier he must present himself at my office. That's my offer."

" You'd accept his word?"

"He's a gentleman, isn't he?" Maier's eyes gleamed with secret amusement. "Tell him to 'phone me, that's all."

"And if he doesn't, you'll put his whole family inside?"

"Yes."

"What if he gives you his word and then breaks it? After all, he'd know his wife and children were safe."

"If he did, I'd nab his brother and work him over— Countess Oldenburg as well. Then I'd get you and Brackwede, too, and the fur would really start to fly."

"I follow you." Lehmann rose and folded his two remaining cigars carefully in a newspaper. "Goodbye, then. I won't say au revoir, just in case."

"One more thing: if Brackwede does come, he needn't worry about his personal safety. I'll welcome him like a valued associate. Tell him that."

Field Marshal Rommel, who had been severely wounded by shell splinters, was finally able to leave the French hospital where he had been convalescing and return to his home at Hesslingen in Swabia.

Here he received orders from Hitler to proceed to Berlin for "an important conference." Well knowing what this meant, he cabled back, regretting that he was unable to attend on account of illness. Friends to whom he confided that Hitler planned to eliminate him scoffed at his fears.

At noon a week later, Generals Burgdorf and Maisel arrived in Hesslingen accompanied by units of the Armed SS, who surrounded the village. Their orders were to open fire on the Fuehrer's erstwhile favourite if he tried to escape.

The two generals announced with due solemnity that they were there on the express orders of the Fuehrer. All attempts to dislodge them were abandoned when they further announced that, if need be, they would have to gain access by force. They were ushered into Rommel's presence.

In the course of a conversation lasting nearly an hour, the Nazi emissaries informed Rommel that he had been accused of complicity in the plot against the Supreme Commander. He was being offered the choice between poison and the People's Court. If he chose poison his family would not be subjected to any form of persecution and he himself would be guaranteed a State funeral. If he chose the People's Court, it would mean disgrace and an excruciating death.

Telling his wife that he would be dead within a quarter of

an hour, Rommel left his home at 1.05 p.m., escorted by the two generals. Twenty-five minutes later his dead body was delivered to a hospital in Ulm. His companions announced—in the name of the Fuehrer—that the cause of death was thrombosis and that no post mortem was necessary.

The State funeral duly took place. The Fuehrer and Supreme Commander was represented by Field Marshal von Rundstedt. Indicating the swastika-bedecked coffin, he declared: "His heart belonged to the Fuehrer."

Field Marshal Model issued a stirring order of the day in which he referred to "one of our nation's greatest military commanders," Goering cabled Frau Rommel "in silent compassion," and Hitler, to all appearances deeply moved, told his intimates that a worthy memorial would be erected in his memory "when victory is ours."

On 30 July, ten days—almost to the minute—after Stauffenberg's bomb exploded in the Fuehrer's Headquarters, Captain Count Fritz-Wilhelm von Brackwede presented himself at the building in Prinz Albrechtstrasse.

"They're expecting me," he told the SS sentry guarding the entrance.

He had his briefcase with him—the one which had been shuttled back and forth between Schifferdamm and the Bendlerstrasse, but there were no papers in it now. It contained a piece of soap, a hand-towel, pyjamas, a set of clean underwear and a pair of socks.

"Sturmbannfuehrer Maier is busy," the SS sentry announced. "He can't see anybody."

"He'll see me," Brackwede replied firmly, suppressing a violent urge to walk out of the building and vanish. "Just mention my name."

His name sparked off a minor explosion. Two SS sentries transformed themselves at lightning speed into watchful escorts. They conducted the visitor to Maier, who came to meet him on the landing with arms outstretched in welcome.

"There you are at last!"

"A bargain's a bargain," replied Brackwede. "Besides, you know how inquisitive I am. I couldn't resist the temptation to see you in your natural habitat."

"You never could resist a joke, either," brayed Maier. "Anyway, you're here—that's the main thing. I take it you're prepared to spare us some of your valuable time. You know how much is at stake, I presume?"

"I know what hostages are," Brackwede said. "That's quite enough for me."

"You only have to read the Germanic sagas . . ." Reichsfuehrer-SS Heinrich Himmler told his fellow-fighters on the total extermination front.

To Third Reich upholders of the final solution, no allusion could have been plainer or more unmistakable. The clan was the ultimate constituent of any community. If it grew and flourished it had to be carefully tended and nurtured. If it did not fit into society, the only answer was to exterminate it.

In accordance with this doctrine, wives, fathers, brothers and sisters, old men and children—even babies—were "taken into custody." All available dependants of the putative ring-leaders of the conspiracy were arrested by the Gestapo. They included at least twelve women aged seventy or over, among them the mother of the two Stauffenbergs.

They were conveyed to gaols, educational institutions and concentration camps, pronounced "racially inferior" and treated as such. No trace of them was found until months after the war had ended, and then only by dint of painstaking investigation.

Countess Nina von Stauffenberg, the colonel's wife, who was expecting her fourth child, was re-named Frau Schank. Through the good offices of her warders she was not maltreated and received almost enough to eat.

Stauffenberg's existing children—two sons and a daughter—were separated from their mother and taught to answer to the name of "Meister." Together with other youthful companions in misfortune they were "administered" by Party organisations and housed in remote and isolated camps, where they were carefully reared in the belief that their fathers were despicable criminals.

"Be broadminded," advised Maier. "Overlook any unavoidable little unpleasantnesses. Think realistically, be smart—turn yourself into what the British call a witness for the Crown. You can name your own price."

"Do you really think I'd be such a swine?" asked Brackwede.

"Don't talk crap!" Maier scoffed. "We're born partners in a damned dangerous line of business, you and I. We both know when it's time to cut our losses. At least, I can't imagine a shrewd operator like yourself not wanting to get out of a bankrupt concern while the going's still good."

"You're obviously having a hard time of it."

The Sturmbannfuehrer nodded. He was so sure of victory that he could afford a little unvarnished candour. "We're operating at high pressure here, twenty-four hours a day. I've only got a couple of hundred men to cope with roughly a thousand suspects."

Brackwede raised his eyebrows. "A thousand, eh? That's a fair number. I wish I'd seen them all in action on the twentieth of July."

"I know, I know—we grabbed everyone we could lay hands on. Now it's a question of screening them, sorting them out, trying to fit the pieces together. It's a damned laborious process, and in my humble opinion we started on it too late."

"You mean Himmler took his time about launching the operation?"

Maier gave an irreverent wink. "You know our Heinrich! If he kept tame Jews for insurance purposes, why shouldn't he have a few stool-pigeons and collaborators among your lot as well?"

"And that could be a source of official embarrassment, eh?"

"Don't cherish any false hopes. my dear fellow. We've covered ourselves against all contingencies—with the Reichsfuehrer's approval, of course. Detailed lines of procedure have been laid down specially for this batch of interrogations."

"I follow. Your instructions are to rule out any form of irrelevant, misleading or embarrassing evidence. All you want are the so-called essentials."

"Precisely."

"If I started to talk about our private agreements, for instance my mouth would be stopped, I suppose?"

"Properly stopped," Maier confirmed. "We don't believe in half-measures here, not that I need to tell you that."

"No, you needn't."

"Then we're agreed on that score." The Sturmbannfuehrer rubbed his hands briskly. "Right, let's get started. How many names can you give me?"

Brackwede shook his head. There was a look of grim determination on his predatory face. "The terms of our agreement were absolutely straightforward. You were to get my family to safety; in return, I was to report to you. Well, here I am, but that's as far as I'll go."

The Sturmbannfuehrer regarded him with surprise and indignation. "Surely you wouldn't try to double-cross me now—not in your position! You'd just be signing your own death warrant—one among hundreds. You wouldn't want it to come to that, would you?"

TWO

"I'm a stool-pigeon," said the man with a face like a sleepy shrew. "My name's Dambrowski—Christian name Alarich, but that's not my fault. You've been warned."

Alarich Dambrowski was scrubbing the floor of the cell assigned to Captain von Brackwede. His bleary-looking eyes darted observantly round the room as he knelt there, emaciated body moving to and fro with a rhythmical, monotonous economy of effort. "They've given you a first-class compartment," he continued. "Did you know that?"

"Consider yourself my guest," Maier had said, and Brackwede had not taken long to realise that he was indeed a privileged visitor. He was surrounded by a certain degree of luxury—a camp-bed with a feather mattress, a hard-backed chair and a table the size of a coffin-lid. There was even a writing-stand under the barred window, and the *pièces de résistance* were a wash-basin and lavatory, both in working order.

"You must be a prize specimen," Dambrowski pursued, "—the brother-in-law of a Reichsleiter, maybe, or something similar?"

Brackwede made no immediate response. Faintly surprised, he watched the man with the body of a starving child shuffling along on his knees. At last he said: "If you've been put here to spy on me you must have been told something about me."

"True." Dambrowski straightened up and looked at him with eyes as opaque as a muddy stream. "You're sharp, aren't you? They say you used to be Deputy President of the Berlin police. Is that a fact?"

Brackwede nodded. "Yes, but it hasn't kept me out of here. Funny, you never waste much thought on prison cells until you see them from the inside."

"You get used to them," Dambrowski said.

"Have you been here long?"

"Nearly five years." The match-stick man in the baggy prison uniform looked almost proud. "It's quite an achievement to survive that long, I can tell you. They call me the best nark in the building, and this bone-and-brain mill rates pretty high in its class, doesn't it?"

"I'm not qualified to judge yet."

"You will be." Dambrowski wagged his head thoughtfully. "You've no idea what the human body can stand, if that's any comfort to you. I've even known times when the Gestapo were almost as done in after an interrogation as the people they were interrogating. It doesn't often happen, but it's lovely when it does."

"I can well understand why you've reached the top of your profession," Brackwede remarked without irony. "Your softening-up technique is beyond praise."

Dambrowski looked gratified. "Thanks for the compliment —you're an expert. I can see we're going to get on like a house on fire. The only trouble is, I don't think we'll have much time together. The Gestapo are working at full pressure. They've just about completed their first consignment for the People's Court."

"Who?" demanded Brackwede.

"Goerdeler, Witzleben, Stieff and Hoepner, for a start." Clearly, Alarich Dambrowski kept his ear to the ground. "There seems to be a mass of evidence against them. As far as a lot of the other traitors are concerned—to use the current term—our friends are still ferreting around. You're supposed to be helping them, aren't you?"

"That's the main idea."

"And will you?"

"You want to know a great deal in a short time, Herr Dambrowski." Brackwede smiled into the informer's expressionless eyes. "However, I quite see that your reputation as the best stool-pigeon in the building depends on your ability to produce results. That being so, you can tell Maier this: I'm not fundamentally opposed to singing in due course, but I shall expect a quid pro quo. He must make up his mind what certain pieces of information are worth to him."

"Herr von Brackwede," Alarich Dambrowski said appreciatively, "I'd like to thank you for being so helpful. If I can ever do anything in return . . ."

"In my eyes, Herr President, you are the most important member of the German judiciary in office today."

Thus spake Adolf Hitler, Fuehrer and Reich Chancellor, unto Dr. Roland Freisler, President of the People's Court. They were once more closeted at Supreme Headquarters, discussing final arrangements for the treason trials. The first hearing was due to be held a few days hence.

"I can assure you that all preparations have been made with due attention to detail," grated Freisler. "I shall mete out justice exactly as you would wish me to, my Fuehrer—Draconian justice."

"Bravo!" exclaimed the omnipresent Bormann, with a sidelong glance at Hitler.

Dr. Roland Freisler was fifty years old, but he had never risen beyond the rank of Under-Secretary of State. In 1942 he had been relegated to what he considered a dead-end job: the presidency of the People's Court. He was destined to be its first and last incumbent, but his sights were set on the Ministry of Justice, and his prospects seemed to be improving.

"There is a wide measure of agreement between the Senior State Attorney and myself," he reported, " —especially as the existing statutes are absolutely unambiguous and leave no room for compromise whatsoever. The penalty for high treason is death. The prosecution will demand the death penalty and I shall pronounce sentence accordingly."

"Thank you for setting my mind at rest." Adolf Hitler's hands trembled convulsively, in contrast to the petrified immobility of his face. "I live and work for Germany—I know no other mode of existence. It is years since I had the opportunity to read a book, visit a theatre or hear a concert."

"The Fuehrer," Bormann said, quietly but distinctly, " sacrifices himself for us all."

"What could be more natural!" cried Hitler. "Our lives belong to the Reich, and I am the Reich. Nothing must be allowed to exist which imperils the Fatherland. You, Freisler, will ensure this in your own sphere."

"I shall exterminate the enemies of my Fuehrer without mercy," Freisler replied simply.

"Have they confessed?" asked Bormann.

"So I'm told," Freisler replied. "The Gestapo seem to have put in some excellent spade-work. I shall complete their task."

"Are we allowing these enemies of the State to have defence counsel?"

"Certainly—in accordance with normal legal procedure." The President of the People's Court looked optimistic. "Most of them will be court-appointed counsel—private representation will only be permitted in exceptional cases. Be that as it may, I guarantee that, at what is probably the gravest and most crucial moment in German legal history, justice will prevail."

"That man is a hundred per cent reliable," Bormann remarked to Hitler, when they were alone again.

And Hitler, soothed and thoughtful, replied: "Freisler is our Vishinsky!"—thereby honouring Stalin's State Prosecutor. Vishinsky's technique impressed him. If anyone could hold a candle to that colossus of the Soviet politico-legal system, Roland Freisler was the man.

"He'll do it!" declared the supreme arbiter of the Third Reich. "He'll see to it that our administration of justice takes the world's breath away!"

In this respect, he was not to be disappointed.

"I'm beginning to lose patience," said SS-Sturmbannfuehrer Maier. His tone was aggrieved. "I want to be easy on you, but I'm only a little cog in a big machine. You know how it is: Hitler whips up Bormann, Bormann puts pressure on Himmler, Himmler reads the riot act to Kaltenbrunner, and Kaltenbrunner comes down on me like a ton of bricks. I'm the one who has to produce results, after all."

Brackwede sat warily on the edge of his chair, trying to look calm. He clasped his hands together to stop them trembling.

"Where are the papers that were in your briefcase?" demanded Maier.

"Somewhere or other."

"What do you want for them?"

"Perhaps they don't exist any more."

"Do you mean," Maier said hoarsely, " —do you mean you've destroyed them?"

"What if I have?"

The Sturmbannfuehrer breathed heavily. "If you have, we'll jog your memory."

"What if I'm suffering from amnesia?"

"Then I'll have to turn you over to Inspector Habecker. Do you know who he is?"

"No."

"Think yourself lucky. I'm easy-going compared with Habecker—you don't seem to appreciate that. I'm sorry, really I am, but if we don't come to some arrangement Habecker will have to take over your case."

"Do you honestly expect me to betray friends of mine—

people I've learned to like and respect? What do you want me to do—deliver them to the scaffold by the cartload?"

" I can see you look at these things far too one-sidedly." Maier seemed genuinely concerned. " Why don't you adopt a more rational approach? Tell yourself you're rendering an important service to the cause of justice, the State, the Fuehrer—take your pick. You needn't claim any direct credit, if that's what's worrying you. I'll be quite satisfied if you simply hand over the contents of your briefcase or reconstruct the lists that were in it. No need to make any personal statement, either—we'll stick to the usual official version and call it a lucky find. Well, what do you say?"

" No," Brackwede replied, " I refuse. Your offer isn't acceptable. My life's worth far less than the original contents of that briefcase."

" All right, I'll make it your life and the Oldenburg girl's— and throw in your brother's for good measure."

" Rubbish!" Brackwede said firmly. " You're talking hot air—you haven't got a thing on my brother and you know it. It was you who turned him into one of the heroes of the twentieth of July."

" Don't be too sure," warned Maier. " Heroes fall harder than most, and don't force me to demonstrate the fact."

One of the first men to face the People's Court was ex-Field Marshal Erwin von Witzleben. Having been dismissed the service by the Court of Honour, he possessed neither rank nor title. He was simply " Witzleben," or " the accused."

Witzleben had considerable difficulty in keeping his trousers up because he had been deprived of his braces. " You dirty old man," jested Freisler, " why do you keep fiddling with your trousers all the time?"

Two hundred-odd spectators, hand-picked for their loyalty to the Fuehrer, gave an expectant titter. Kaltenbrunner leant back in his front-row seat, stroking his chin and surveying the scene with veiled eyes.

Freisler embarked on the first of his numerous performances. He announced in a positively plaintive tone that in 1940, as an erstwhile member of the Reichstag, he had been profoundly moved when the Fuehrer promoted Witzleben to the rank of field marshal. " And how scurvily he repaid the Fuehrer's generosity! He established treasonable relations with an individual named Beck."

Erwin von Witzleben, racked with pain and hunger, attempted to explain his personal attitude. He had been driven to the conclusion that errors had been made during the course of the war—grave errors. He refrained from mentioning Hitler's name.

Freisler shouted him down. "What unparalleled arrogance to assert that you could have done better than him who is the Fuehrer of us all! Did you imagine that the Fuehrer would let himself be taken without a struggle—well, did you?"

"Yes," Witzleben replied, "I did think so at one time."

"You did think so at one time!" Freisler repeated acidly. "What a mixture of criminality and stupidity . . ." He proceeded to dwell at length on ridiculous minutiae such as the field marshal's alleged squandering of petrol. The field marshal politely informed him that his car ran on gas, not petrol.

"You can economise on gas, too!" was Freisler's rejoinder.

The proceedings were enlivened by malicious, mocking exchanges. "You suffered from abdominal haemorrhages?" inquired Freisler. "Were you gravely ill?" When Witzleben confirmed this, Freisler pounced triumphantly. "So you resented the fact that illness prevented you from taking up a military command!

"You wanted to rule against the will of the people!" the President exclaimed with every sign of horror. He hissed at Witzleben like a locomotive under a full head of steam, employing words such as "ambition," "felony" and "senility," but perhaps his most dramatic cry from the heart was reserved for his concluding address:

"We are returning to life, to the fray. We have nothing in common with you . . . We are marching with all our might towards total victory!"

A few minutes earlier, he had condemned Field Marshal Edwin von Witzleben to death by hanging.

"You know all about these things," Lehmann said to the playwright. "What are your views on justice—the divine variety, I mean?"

The playwright shook his head. "You expect too much of me, my friend. My business is human nature. I merely try to portray it. I'm quite incapable of explaining it."

Lehmann had turned up at the slogan-painters' basement headquarters long before the normal hour. The playwright, who was as usual engaged in covering small pieces of paper with notes, was the only other occupant. He concealed his keenness to be there on time by telling Lehmann that he found the basement a stimulating place to work.

"Why are we doing all this?" mused the ex-corporal. "Why aren't you having a rip-roaring time with one of your actress friends? They always say an actress'll do anything for a good part. Why don't I take one of the girl students out to supper and then back to my room—why slosh paint on walls instead? Why is an intelligent man like Captain von Brackwede hellbent on dying a hero's death? He could have had any job he liked, but he wasn't interested. Why not? Why didn't Stauffenberg run errands for Hitler and sit behind his desk waiting for promotion?"

The playwright shuffled his notes together in silence.

"At least try to give me a rough explanation, won't you?" Lehmann insisted. "If you're good at your business you must know what makes people tick."

In a quiet, almost anguished voice, the playwright said: "I think you're trying to pin down the meaning of life. It's—" he groped for his words " —it's a refusal to surrender to aimlessness."

"What does that mean, in plain language?"

"Well, painting slogans on walls, for one thing."

"Or blowing up a man like Hitler?"

"That too."

"I follow," Lehmann said. "Everybody's got to cope with himself and his surroundings in his own way—preferably so he's not ashamed to look himself in the face afterwards."

The playwright nodded. "You've said it."

Lehmann busied himself with the suitcase he had brought along. It contained British plastic explosive of an amount and quality similar to the charge used by Stauffenberg.

"Whose backside can I shove this under?" he pondered aloud. "You never know—it might give me some idea of the meaning of life after all."

"Who is Inspector Habecker?"

Alarich Dambrowski surveyed Captain von Brackwede with compassion as he mechanically scoured the lavatory-bowl. "Have they threatened you with Habecker?" He wagged his head sorrowfully. "They mean business, then. Officially, he's the most successful interrogator in the building. Off the record, he's one of the devil's own. There are only two alternatives with him—either you sing like a canary or they carry you out in a sack."

Brackwede, now clad in a crumpled grey civilian suit and an open-necked blue shirt, rose uneasily from the camp-bed and walked over to the little man with the wizened face. "Do you know a Countess Oldenburg?"

Dambrowski raised his cobweb-thin hands in a gesture of regretful assent. "A very nice lady," he said. "We don't often have high-class specimens like her in here. She had such a sensitive face, too."

"Had? Do you mean they've ill-treated her?"

"They've interrogated her a few times—not with much success, as far as I know." He turned on the tap. "The Countess is in the cell next door," he continued above the noise of running water. "I've been told to leave both doors open—accidentally on purpose—and then push off for a while so you can have a chat together. Instructions from Comrade Maier."

Brackwede, who began to have an inkling of what was expected of him, realised that he wanted to postpone the meeting as long as possible. Agonisingly aware of his weakness, he asked the informer where he came from.

"Hamburg—I used to be a stevedore at the docks there, not that you'd know it to look at me now. All the same, I've still got some strength left. I twisted someone's neck the other day—he tried to commit suicide and made a hash of it, so I helped him out. Apart from that, I'm a Communist—that's to say, I was one, officially speaking. I've been maintained by the tax-payers of the Third Reich since nineteen-thirty-three. I started off at Dachau, got moved to Flossenbuerg, graduated from Ploetzensee and finally landed up here."

"Your ambition is to survive, I take it."

"You probably think the same way as I do, Herr von Brackwede." Dambrowski blinked wearily. "The Thousand-Year Reich has got to end sometime—maybe in the next few months. Till then, it's just a question of scraping through and taking what comes—including the sight of Countess Oldenburg's face. Don't ask me to spare your feelings unless you want to ruin my reputation as the best stool-pigeon in the business."

A few moments later, Brackwede slipped into the cell next door. Elisabeth was lying on the bed, scarcely able to move. With an effort, she raised a hand in greeting. Something like a smile passed across the puffy red mass which was all that was left of her face.

Brackwede stood looking down at her. Timidly, he touched her hand, and her fingers stirred a little. He closed his eyes for several seconds as though dazzled by a blinding light, but his voice was calm.

"Don't say a word, Elisabeth—I know what you want to tell me. Thanks for everything. You'll be released before the day is out."

She gazed at him in silent entreaty, but he shook his head. Then he bent over her and gently laid his cheek against hers.

Brackwede left the cell without a backward glance. To Alarich Dambrowski, who had been eavesdropping in the corridor, he said: "I'm ready now. They can have all the evidence they want out of me—pass that on."

Karl Theodor Huber regarded himself as the most harassed man in the whole of the Third Reich. His eyes were glazed with consternation, his hands fluttered nervously and cold sweat trickled down his face.

Huber was the scion of a respectable South German peasant family. He was also a recording supervisor with the Greater German broadcasting service, and it was his duty to capture the proceedings of the People's Court for posterity. Addressing him and the other members of his team, Reich Broadcasting Director Hadamovski had stressed the unique nature of their assignment, which was, he said, tantamount to working "for the Fuehrer's private ear."

Everything seemed to go swimmingly at first. Numerous microphones were installed in the court-room and carefully checked. Huber sat in the President's chair and carried out volume tests. His assistants took the place of accused and defence counsel, and a court reporter played the State prosecutor's part with verve, repeatedly calling out: "I therefore demand the death penalty!"

"Terrific!" Huber commented in his improvised control-booth. "That ought to do the trick. We should get everything, deep breathing and all."

On 7 August, however, at the very first session of the People's Court *in re* "attempted assassination of the Fuehrer, treasonable conspiracy and persistent high treason," the recording supervisor's dreams of technical perfection collapsed in shards.

In the first place, the President almost invariably bellowed at the top of his voice, causing the overloaded microphones to vibrate in sympathy. In the second place, many of the accused spoke too softly, some of them hardly above a whisper. Karl Theodor Huber found it an almost superhuman task to strike an appropriate balance.

The recording supervisor's hand-wringing rose to a pitch of desperation during the cross-examination of General Paul von Hase, formerly in command of Berlin District. Far from producing the volume of sound which might have been expected from a general, he spoke with an indistinctness and hesitancy which often verged on the inaudible.

"So you were involved in the plot," said Roland Freisler.

Closeted in his control-booth, Huber winced yet again. This time, it was the President who spoke with unexpected moderation.

"So you were involved in the plot," Freisler repeated.

"Plot" was the term most favoured by the President during the course of this hearing. The accused, he claimed, had not rejected the order to occupy the government quarter with sufficient speed or firmness. His words came faintly to the ears of the recording supervisor like the howl of a distant jackal. The needles of his various dials flickered feebly.

"At first," Hase said, "I remained at home. I had some official business to attend to."

"Ah!" Freisler's voice rose to a siren-like scream. "You had some official business to attend to. What else did you do besides eat lunch?"

"Nothing in particular," Hase replied submissively.

Swift as a hawk, Freisler swooped down on his helpless prey, his voice shrilling like an alarm-clock. Huber feverishly manipulated his volume controls.

"Nothing in particular, eh? How strange! I should have thought that the following realisation would have been staring you in the face: every minute that passes means that I'm more of a rogue, a traitor, a scoundrel, and more than ever responsible for the fact that someone may be assassinating the Fuehrer . . ."

"Of course, Herr President," General von Hase replied quietly, "those thoughts did pass through my mind."

Freisler trumpeted on. He called Hase a criminal, accused him of abusing his position and distorting the meaning of words. Finally, he hissed: "Once treachery had entered your breast you were no longer a soldier . . ."

The death sentence was followed by another harangue "Perjured, ambitious and dishonourable men have betrayed as no one in the whole course of our history has ever done, the sacrifices of our soldiers, people, Fuehrer and Reich . . . Traitors to everything we live and fight for, they will all be punished with death. Their property is forfeit to the Reich."

"The man's a complete fiasco!" moaned Recording Supervisor Huber, now at the end of his tether. "He hasn't a clue what this is all about."

"I'm deeply hurt," said Sturmbannfuehrer Maier. "Why are you forcing my hand like this? What have I done to deserve it, after the way we've always got on together?"

"Stop beating about the bush," Brackwede told him impatiently. "You'll get a full and legally watertight confession from me on one condition: that you release Countess Oldenburg-Quentin immediately."

"Only a confession? What about your co-operation—what about those lists of yours?"

"One thing at a time—and don't look so damned surprised. Anyone would think you didn't know that I aim to sell my skin for the best price I can get. All right, let's get on with it."

"Have it your own way," Maier said, looking disappointed. "Don't say I didn't warn you, though. I've done all I can. Anything that happens from now on won't be my fault."

He gave orders that Countess Oldenburg-Quentin should be released at once and allowed to leave the building unescorted. The file on her was closed. "And get Lieutenant von Brackwede to see her home. —All right?" he added, glancing at Brackwede, who nodded.

Two Gestapo interrogators appeared. One of them dictated a prepared statement which the other typed direct on to his machine. Captain Count Fritz-Wilhelm von Brackwede's deposition was as follows:

"I was closely concerned with the plans and preparations for the attempt on Hitler's life. I played an active and leading part in the Bendlerstrasse revolt of twentieth July nineteen forty-four. I am fully aware of the implications of my activities, and of the significance of this confession."

When Brackwede had signed this document in quintuplicate, Sturmbannfuehrer Maier took charge of it and dismissed the two men. He stared moodily round his sparsely furnished office, with its smell of stale cigar-smoke and dusty files. Then he picked up the five copies of the brief but deadly statement and weighed them in his fleshy hands.

315

"I could tear this up," he said. "All you have to do is say you'll work with me from now on."

"Don't tear anything up," Brackwede replied sharply.

Maier shrugged. "In that case, your next stop is Habecker."

President of the People's Court Roland Freisler was flanked by two "observers," namely, General Hermann Reinecke and Councillor Lemmle. One was a soldier who believed implicitly in Hitler and the other was a legal functionary. Both, as they subsequently stated, were merely doing their duty.

General Reinecke, newly-appointed chief of the General Armed Forces Office at Supreme Headquarters, regarded the succession of doomed men with distaste. They made—with few exceptions—an extremely poor impression on him.

"The path of truth," intoned Freisler, "is hard because it is narrow but easy because it is straight. Tread that path!" The President loved his quotations, which ran the gamut from the Nibelungen to Hitler.

General Reinecke remained as unimpressed by Freisler's quotations as he was by the harsh glare of the floodlights, the whirring cameras and the three broad swastika banners behind him. Only when they lighted on the court-room bust of Frederick the Great, King of Prussia, did his eyes grow mild.

"A dastardly act, an act which breaks all bounds and makes mock of moderation . . ." declaimed the President, who spoke far more in the course of the hearings than all the accused, defence counsel and prosecutors put together. "These craven assassins tried to rob us of our Fuehrer!"

With an earnest and imposing mien, General Rienecke pondered on the oath of allegiance and came to the conclusion that it had been shamefully broken. He pondered on the inviolability of a Head of State and came to the conclusion that, much as this judge in his blood-red robes grated on his nerves, those on trial here could not be genuinely representative of Prusso-German military tradition.

It was now the turn of ex-Major-General Helmuth Stieff. A thin and slightly hunched figure attired in a shabby civilian suit, he stood there, frozen-faced and silent, while Freisler called him a filthy liar.

". . . it would be no exaggeration to say that when you were first interviewed by the police you lied fit to bust a gut." Freisler unblushingly referred to the Gestapo as "the police." "Well, would it? Am I right? Yes or no?"

"I kept quiet about certain things," Stieff conceded.

"Yes or no!" Freisler roared. "There's no half-way house between truth and falsehood. Did you lie or did you tell the whole truth?"

The accused said that he had told the truth at a later stage. He stood mute and motionless—almost paralysed—as Freisler went on to call Colonel von Stauffenberg a cut-throat and a criminal, but when he spoke of National Socialist "manly loyalty" Stieff suddenly interrupted him with a reference to "one's responsibility to the German people."

Reinecke pricked up his ears incredulously. For a traitor who had been convicted out of his own mouth, this was going too far! What went on in these people's heads, he wondered. Hopefully, he glanced at the President.

Roland Freisler more than fulfilled his expectations.

"Fuehrer and people are always one!" he bellowed. "What sort of Jesuitical-reactionary quibble is that? What do you think would have happened if one of the last Goths on Vesuvius had made such a reservation? What do you think would have happened to a member of the wandering Germanic tribes if he'd said such a thing? He'd have been left to drown in a swamp, and that would have been the right place for him!"

Reinecke sat back, regarding the accused with a faint smile of bitter, melancholy contempt. Then he closed his eyes briefly.

Yet another candidate for the meat-hook.

Alarich Dambrowski's sphere of weasel-like activity extended to the sub-basement at the rear of the Gestapo building in Prinz Albrechtstrasse. "I'm indispensable," he told Brackwede with a wink. "They've left me in charge of you because I did such a successful job on you upstairs."

The cell which now housed Captain von Brackwede was as cramped and dirty as a carelessly-emptied dustbin. His hands were fettered and the iron chain round his body bit into him agonisingly whenever he moved.

"You've got to learn to eat and write under these conditions," the informer told him. "Practice makes perfect, and nothing's impossible as long as you're still alive. What about that strange colonel of yours—Stauffenberg? He only had one hand, didn't he?"

"One hand with three fingers on it," Brackwede replied.

"There you are, then!" Dambrowski gave him an encouraging smile. "Here, take this." He fished in his pocket and produced a crust of bread and a piece of sausage the size of a baby's fist. "You'll need it—the food here isn't enough to keep body and soul together. Goerdeler moans with hunger every night. Besides, you're due for a visit to that bastard Habecker today. Be prepared for the worst, and watch out for Elfriede."

Brackwede's initial impression of Inspector Habecker was of a calm, equable man with a friendly voice. He had the robust and honest visage of a "regular" in a country inn.

He opened with an official preamble.

"I have to inform you that you are charged with complicity in the twentieth of July conspiracy. We have your confession and a mass of corroborative evidence, so there's no point in trying to retract. Right, let's get down to a more detailed statement."

Brackwede stared round the room. It had clean white walls and a scrubbed wooden floor, like nearly all the other rooms in the building. Habecker was standing opposite him, a harsh beam of light shone in his eyes, and a Gestapo man with a torso like a bulging sack was stationed behind him. Habecker's secretary, a green-eyed girl with smoothly-combed brown hair, was lolling in a corner, looking bored. This, presumably, was Elfriede.

"I retract nothing," Brackwede said, "but I'm not making any further statement."

Habecker hit the handcuffed man in the face with the flat of his hand. Brackwede tried to elude the blow, but a fist crashed into his neck as the Gestapo man behind him went into action. Habecker struck again, this time drawing blood from Brackwede's aquiline nose with his clenched fist.

"That ought to dispel any possible misunderstandings," said the inspector. "Now we can start to talk frankly. Your statement, please."

"I've no statement to make." Brackwede found it hard to breathe. The blood running down his throat made him gag. "No statement!" he repeated.

"Take a closer look at this big-mouth, Elfriede," recommended Habecker, lighting a cigarette. "You've got a weakness for his sort, haven't you? All right, don't stand on ceremony —make friends with him."

Elfriede rose, smoothing down her skirt, and advanced on Brackwede with a dancer's step. Her glittering eyes seemed

318

to probe every part of his body. Then she removed the cigarette from Habecker's mouth and stubbed it out on Brackwede's manacled hands. He silently gritted his teeth and closed his eyes. The man behind him clamped his arms round him as a precaution.

" He refuses to gaze into your gorgeous eyes," Habecker remarked encouragingly. He leant back against his desk with his legs slightly apart. " He doesn't seem to have a proper appreciation of your special charms . Hardly gallant, is he?"

Brackwede opened his eyes and saw Elfriede's forked fingers a few inches away. They quivered as they approached his face, moving towards it with the inexorability of a conveyer belt. Then a stabbing pain ricocheted from his eye-balls to the back of his head.

" A modest beginning," Habecker observed casually. " Just a little taste of the feast to come—personally prepared by me."

Elisabeth lay on her bed like a broken doll, unmoving, scarcely breathing.

The doctor whom Konstantin had fetched was sitting wearily beside her on a chair, grey-faced with fatigue.

" How on earth did it happen?" he asked.

" She was with the Gestapo."

The doctor rose to his feet. He clenched his fist in silent outrage and bowed his head, vainly striving for words. At length he said quickly: " She ought to be admitted to hospital at once, but I don't know of one that can take her—they're all overcrowded. She ought to have a shot of morphine, too—at least one—but I can't give it to her. It's been a long time since I had enough drugs."

" Is she in danger?" Konstantin asked anxiously.

" Who isn't, these days?" The doctor bent over the broken body. He put out a hand tentatively and then withdrew it. " I'll do my best to procure some drugs. Maybe there's a hospital bed free somewhere, too, but I can't promise anything."

" What happens meanwhile?"

" Pray—that's probably the only thing you can do. Giving that sort of advice comes hard to a doctor, believe me, but at the moment I can't think of anything better."

The doctor hurried off with a hunted air, promising to return soon—probably some time next day. Konstantin did not hear what he said.

He bent over Elisabeth and stared down at her face. It was swollen and unrecognisable, like a lump of congealed and fissured wax. The long, agonising minutes went by in dream-like succession, leaving them alone with each other and their powerless thoughts.

And then it seemed to him that she began to smile, to dissolve into rapturous tenderness, into sweet abandon, as she had done once upon a time—only a few days before.

"I love you, Elisabeth," he said, putting his face down to hers.

But Elisabeth, Countess von Oldenburg-Quentin, was dead.

SS-Sturmbannfuehrer Maier was not only alive but indignant. Kaltenbrunner had stepped up pressure on his divisional chiefs, informing them that the Fuehrer not only expected detailed reports but was insisting on concrete results. And yet, in a matter which was, for Maier, of the utmost importance, even Habecker was failing to make progress.

"Why aren't you getting any further with Brackwede?" he demanded.

Inspector Habecker looked slightly depressed. "He's a damned tough proposition. I've pulled out all the stops, but he still won't sing."

"How long will it take you?"

"I really can't say."

Maier knew what this meant. If Habecker made such an admission, no results could be expected—at least in the foreseeable future. The results for Maier, on the other hand, would be positively catastrophic.

"Have you tried everything?"

"Not quite. Shall I?"

"Yes," Maier said harshly.

This was the equivalent of giving Habecker carte blanche but Maier felt that it was an unavoidable step. After all, he had warned Brackwede. "What do you think, Habecker—will he talk?"

"It's an open question, I'm afraid. Cases do exist where . . ."

"Do you know what this means?" Maier interrupted him angrily. "Have you any idea what's at stake—for you, for me for us all? You've got to get him to talk, I tell you!"

"I'm doing my level best," the inspector replied. His professional pride seemed to be hurt. "I've always demonstrate my abilities in the past, but there are exceptions. Take Juliu Leber, for instance."

320

"Leber!" the Sturmbannfuehrer ejaculated bitterly, recalling one of the darkest hours in his Gestapo career. "Don't start quoting him—he's a unique case. There can't be another one like him."

"It's not beyond the bounds of possibility, I'm afraid—Brackwede is a similar type from that point of view." Almost meditatively, the inspector added: "Just imagine those two as Minister of the Interior and Secretary of State . . . What an unbeatable combination they'd have made!"

Maier brusquely waved the remark aside. "Stop daydreaming and concentrate on your job. Either you get Brackwede to talk or you end up as untalkative as he is."

Habecker withdrew, looking affronted. The Sturmbannfuehrer stared after him with a vaguely hopeful air, pleased at the effect of his words. Then, remembering that he had scant grounds for optimism, he grimly buried himself in his work and prayed for a ray of light.

The ray of light seemed to dawn later that day, when he was informed that a man called Lehmann wanted to speak to him on the telephone. The Sturmbannfuehrer took the call on the spot, even though he was in the middle of an interrogation.

"Remember me?" asked Lehmann.

"Do I, you young dog!" Maier replied genially. "To what do I owe the pleasure? I don't suppose you rang to inquire about the state of my health."

"No, I was going to suggest a deal."

"Why not? What are you selling and how much do you want for it?"

"My asking-price is a valid passport, safe-conduct to the Swiss frontier and a thousand dollars in cash—genuine dollars, of course."

The Sturmbannfuehrer was reduced to stunned silence for a few moments. "You want your bread buttered on both sides, don't you?" he jested feebly, but Lehmann continued in businesslike tones: "I'm offering you Count von Brackwede's papers and an exact reconstruction of the Stauffenberg bomb."

"You mean it?" Maier said breathlessly. "When?"

"The sooner the better. Is it a deal?"

"Yes—you can deliver right away, as far as I'm concerned."

"Done," Lehmann replied. He sounded satisfied. "Expect a call from me inside the next twenty-four hours—but my offer only extends to you. You mustn't bring more than two men with you."

"Agreed," Maier said promptly. "I'll make the arrangements straight away."

"Fine—but don't try to diddle me. I'm not an aristocrat like Brackwede. I've got no manners and I shit on gentleman's agreements. I want to deliver and collect, period. I'm sure you can understand that."

The chief prosecutor at the People's Court trials was a man named Lautz—Senior State Attorney Lautz, a lawyer of dignified appearance who survived the fall of the Third Reich to enjoy a pension commensurate with his former status. He, too, declared that he had only done his duty, and that if he had not done it someone else would have.

His position was crystal clear. All he had to do was to follow the existing laws, and he did so to the letter. Death being the penalty for high treason, he demanded it with monotonous regularity.

"Justices of the People's Court of the Greater German Reich! In all the history of the Prusso-German armed forces, so rich in examples of courage, gallantry, loyalty and honour, there is no precedent for the occurrence which has been unfolded before you with such force today. In describing the accused and their crime, therefore, one finds continual difficulty in preserving a moderation proper to the dignity of this court of law . . .

" . . . A small circle of unprincipled scoundrels . . . hatred for the Fuehrer . . . a consuming urge for self-aggrandisement . . . human shortcomings at their most extreme . . . an abysmal lack of regard for the German people . . .

"They endeavoured, by means of an attempt on the Fuehrer's life which was craven in conception and, by the grace of God, unsuccessful, to gain control of the army and our homeland. They then planned, by concluding a cowardly pact with an enemy . . . to deliver the Reich into hostile hands. They are, therefore, not only guilty of high treason but betrayers of their country as well."

And so it went on, almost every day: deprivation of civil rights in so far as the Wehrmacht's "Court of Honour" had not already done this, confiscation of property, and, finally, the death sentence. In acceding to the Senior State Attorney's demand for the supreme penalty, Freisler concluded: "There can be no question of death by shooting. However, the State has passed a law designed to deal with acts of particular infamy. Under its provisions, sentence of death may be carried out by hanging. And with that, we have said all there is to say on the matter."

Such was the pattern of a normal day's hearing. All present merely "did their duty" and "served the ends of justice." It was not until some time later that they pronounced the whole proceedings "tragic."

There were amusing interludes from time to time. On such occasions the packed auditorium rang with lighthearted merriment and even the Senior State Attorney permitted himself an indulgent smile—as, for instance, when President Freisler summoned "People's Comrade Else Bergenthal" before the bench to give evidence.

Freisler treated this modest and unassuming woman with elaborate courtesy. Leaning forward in his chair, he declared himself "ready and willing to respect the personal integrity of People's Comrade Bergenthal as a German woman."

"We assume that, in view of your personal integrity, you will tell the truth."

"Yes," Frau Bergenthal assured him.

There was a rustle of expectation among the two hundred spectators, most of them in uniform. A special treat seemed to be in store.

"You were housekeeper to this man Beck," Freisler began in mellifluous tones. "Would you say he was a strong, forceful personality—the sort of man who would make an impression if he presented himself to the people and demanded something of them?"

"I don't know," replied Frau Bergenthal. "I couldn't venture an opinion on that."

Freisler graciously accepted her inability to pronounce on the question. He was not interested in personal evaluations, he assured her, merely in certain details of a potentially indicative nature. For instance, when she came to make Beck's bed in the mornings, did it show traces of "tossing and turning"?

People's Comrade Bergenthal was forced to confirm this. She reported, reluctantly but truthfully, that he, Beck, had "sweated frightfully at nights" and that he seemed "terribly agitated."

"So that in the morning," Freisler amplified with relish, "when he got out of bed, it was sopping wet?"

The witness replied in the affirmative. Good-naturedly, the President expressed his thanks, discharged her from her oath and bade her farewell in terms of the utmost warmth and cordiality.

Triumphantly, he made his point: a man who "tosses about in terror at night so that his bed is sopping wet for a fortnight" could not be "a man of strong personality." Yet a flabby wretch like that had had the effrontery to set himself up against the unique, the incomparable Fuehrer . . .

The spectators murmured their approbation.

"Still bright and cheerful," Habecker inquired with a yawn, "Or are you ready to see sense at last?"

"I have no statement to make," Captain von Brackwede said resolutely. Pain and hunger had transformed his face into a mesh of wrinkles and dulled the light in his red-rimmed eyes.

He had been compelled to spend three days and nights chained up like an escape-artist. The harsh and dazzling glare of the light in his cell was never extinguished. Meagre, unsustaining food had left him limp and enervated. He had been beaten, kicked and spat on. Elfriede, Habecker's secretary, had tried to pull his tongue out with a pair of pliers and drill a hole in his testicles with a pencil.

Three interrogation experts apart from Habecker had been working on him incessantly. One bellowed at him and plied him with kicks and punches, another simulated a kindly, humane approach, and the third made heartfelt appeals to his integrity, conscience and any other moral values which sprang to mind. Brackwede never said a word.

"You must try and think up some way of taking your mind off things," Dambrowski told him as he carefully washed the blood from his body. "Couldn't you throw them a sop of some kind before they turn you into bone-meal? You know your best bet? Incriminate someone who's already dead."

"Not even that," Brackwede groaned.

He was dragged before Habecker again.

"It's a long time since I had anybody like you to contend with," the inspector said in a mildly admiring tone. He looked down at his nibbled finger-nails. "You've become quite a point of pride with me. I'm disappointed in you, though— I thought you had more intelligence. You must have a fair idea of our methods by now. Well, how about it? Do I get some names or don't I?"

Brackwede closed his eyes and shook his head in a gesture of uncompromising refusal. His bruised lips were compressed into a thin, hard line.

"One last try," said Habecker. "We're in possession of a statement by Goerdeler which gravely incriminates you."

"It must be forged," Brackwede said in a muffled voice. He knew that ruses of this kind were common practice at Prinz Albrechtstrasse. "Confront me with Goerdeler and we'll soon see if it's genuine or not."

Habecker shrugged. "Very well, since you insist, we'll have to try some more effective methods of persuasion."

Four men went to work on Brackwede for a full night, panting with destructive fury. They drove pins into his fingertips, hips and legs. They secured him to two beams with cord and stretched his limbs, slowly at first, then with a series of jerks. They lashed him up with cord until he was a tottering bundle of flesh and bone and beat the back of the neck with truncheons until he lost his balance and crashed to the floor on his face. Blood spurted from his nose, mouth and ears.

Such were the "four degrees" of torture in current use at Prinz Albrechtstrasse. They had not been devised by the Gestapo but borrowed from the Middle Ages.

Brackwede's heart pumped madly and a volcano seemed to erupt inside his skull. Then he lost consciousness and collapsed with a bubbling groan.

He lay in the corner of his cell for twelve hours, stiff and contorted as a dead insect. When he came to his senses again he crawled to the door on mutilated limbs.

"No!" he screamed, spitting blood. "I won't talk! Less than ever, now!"

Ernst Kaltenbrunner, chief of the Central State Security Bureau, sent his Fuehrer a lengthy written report every day. Place of origin: 8 Prinz Albrechtstrasse, Berlin S.W.11. Signed: Kaltenbrunner, SS-Obergruppenfuehrer and General of Police.

The contents of these missives appeared under headings such as "Effects on Popular Moral," "Summary of Press Comment," "Interrogation Reports," "Background Information," "Detention Lists" and—over and over again—"Public Opinion."

Adolf Hitler evinced particular interest in the latter subject, so Kaltenbrunner's reports took this into consideration and told the Fuehrer precisely what he wanted to hear.

It was reported that an army officer had said: "Those swine ought to have been drowned at birth." Newspapers proclaimed that the public was "seething with righteous indignation," and that the soldiers at the front were "behind the Fuehrer to a man, filled with disgust . . ." Kaltenbrunner's reports further claimed that a number of People's Comrades had unanimously declared that "bastards like those ought to be subjected to medieval torture."

"The voice of the people" was diligently recorded in private homes, barracks, inns, factories and among "combat soldiers in the front line." Germany, it appeared, gave thanks to God for the Fuehrer's deliverance. If that was what he wanted, that was what he should have.

Hitler also learned that a woman had been detained at Halle for having expressed regret at the failure of the attempt on his life, and that another woman had been arrested in Vienna because she had said: "It had to come sometime!" —but these were the only dissentient opinions quoted in the reports submitted for the Fuehrer's delectation.

Apart from that, so Hitler was informed, "terrible fury" reigned supreme in the hearts of all good People's Comrades, coupled with gratitude. It was reported from Schwerin that "women, in particular, are saying that the Fuehrer must have a good guardian angel," and the view of "other ranks and young officers" was represented as being that "death by hanging is an entirely fitting—indeed, mild—punishment for those treacherous creatures." Older officers, by contrast, gave it as their opinion that "those people ought to be granted a bullet."

Finally, there was a never-ending inventory of the "outspoken and unanimous" remarks uttered by the outraged German people, e.g., "Clear the decks!," "Make a clean sweep!" and, last but not least, "Better string up one too many than one too few!"

"Can you move again?" asked Alarich Dambrowski, bending over Brackwede with a worried frown. "I thought you'd had it, but you crawled on to the bed by yourself last night."

"I'm feeling a bit better."

"Don't let on," advised the scrawny little man. "Stay lying down as long as possible—act as if you can't lift a finger. I'll tell them I dragged you on to the bed myself."

Dambrowski began to probe the maimed body with deft

and delicate movements of his spidery fingers. Brackwede cried out in agony.

"You're in a bad way," said the informer. "How's your head—can you think straight?"

"I don't want to."

"That's good." Dambrowski pulled a bottle out of his trousers pocket. "I can't do much for you, I'm afraid. You'll have to make do without bandages and so on, but I can offer you a little pick-me-up. Here, it's cod-liver oil—no one here'll drink the stuff. It isn't much, but it's better than nothing."

"I've got to get on to my feet again as soon as possible."

"So they can put you through it again?"

"I must speak to one of my friends."

"Who, for instance?"

"Any one."

"There must be quite a lot of them on the premises. Can I help?"

Brackwede asked to be taken to the wash-room next morning. Several detainees were always in there at the same time, which made it possible to exchange a word of information or a warning glance, and brief conversations could be held under the shower in the corner.

"I should take it as easy as you can," recommended Dambrowski, folding Brackwede's coat into a cushion. "If you really want to pass something on, why don't you let me do it for you?"

"What's this—another trick?"

Dambrowski gave a wry smile. "You really are feeling better, aren't you? All right, who do you want me to pass a message to? Moltke, Uxkuell—Berthold Stauffenberg? Dr. Mueller from Munich is here, and so is the Doctor."

"Eugen G.?"

"He's a real card, the Doctor." Dambrowski's chuckle turned into a violent spasm of coughing. "Do you know what he's been up to, among other things? Pastor Delp spends the night writing notes, and he pinches them out of his pocket every morning. The guards haven't caught on so far. How do you like that?"

Brackwede gritted his teeth and sat up with the cold sweat pouring down his face. "Speak to one of them—it doesn't matter which one. Tell them I haven't given them a single name—not one."

"Haven't you really?" Dambrowski asked incredulously.

"No, not a single one."

"And you think you'll get anywhere like that?" The stool-pigeon threw up his hands. "Goerdeler's been operating on quite a different tack. They say he's given them lists a yard long, full of the most fantastic names—Himmler's included. If that isn't method, what is? You might try the same dodge."

"Each man to his own system," Brackwede said, falling back exhausted. "Mine is silence."

"It hurts me to have to tell you this, but your brother has confessed." Sturmbannfuehrer Maier's voice rang with regret. "I'm afraid you'll have to make up your mind, once and for all, between family loyalty and loyalty to the Fuehrer. I trust you won't find it a hard choice."

Konstantin von Brackwede, summoned to the Prinz Albrechtstrasse headquarters, took the file which Maier had handed him and leafed through it stiffly. What he read seemed to evoke no reaction in him at all. He handed it back without a word.

"I can understand what a shock this must be," Maier went on. "However, I'm sure nothing will deter you from doing your duty."

"What do you expect of me?" Konstantin asked, not looking at him.

"Bring your brother to his senses. You must even be prepared to give evidence against him if the need arises. I'm asking a great deal of you, I know, but I want to save him from the worst and I need your assistance. Are you prepared to speak to him?"

Konstantin nodded and got up. A guard escorted him to the sub-basement, where a warder conducted him the rest of the way. When they entered Brackwede's cell a doctor was hard at work on him, trying to get his patient ready for the next session of torture as soon as possible.

Konstantin stared at his brother in helpless amazement. He was lying there like a dead man. His eyes were closed, but a faint snoring sound emerged from his gaping mouth. Konstantin moved closer. The doctor and the warder withdrew, closing the door behind them.

Minutes passed. Then Konstantin knelt down and bent over his brother's battered face. "Fritz!" he called softly.

Brackwede groaned. His hands started to twitch convulsively. Then his eyelids flickered and he opened his eyes.

"Hello, youngster," he murmured.

"Don't say a word, Fritz," Konstantin said with agonised tenderness. "There's no need—I understand"

"I'm not done for yet," Brackwede told him.. "Don't pity me—anything but that."

"No," said Konstantin. "I just wanted to tell you—I'm your brother now, in every way."

"That's bad." Brackwede gasped as he tried to sit up. His face twisted suddenly as if a wave of pain had engulfed him, and he fell back unconscious on the bed.

Konstantin left the cell and the Prinz Albrechtstrasse. Going back to the room that had once belonged to Elisabeth Oldenburg, he shot himself.

"It's time," Lehmann announced. "Drive to Savignyplatz and stop at the public call-box by the round-about. I'll 'phone you there in half an hour."

Sturmbannfuehrer Maier felt sure that his goal was in sight. Lehmann was a realist, the sort of man who would sell his own mother if there was a profit in it—of that Maier was convinced.

Safe in this conviction, he observed Lehmann's instructions to the letter. The only men he took with him were Voglbronner, his closest associate and confidant, and an SS-Standartenfuehrer who was the Prinz Albrechtstrasse's best explosives expert.

Punctually at the prearranged time the telephone rang. The corporal named an address in the neighbourhood, and Maier reached the spot within five minutes. Another minute, and he found himself face to face with Lehmann in an upstairs room.

"Nice to see you," Lehmann said.

On the table in front of him lay a thick wad of papers and beside it a briefcase of the type used by Stauffenberg and Brackwede.

"Come closer, gentlemen—I think I've got something that'll interest you here."

The room in which Lehmann and the three Gestapo men were standing was an attic room with sloping walls. It was virtually empty.

"These papers are exact copies of the documents Captain von Brackwede wanted to hide in a safe place, and this briefcase is an exact replica of the one which was supposed to blow up our beloved Leader."

329

"Very good," the Sturmbannfuehrer remarked graciously. "Let's get down to business straight away."

"Let me give you a short run-down first," Lehmann told his visitors, who were standing nine or ten feet away. "—And kindly stay where you are. Don't come any closer or try to leave the room, otherwise there may be an unfortunate misunderstanding."

"Stop beating about the bush, my friend," Maier advised. "Get to the point."

"Just what I am doing," Lehmann assured him. "I'd like to draw your attention to this briefcase. It contains the same type and quantity of explosive as was used on the twentieth of July, so we all know what its potentialities are. An acid-operated detonator of the same series is also incorporated in the charge. However, as a special favour, I've taken the liberty of adding a little surprise attachment of my own. Take a look at this gadget in front of me."

He pointed to a palm-sized instrument resembling a Morse key. It was connected to a torch battery, and two wires led from it into the recesses of the briefcase.

"A contact-breaker," the Gestapo explosives expert observed in a flat voice.

"Precisely," replied Lehmann, "simple but effective. One little press, and the whole room goes up. I don't advise anyone to pull a gun or run for it, either. I'd be far too quick for you."

Voglbronner blanched. "He'd do it, too!"

"Don't lose your nerve," Maier warned him in a shaky voice. "This is typical Lehmann," he pursued, trying, without conviction, to assume a bantering tone. "Didn't I tell you he was as artful as a wagon-load of monkeys!"

"Don't prove it by coming any closer," advised Lehmann.

The Sturmbannfuehrer managed a laugh. "I'm not crazy! I accept the fact that you're not bluffing, but I'm also aware that you're not an idealist or an idiot. You want to guarantee your own safety, that's all."

Voglbronner breathed a sigh of relief. Maier, the ever-practical, seemed to have hit the nail on the head. He said: "I thought there was something funny going on when we walked in here and saw his surprise packet lying on the table like a Christmas present."

"You keep your trap shut!" snapped the Sturmbannfuehrer. Turning to Lehmann, he said ingratiatingly: "We've brought everything with us, as agreed—a passport, a thousand genuine dollars, a first-class railway ticket and a travel permit with a special exit visa valid for Basle."

"I'd have liked to see Basle," said Lehmann.

"Off you go, then!" Maier's voice had regained its genial timbre. "And now take your paw off the knob—it's making me nervous. A bargain's a bargain, after all."

"You won't follow me?" Lehmann insisted. "You won't seal off the frontier and put the number of my passport on the wanted list—always providing I manage to leave the house at all?"

"I give you my word," replied Maier.

"The word of a lying bastard," Lehmann said softly.

The blood rushed to Maier's face. "Don't push me too far, little man!" he growled.

"He doesn't care!" Voglbronner said in a horrified whisper.

"Don't move!" warned the explosives expert. "Only a fraction of a second . . ."

"Lehmann," the Sturmbannfuehrer said hoarsely, "be reasonable, for God's sake!"

"What do you mean, reasonable?" Lehmann surveyed him with contempt. "What's the point of being reasonable when you're surrounded by a pack of wolves? The only thing to do is take a few of them with you when you go."

"He means it." Voglbronner's voice had dwindled to an inaudible murmur.

"He just wants to see us shit our pants," Maier sneered, half-hopefully.

The explosives expert licked his dry lips. "That charge would demolish half the house . . ."

"Who cares?" Lehmann replied with a shrug. "Didn't you see the sign? This is a local Party office. A member put this room at my disposal and called a meeting in the cellar for this time. We've got the place to ourselves."

"What do you want?" Maier asked humbly. "Name your own price."

"Three human lives." Lehmann's voice was steady. "Countess Oldenburg, Lieutenant von Brackwede and his brother. Two of them are dead and the other's on the way."

"But that's impossible . . ." Desperation shone in Sturmbannfeuhrer Maier's eyes. His face had gone blotchy and his whole body seemed to shake. "You can't mean it!"

"Apart from that, I want my home in the East back—the one you've helped to hand over to the Russians."

"My God!" Voglbronner gurgled in a choking voice.

"Go to hell, the lot of you!" Lehmann said cheerfully, and pressed the knob.

The house shuddered. The attic became a ball of flame and exploded into a myriad fragments. Not a trace of its occupants was ever found.

Roland Freisler was extracting a great deal of entertainment from ex-General Erich Hoepner, whom he had singled out as a potential figure of fun as soon as he read his file.

"Right!" said the President. Without referring to his notes, he stated that the accused had arrived in Berlin on 19 July, two days before the revolt. Why?

Hoepner, with a touch of eagerness: " Salbach's, my wife's furriers, asked her to call in during the first half of the week to try on the fur she had inherited from her mother . . ."

Freisler's eyes gleamed with satisfaction. Hoepner was falling into his trap. A man like this might even tickle the Fuehrer's sense of humour. "So you drove to Berlin firstly on account of your wife?"

"Yes," Hoepner agreed. "Secondly, I wanted to put through a 'phone-call from Berlin to Schlawe, thirdly, I wanted to buy myself some cigars, and, fourthly, I wanted to be of assistance to my wife."

"That was firstly," Freisler remarked with sarcastic glee.

The two hundred spectators tittered, and a ripple of sub-dued merriment broke over the judge's bench. Hoepner, still unaware of what was happening to him, looked slightly be-wildered.

Mouthing into the microphone as though it was the Fuehrer's private ear, Freisler shamelessly exploited Hoepner's ingenuous attitude. The former general stumbled into one trap after another, abused, reviled, a prey to the mocking laughter of the spectators who had been detailed to attend the trial. He was described as a coward, an ambitious scoundrel, an insane traitor, a turncoat, a murderer's accomplice and a coward who had been dismissed the service for insubordination. Despite, this, Hoepner attempted not only to defend himself but to justify his actions.

"I believed the Fuehrer to be dead."

At this, a recitation of the National Socialist creed gushed into the microphones like water from a trap: " The Fuehrer exists in the German people eternally. When the Fuehrer dies, his work must remain in our hearts like a testament . . .

loyalty . . . marching along the road to the future . . . any fool would have known what was afoot, but you stayed sitting on your backside . . ."

Hoepner did not deny this, but he repeatedly stated that he had acted in good faith, with a clear conscience. He could not have known . . . No, he did not regard himself as an unprincipled swine.

" No !" queried Freisler. ." What form of animal life would you consider more appropriate?"

Hoepner, who was totally unequal to the President's mordant sallies, furrowed his brow in an endeavour to find an answer to the question.

" A donkey, perhaps?" suggested Freisler.

" Yes," Hoepner replied bitterly, " a donkey."

But not even this saved him from the gallows.

The first death sentences imposed by the People's Court in connection with the events of 20 July were passed on 8 August. The first executions took place at Ploetzensee a bare two hours later. Not all those who had been condemned were allowed to die immediately, however. Some of them were kept on ice, like Goerdeler, who wrote several more monographs and filled hundreds of pages with his ideas on " spheres of national life," including a proposed financial reform. He was executed on 2 February 1945, and others were not put out of their misery until a few days before the war ended.

The roll-call of suicides included several dozen names, among them those of the two field marshals and four generals who took their lives in the weeks immediately following the revolt. They were joined by about a hundred soldiers and diplomats, civil servants and academics, former ministers, trade union officials and ex-members of parliament who leapt to their deaths, slit their wrists, shot themselves through the head, took poison or deliberately turned on their tormentors.

On 29 August the Paris group stood trial. When Stuelpnagel, Finckh and Hofacker came to plead, the blinded general tersely acknowledged his complicity. Finckh preserved a contemptuous silence and Hofacker boldly regretted that the attempt had failed. They were all hanged.

Before, with, and after them, numerous men were brought to book who had known nothing of the events of 20 July. They were ignorant both of the preparations for the coup d'état and of the identity of the conspirators, but they happened to be on some list which designated them for high office after the insurrection. Hence, they had to die.

Although very few of the conspirators remained undiscovered, one or two escaped with their lives because documentary evidence of their guilt could not be produced. A mass of material was assembled, but Captain von Brackwede's papers, which probably constituted the most important link in the chain of evidence, were never found.

Gestapo efficiency manifested itself clearly in the courtroom, not only in the bulky dossiers provided for the prosecution's use but also in the faces of the accused, which bore the marks of brutal interrogation. Some of them were shattered wrecks who could scarcely stand upright.

Even so, many fought back.

" I did it," said an embassy official, "because I consider the Fuehrer to be an agent of the Devil . . ."

Helmuth von Moltke also essayed a brief duel with Freisler, who angrily tried to shout him down. Ambassador von Hassel maintained an unshakably dignified front, and Julius Leber stood firm, treating Freisler's jackal-like howls of abuse with leonine disdain.

When judgment was being passed on General Fellgiebel, the Signals chief called out: "Hurry up with the hanging, Herr President, or you'll hang before we do!" In the closing minutes of his trial, Field Marshal von Witzleben excelled himself by telling Freisler: "Within three months the people will call you to account and drag you alive through the mire of the streets."

This prophecy was not fulfilled. Freisler died on 3 February 1945, during an air-raid on Berlin, just as he had hurried down to the cellar in the middle of a hearing. The courthouse shook to its foundations and collapsed "with an ear-splitting crash." A huge beam fell from the ceiling and crushed Freisler to death.

The Gestapo headquarters in Prinz Albrechtstrasse were destroyed in the same raid, but the dungeons in the basement survived and torture was resumed there without delay.

Months elapsed before this happened, however, and scarcely a day passed without a new crop of death sentences.

Freisler, formerly a Communist but a member of the Nazi Party since 1925, presided at every session and passed approximately one hundred sentences of death. When sentencing Joseph Wirner, a lawyer who belonged to the conspirators' circle, he shouted: "You'll soon be in hell!"

"It will be a pleasure, Herr President," Wirner retorted, "—as long as you follow me soon!"

Count Fritz-Wilhelm von Brackwede, restored to comparative working-order by injections, medicaments and supplementary rations, was taken to a waiting truck, manacled as usual, and dumped on the floor. A guard stood over him with a drawn pistol.

Brackwede tried to peer through the barred windows, but they were covered with dirty green hessian. Half-asphyxiated by the stifling heat, he asked: "Where are we going?"

The guard maintained a wary silence. His pistol-barrel wavered as the van bumped over worn and rutted roads, and Brackwede's head thumped against the floor-boards.

Some time later he was prodded into the open air. He looked round. Behind him was a thick, grass-grown mound, pock-marked with bullet-holes. Dark brown patches stained the sand at his feet.

"Know where we are now?" his escort inquired with a grin. "Seen a rifle-range before, haven't you?"

For more than an hour, Brackwede stood under the pale sky with tall bullet-torn banks surrounding him and blood soaking into the crisp yellow sand beneath his feet. From near at hand came the crack of rifles, smothered cries, the dull thud of falling bodies and the sound of cheerful conversation. Evidently, there were people to whom killing was all in a day's work.

After that, he was led into a squat, windowless shed. Recoiling at the stench of decay and formalin, he saw two crude containers like long packing-cases and, standing between them, Inspector Habecker.

Habecker beckoned to him. "Come here," he said in an off-hand voice. "I want to show you what you've done."

When Brackwede reached his side, Habecker raised the lid of one of the packing-cases. It contained a woman's corpse. The features were unrecognisable, but Brackwede sensed that it was Elisabeth von Oldenburg—or what was left of her.

"She died," Habecker announced in the tones of a museum guide, "because you, Brackwede, wanted to live the easy life."

He closed the lid, only to raise the other with a reciprocal movement which was positively rhythmical in its execution. Another corpse came to light. This one belonged to a young man with an unblemished face of waxen smoothness. The only

335

thing which marred the picture was a bluish-red hole in the right temple.

"Your brother shot himself because he couldn't live with the disgrace you brought on him and his family." Habecker slammed the lid shut. "Are you satisfied now?"

There were moments when President Roland Freisler felt he was reaping a rich harvest, especially when he succeeded in conjuring National Socialist noises out of some of the accused. What did it matter if such confessions and admissions were prompted by naked fear and the urge for self-preservation? The main thing was that they were made.

Von Popitz, for instance, declared that he "approved of the National Socialist State in every respect," and Count Helldorf asserted that he, too, "approved" of National Socialism. Goerdeler's formulation was that "the Party's fundamental tenets" had been "held up as an example to him in his family home."

Freisler had phrases of this kind underlined in the official record.

"Acknowledgements of guilt" were carefully collected, among them a letter from General Stieff, who had written: "My life is finished. The main hearing took place yesterday and today. The prosecution are demanding the death penalty, and it can hardly turn out otherwise. It is just . . . I am going, calm and composed, to the death which I have brought upon myself by my guilt."

In the official Gestapo report to the Fuehrer, special emphasis was imparted to two words in this letter by means of italics. The words were " just " and " guilt," though it remains exceedingly questionable whether the general ever wrote such a farewell letter at all.

Further quotations in the same vein were admitted in evidence at the behest of the presiding judges. A man named Leonrod was alleged to have expressed the hope that his name would be obliterated from his family tree because it would be "a stain " upon it. Jaeger: " . . . my complicity . . ." Helldorf: " . . . acknowledge my guilt . . ." Smend: " . . . I too am guilty and must die . . . And so I leave this life a dishonoured man, having gambled away everything . . ."

"I think we're entitled to feel satisfied," Freisler told his associates in the ante-chamber after a day's labour. "The Fuehrer has expressed his appreciation to me, and, through me, to you. His instructions are to keep up the good work."

He allowed an usher to help him out of his crimson robes, conversing with the Senior State Attorney meanwhile.

"One or two defence counsel sound strangely un-German, don't you agree?"

"One or two, yes, but they're exceptions."

"Even so, we ought to put a stop to anything which might detract from the dignity of the court, oughtn't we? Defence counsel are as much servants of justice as you or I."

The Senior State Attorney nodded. "A few of them don't seem to grasp the point of the proceedings, I must admit. I'll call them to order when necessary, as you suggest."

Freisler took leave of his associate judges, the Senior State Attorney and the Senior State Attorney's assistants.

"Who's on the list for tomorrow?" he asked the clerk of the court.

The clerk of the court reeled off half a dozen names, among them that of Captain von Brackwede.

"No one of note, then," said the President, closing his brief-case.

The public executioner of Berlin had problems of his own, but he felt profoundly honoured by the Fuehrer's personal interest and was determined not to let him down.

At the moment, he was holding a professional consultation with his two assistants. They were seated at a table in the execution block at Ploetzensee, drinking an excellent brandy which was one of the perquisites of their job.

"I've seen the films of the preliminary executions," reported the chief executioner, "and I must admit, I'm not entirely satisfied."

"Why not?" said the first assistant. "Everything's gone all right so far, hasn't it?"

"Technically speaking, yes, but visually—well, there's room for improvement."

The three men might have been cronies who had gathered for a quiet game of cards. The chief executioner looked like a middle-aged civil servant on the verge of honourable retirement. His two assistants had respectable working-class faces. One of them was the father of four children and the younger was just about to get married. His fiancée worked in a florist's shop.

"But we've been breaking records day after day," protested the senior assistant. "I challenge anyone to do better."

"I know, I know," replied the chief executioner. "All the

same, I can't expect the Fuehrer to put up with the sort of defects that show up in these films. We've got to iron them out somehow."

"Maybe it's the camera-man's fault," hazarded the junior assistant. "He's always getting in the way. Why doesn't he take his cue from us?"

The chief executioner frowned. "I know we're working under very difficult conditions, but we've got to allow for them. The hooks are too shiny, and so are the wire nooses—they reflect too much light and spoil the picture."

"In that case we'll simply paint over the hooks and nooses or round up some different materials. We should be able to get some from somewhere."

"Good idea," the chief executioner said approvingly. "There's something else, though. One of you always stands with his back to the camera when the execution is taking place, and that won't do."

"But we can't change our system at this stage!" The senior assistant looked worried. "After all, it's the traditional method —one of us stands in front of the prisoner and clasps him round the hips and the other grips him under the arm-pits. It's the only way to hoist him and drop him properly."

"That's all very well," replied the chief executioner, "but the one in front of the prisoner obscures his face. It ruins the film, and the Fuehrer isn't going to like that. He wants to see everything in detail."

"Bugger it!" said the junior assistant. "That's means we'll have to go back to square one again."

Captain Count Fritz-Wilhelm von Brackwede stood in the main chamber of Berlin's Supreme Court, flanked by two policemen.

His handcuffs had been removed, and he massaged his flayed wrists mechanically as he surveyed his surroundings—the blood-red swastika flags, the fiery crimson of Freisler's robe, the bright red collar-tabs of the general who was acting as an observer. Prosecuting counsel, clad in raven-black, lolled sideways in his seat with an air of ennui.

Freisler took his time. He leafed methodically through the papers in front of him and came to the conclusion that the prisoner was of no particular importance. He was merely one nobleman among many, a former administrative official from the East Prussian and Silesian area who had served in the army since the outbreak of war, with one or two interruptions—

in short, someone whom he could handle with one hand tied behind his back.

"Come here," Freisler began casually. He usually came straight to the point when dealing with generals, ambassadors or other senior officials. "You know why you're here?"

"No, I don't," answered Brackwede, " —particularly as I find myself confronted by the busts of Frederick the Great and Adolf Hitler. One abolished torture and the other reintroduced it. I call that a retrogressive step."

Roland Freisler, whose attention had evidently been wandering, looked bemused. "What was that? Did I mishear you? I sincerely hope so! What are you—a frustrated historian or something? If so, let me inform you that we're not interested in historical theory. Facts are all that count here."

"Just the point I wanted to make," Brackwede replied firmly. "I have been tortured. I did not make the statement presented in evidence until after I had been tortured. Consequently, that statement cannot serve as a proper basis for this hearing. Apart from that, I consider this court to be prejudiced, biased and not competent to try me. I therefore reject it."

Freisler drew himself up with an expression of boundless amazement and gazed helplessly round the court-room. He saw incredulous surprise, bewildered concern and, in a few isolated cases, ill-concealed grins. In an attempt to reassert his authority, he switched on the sarcasm.

"You're a comedian, I take it?"

"Possibly, but I've read Adolf Hitler's *Mein Kampf,* and he says that if a nation is being led to destruction by its government, it is not only the right but the duty of every member of that nation to rebel . . ."

"This is pure and unmitigated impertinence!" roared Freisler.

"Adolf Hitler also wrote that human rights transcend State rights, and any course of action which strengthens human rights is permissible. Indeed, not to take it is a symptom of criminal disloyalty."

"You're a bounder!" Freisler shouted excitedly. "How dare you, a criminal, misappropriate the Fuehrer's words for your own infamous purposes? You ought to be ashamed of yourself!"

"Perhaps I should," Brackwede conceded, " —for having quoted a man like Hitler in the first place."

Freisler bellowed, the microphones danced, and in the control-booth the next few sentences were obliterated by distortion.

"You are refused permission to speak," Freisler yelled at Brackwede in a voice which shook with fury. "The court is adjourned for half an hour."

"God Almighty!" hissed one of the policemen guarding the prisoner. "You can't afford to do that! No one's had the nerve to behave that way before."

"Then it's high time someone made a start," Brackwede said resolutely. Turning to his court-appointed counsel, he went on: "Better get out while the going's good—I'll conduct my own defence from now on."

"But I want to defend you," protested the barrister. "Your reference to torture could create an entirely new situation, always provided we can make your allegations of maltreatment stick."

"Are you a married man?" Brackwede asked. "Any children?"

The barrister looked surprised. "Yes."

"Are you an opponent of National Socialism?"

"How could I be!"

"Without risking your neck—no, of course you couldn't." Brackwede gave a faint smile. "In that case, why get involved unnecessarily? You have everything to lose—I have nothing. Keep out of this and leave the field to me."

After an uneasy half-hour, Freisler resumed the presidential seat. He had spent the interval in re-reading Brackwede's file but had failed to discover any special feature. It contained a straightforward confession, nothing more, but that was quite enough.

"Prisoner Brackwede," he began, "let us come to the point. Are you trying to assert that you took no part in the events of 20 July?"

"Far from it," replied Brackwede. "I took an exceedingly active part in them. It was my conviction that Hitler had to be eliminated because that was Germany's only chance of survival."

Freisler not only accepted this but breathed a sigh of relief. Such an admission was quite enough to warrant a death sentence. Now that the main issue was decided he could afford to indulge in a few of his favourite platitudes.

"The court is in possession of a treasonable plan to simplify the administration of this country. Do you admit to being its author, Count Brackwede?"

"Prisoner Brackwede, if you don't mind," amended the accused. "As far as the plan is concerned—yes, I gladly lay claim to it. It was designed to create a new and rational system of government which eliminated corruption, popular deception and abuse of power. However, the first essential was to get rid of Hitler."

"I see you don't attach much importance to oaths, Brackwede—Prisoner Brackwede, if you prefer."

"It wasn't we who broke that oath but Hitler and people like you. Criminals have no claim on the loyalty of others."

There was a roar of protest at this. Prosecuting counsel thumped the table with his fist, the associate judges flushed with shame and indignation, and a number of spectators leapt to their feet.

Roland Freisler vacillated for several seconds. He felt tempted to adjourn the hearing, but that might have been construed as weakness on his part. To a man whose enemies and professional rivals would relish his discomfiture, there was only one course of action open, and that was to demonstrate his complete mastery of the proceedings. Raising one hand in a placatory gesture, he addressed the excited spectators.

"People's Comrades," he said with a supercilious smile, "we must never forget that we are dealing here with people who cannot, in the very nature of things, be normal—in fact some of them must be positively deranged. It is obvious that we are confronted by one such specimen at the moment."

"That remains to be proved," Brackwede replied. "However, even a bird-brained idiot could see that we've lost the war. Prolonging it will only mean more mass-murder and total annihilation. The losses of the past five years may well be doubled in the few months that are left to us."

His estimate was virtually correct. Almost as many people lost their lives after 20 July 1944 as had died in the preceding years of the war, and the devastation of towns and cities redoubled in intensity.

Freisler glared at the prisoner with what he hoped was withering scorn. "This self-confessed scoundrel is a living demonstration of how necessary it has become to mete out Draconian justice. Vile, criminal elements have made repeated attempts to stab our Fuehrer in the back—congenial criminals who did not balk at pretending to be loyal National Socialists. Do you deny that, Prisoner Brackwede?"

"No," Brackwede replied, bowing his head. "I did believe in Hitler and National Socialism once, until I realised what

341

the man was and what he was doing. Then I became his opponent. I had no choice.

"Like many of my friends, I became convinced that he had to be eliminated—not merely when his defeat seemed certain but long before the war.

"We owe allegiance to God, justice and liberty—not to a criminal."

Captain von Brackwede's defence counsel looked profoundly worried. "What shall I do now?" he asked. "Give me a free hand and I'll try to shake the indictment—or at least cast doubt on it."

"What do you hope to achieve?"

The lawyer gave Brackwede a searching stare. His weary indifference had been dispelled by the prisoner's adamantine poise. "Do you know what I feel at this moment, Count von Brackwede?—Shame, at not being in your place."

"Try to survive, so that you can talk about it afterwards."

"But I don't want to be a coward—I want to do my best for you."

"Thanks," replied Brackwede. "Just answer me one question, though: do you think anything you can do will save me from a death sentence?"

"No."

"I didn't think so," Brackwede said. "I had a friend once, a corporal Lehmann. He had a bigger heart than most, but he also had a healthy dose of common sense. Do you know what he told me? Any sacrifice made in a good cause is justified as long as it's worth-while. Pointless sacrifices, however heroic, are pure idiocy."

"I understand," the lawyer said humbly.

Brackwede knew that it was different with some of the other defence counsel, who were more often concerned to protect their own interests than those of their clients. They were averse to being tarred with the same brush as the defendants, however indirectly.

One of them, and he was not alone, began his speech for the defence with the words: "Why any defence at all, you may ask?" He then explained at length that a defence counsel's most important task was to "assist the court in reaching a verdict." However, situations sometimes arose in which "the best defence counsel found it impossible to say anything in favour of the accused man represented by him . . ."

A Dr. Falck explicitly stated: "As a court-appointed defence counsel, chosen by lot, I espouse the view that defending counsel should do his best to avoid becoming a second prosecutor . . ."

A defence counsel named Dr. Bergmann: ". . . I therefore find myself unable to put forward a plea which differs from that of the Senior State Attorney."

Defence counsel Dr. Weissman: ". . . the inevitable sentence of death . . . I am certain that you . . . will arrive at a right and just verdict."

"Another of my friends," Brackwede told his defence counsel, "commonly referred to as 'the Doctor,' was a moral philosopher and strong believer, but do you know what he told me? Liars can't be fought with truth alone and crime can't be stamped out by decency—that's what he said."

"Your friend is alive," the lawyer said in a low voice.

Brackwede beamed with delight. "You don't mean it! How did he manage that?"

"He was arraigned before the People's Court like many others. He stood there like a lion at bay, just as Julius Leber, Uxkuell and Hofacker did—not to mention you, Count von Brackwede—but he was almost the only one to be sentenced to a short term of imprisonment."

"That's good. At least there'll be one of us left to testify later on. How did he get away with it?"

"He married the right wife. She has a childhood friend who happens to be a friend of Freisler."

"Splendid!" said Brackwede. "It's odd coincidences like that which help to shape the history of the world. However, we mustn't let ourselves be distracted by it. There aren't any exceptions to the rules governing my case."

According to extant records, seventy-six " official " executions took place during the months that followed the twentieth of July. Recorded murders and suicides among those immediately involved took the total to one hundred and forty-seven, but conservative estimates of the number of violent deaths run to two hundred at least.

Admiral Canaris was led naked to his execution in the closing days of the war. Numerous other prisoners were driven into the open at gun-point and then shot " while trying to escape." General Fromm, condemned to death for cowardice, was executed in Brandenburg Penitentiary on 19 March 1945. He died crying " Heil Hitler!"

Among those who met their end were children, old men,

youths, girls and mothers. Not all of them knew why, but their deaths were only a drop in the ocean of mass-killing that engulfed the fighting fronts, the home front and the concentration camps.

Adolf Hitler, himself on the threshold of death, proclaimed: "We shall win because we must win! If we did not, world history would have lost its meaning."

"The accused may address the court," said Roland Freisler, determined to maintain an outward show of justice. "But it must be a final word," he added quickly, "not a closing address. I won't tolerate any long-winded digressions."

Brackwede said:

"We assumed responsibility for this act in order to save Germany from a terrible misfortune. I fully realise that I shall be hanged, but I do not regret the part I played. I hope that, at a more auspicious moment, another man will complete our work."

"Death by hanging!" shouted Freisler. "Sentence to be carried out forthwith!"

Barely two hours after being sentenced, Fritz-Wilhelm von Brackwede was driven up to the red-brick bulk of Ploetzensee Prison, where all was in readiness for his execution.

The building in which the executioner and his two assistants awaited him stood a little apart from the main block, surrounded by trampled grass and gnarled pine-trees. The execution chamber measured twelve feet by twenty-five.

Those present included the Reich Attorney-General, the executioner and his assistants, two prison warders and two camera-men. On a small table situated against one of the longer walls stood some glasses and a bottle of brandy, destined for the witnesses of the execution.

Pale shafts of daylight entered the room through two narrow barred windows. Let into the roof immediately above them was a girder made of T-iron with eight sturdy butcher's hooks suspended from it.

Brackwede entered the room with head erect.

"Prisoner," said the Reich Attorney-General in routine tones, "the People's Court has sentenced you to death by hanging. Executioner, do your duty!"

The executioner placed the wire noose round Brackwede's neck. "It tickles a bit," he murmured, being a man known for his sense of humour, "but it doesn't last long."

344

The executioner's assistants, who received 50 marks per execution as compared with their chief's 300, took hold of Brackwede, lifted him so that the other end of the wire could be placed over the butcher's hook, and let him drop " with great force."

His last words were: "What a world!"

AUTHOR'S POSTSCRIPT

FRITZ-DIETLOF, COUNT VON DER SCHULENBURG

Born in London, 5 September 1902; executed in Berlin, 10 August 1944

The fictional character of Count von Brackwede is modelled, however imperfectly, on this unique member of the German resistance movement.

Invaluable information about Count von der Schulenburg was supplied by Dr. Eugen Gerstenmaier, who described him as a wonderful friend and one of the finest representatives of " the other " Germany. Further important leads were provided by Eberhard Zeller's remarks in *Geist der Freiheit*, probably the best account of the events in question, and Annedore Leber gives a compelling portrait of Schulenburg in her book *Das Gewissen steht auf*.

Numerous long talks with his friends, brother officers and relatives and with Countess Charlotte von der Schulenburg not only filled the author with gratitude and admiration but helped to complete his half-formed picture of a man who was not only symbolic of a new, different and better Germany but a strong individualist with a fascinatingly complex personality.

Albert Krebs's biography of Schulenburg gives an admirably accurate account of his life. A novel, however, is governed by its own laws. It must strive to go beyond recorded facts, to shed light on underlying factors, interpret the climate of the time, capture historical trends in a single character.

This makes it necessary to exceed the bounds of what is historically demonstrable: hence the figure of von Brackwede— an amalgam of Schulenburg, Schlabrendorff, Yorck and Uxkell, a Prussian, an aristocrat and a soldier of the type which Schulenburg actually represented to such perfection.

When Fritz-Dietlof von der Schulenburg was born in 1902, his father, Friedrich Bernhard, was the Kaiser's military attaché in London. Friedrich Bernhard was a cavalry general and a Prussian officer in the tradition of Frederick the Great. Ludwig Beck was one of the fellow-officers whom he most respected and admired. Towards the end of his life he was appointed an SS-Obergruppenfuehrer, and when he died in 1938 he was accorded a State funeral.

Fritz-Dietlof's mother, Freda, née Countess von Arnim-Muskau, was an energetic woman with a fiery temperament. She was sometimes accused of being a "Red aristo," but her marriage to the stern and upright Prussian nobleman was entirely harmonious.

Fritz-Dietlof himself showed signs of an unusually self-willed temperament at an early age. He rebelled against his English governess, kicked against the pricks generally, fought with his fellow-pupils and was noted for his "marked passion for reading."

He had three brothers and one sister. One of his brothers died in an accident, another of a fatal illness and the third in action on 14 July 1944, a month before Fritz-Dietlof was hanged. His sister Elisabeth, a woman of considerable artistic ability, now lives in a convent.

The Schulenburgs belonged to the old-established *Schwertadel*, or military nobility. As befitted men whose ancestors had served Prince Eugene and Frederick the Great, they administered their estates, entered the civil service or joined the army. Fritz-Dietlof matriculated "with ease," fought a number of successful duels as a student and passed his law finals "on his head."

In 1932 he joined the German National Socialist Labour Party. Despite "strong misgivings about Hitler and certain others," he felt convinced that Germany was on the threshold of a new and momentous future, and that what had once been "Prussia" would become "the Reich."

In 1933 he married Charlotte, a girl student from a solid middle-class family. She bore him six children, five girls and—the third-born—a son. All have survived and are variously resident in America, England and Munich.

This marriage, with its studiously unpretentious mode of existence, represented a treasured haven of repose in Count von der Schulenburg's life. At home, he could be gay and carefree, warm and open-hearted, an uninhibitedly cheerful companion, a dancer of impromptu dances and a teller of fairy-tales. Shortly before his death, he described his family as "a world in itself."

When, in 1933, he was posted to the East Prussian domain of Gauleiter Erich Koch, he temporarily succumbed to the then widespread misconception that flagrant abuses are an inevitable concomitant of change, that mistakes must be accepted and that to err is human. The rapid growth of corruption among the "brown bureaucrats" disgusted him, however, and he soon began to have qualms.

On leaving the province of East Prussia he became chief administrator of the Fischhausen district, where he spent a successful tour of duty. He showed himself liberal in matters of detail, meticulous where important issues were concerned and helpful to all and sundry—a district administrator in the traditional Prussian mould.

His metamorphosis into an opponent of National Socialism was clearly the outcome of a complex and painful mental process. He did not sever his links with the Party at once because he initially believed that opposition from within the movement would bear more fruit. Years elapsed before he was ready to take the ultimate step.

During his early days as an administrative official at Potsdam, Fritz-Dietlof had spent a great deal of time with the officers of the 9th Infantry Regiment, which was General von der Schulenburg's family regiment and became one of the germ cells from which the events of 20 July 1944 ultimately sprang.

It was at Potsdam that Fritz-Dietlof later joined the army, and there, too, that he met people who at once aroused his sympathies. These included Plettenberg, Klausing, Busche, Willessen, Hammerstein and Kleist—all men of aristocratic birth—and one middle-class officer for whom Schulenburg formed a particular liking, namely, Lieutenant Fritsche, who was one of those entrusted with the detention of Fromm and other generals in the Bendlerstrasse on the day of the revolt.

1937 brought a clearly discernible turning-point in his career. When he was appointed Deputy Police President of Berlin, he told his friends: "I had to decide whether to leave the service or become Hitler's Fouché. I chose the second alternative." The events of the *Kristallnacht* affected him deeply, and thereafter his course was set. A little while later a secret Party document pronounced him "politically unacceptable."

On the outbreak of war, Schulenburg volunteered for active service—his own form of "emigration." Professional soldiers found him defiantly casual. The monocle screwed into his defective left eye irritated them, as did his friendly attitude towards the lower ranks. He became very attached to a lieutenant named Konstantin, a very young man "of heroic disposition." When he was killed, Schulenburg wrote a poetical appreciation of him which was published in pamphlet-form in 1942.

Shortly afterwards, his services were requested by administrative departments in Berlin. He worked in the Ministry of Economics, drafted a plan for far-reaching administrative reform and was assigned to General von Unruh, whose job was to free men in the rear echelons for combat duty. While engaged in all these activities, Schulenburg continued to seek out and recruit men of similar convictions. He became renowned for his unerring instinct and spell-binding eloquence, and before long he was the main link-man between resistance groups of the most varied complexion.

His personal contacts ranged from the Gestapo to General Beck. The uninitiated, who regarded him as enigmatic, shrewd and, at the same time, stimulating, christened him "Sphinx-face" or "the wild man of the woods" and credited him with a reputation both for biting sarcasm and gentle irony. He spoke to generals "as an equal"—also to corporals.

To the few friends who got to know him really well, he opened his heart with complete and unqualified affection. Once they had gained his confidence they belonged, as it were, to his family circle. It was no coincidence that these friends were among the leading figures of 20 July 1944. Caesar von Hofacker was a witness at Schulenburg's wedding and godfather to his son. His co-godparent was Peter von Yorck. Count von Uxkuell also belonged to Schulenburg's circle of friends, and so, last but not least, did the brothers Stauffenberg—Claus and Berthold.

All these men used to enjoy convivial evenings in each other's country homes, spent much of their leisure time together, and met frequently at family gatherings years before the outbreak of war. Their conversation became grimmer, more sombre, more determined. They conspired together and agreed to take concerted action on the day of the revolt. None of them survived.

Count von der Schulenburg possessed the strength of mind and intellectual daring to project his thoughts far into the future. He readily assimilated new ideas. As a young lawyer he was an admirer of Winnig, a Socialist. He read Marx and Hegel, Kant and Engels, Freud and Lenin, St. Thomas Aquinas and Plato. He also made the acquaintance of Julius Leber, a much-venerated and seemingly indestructible figure whose attempt to reconcile Prussian nationalism with Social Democracy Schulenburg saw as the harbinger of "a radiant future."

"I often think back on those events," Dr. Eugen Gerstenmaier told me, while this book was being written. "Much of it is past history—unforgettable, but hidden behind a sort of veil. Even so, I often catch myself wondering what Fritz Schulenburg would have said about the things that are happening now, and what his advice to me would have been." Quietly, he added: "I wish those people were still alive—we need them."

On 20 July 1944, when he realised that the military revolt had failed, Schulenburg's verdict was: "We must sacrifice ourselves. People will understand us later on."

His last proud words, uttered before the People's Court, are quoted in this book but attributed to Count von Brackwede. An attempt has thus been made, through the mirror-image of a fictional character, to interpret the mentality of a wholly exceptional human being and of those who shared his convictions. Although this fictional character was conceived before the author was in possession of all available documentary evidence, it required little modification.

This book is therefore dedicated, with deep respect, to:

FRITZ-DIETLOF,
COUNT VON DER SCHULENBURG,
AND HIS COMRADES

THE END